FROGS DON'T CROAK IN THE WINTER

BOOK FOUR

THE BOB ROOSEVELT MYSTERY SERIES

by

Robert K. Swisher Jr.

OPEN TALON PRESS

OTHER PUBLISHED NOVELS BY ROBERT K. SWISHER JR.

Historical Fiction: Trade and E-book
Published by Sunstone Press
The Land
Fatal Destiny

Contemporary Western Fiction: Trade and E-book
PUBLISHED BY SUNSTONE PRESS
How Far the Mountain
The Last Narrow Gauge Train Robbery
The Last Day in Paradise
Love Lies Bleeding
The Man From the Mountain

Literary: Out of Print
Published by Samisdat Press - Canada
American Love Story

Young Adult: Trade Only
Published by Echo Press California
The Weaver
Published by Sunstone Press
Only Magic

Humor: E-book only
Conversations With the Golf God

Mystery Series: E-book and Trade
Bob Roosevelt Mystery Series – 4 novels

Contemporary Fiction: E-book only
Hope
A Circle Around Forever

Trade and E-book
Published by Open Talon Press
Vent
Grammar Nazis Are Not Always Rite, Right, Write
Vent Revisited
The Lonely Cowboy
How Bridge McCoy Learned to Say I Love you

Short stories and poetry in literary journals, articles in outdoor magazines. Reviews by Publishers Weekly, Best Sellers, Library Journal, and many others.

PUBLISHED BY
OPEN TALON PRESS

EDITORS: Sheila Awalt

COVER DESIGNER: Samantha Fury...Mike Nguyen
PRINT FORMAT: Samantha Fury

Library of Congress - In Publication Date

Swisher, Robert K, 1947 -
FROGS DON'T CROAK IN THE WINTER: A novel / by Robert K. Swisher Jr.
Summary: mystery, humor, satire
ISBN is 978-0-9979096-8-5
LCN is 2021901002

DEDICATION

FOR THE LITTLE BOY WITH THE SAD EYES AND THE OLD LADY ON THE CORNER TALKING TO THE MOON - THE LONELY AND THE SIMPLE ARE THE CLOSEST TO GOD

FROGS DON'T CROAK IN THE WINTER

BOOK FOUR

TABLE OF CONTENTS

CHAPTER ONE
HELP ME FIND MY HEART

The sign stated Saint. Ansgar, Minnesota, population 564. "This is it, this is where I'm going to stop for a while," I said with enough force to convince my Guardian Angel there was no room for argument.

"No, take my advice and don't stop here," he said in a worried tone.

"But I feel drawn to this place," I argued.

"If you stop here you are going to freeze your 62 year old, long haired, old hippie, Vietnam vet, private investigator stupid self, right into the middle of a murder, a stolen heart, more missing money than you can count, witches, and everyone you meet, let me repeat, everyone you meet, is going to try and kill you. In fact, this could be your boot hill," he warned.

"There are no witches anymore," I said.

"Says who?" he said.

Do I follow my instincts or do I listen to my Guardian Angel? My Guardian Angel has seldom steered me wrong. "I'm going to stop and follow my feelings," I told him - taking good advice has never been one of my strong points.

"What are you going to do here?" my Guardian Angel asked, rolling his eyes back in his head like he knew I did not have a good reason.

"You told me in Phoenix I should go somewhere where frogs don't croak in the winter," I replied.

"Roosevelt, it's January and we're in Minnesota. Instead of stopping here why don't you keep driving to the North Pole? There might not be as much snow."

I pondered his question while ignoring his lousy try at sarcasm. "You're right," I answered nonchalantly, "It might be warmer at the North Pole."

"When I told you, you should go somewhere where frogs don't croak in the winter, I was only trying to cheer you up after your bummer in Phoenix. I can see now I should have told you to get over it, you big crybaby."

"Don't call me a crybaby!" I ordered angrily.

"You can't tell me what to do," he retorted.

"You're my Guardian Angel!" I snapped back. "I can tell you whatever I want, order you to do whatever I want and"......my Guardian Angel cut in...."There is nothing in my contract that states I have to take orders from you."

"What are you the union boss of Guardian Angel contracts?" I steamed.

"No, I'm a monk."

"Show me the contract!" I demanded.

"You can't see the contract?" he said, as if he is a wise sage who was tired of trying to help stupid people, me, of course, being the stupid people.

I am the only one who can hear my Guardian Angel and when I talk to him it is only through my mind, which is a good thing, if not, people would think I talk to myself all the time. And, thank God, I am the only person who can see him. He is not a pleasing sight. My Guardian Angel is a 14th century monk with a shaved head. He is 5'2" tall and in his early 60's. His eyes are tiny brown slits that show he is not to be trusted. His eyebrows are so bushy birds could nest in them. He has a splotchy uneven black beard and his complexion is close to watery flour paste. He wears sandals with no socks and a knee length, stained, brown wool robe, which exposes mats of black curly hair on his bowed leg. To top it off he does not bathe. He is also not the best Guardian Angel - he is snide, sarcastic and lecherous - he informed me it makes him feel like an individual. For many years he would not tell me his name saying it was none of my mortal business, but then in a weak moment, which we all seem to go through, he informed me his name was Wright, which is completely out of character, so I nicknamed him Pea Brain. A name he does not really like, but what the hell, I am his boss, and how many people in life like their boss? But in an effort to be nice, I only call him Pea Brain when he peeves me off. I have also discovered he used to take money to forgive sins and slept with as many women as he could informing them he was a blessing from God. In a lame excuse he told me the Bishop made him do it.

Looking out the window I felt my Guardian Angel might be correct about Minnesota. Even snowflakes and ice don't like being in Minnesota in the winter. They would rather be in Florida taking Hebrew and Spanish lessons. Besides, all I had for a winter coat was a lined Levi jacket and a lined Levi jacket only keeps me warm when you are sitting in a bar next to the heater.

I have been on the road since leaving Phoenix - the past month is a blur of fast food restaurants, highways, and dim lit bars. I am once again lost, disillusioned, searching for love in all the wrong places and trying to remember the feeling of the hippie days when I went from day to day happy and carefree and life was nothing but flowers and women who read tarot cards and made me eat bean sprouts.

"Blame it on smoking 62,000 pounds of pot," my Guardian Angel told me.

"I haven't done drugs in over thirty years," I said.

"You have thirty years of residual effects left in your lungs," he said.

I had accomplished one thing in the past month. I spent some of the $25,000 I had earned solving a murder and bank robbery in Phoenix on my 1966 black Volkswagen bug - good old Matilda, the woman of my life. Matilda has always started. Out of appreciation I got her a face lift, tummy tuck, and breast job - a new fender and bumper and new rings.

"If you truly are an old hippie you would be walking or riding a bicycle and not driving a machine that helps deplete the ozone," my Guardian Angel had told me after I paid the bill.

"Life is nothing but a dichotomy," I had replied.

"If you want to waste your money you should give it to

Greenpeace or a church made up of old hippies who believe they can learn how to levitate," he had said.

"Listen, I am an old hippie, but I don't have any answers and I don't have the desire to levitate or live on rice, and I can't solve the world's problems," I said trying to defend my materialism.

An old hippie has times when materialism is a problem, unless it comes to spending money for good beer or bongs.

"Why are you a private detective if you can't solve problems?" he asked smugly.

"I'm not anymore. My license is expired and I don't want to get involved in any cases. I want to fall in love with a down home woman and live a peaceful normal life."

"How many years is it going to take for you to realize your search is hopeless?" he asked.

Sometimes I think my Guardian Angel, not me, is the old hippie, and it was he who took too many hits of cheap acid. What I can't figure out is why after so many trips he can still think straight and has good reasoning? Life is not fair.

I drove into Saint. Ansgar feeling as though I was being pulled into town by a being far greater than myself who would give me a purpose in life and lead me to the lady of my dreams. I don't want to call the feeling destiny. About the only thing following my destiny has ever led me to is poverty.

"You're heading for trouble, murder, witches, maybe your own death," my Guardian Angel warned again.

The sky, which for several weeks had been nothing but a dank, dark carpet of gray clouds, suddenly cleared and the sunlight glistened off the snow. It was like Mother Nature was rolling out a sparkling welcome mat for me. "It's a sign things will be good here," I told my Guardian Angel.

"The only sign that would be good here is one stating, Roosevelt, get out of town," my Guardian Angel said.

Snow banks, over ten feet tall, were on either side of the road, the remains of what is called in Minnesota, a light dusting. Icicles, so big it would take two men to carry one, hung from the rainspouts of houses. Naked Christmas trees were tossed in front yards waiting for their pilgrimage to the dump - Santa Claus is dead - good will for another year goes to the garbage. Sidewalks and driveways were mere trails cut through the deep snow. The houses were surrounded by large oak, maple and cottonwood trees. Their leafless branches reached out like the tortured arms and hands of giants suffering from arthritis. I stopped at the only red light in town. No moving cars were in sight.

"It should be a blinking red light," my Guardian Angel said.

For a Guardian Angel he has about as much patience as a mouse.

"While we're here you can run for the city council and change it," I replied.

"While we're here you'd better get a girlfriend that is better looking than a walrus. I need some cheering up," he said sternly.

My Guardian Angel is different. Most 14th century monks spent their time copying bibles and painting beautiful flowers in the margins. Mine spent his time copying the Kama Sutra and drawing dirty pictures in the margins.

The light changed and I drove past a red brick bank, a convenience store with six gas pumps in front, a small cafe, a hardware store, a grocery store, a bar with a sign so faded I couldn't read it, half a dozen empty store fronts, and to my surprise, a red brick two-story Victorian home with a professionally painted sign hanging from the front porch stating in large letters: THE HOME OF HEARTS - HEARTS OF EVERY SHAPE - and in smaller letters - TEA ROOM. Painted hearts in rainbow colors bordered the sign. "Who would want to buy hearts in a red neck town like this?" My Guardian Angel asked disdainfully.

"How do you know it's a red neck town?" I asked.

"Please, Roosevelt, try to show a small amount of intelligence," he replied.

A dozen or so pick-up trucks, which had more rust on them than paint, lined the street. After the downtown section there were a few more houses and the town ended abruptly - reminding me for some strange reason of unfulfilled love. The road continued on, a ribbon running through an endless white flat plain which would go forever and lead to nothing - no tomorrow, no dreams.

I drove on and a mile from town there was a large church. The church was built from light brown limestone cut in three foot by three-foot blocks. Stained glass windows reached out to the world.

The steeple strained to touch the sky. The large dark gray bell in the steeple rested in mute silence waiting to call in the believers. A sign in front of the church proclaimed - Saint Ansgar Church - The Sword of the Lord. Behind the church was a house also built out of blocks of limestone. A green Chevy four door and a white Ford Van with a dent on the right side were parked by it. Smoke drifted lazily out of the chimney.

Turning Matilda around in the church parking lot I drove back through town. The town ended like a carbon copy of the other side. "You should have known that," my Guardian Angel remarked. "You came in this way."

"Coming, going, what difference does it make in this confusing world?” I asked him.

"Ever hear of the Oh Oh bird?" he asked.

"Truthfully, no."

"The Oh Oh bird is a bird that flies in circles. He keeps flying in smaller and smaller circles until the circles are so small he ends up with his head stuck up his rear. Thus the Oh Oh bird."

"Are you insinuating I spend my time with my head up my rear?"

"Not me, oh wise one who thinks he will find meaning in his life by living in a refrigerator. But you are good at going around in circles."

I turned around and drove up and down the side streets. I was surprised to pass a fire station, a new two-story brick school serving all grades, and a Sheriff's Office too small to include jail cells - no cop cars were in front. When the paved side streets reached the edge of town the roads turned into gravel and continued on between snow-covered fields. Scattered on the horizon were farm buildings, their images shimmering in the ice crystal air like they only existed in dreams and would vanish when the snow melted.

"What do they grow up here?" my Guardian Angel asked. "Desolation?”

I have never understood why people ask questions if they are going to answer them themselves.

I drove back to the center of town. Four men waved at me as they walked across the street. They were all wearing parkas and insulated boots an Eskimo would kill for. I waved back. "Strange," my Guardian Angel said. "You'd think men from this part of the world seeing a long hair driving a Volkswagen would want to kick your face in."

"People aren't hung up on long hair now," I told my Guardian Angel.

"Too bad," he replied.

My Guardian Angel has been with me since Nam. I owe him. He saved my life through the war and other happenings in my life too boring to tell. But, deep in his lecherous and larceny filled heart he would like to see me bite the bullet so he could get assigned to somebody who is not as boring - he does not like the fact I am moral and upright and have taken a vow I will only sleep with a woman if I love her. He thinks my morals are disgusting.

For some strange reason I felt compelled to go into the HOME OF HEARTS and parked Matilda in front of the shop. "Where are you going?" my Guardian Angel demanded.

"I'm going to look at the shop and drink a cup of tea."

Me drinking tea shocked him so bad he decided to stay in the car. Which, if he was a class A guardian angel, and not a class D, would be called dereliction of duty.

The two-story red brick Victorian home was pretty in a castle sort of way. I imagined men clad in armor and waving six-foot long swords clamoring up a ladder to breach an upstairs window and abduct a screaming fourteen year old virgin. This picture was formed in my mind figuring there had to be a few fourteen year old girls in Europe the knights had missed as they raped their way from country to country under God's banner.

There was a large foot mat in front of the door with, WELCOME ALL LONELY HEARTS, printed on it. I wiped my feet carefully. The door groaned as I opened it. I entered a large room and was greeted by a glistening world of hearts. Hundreds of heart pendants in every color and size imaginable hung from hooks in the ceiling. The large dormer windowpanes were covered with hearts held to the glass by clear suction cups - the sun hitting the hearts sent rainbows dancing around the room. There were small tables scattered around the room with hearts lying on black velvet pillows as if waiting for a prince on bent knee to present them to his princess. The sight took my breath away. It was Tinker Bell's home - an ice palace of hearts - a glistening twilight zone of fantasy and far away worlds.

I noticed a door to another room, the frame circled by hearts. The room was smaller, pendant hearts strung on clear fishing line of different lengths hung from the ceiling. The hearts were so close together the room reminded me of a den of a large and beautiful spider that spins webs of hearts. The lighting sent red, yellow, blue, and colors I couldn't name reflecting off the walls. Years ago I would have said, "wow, groovy, far out man," now it was beautiful.

I went into another room. In the center of the room was an oak table with glass claw feet. On the table was a glass dome about six inches around and a foot tall. There is only one light in the room. It is set in the middle of the ceiling and shines in one straight beam down on the dome. The glass dome is the kind a dried flower would be kept under or a porcelain figurine so fragile the owner do not want touched. There is a brass nameplate on the walnut base that reads: THE QUEEN OF HEARTS. But the glass dome is empty.

Looking at the dome feelings of loss, sadness, disillusionment, and loneliness, swirled through me all at the same time. I felt something was wrong - terribly wrong.

"What's wrong is that you are in Minnesota and headed into deep trouble," my Guardian Angel said.

"I thought you were in the car."

"Even a being that can't feel anything physical gets cold in this place," he replied. "It couldn't be more than zero out."

In the corner of the room is a black metal bird stand for a large bird, but there is no bird. Leaving the room I saw a door with a wood plaque over it stating: TEA ROOM.

I can hear faint sobs from a crying woman.

"Abandon ship! Abandon ship!" my Guardian Angel warned. "Retreat, the battle is lost! Beat feet! Dive! Dive!"

Would I listen? No. Should I listen? Probably!

I went into the Tea Room. In the room are three black wrought iron patio tables with four matching chairs around each one. A chandelier of crystal hearts hangs over every table. At one of the tables a woman is sitting, her shoulders are hunched over, her head is buried in her hands and she is sobbing. A black raven, over a foot tall, with red beady eyes, stands on the table looking at the lady like he wished she was a large juicy grasshopper.

"Roosevelt, don't even think about the woman," my Guardian Angel said with a cautious tone to his voice.

I should take his advice and turn and run from the crying woman. But, I feel sadness for the crying women. She is lonely. I am lonely. I went over to the table. The raven looked at me, ruffled his feathers, and squawked, "Me love you."

"It's your lot in life, Roosevelt," my Guardian Angel said. "Only a big dumb black bird could love you."

I ignored the bird. Talking to birds has never been one of my strong points.

"Is anything wrong?" I gently asked the crying lady.

She took her face out of her hands. She looked up at me with red swollen eyes, the tears running down her cheeks, anguish written on her face like a blinking neon sign. "Hell no, you dumb jerk, everything is just peachy keen!!" she snapped.

"I like this one," my Guardian Angel smiled. "Without even knowing you she knows you make a toad look smart."

I don't know how to reply to the lady. I feel like my feet weigh 300 pounds each and I will never be able to move again. In my bewildered state I studied her. She is in her early forties, five feet three or four. She has long dark hair that reaches to the middle of her back. Her eyes are dark with long black eyelashes and she has full pale lips that blend well with her round face. She has no makeup or lipstick on but her complexion is clear and alive with a touch of red on her cheeks. She is wearing a long, pine tree green, sack dress, with long sleeves that any peasant in Chile would love and in no way hinted at her charms. She is big-boned, strong, blocky, but not overweight, and attractive in a farm girl sort of way. My heart stirred then fluttered. I feel like I know her. I want to know her more. Is she the reason I was drawn to Saint Ansgar?

"Roosevelt, you are a dreamer," my Guardian Angel said.

The lady took a white handkerchief out of a pocket and blew her nose loud enough a lumberjack in Alaska would be proud, wiped her eyes, took two deep breaths, sobbed once more, and said in a lonely voice. "Please sit down. I'll make us a cup of tea. I need somebody to talk to. I didn't mean to be rude. Thank you for showing concern."

Her voice is like a song.

"A death march," my Guardian Angel said.

I smiled at her and sat down with a deep feeling of hope and warmth in my heart.

"Roosevelt, I'm telling you," my Guardian Angel said sadly, "You should keep going to the North Pole."

A few brain cells in my lost and bewildered mind know he is right, but there is something about the lady - something special. The lady stood and the raven flapped and perched on her shoulder. There is a counter in the corner with steaming pots of water and she brought back two cups of tea and set them on the table. The raven flapped onto the back of a chair. My cup has little yellow hearts on it and the handle is so small I can't get my little finger through it. I feel like a little boy who is playing house with his sister. I sipped the tea. It tastes like dried weeds with a little dirt tossed in.

"It's a special blend," she said. "It helps one think clearly and stimulates your endorphins."

"To Roosevelt that's beer, not tea," my Guardian Angel said.

"Very nice tea," I told the lady. I have always been a good liar.

"Good tea," the raven squawked.

I wanted to give him mine.

The lady looked at me over the edge of her teacup. Her dark eyes seemed to probe every one of the long shoulder length graying hairs on my head, pick apart the green of my eyes, devour my white neatly trimmed beard, sigh distastefully at my long-sleeved cowboy shirt and Levi’s, and wonder what kind of idiot I am to only be wearing a lined Levi jacket. She looked at my cowboy boots, looked me in the eyes and started to laugh. Not a mild he he, type laugh, but a, har har har, type laugh. "You're a dumb cowboy!" she he, he, har, har'd, like being a cowboy is funnier than being the president.

"He is a funny looking," my Guardian Angel agreed.

"Cowboy," the raven squawked, which sounded like kawba.

"No, I'm a cowboy who at one time was a hippie," I said.

She laughed harder which hurt my feelings. I had the urge to be rude, not finish my tea and walk out. On the way I'd punch my Guardian Angel in the nose and swat the bird. Roosevelt with hurt feelings is not a good boy. The lady suddenly stopped laughing and started bawling. Not a, my cookies burnt bawling. Not a, my car keys are locked in the car bawling. But a pure tour de force bawling. The anguish of a woman's world poured out of her mouth.

I feel like the Pope wondering how to talk to a Hare Krishna. What could I say? Need some new symbols son? How's your bongo holding up? Doesn't dancing all the time with sandals on give you falling arches? You know if you didn't wear white your cleaning bill would be less.

"Do something Roosevelt," my Guardian Angel pleaded. "I can't stand to see a woman cry."

"You couldn't care less about women crying all you want is to see them naked," I said.

"So?"

"Shut up," the raven squawked.

The bird isn't as dumb as he looks.

The lady kept crying and was shedding so many tears I knew she would dehydrate within three minutes if she kept it up. My mind raced to think of something to say. But I could think of nothing, which, when it comes to women, is normal. Feeling as useless as Billy Graham in Saudi Arabia I got up to go get myself another cup of dried weed, dirt flavored tea. The lady leapt out of her chair and threw her arms around me, pinning my arms to my side in such a fierce hold I feel like a pro wrestler who was about to be picked up and tossed to the mat by a guy who had eaten so many steroids his arms are so big he can't scratch his nose. My teacup shattered on the floor. "I need a friend," she bawled. "Nobody loves me. I am so lonely."

The raven flew off the back of the chair and landed on my head. "Me love you," he squawked.

I would have held the lady, patted her head, touched her cheek, swatted the raven, but I couldn't move my arms and my fingers are getting numb from lack of blood circulation. The lady sobbed several more times, released me, and sat back down. I picked up her cup and walked over to refill it with the raven still on my head.

"You are one funny guy," my Guardian Angel laughed.

When I set the cup in front of her and sat back down she was cried out and the raven hopped back to his chair. The lady's face is so red and puffy she could make a commercial for hay fever. "It can't be all that bad, turn that frown upside down, sunrise always follows the dark, a stitch in time saves nine," I said trying to cheer her up.

"What does knitting have to do with it?" she demanded.

"Yea, what does knitting have to do with it you idiot?" my Guardian Angel also demanded.

"Crap," the raven squawked.

The bird is getting on my nerves.

"Just trying to help," I told the lady.

She was about to say something, stopped, and then looked at me with a puzzled look on her face. "I know you," she said like she didn't know if she did or not.

"No, I don't think so," I said.

"I know you," she said again, but more confidently.

"No, you don't," I said.

"How many past lives do you remember?" she asked me.

"He doesn't remember yesterday," my Guardian Angel said.

"I don't believe in that past life stuff. This one is tough enough," I replied, keeping my answer short. I don't feel like getting into a deep conversation concerning past lives. Years ago, a guy accused me of having an affair with his wife in our past lives - only he was going to shoot me in this life.

She looked at me and I could see the puzzled look on her face slowly piece itself together. "I'll be," she said.

"I'll be rolled in flour," she said.

"That would be different," my Guardian Angel said.

"You're Bob Roosevelt," she said. "You're the detective that was on TV for solving that kidnapping in Florida."

My fifteen minutes of fame had caught up with me again. It's hard to run from a sordid past.

"Now that you know he is Roosevelt, famous for fifteen minutes and two reruns, be a detective groupie and rip your clothes off and make mad passionate love to him on the floor," my Guardian Angel said. "Or better yet, stand up on the table and do an exotic dance with that bird on your head and then attack Roosevelt with such enthusiasm he will never be able to look at another woman."

"That's me," I replied to the lady, trying not to sound proud and stuck up while ignoring my lewd Guardian Angel.

A person, just by getting his or her face on the boob tube, is thought to know everything and be blessed by whatever deity controls the TV remote. It's strange but every man or woman TV personality with at least six divorces is an authority on relationships and every politician who has lost the race is an authority on government.

"You are just the person I need," the lady said with such a tone of relief in her voice it made me nervous.

"Let's get in Matilda and get out of here," my Guardian Angel warned me. "Remember, murder, stolen big money, your death, witches."

The lady leaned so far forward that if she would have had on a low cut dress I could have seen her belly button. "You will help me, won't you?" she asked in a voice somewhere between Cinderella and the lady who was the star in Betty Does Boise.

I looked into her pleading eyes. I looked at her big strong bones and thought to myself. Self, if you help her, this Minnesota lady who for some reason has made your old gray heartstrings at least vibrate might be the lady you are looking for.

"I might be able to help you," I replied, "but first I have to know what kind of help you need."

"She needs joy jell rubbed all over her body," my Guardian Angel said.

"Money," the raven squawked.

She started to cry. "I'm so relieved," she sobbed. "I have a friend," she blubbered happily.

Why women smile when they are crying I have never been able to figure out?

I smiled at the lady. I don't know exactly why? But something about the lady made me smile. Maybe in some small way I have touched her loneliness. Maybe she has touched mine.

"Don't make me gag," my Guardian Angel said. "I know your heart is colder than the arctic."

"It's not something I'm proud of," I replied sadly.

The lady stood. "I'll be back," she announced, looking at the bird and pointing at her shoulder. The raven flapped to her shoulder. There is a set of stairs in the corner and the lady went upstairs.

I needed a cup of dried weed, dirt tea and I poured myself another cup. I could hear every step the lady made upstairs and then water being turned on and rushing down a pipe. I looked out a window at the frozen backyard.

The lady came back. The raven on her shoulder looked like a modern piece of jewelry. She sat down and smiled at me. She had washed her face. "I suppose you should know my name before you help me," she said with a small smile. "I am Fanny Ruth. People in town call me Fanny. But they all think I'm crazy."

"Crazy is not half bad," I said, returning her smile.

"This is Clyde," she said, looking at the raven who now sat on the table. "He is my only friend."

"Me love you," Clyde squawked.

"Stupid bird loves everybody," my Guardian Angel said.

"As you know I'm Bob Roosevelt," I said.

"Introduce me, without me you are nothing - a ship without a sea - a plane without the sky. A hummingbird without a flower," my Guardian Angel said.

"A happy man without distractions," I replied.

"Fanny, how can I help you?" I asked trying not to sound like a shrink.

She hesitated and said barely above a whisper, "You have to help me find my heart, somebody stole my heart."

I remembered my first love - a distant feeling, a feeling so dim now it barely glows, but still a warm, happy feeling. But, even feeling warm, I couldn't think of anything to say. Fanny, I can't find my own heart, didn't sound right.

"You have to help her, Roosevelt," my Guardian Angel said. "A person without a heart is nothing. Ask the Scarecrow?"

I wanted to tell her Fanny, we all have a heart, it's there we only have to hold onto it during this life. I feel like holding her, telling her bedtime stories, telling her the Wicked Witch of the North has flown away. But, as usual, I couldn't express my feelings.

Fanny stood and took my hand as Clyde jumped, with great difficulty, onto her shoulder. Fanny's hand is warm, warm like the inside of a fur-lined glove, warm like a mother's hand on the forehead of a sick child. She pulled me up and I followed her, hand in hand, to the room with the empty dome. Clyde flew to his perch zigging and zagging like he is drunk. "Not you, not you, not you," Clyde squawked as he walked nervously back and forth on his perch.

Fanny released my hand and pointed at the glass dome. "There was a heart in there. A small diamond heart, on a white gold chain, it belonged to my grandmother. She gave it to my mother who gave it to me. Somebody stole it sometime yesterday." Her words were low and distant, mysterious, filled with longing and sadness.

"How much was it worth?" I asked.

"Not much, maybe a couple of hundred dollars, but it was special, it was my heart."

She turned from the table and I followed her. Clyde stayed on his perch. We went outside through the front door and walked around to the side of the house. On the side is a set of steps leading to the porch. Beside the steps were two coal black cats. They were frozen solid and laid out back to back on their sides. Their legs are stretched out straight. What didn't seem like enough blood from their cut throats stains the snow. "Whoever stole my heart also killed my cats and put them here," Fanny said holding back a sob.

I feel her loss. I feel her sadness. I wondered who would be vile enough to kill her cats. It made me angry. I swore to myself I would find the culprits. In a small town it couldn't be that hard to find the killer or killers and also recover the diamond.

Fanny turned to face me. Two teardrops were frozen on her face. I reached out and touched them gently and they fluttered to the ground like ice butterflies.

"You're a good man, Roosevelt," my Guardian Angel said, "even if you are a jerk most of the time."

"You will help me?" Fanny asked.

"I'll do my best," I promised her. "For all the lost hearts, I'll do my best."

A lonely smile creased Fanny's face. I suddenly had an eerie feeling in my stomach. It felt like the grim reaper was beckoning me. I wondered if I could get killed over a lost heart and two dead cats.

"You bet your booty," my Guardian Angel said.

CHAPTER TWO
HAIR BALLS

Clyde and I are sitting in the Tea Room looking at each other. Fanny had made herself tea that looks like weak pea soup and is supposed to keep a person regular. Fanny was making me a cup of instant coffee. "I only keep this for customers who don't drink tea. Coffee has no redeeming value, especially instant," she informed me as she set the cup in front of me like it was a cow pie. "It's full of caffeine and they make instant coffee using methylene chloride, which, if you didn't know, is paint stripper."

"I like strippers," my Guardian Angel said. "Fat strippers, skinny strippers, old, young, black, blue, orange, gold, it doesn't make any difference, as long as they strip."

I want to tell Fanny I can only take so much tea and tea in all reality is only for the English. I want her to think seriously about what tea had done to the English. I cannot imagine sitting around all day saying - "damn Americans or, isn't it a lovely rainy day and, pass the crumpets."

I sipped my instant coffee, which, truthfully, is foul stuff, and should only be served to people in jail who will drink anything, including liquid shoe polish, but I am not going to tell Fanny and taint my male ego.

"Not you! Not you! Not you!" Clyde squawked.

"I didn't know ravens could talk," I said to Fanny.

"A farmer found Clyde when he was little. He had a broken wing and he couldn't fly. The farmer slit the tip of Clyde's tongue about a quarter of an inch, which causes vibrations and enables him to talk."

"I'll be," I said.

"Damn farmer," Clyde squawked.

"Better not let the cruelty to animals people hear about this," my Guardian Angel said. "They'll want to send Clyde to a raven plastic surgeon to have his tongue sewed back, which will end up costing the tax payers about 3,000 big ones. Then they will want to release Clyde in some national park where he will spend his time pooping on people's heads in retaliation because he can't communicate anymore."

"How did you get Clyde?" I asked.

"A farmer traded him for a heart pendant for his wife's birthday."

Fanny stroked the bird's back. "Me love you," Clyde squawked.

"How do you think your heart got stolen?" I asked Fanny.

"I don't know. Nobody in town likes me but I don't know of anybody that would steal from me. Although there are a lot of weird people around here," she answered sadly.

Fanny seems lonelier than the ice cream man during the winter and I wondered why she feels nobody likes her.

"Take me on a tour of your house," I said.

"Take him to your bedroom," my Guardian Angel said.

"Bad cat, bad cat," Clyde squawked.

"Is seeing the house part of your investigation?" Fanny asked.

"It might help," I replied. "But older houses have always intrigued me."

"We'll start with the outside," Fanny said happily, which seemed like a strange thing to be happy over.

"Too cold, too cold," Clyde squawked and did not move from the back of the chair when we walked away.

Fanny did not put on a coat. People in Minnesota probably have hot flashes when it is zero. We went out the front door, down the porch steps and to the left of the house. "The porch goes two thirds around the house," Fanny pointed out. "There is a door that goes into the Tea Room on this side," she pointed at the door.

Fanny didn't glance at the frozen cats by the steps. I knew it was painful for her. We walked around back. There is no back door. There are two small houses behind Fanny's - one is white and one is yellow - the closest one is white. "Who lives in those houses?" I asked.

"A single mother and her ten-year-old son live in the white house. The boy is very nice and very lonely. An older, retired couple, live in the yellow house."

"Why are there gates in their fences that open to your yard?" I asked.

"Who knows," Fanny replied.

"So they can let their dogs out to poop in somebody else's backyard," my Guardian Angel said.

There is a cellar door in the back of the house. "What is in there?" I asked Fanny.

"It used to be an old root cellar but now it's where the gas heater is."

"Is it an old heater?"

"No, I had a new one put in two years ago."

There is no door on the right side of the house - only large bay windows.

We went back inside. The first room has three windows in it. I noticed none of the windows have curtains. In fact, none of the windows on the bottom floor of the house have curtains. "None of the windows open," Fanny told me. "They have been painted so many times they are stuck shut. In the summer I open the doors to keep the house cool."

The middle room with the spider web of hearts has a window on the left side. The room with the raven's stand and the bell dome has a window on the right side. "At one time this was the kitchen," Fanny explained when we were back in the Tea Room. "The other three rooms were the dining room, sitting room, and living room."

We went up the stairway that is in the corner of the Tea Room. There are four rooms off of the hall - two on the left and two on the right. "This is my bedroom," Fanny pointed to the first door on the left.

"Now we are getting somewhere," my Guardian Angel said.

The room is small, spotless, and everything is neat.

The first room to the right had been converted into a kitchen.

The third room, on the left, is a guest bedroom and is round - the room I had pictured knights storming in search of a fourteen-year-old virgin.

"The fourth room is filled with cardboard boxes stacked in no particular order.” This is where I keep my inventory," Fanny informed me.

We went back to the Tea Room. Fanny made me another cup of methylene chloride and herself another cup of green, keep one regular, tea. If she kept it up she wouldn't have to worry about being regular - she would have the trots. "Do the windows upstairs work?" I asked.

"Only in my bedroom. I put a fan in the window in the summer."

"Is it ever summer here?" my Guardian Angel asked.

"It's a lovely home," I told Fanny.

"It belonged to my grandparents. They came here from Sweden in the 1860's. My grandfather ran a butcher shop. He was good with money and they built this house in the early 1880's. My grandparents were killed in a car wreck when I was little. My mother and father had a small farm but they were very poor. My parents rented the house for a long time but when my father ran away with a woman from Minneapolis my mother and I moved here. I have never heard from my father. My mother sold the farm to pay off the debt and worked as a waitress. She died from cancer when I was sixteen. I have lived here by myself ever since."

"You seem to have done a good job with your life," I said, feeling sad for Fanny and my words seeming hollow and useless. It is difficult to make a statement that will make everything seem ok when somebody tells you a sad tale of life.

"I get by," Fanny replied simply.

"Me love you," Clyde squawked.

"Three years ago I opened my shop," Fanny said. "In the summer time we get a lot of tourists from Minneapolis."

"I bet you sell a lot of hearts."

"Enough to pay the bills and get through the winter plus it keeps me busy and I meet some interesting people. Not like all the ignorant red necks around this place," she said bitterly.

"I told you this town is full of red necks," my Guardian Angel said.

My Guardian Angel never forgets and if he can pull up a jab from the past he does it with relish. It's a good thing he is not the Guardian Angel to a marriage counselor.

"Is there somewhere in town I can stay while I sort things out?" I asked Fanny.

"Aren't you going to ask me a lot of questions?" she asked me, with a puzzled look on her face

"Not now, but I will."

She seemed relieved and then looked at me hopefully. "You can stay in my guestroom."

"I don't think that is a good idea," I said, although I wanted to. "If I'm going to help you it is better if I'm not so close. I try not to mix business with pleasure."

"Roosevelt, Roosevelt, reconsider. You have one lonely girl here that you could have in the sack faster than Tiger Woods makes a putt. Are you sick? Don't let me down," my Guardian Angel said.

"Shut up," I told him.

"You owe me," he said.

"I'm not paying," I said.

He stammered, "but, but, but."

"There is a widow lady in town who rents rooms. I'm sure you could make a deal with her since it's the off season," Fanny said, sounding disappointed.

"A seventy-year-old widow lady who listens to church music all day on the radio," my Guardian Angel commented disgustedly.

"Where does she live?" I asked.

"Go to the red light and turn left. It's the third house on the left. There is no sign out front."

"Would you like me to bury your cats for you?"

Fanny laughed, which I thought was strange. Dead cats aren't the funniest things in the world unless, of course, you are a dog.

"The ground is frozen three-foot deep. It will be months before I can bury them," Fanny explained.

"You silly boy," my Guardian Angel said.

I am getting sick of my Guardian Angel running his head.

"I'll put them in the cellar so you won't have to look at them," I volunteered.

"That would be nice," she smiled shyly at me.

"Bad cat, bad cat," Clyde squawked.

Would you like to come to dinner after you are settled in? Say around six?" Fanny asked with a pleading look in her eyes.

"I'd like that," I replied.

I wanted to hug her but I only smiled at her and left.

"I wonder how baked raven would taste?" my Guardian Angel asked as I went outdoors.

I once again noticed there was very little blood around the cat's heads. I picked the two frozen cats up by their tails and put them in the corner of the cellar.

"Those are the kind of cats I like," my Guardian Angel said.

"Fanny loved those cats," I said. "That isn't a nice thing to say."

"Hairballs aren't nice," he said.

"Cat poo on your carpet isn't nice," he said.

"Cat hair floating through the air and getting on your food isn't nice," he said.

"Dead birds left in your closet aren't nice," he said. "Claw marks on your new sofa aren't nice," he said. "Curtains ripped to ribbons aren't nice," he said.

"Get yourself a dog," I said.

Back outside I looked at the gates to the chain link fences of the neighbors. The one where the little boy and his mother live is open and there is a well-used trail through the snow that leads to the door to the Tea Room and also the cellar. The other gate is piled with snow.

Matilda was her ever-reliable self and started right up. I let her idle. She is getting old and it takes longer for her blood to warm up than it used to. "I can't believe you are going to try and find Fanny's heart," my Guardian Angel said.

"You told me I should help her."

"I've changed my mind. There's no money in it and I still feel you might get boiled by witches."

"I feel like I have been sent here on a mission," I said.

"Roosevelt, Roosevelt, Roosevelt," my Guardian Angel muttered sadly.

"Besides," I said. "I have a warm feeling for Fanny."

"She isn't your type."

"How do you know?"

"I don't really know but I feel certain she isn't your type."

"You don't want to see me fall in love," I said.

"It would be boring."

"It would be wonderful," I replied.

He was quiet for a moment. "Since you are going to try and be a famous cat murder solver you could have at least stayed with Fanny and given me a thrill or two."

"She doesn't need a man pawing her. She needs a friend."

My Guardian Angel started to wretch.

Driving toward the widow's house I had a strange thought: I hadn't seen a TV or a phone at Fanny's.

"Some people aren't tied to modern conveniences like one old hippie I know who has completely sold out," my Guardian Angel said in a taunting voice.

"I'd like to slap you one time," I said.

"Peace brother," my Guardian Angel snipped.

"What do you know about selling out? We had to sell out." I am as bad as my Guardian Angel. I also answer my own questions.

"No you didn't. Nobody had to sell out. You all gave up. It was too tough on you poor, poor baby boomers who had been given everything your whole life. Without big brother's food stamps you wouldn't have lasted as long as you did. And, you hippies created two of the biggest materialistic markets there are?"

"What's that?"

"Drugs and organic food."

I tried to think of a comeback. My mind reeled in confusion. "I'll have to think about it," I finally said.

"Think, that's a good one," he snickered.

I looked at the house I had driven to. There is nothing special about it. It is a normal one story Midwestern house. There is one thing out of the ordinary though. At the end of the gravel driveway is a two-car garage. Parked in front of one of the doors is a new four door baby blue Mercedes - a new Mercedes in the Midwest is as normal as a rich guy in L.A. driving a Ford tractor.

There is a sign on the front door. "Ring Bell."

"Well, duh," my Guardian Angel said.

I did what the sign instructed.

I heard footsteps coming to the door. "Here comes the seventy-year-old widow with white permed hair. She is wearing three sweaters and will cook you poached eggs and oatmeal for breakfast," my Guardian Angel said in a dejected voice. "You are missing out on a not beautiful, but not bad looking, single lady who is lonely, who probably hasn't been with a man in ten years and would make love to you so fiercely your voice would raise three octaves."

The door opened and my Guardian Angel's lower jaw dropped far enough he looks like a large mouthed bass. This seventy-year-old widow is about thirty. This seventy-year-old widow is close to six feet tall. This seventy-year-old widow has legs taller than a pine tree. This seventy-year-old widow has blue eyes, a fine chiseled face, long blond hair that reaches the middle of her back, and a chest that has sent fourteen men to jail and caused seven divorces. "You're the only seventy-year-old woman that should be on the cover of Cosmopolitan," I said to her.

"What?" she said in a voice that would melt steel.

"Inside joke" I said. "I was told I might be able to rent a room here."

"I don't rent rooms to dumb looking cowboys who need a haircut," she said. "And dumb looking cowboys don't read Cosmopolitan."

"Tell her you'll do the dishes, scrub the floors, anything she wants you will do," my Guardian Angel urged frantically.

I didn't want to tell her anything. I don't consider myself dumb looking. Maybe ugly? Maybe simple? But not dumb. Although she was right about cowboys reading Cosmopolitan - they only look at the pictures - the pictures are better than Playboy.

She looked down at my boots, her eyes moved up my legs, settled on my crotch, up my belly, to my neck, looked into my eyes, looked at my hair. I feel like a piece of meat.

I looked at her. Fair is fair. She is wearing brown leather boots. She has on brown wool slacks that fit her like they were tailored. A light blue long-sleeved sweater that is so tight it is part of her skin. She has on no rings or jewelry of any kind. It is strange though. Her face and hands are tanned, tanned a golden brown.

Nothing is tanned during the winter in Minnesota. A tan is called windburn and is the color of cheap red lipstick. The only makeup she has on is a pale red lipstick that gives her lips the wet look.

"Come on in, we can talk," she said.

I guess I am at least prime B beef.

"Talk, smock," my Guardian Angel slobbered. "Talk is for sissies, let's just get it on."

It's a good thing my Guardian Angel was a monk. With his style he would have never been able to get a date unless her favorite thing to do was sit in the dog pound seats at a Green Bay Packers game and scream, "The refs suck."

The house smells like roast beef and gravy. It smells wonderful. I have never walked into a house and said, "Boy, that tofu sure smells good."

"Follow me to the kitchen," Miss Cosmopolitan ordered. "I have to check the roast and then I'll give you a tour."

The kitchen is large, with a table that would seat six comfortably. I sat down at the table while she checked the roast. When she was done she turned to me and smiled a smile that would make a Born Again Christian lie. "I'll show you my rooms," she said.

"Let's start with your belly button room," my Guardian Angel said. "Then your bare stomach room, then your...."

"Shut up," I cut in.

A hallway ran away from the living room with three rooms off of it. "Forty bucks a night for the first room and you get breakfast and dinner. Forty-five bucks a night for the second room you get breakfast and dinner. Fifty bucks a night for the third room and you get breakfast and dinner," Miss Cosmopolitan informed me.

"Why is each one higher as you go down the hall?" I asked.

"The most expensive room is next to the bathroom," she said like even a worm would have known the reason.

There is a bathroom at the end of the hall two people wouldn't fit in unless one was going to the bathroom while the other was taking a shower. "Towels are included," she said.

"Where do you stay?" I asked.

"Downstairs," she replied.

"I bet she has a round bed surrounded by mirrors, a Jacuzzi, large screen TV, a shower large enough for two people and a refrigerator stocked with beers from around the world," my Guardian Angel said.

"I'd like to look at the room closest to the bathroom," I told Miss Cosmopolitan.

"Anything you want, it's your money," she said.

We went into the third room, the fifty-dollar special. There is a queen-sized bed with a purple quilt, a small dresser, an overstuffed chair and a large closet.

"I don't think you should take this room," my Guardian Angel said.

"Why?"

"I really don't know but I have a feeling a monster might be in the closet."

"Is he green with big yellow eyes and likes to eat children?" I asked sarcastically.

"You'll be sorry oh wise one," he said.

I started to open the closet. "Don't," my Guardian Angel warned.

I hesitated.

Miss Cosmopolitan is standing only a few feet from me.

I once again started to open the closet door.

"Don't," my Guardian Angel warned again.

I hesitated again.

"There are no monsters in there," Miss Cosmopolitan said like I am a sissy.

What am I a man or a mouse? I opened the doors. Miss Cosmopolitan screamed, stepped backwards and fell on the bed in a stone cold faint. In the old days, when fainting scenes were romantic; it was called having an attack of the vapors.

I feel dumb. I am dumb. God had sent me one of his angels to protect me and guide me through life. I once again have not listened. It is a nice closet, there are ample hangers, even the big plastic kind to hang slacks on so they won't get a hanger mark. What messes it up is the man lying on the floor. A man lying on the floor, in itself is not that unusual, but when their throat has been cut and their dry tongue is sticking out of their mouth it changes the tune.

"I told you," my Guardian Angel said. "But no, you never listen. You never listen to me, me who has been with you all these years, nursed you, defended you, and stood by you. What do I get? Nothing. Nothing. You are a hard man to protect Roosevelt."

I looked at the man. I looked at his open, surprised eyes. I looked at the blood. I turned and looked at Miss Cosmopolitan. No matter how beautiful a woman, if they are passed out and have drool running out of the corner of their mouth, it is not a pretty sight. I shut the closet door.

"That will teach you to try and solve a cat murder," my Guardian Angel said.

"I should have listened to you and gone to the North Pole. I could have moved in with an Eskimo family. I could have sat around all winter freezing, eating raw whale fat and carving peace signs from walrus tusks and then this summer taken them to Seattle and made a small fortune."

"No, my disillusioned, lost in time and space, caught somewhere between being a cowboy and hippie, friend. If you would have gone to the North Pole you would still have found a way to muck it up," my Guardian Angel said with a tone in his voice that I knew I was destined until death takes me to always fall into a bucket of mud.

I am speechless. I am lost. I am three steps beyond confusion. But, I do know one thing. My Guardian Angel seldom calls me friend. There is no doubt about it. I am in for a rough time.

CHAPTER THREE
MISS COSMOPOLITAN

Miss Cosmopolitan moaned three times and sat up on the bed. She wiped the drool off the corner of her mouth with the back of her hand. "Is he dead?" she asked in a dreamy far away manner like she had been eating mushrooms but not the ones that come from Korea and are packed in water.

"Good thing she is good looking because she might lack a few brain cells," my Guardian Angel said.

"He is dead as dead can be," I replied, wondering if it was too late for me to bolt to the door, crank up Matilda and book it down the road even if I might be falling in love?

"You had your chance, Roosevelt," my Guardian Angel commented dryly.

"My lord! My lord! My lord!" Miss Cosmopolitan screeched sounding like an echo. She stood up and started jumping up and down with her legs close together it was like she had to urgently go to the bathroom, but had forgotten how to walk.

"What am I going to do? What am I going to do? What am I going to do?" she stammered, still jumping up and down.

"You are going to have to rid her of this repeating phobia and tell her, her interpretation of a rabbit is far from perfect," my Guardian Angel said.

"Calm down and call the cops," I told her.

"Of course, of course, of course," she agreed and hopped more than ran to the living room.

Following her, she picked up the phone, dialed, waited a few moments, all the time hopping, and then blurted. "There's a body in my closet. Come quick! Come quick! Come quick! Yes, of course, it's 311 Elm Street. Saint Ansgar."

She hung up the phone and fell back into an off purple recliner. She reminded me of a rabbit who had been drinking coffee for three days and finally crashed.

I went back to the bedroom and opened the closet. "I bet he is still dead," my Guardian Angel said.

His sense of humor is warped.

The body is lying on a king-sized yellow sheet that was doubled up but was not folded over the man. He is in his late twenties or early thirties. He is lying flat on his back and his arms are straight down his sides like he is standing at attention only lying down. He has black hair, cut the way marine sergeants like to cut their hair. He is clean-shaven. Forget the myth a beard grows after you are dead. He is wearing a long-sleeved white shirt with gold heart-shaped cuff links and a blue silk tie, tied in a perfect Windsor with a gold, heart-shaped tie tack. His throat had been cut cleanly. The wound is not jagged at all. It had to have been a sharp knife. I noticed the cut started just below his right jawbone and slanted downward through his Adams apple and stopped at his collarbone. There is blood on the front of his shirt, around the cut, but nowhere else. The blood is dry and has turned black in several places. He has on expensive gray slacks, an alligator belt and matching socks. His shoes are alligator loafers with a nice shine on them. He has on a gold wedding band, a gold link bracelet on his left wrist, and a gold Rolex on his right wrist. I rolled the body over enough to pull an alligator leather billfold out of his back pocket. Some poor alligator is swimming around Florida with a six-foot patch of skin missing from his back. The billfold is empty. I put it back. His other back pocket is empty. I let the body settle back into its original position. His front pockets are empty. I checked his shirt pocket and they are also empty. All I have discovered is that he is cold and stiff - the man has been in the closet for more than a day. I shut the closet door and looked at the carpet in the bedroom and checked the floor all the way to the front door. There are no blood spots. I checked the floor from the bedroom to the kitchen back door. There are no blood spots.

"This guy didn't float into the closet," my Guardian Angel said.

"No, and he didn't get killed in the closet either," I replied.

"Maybe aliens killed him in South Dakota and transported him to the closet with some molecular beam," he said seriously. "He saw them land their spacecraft, raid a closed McDonald's to see what you humans subsist on, and they had to kill him so he wouldn't tell the government aliens don't like French fries."

"You bet, and ravens can read the future," I said.

"The plains Indians believed ravens could see all and knew all," he replied.

"You're making that up?" I asked.

"No, it's true."

The thought intrigued me. It is a good setting for a novel. Too bad Edgar Allen Poe is dead.

I went back to the living room. Miss Cosmopolitan was still in the chair. I was about to say something when we both heard the siren. "I didn't do it. I didn't do it. I didn't do it," Miss Cosmopolitan pleaded. "You have to believe me, I didn't do it. I wanted him dead but I swear I didn't do it."

I was about to ask her who he was she wanted dead, but the doorbell rang. Police coming to a homicide scene in Saint Ansgar are polite. The city should ship a few of them to the Houston and L.A. police departments for a few lessons in humanity. Thinking about though, it isn't such a good idea. The Houston cops and L.A. cops would kill them for saying please and thank you.

Miss Cosmopolitan bunny hopped to the door. "He's in there, he's in there, he's in there," she stammered, pointing at the bedroom door.

The Sheriff is wearing an unzipped military brown parka that is bulky enough for a polar bear and has rubber boots over his boots. He has on a brown fur lined hat with the earflaps tied up. He is tall and skinny and has a thin light brown moustache. His face looks so innocent he could have been a male cheerleader in college. He couldn't be over 22 years old. The only thing that stops him from being a kid is the 44-colt magnum with an eight-inch barrel on his hip. The pistol is so long it almost hits him at the kneecap. With a gun that big who cares if he only has to shave once a week. He also has a cell phone on his belt. I take it Saint Ansgar doesn't have a dispatcher. The officer gave me a look that said you are a suspect, don't go anywhere.

"In the closet. In the closet. In the closet," having to go to the bathroom, bunny hopping, Miss Cosmopolitan said.

I followed the Sheriff with Miss bunny hop, hop, hop, hopping behind me. The Sheriff opened the closet door, looked at me, looked at Miss Cosmopolitan and then fainted. Real men don't get the vapors. Of course, real men don't have to carry a pistol that will blow holes the size of your head through a concrete wall. The Sheriff has to have an identity problem.

"That's wasted government money," my Guardian Angel said looking at the sprawled out Sheriff.

Miss Cosmopolitan looked at the Sheriff, looked at me, looked in the closet and crumpled to the floor like a dandelion hit with a shot of Round Up.

"Why don't you faint," my Guardian Angel said to me. "Then it would be a threesome."

"I'm not into threesomes."

"You are a boring person, Roosevelt."

"The older I get the more boring suits me."

"How well I know."

Miss Cosmopolitan sat up. If she said anything to me in triplicate I would scream. Holding out my hand I helped her up. "Why don't you make some coffee and check your roast," I said.

In the early days of TV shows this would have instantly calmed down a hysterical woman. In our modern day I expected her to yell at me. "Make your own coffee bonehead."

But she walked away like making coffee and checking a roast is what everybody does after they find a dead body in their closet.

The Sheriff moaned. I sat on the bed. If I smoked it would be a perfect time to light up.

The Sheriff moaned again and opened his eyes. He sat up slowly, rubbed his head, made sure he still had his pistol and stood. "I take it you've never seen a man with his throat cut before?" I said.

He smiled sheepishly and nodded his head. I didn't want to tell him about Nam.

He sat on the bed next to me looking embarrassed and lost at the same time. His face is the color of dirty snow - not the yellow kind. "I don't know what to do," he said to me.

"Take three aspirin, go home, drink a lot of water and call me when the fever goes down," my Guardian Angel said.

"Take your coat and hat off. It will make you feel better," I told the officer.

"Why?" my Guardian Angel asked.

"I don't know."

The cop stood and took his coat and hat off. I read his nameplate. Jack Benning.

"Take a few deep breaths, Sheriff Benning," I instructed.

He took several deep breaths and sat back down on the bed. The color is coming back to his face. "You should call the homicide boys," I told him.

"I'm the only cop in town," he replied.

"Where is police headquarters?" I asked.

"Albert Lee, about 90 miles north of here."

"You'd better call them and tell them their coffee break is over."

"I should look at the body," he said sheepishly.

I opened the closet door. Sheriff Jack Benning shook his head several times. "I'll be damned," he said.

"I'll be damned," he said again.

"I'll be damned," he said again.

"I wonder if there is a common gene around here that makes people repeat themselves?" my Guardian Angel asked.

"That's Carol's husband," Jack Benning said.

"Carol who?" I asked.

"You sound like an owl," my Guardian Angel said.

"Carol, the lady who lives here."

"What is his name?"

"Franklin."

"I'll be damned," I said.

"I'll be damned," my Guardian Angel said.

"I'll be damned," Jack Benning said.

I shut the closet door. I am about damned out.

"I'll call in," Officer Jack Benning said.

Officer Benning went outside to, I presume, call in on his radio. I went to the kitchen.

The roast is on a large platter on the table. Potatoes, onions and carrots are piled around the meat. There is also a steaming bowl of brown gravy. There are three place settings with the knives, spoons, and forks placed properly for a formal dinner.

"It's a happy murder dinner," my Guardian Angel said.

"It might be an early wake," I said.

I sat at the table, murder or no murder I am not going to miss out on a home cooked meal. Carol brought me a steaming cup of coffee. "It's not instant is it?" I asked.

"I grind my coffee from real beans," she said, insinuating that anybody who didn't grind their own beans is lower than a tomato worm.

I am in heaven. The older a man gets, the way to his heart his through his stomach is true. The stomach gets bigger, the lead pencil gets smaller.

Officer Jack Benning came into the kitchen and sat. "That's one good-looking roast," he told Carol.

People in Saint Ansgar don't let a little thing like a dead body in the closet ruin their appetites.

Carol beamed like Betty Crocker's daughter as she set a warm loaf of homemade white bread on the table and a stick of real butter. It is cholesterol heaven. She piled our plates with enough food for a Boy Scout troop before she sat.

We all ate like it was the last real food we would ever eat. The government was about to pass a law everybody had to eat bean sprouts, garbanzo beans, tofu, and vegetables pressed into the shapes of pork chops and chicken legs. A senator from California, who pushed the law, was proclaiming although vegetarians were a minority, we all had to do as they do so they didn't feel so alone.

Keeping good dinner etiquette we only talked about things that could not be argued over: the weather, the pro's and con's of the Minnesota Vikings playing in an indoor arena, how come The Doors were becoming popular again, body piercing, face tattoos, and how bad modern TV was even if you did get 3,157 channels.

About an hour after we started eating the doorbell rang. Carol went to answer the door. Three men followed Carol into the kitchen. They all have on dark suits, white shirts and ties, and knee length lined overcoats some color between beige and coffee brown. They'd been watching too many New York City based cop shows.

"Where's the body?" one of the men who must have been the senior detective demanded.

I guess he had to come all the way to the kitchen so he could smell the roast before he asked the big question.

Sheriff Jack Benning jumped up so fast he almost tripped and led them to the body. Carol and I stayed at the table. "Did you kill your husband?" I asked seriously.

"No," she answered simply.

"They might arrest you, you know?"

"Why? I didn't do it."

"You don't know our wonderful legal system. They don't care if you didn't do it."

"I don't want to go to jail," she said and started crying.

It is a good cry. Tears the size of grapes splashed on the table. Snot started to run out of her nose.

I handed her my handkerchief. Snot, like drool, is not a pretty sight, no matter how beautiful the woman is.

"A regular Sir Walter Raleigh," my Guardian Angel said.

"Do you know anybody who would post your bond?" I asked.

"I....sniff...sniff...sniff....have...honk into my handkerchief ...splash....splash...splash, grape size tears hitting the table...enough money....to make bond."

"If she would get naked I would put up her bond," my Guardian Angel said.

Sheriff Jack Benning and the officer who had to be the boss came back into the kitchen. The Officer Boss looked at Carol. "We know you didn't do it, Carol," he said soothingly and handed her another handkerchief, mine was wetter than a washcloth.

How he knew she didn't do it I don't know, but it is always wise to not ask cops questions, especially if you are a stranger in a small town.

"Thank you, thank you, thank you, Bill," she said dabbing her eyes.

Sheriff Jack Benning and Officer Boss, also known as Bill, sat down. Carol got Bill a cup of coffee. Bill looked at me the way a praying mantis looks at a cricket. "Bob Roosevelt, what are you doing in Saint Ansgar, Minnesota?"

"I asked him that myself," my Guardian Angel said.

Sheriff Jack Benning looked puzzled.

Carol looked puzzled.

"I don't know. I should have gone to the North Pole," I answered truthfully.

"This is Bob Roosevelt, he's a private detective," Bill said to Jack Benning and Carol. "He's an old hippie that became a detective and solved a kidnapping case in Florida and got on TV."

Sheriff Jack Benning was impressed.

"Don't ask for his autograph," my Guardian Angel said to Jack Benning, "you'll only make his head swell."

Bill held out his hand to shake. I hadn't noticed before but he is a big man, almost six feet tall and in his early fifties. He looks like an old guard for the Iowa Hawkeyes. One of those guys who don't know what a neck is and played football before sissies took over the game and had to wear facemasks. "I'm Bill Buffalo, Chief of Detectives out of Albert Lee," he said in a calm controlled voice.

"Glad to meet you," I replied, lying through my teeth.

Meeting detectives is never good unless you are the kind of person that enjoys going to police fundraisers or getting locked up.

The formalities done, Bill Buffalo asked me again. "What are you doing here?"

I decided to cut to the chase and leave out all the cosmic reasons that caused me to stop in Saint Ansgar. "I came by to rent a room."

"It's true," Carol said. "I have never seen him before today."

"I didn't ring the doorbell with a body under my arm and ask Carol if I could hide it in her closet while I went cross-country skiing," I said.

Jack Benning laughed. Carol laughed. Bill Buffalo didn't.

"I thought you were on vacation in Florida?" Bill Buffalo said to Carol.

"That explains the tan," my Guardian Angel said.

"I came back late last night. I've been gone for two weeks."

"How was it?" Bill Buffalo asked her.

I wondered why he didn't ask her if there was anybody who could verify her story.

"Wonderful, the sun was always out, the beaches weren't crowded. I didn't do anything but lie on the beach and read."

The detectives, the sheriff and I had the same vision at the same time - Carol lying on the beach in a string bikini so small it was useless.

"I don't see any reason to take you in for questioning," Bill Buffalo said to Carol.

"Or you," he said to me. "But I don't want either one of you to leave town until our investigation is over."

I nodded my head like I have super glue on my feet and couldn't leave if I had to. "Thank you, Bill," Carol cooed like a morning dove that had fallen in love for the first time.

We sat in the kitchen talking small talk while I presumed the other two detectives did the investigating thing. The conversation was starting to wane when they came into the kitchen. "We're all done. The boys from the morgue have picked up the body," one of the detectives said.

He looked at me, smiled like he had shot a cat burglar, and said. "Bob Roosevelt, the detective that was on TV, I'll be, what are you doing in a berg like this?"

"Learning how to treat frostbite," my Guardian Angel said.

"This is Pete Rosebet and Paul Binyon," Bill Buffalo introduced me. "They are two of the finest men on the force."

Pete Rosebet is thin and has a tiny moustache. He reminds me of Charlie Chaplin but I doubt he has as many young girlfriends. Paul Binyon is slightly overweight, blond headed, and has happy eyes. I stood and shook hands with each man.

Officer Bill Buffalo took a card out of his billfold and handed it to me. "Call me if you come up with anything," he ordered like I was going to try and find out who killed the husband, whose wife didn't do it, but wanted him dead.

"And don't you worry your pretty little head," Bill Buffalo said to Carol.

Pete Rosebet and Paul Binyon looked at her like they are her long lost brothers but I knew they were only looking at her body.

Carol led the long arms of the law to the door. When she came back she is as happy as a cheerleader even though she doesn't know how the score is kept.

"So you are a famous detective," she smiled at me as she sat. There is no trace of fear in her eyes.

"We don't get too many famous people around here," Sheriff Jack Benning said.

"Oh, it isn't much," I said, trying to act humble.

"Can I have your autograph?" Jack Benning asked as he took a note pad and pencil out of his breast pocket.

'To the most professional Sheriff I have ever met, Bob Roosevelt,' I wrote and handed the pad and paper back.

He read it and his face lit up like a little kid looking at his first Christmas tree. He put the pad and pen back in his pocket, stood, smiled at Carol, shook my hand, and started to leave, stopped, took a business card out of his pocket and handed it to me. "This is my cell phone number. I always have it with me. I have a feeling you might need it," he told me as he gave me the card.

"That is your second business card of the day. These fools must think you can make them some money," my Guardian Angel said.

Walking down the hall to get his coat I heard Jack Benning muttering, "I'll be, Bob Roosevelt, I'll be, I'll be."

"You be a fool, you be a fool, you be a fool," my Guardian Angel hollered at his back.

Carol is looking at me like a freshman girl looks at a senior boy who is the football team's starting quarterback. The guy, who in high school, is voted the student most likely to succeed, but ends up doing three years for statutory rape and when he gets out of the pen sells used cars at Joe's Car Lot where everybody gets credit.

"It must be wonderful to have been on TV. I have always wanted to be an actress. I studied drama in college and was in all of the plays," Carol said, sounding sad.

"One can never let go of their dreams."

"I don't. But the older I get my chances get smaller and smaller."

I take it nobody has told her that in order to be an actress she should move to Minneapolis.

Because I was the one that found the body in the closet I feel obligated to get involved.

"Don't," my Guardian Angel warned. "Stick with finding a heart and solving cat murders. It will be safer."

He is smart. He is wise. He rarely gives me bad advice. Do I listen?

"So that was your husband in the closet?" I said to Carol.

"We were in the process of getting a divorce, but that was him," she said, but not sadly. "He was a two-timing low life that didn't have the decency to take it out of town."

"I take it he had an affair with a lady in town?"

"One, how about three, three that I know of."

"How did you find out?" I asked, which as soon as the words were out of my mouth I knew the question, on the stupid question scale of one to ten, is about a nine.

Carol looked at me like I have to be the stupidest private detective in the world - which I am. "Roosevelt, this town only has 564 people in it. People around here know when you turn on the TV."

"Who was the last lady he had an affair with?" I asked, trying to save face.

"That pig who owns the HOME OF HEARTS, Fanny Ruth."

"When a person tosses his life to the wind, freeing up all the potential he possesses, letting life take him on his true destiny, that person more often than not wishes he would have been a shoe salesman in Topeka," my Guardian Angel said.

"Do you think it's too late in my life to move to Omaha and sell mobile homes?" I asked him.

"Once again a budding love for you is nipped in the bud," he said.

I feel lost, my feet are off the ground, my head is in the clouds, a normal state when I was a pot head and making leather pouches to put tobacco, bottle caps, shiny pebbles and roach clips in, and hang around my neck to keep the evil spirits away.

"By the expression on your face you look like you know Fanny Ruth," Carol said.

"I stopped to have a cup of tea and met her."

"You're lucky she didn't toss your longhaired cowboy body down on the floor and rip your clothes off. She'll sleep with any man that can walk."

"I take offense at that statement," I said.

It's not nice to make jokes about a man's libido and, besides, I'm not just any man.

Carol apologized. "I didn't mean it to sound the way it did. To tell you the truth, you're kind of good looking for a man your age."

"Call him sir and really rub it in," my Guardian Angel said.

"Actually, I like older men," Carol said. "They are more caring. They really want to get to know a woman. They want to see into her brain and see what she sees. They like to hold hands, send flowers, and drink champagne. All those little romantic things that are special in a relationship."

"Go get 42 dozen long stemmed red roses, 16 dozen white carnations, 14 dozen mixed mums and a case of the cheapest champagne you can find," my Guardian Angel said and started dancing a jig that male English pagans danced before the ceremony when all the men in the village were going to sleep with all the young maidens so the wheat would grow. They also had this ceremony for corn, squash, cabbage, radishes, onions, the new moon, the quarter moon, the half-moon, the full moon, rain, snow, sleet, hail, wind and on and on and on. This is the real reason most pagan men died in their 30's.

"Roosevelt, can you do me a favor?" Carol asked. She already knew the answer and went on without giving me a chance to say anything. Women are good at this. "Will you find out who killed my husband for me?"

"Say yes," my Guardian Angel begged.

"You told me to stick with cat murder," I said.

"That was before I knew Carol liked older men," he replied.

Carol's eyes beseeched me.

"I'll find out who killed him," I answered.

"Yes....yes....yes...." my Guardian Angel was giving himself high fives.

"You can stay here for free and I will cook for you," Carol said.

"Yes....yes...yes...." my Guardian Angel is smiling bigger than little Donny Osmond.

"I'll even pay you," Carol said. "When you solve the case I'll give you $3000."

"Tell her you'll find the killer for free," my Guardian Angel said.

"This is America, nothing is free," I told him.

"I'll take the room farthest from the bathroom," I told Carol. "But you should know I never mix business with pleasure."

She smiled at me, like yea, right, wait till you see me naked.

Looking at my watch it is 4:30. I am going to see Fanny Ruth at 6:00. "I'll get my things out of the car," I said to Carol.

"This deal with Fanny Ruth and Carol could get to be a problem," my Guardian Angel said to me as I got my things.

"I don't think 'could get to' is the right phrase. How about, already is a problem," I said.

Carol watched me hang my few things in the closet. She seems to have completely forgotten her husband had been found dead in the next room - at least she didn't have to wait for the divorce to be completed.

"By the way. Since I am going to be sleeping and eating here what is your last name?" I asked.

"Trouble. My name is Carol Trouble," she said and smiled at me like a Texas cat smiles at a slow lizard.

"Oh, oh, Roosevelt," my Guardian Angel said.

CHAPTER FOUR
A WHITE KNIT BIKINI

It didn't take me long to straighten out my things in the closet. An old hippie, only partially sold out, does not own much. A few western shirts, three pairs of Levi's, underclothes, a pair of stepping out boots, shave kit, a 9 m.m. pistol and a box of shells, a notebook and a pencil. What else do I need in life?

"A brain, common sense, a few bucks unless you are born with a silver spoon, luck, food, water, sex, Vitamins A and E, zinc, need I go on?" my Guardian Angel asked.

"You are not good for helping me hold onto a small amount of identity," I told him.

"You have to have a small amount of identity first," he replied casually.

I checked the time on my ten-dollar Kmart watch. I have an hour before I go to Fanny Ruth's. Carol had gone to the basement to, as she said, "to freshen up."

"Why don't you go down and ask her if you can help her freshen up?" my Guardian Angel asked.

"Why don't I go to the bedroom where the body was and see what the detectives did and maybe find out something?" I said.

"You can start on the murder after you see Carol naked," he said.

Sometimes my Guardian Angel's priorities are not always in the right order.

"You really know how to bum an angel out," he said, feeling

sorry for himself.

The bedroom hasn't changed except there isn't a body in the closet. There is a trace of fingerprint powder on the windowsill and surprisingly, when the detectives were done they had cleaned up. The detectives had not drawn a circle around the body. But, I suppose, if there is a body in the closet there is no need to draw a circle around it. I've always wondered why cops draw circles around dead bodies anyway. Is it to remind them there was a body there? If so, how could they have forgotten? I went through the dresser, each drawer is empty. The closet is empty. There is nothing under the bed or under the mattress. "Oh great private detective who is wasting time when he should be downstairs helping a gorgeous woman freshen up, what now?" my Guardian Angel asked.

I ran my hand inside the creases of the chair as far as I could push it down. Deep in the back crease I felt something hard and smooth. With a lot of twisting and turning I managed to pull a smooth, dark blue glass heart, about the size of a half dollar, out of the crease. There is a gold clasp on the heart but no chain. Back in my room I put the heart in my suitcase.

"Now go help Carol freshen up," my Guardian Angel said.

"I'm going to take a shower."

"Alone?"

"Yes."

"Bummer."

The sun was setting as I was about to leave the house. I have on clean clothes and my stepping out Ostrich cowboy boots. Some Ostrich isn't happy but they are great boots. "Aren't you forgetting something?" my Guardian Angel asked.

"I should get a key to the front door from Carol."

"True, but aren't you forgetting something more important than a key?"

I had to think. I have money. I have my car keys. "Not that I know of," I replied.

"Your pistol, you idiot, you're forgetting your pistol."

"I don't need my pistol. I'm going to dinner at a Tea Room."

"Ok, have it your way. I'm only trying to help."

Sometimes I think my Guardian Angel should have been a

woman.

There are two cars parked in front of the HOME OF HEARTS, a new dark green Buick and a new bright yellow Volkswagen bug. Parking beside the new bug I thought I heard Matilda tell it, "you look cheap."

Older Volkswagens can be kind of gnarly to young Volkswagens.

A man and women in their early to mid-fifties are looking at the hearts in the first room. The lady is dressed expensively and is refined. The man, short and dumpy, and almost bald, has an air of importance that floats around him in an impenetrable cloud. The lady smiled at me and went back to looking at the hearts. The man glanced at me with no expression on his face. "Lovely, they are lovely," I heard the woman comment.

"Buy a few and let's get out of here," her husband said gruffly.

A young lady, around eighteen, is in the middle room. She is thin and pretty and looks innocent in a way only the young can. She has long auburn hair, is wearing wire rimmed glasses, has peace sign earrings in her ears, a peace sign strung on a leather cord hanging from her neck, and has a small multi colored beaded purse. She is mesmerized by the hearts. As I went by her she gazed at me with far away eyes and said, "Peace."

I smiled at her and formed my fingers into the peace sign and hoped she could hold onto her dreams in this world of wars.

"Poor thing, the world is going to beat her up," my Guardian Angel said.

What could I say?

When I walked by the room where the QUEEN OF HEARTS had been the light that shone down on the glass dome was turned off.

Fanny and Clyde are in the Tea Room. Fanny is standing by the cash register and Clyde is perched on top of it. "I'm so glad you came," Fanny grinned at me in a way I knew she was relieved I had shown up.

"Crap," Clyde squawked.

Fanny had changed clothes. She is wearing bib overalls over a white, cotton, long underwear top, with three of the top buttons unbuttoned. She looks sexy in a milkmaid kind of way and I smiled at her.

"If you were going to take one home to mama this would be the one," my Guardian Angel said. "If you were going to take one to Vegas and throw away all your money it would be Carol. Myself I am more into the Vegas type."

The older couple walked into the Tea Room. The lady put a handful of hearts on the counter. "These are nice, Mrs. Boraxe," Fanny told her.

"I so love your shop, Fanny. When we travel I tell all my friends about it," the lady said. "You should try mail order or get on the web to boost your sales."

"It's in the planning stages," Fanny answered.

I saw Fanny glance at the man the same time he glanced at her. I don't know what it was, but something passed between them and I sensed that something isn't good.

The lady smiled at me as the couple left. The man walked beside her like it pained him to be seen in public.

"Who are they?" I asked Fanny.

"That's Merriam and Dale Boraxe. He is the mayor. They have more money than God. Mr. Boraxe owns over 5,000 acres in this county."

"I should talk to him about making the red light in town a blinking light," my Guardian Angel said.

I sat at the table. Fanny headed toward me with a cup. I was about to tell her no more tea as she set the cup down. "I made you real coffee, real men need real coffee."

"Coffee sucks," Clyde squawked.

"Real men should be more sensitive to the needs of their Guardian Angel," my Guardian Angel said.

"Real Guardian Angels should shut up," I said.

The hippie girl walked into the Tea Room. She smiled at me as she headed to the counter. Reaching the counter Clyde flopped onto her shoulder. "Me love you, bad cat, bad cat, crap, too cold, too cold, damn farmer, cowboy, not you, not you, not you, pretty, pretty, coffee sucks, good, good, good tea, shut up, peace," he squawked.

Young cute innocent looking hippie girls must excite him.

"I love you too, Clyde, you are a creature of the universe, not more important or less important than any of us," the girl said to the raven.

"Crap," Clyde squawked.

"I'm glad to see you are doing fine, Sheila," Fanny said.

"It's good to be home," Sheila replied, setting a glass heart on the counter.

Clyde hopped from her shoulder down to the heart and looked at it. "Pretty, pretty," he squawked.

Fanny rang up the heart and put it in a small case before giving it to Sheila.

Sheila gave her money from a beaded purse. "Where is the QUEEN OF HEARTS?" she asked, putting the purchase in her purse.

"I'm having it cleaned," Fanny answered. She looked at me letting me know to keep my mouth shut.

Sheila gave me a faraway smile.

"This is Bob Roosevelt. He is an old friend of mine," Fanny told Sheila. "Bob this is Sheila Harberts."

"It's nice to have friends," Sheila said in a dreamy voice before she left.

Fanny came over and sat. "She is such a nice girl. It's too bad what she has done with her life."

I didn't want to know what she had done, but Fanny went on. "Earl Harberts is president of the bank and Brenda, her mother, owns the bar in town. Sheila has always been different - the quiet loner type. After Sheila graduated from high school she fell heavy into drugs. They found her one night wandering around a field completely naked and screaming at the sky over and over, "why can't we live in love?" Earl had her committed to the nut house in Rochester. It's been a year and she just got back last week."

"It's a good question she asked," I said.

"I know," Fanny replied sadly. "She is living with her parents for now. They just bought her a new Volkswagen."

I wondered if the new car would help solve her problems. Why is it in the modern world that we think if we go shopping life will get better?

Clyde walked across the floor and hopped up onto a chair bottom and then using his beak swung up onto the top of the table.

"Where does Clyde go to the bathroom?" I asked Fanny. I have to know, the question has been bothering me.

"He goes upstairs and uses the toilet."

The image of Clyde sitting on the edge of the toilet and pooping made me laugh.

Fanny laughed.

My Guardian Angel laughed.

"Not you, not you, not you," Clyde squawked looking at us like we are dumber than sparrows.

"Let's go upstairs, I have dinner in the oven," Fanny said as she stood. Clyde flopped to her shoulder.

Fanny was baking pork chops. Roast beef for lunch and pork chops for dinner. I am in double heaven.

"I wish I could eat," my Guardian Angel commented sadly.

Fanny put the chops on the table and sat. She looks like the grace saying type so I waited for her to say grace.

"Go ahead and serve yourself. I don't believe in grace," Fanny told me with a slightly caustic tone in her voice.

Clyde sat on the edge of the table and ate tid-bits of food Fanny gave him. While we ate I studied Fanny's face. It is a sad face, a lonely face, but a good face. If she had slept with Carol's husband I felt she had been used or caught in a moment when her loneliness was too much for her to handle and any touch, even a married man's touch, took the loneliness away if only for a few moments. Her loneliness drew me to her. "Do you know Carol Trouble's husband?" I asked her.

Fanny was not alarmed by my question. "Of course I know him. He lent me the money to buy my first inventory for the store. He has always been nice to me."

"She slept with him out of thanks," my Guardian Angel said.

"You are a heartless angel," I told him.

"Most people in town were afraid of him," Fanny went on. "He was a big gambler, a good gambler, and some say he was a hood, but he was never arrested. If he was a hood he kept his business out of town and he really didn't care what people thought about him."

"Where did he gamble?" I asked.

"There are Indian casinos all over the state, but I think he gambled mostly in private poker games. Games set up by people he'd met through the years."

The gambling explained his good shoes and expensive jewelry.

I finished eating. Fanny poured me a cup of coffee.

I could see no reason to beat around the bush although I didn't like being the one to break the news to her. "Franklin Trouble was found dead in the closet of Carol's house this afternoon," I told Fanny.

Fanny looked at me in disbelief. "No, no, it isn't true," she stammered but didn't cry.

"I found him. His throat had been cut."

She took a deep breath. "That's what the siren was for I heard this afternoon," she said to herself more than to me. "He was a friend. I have so few friends," she sighed then looked at me quizzically. "I thought you went to Carol's to rent a room?"

"I did."

"He didn't live there. They have been separated for months. The final divorce papers were due in a few weeks. He bought a house in the country a few months ago and lives there."

I wondered why Carol hadn't told me about the house. I wondered why Fanny didn't seem to be overly shocked over Franklin's death. I wondered if the cops knew about Franklin and Carol getting a divorce and Franklin living in a house away from his wife.

"Did he mess around on Carol when they were together?" I asked.

"Mess around, they both messed around, Carol is hotter than Thai food. All you have to do is put your finger on her and her pants come off."

"Drink your coffee and get back to the house and put your little finger on Carol's forehead," my Guardian Angel ordered.

"Did you sleep with Franklin?" I asked.

Fanny thought to herself for a few moments and then said. "He came over here one night a few months ago. I had paid him back the money he loaned me but he would come over every so often to see if I needed anything. We talked awhile and he bought a set of heart shaped gold cuff links and a heart shaped gold tie tack. One thing led to another and we ended up in bed. It wasn't what you think or read in a romance novel. There was no great amount of passion. It was more like two lonely people, who for a brief moment, keep the loneliness away."

I smiled at her and said, "I understand completely."

She reached over and touched my hand, smiled sadly at me and said. "I feel a deep warmth in you, an understanding. I think we could be good friends and maybe more."

"I hope so," I replied.

"Does Carol work?" I asked Fanny.

"She has never worked. Franklin always had a lot of money. While he was off gambling she went on trips. She loves Florida. When they separated he gave her the house in town."

"Strange," I muttered, but thought to myself, he must have given her a lot of money for her to have a new Mercedes.

"Weird that she rents out rooms," my Guardian Angel muttered.

"Crap, cowboy," Clyde squawked.

"Crap, cowboy," is right, I agreed.

Fanny poured me another cup of coffee. "A murder in Saint Ansgar, this will shake up the old town," she said in a manner like it made her happy.

"Why didn't you call the police when you found your heart missing and the cats were killed?" I asked her.

"I presume you met Sheriff Jack Benning. He couldn't find his butt if somebody didn't tell him it was in back of him. All he would do is look around, scratch his head, and play with his pistol and leave."

"I wish Roosevelt would let somebody play with his pistol," my Guardian Angel said.

"If you hadn't walked in I wouldn't have any hope of getting my heart back?" Fanny said to me, her sad eyes burning into mine. "It was destiny you showed up."

"It was stupidity," my Guardian Angel said.

Destiny or not I don't know what to do or where to start. There are two dead cats that died from their throats being cut, a stolen diamond heart, a dead man who died from a cut throat, a separated wife hotter than Thai food who wanted her husband dead but said she didn't do it, and Fanny, who did sleep with the dead man and who makes my old heart twang.

"Do you dislike Carol?" I asked.

"No, I've never really known her. She probably doesn't like me though. Franklin told her we had an affair. If sleeping with a man who is separated is called an affair?"

"I think it's called a separatedfair," my Guardian Angel said, "and is one sin level down from true adultery."

"Have you ever been married?" I asked Fanny.

Fanny shook her head. "Not even close. Oh, I've loved a few men but the men I loved didn't know I existed."

There was a trace of bitterness in her voice.

"What were the names of your cats that got killed?" I asked.

"Lucifer and Black Magic. They were nice cats. I had them since they were kittens."

"Witch cats," my Guardian Angel said.

Looking at my cheap Kmart watch it is almost 9:00. "I'm tired and should be going," I said. I had asked enough questions for one night.

"You could try to get it on with Fanny and then go have some Thai food for a snack," my Guardian Angel suggested.

"Do you think you'll find my heart?" Fanny asked me as we both stood.

"I hope so," I told her.

She walked with me to the front door. I feel she wants me to stay. I feel she is deeply grieved over Franklin's murder. She looks lost, alone. Tears are forming in her eyes. Smiling sadly at her I left feeling useless.

"I don't want to get in the way of your heart," my Guardian Angel said. "But I think there are some deep dark things about Fanny you don't want to get involved with."

The cold felt good on my face as I walked to Matilda. There are no clouds and the stars are bright burning embers. They aren't embers of hope, though, they are dying embers.

Driving to Carol's I started to turn into the driveway, but decided not to and drove to the edge of town. I stopped when the pavement ended, left Matilda running, turned off the headlights and got out. I walked several yards down the road. I am bothered.

I have a feeling that whatever is bothering me is something I really don't want to find out. I looked up at the millions and millions of stars. What are dreams and hopes and needs and desires when we can be snuffed out so quickly without a last flash of glory like a falling star? We are not stars. We are not planets. We are not light years. What are we?

"You're a mushroom trip that never ends," my Guardian Angel said.

A set of headlights came toward me from town. I started back towards Matilda. "Lock and load!" my Guardian Angel yelled. "Commies at six o'clock!"

The car sped up and I dove for the ditch as the car raced by. I didn't have time to look at the car. Three loud explosions interrupted as I rolled down the ditch. The car did not slow down. Jumping up I reached for my pistol. I could get a few quick shots off at the rear of the car but my pistol was in my room.

"Told you to bring it, told you so, told you so," my Guardian Angel taunted.

The taillights to the car faded in the distance. I hadn't had time to see what make the car was or its color. I knocked the snow off of me, got a flashlight out of Matilda and looked at the snow packed road. There was no way to make out a single tire tread from all the tracks already in the road. I searched for several minutes but didn't find any spent cartridges. They must have been extracted in the car. I drove to Carol's. If the shots had been heard nobody was standing on their porches to see what had happened. People in Saint Ansgar probably thought it was deer poachers.

I parked in Carol's driveway with one thought burning in my mind. There are not many people in town who know I am a detective.

The baby blue Mercedes was not in the driveway. Before going to the door I looked in the garage. The Mercedes is in the garage. I went into the garage and felt the hood of the car. The metal was cool.

The front door to the house is locked. I would have to get a key. I once again followed the instructions on the door and rang the bell.

The door swung open, if my tongue wasn't attached it would

have hit the floor. "Hello sailor boy," Carol said.

She is barefoot, wearing a white knit bikini so small it would have looked big on a flea. "I heard your ship came in and I knew you would be by to see me."

"Throw money at her feet, toss her diamonds, give her a car," my Guardian Angel stammered.

"Follow me sir, your table is right over here."

I followed her like a hypnotized moose. We went down into the basement. On the walls are painted ocean scenes. Palms swayed with the wind. Parrots perched on Mango trees. The ocean stretched out beyond sight. A round bed, big enough for the Chicago White Sox baseball team to sleep in is in one corner. The walls around the bed and over it are covered with mirrors. A Jacuzzi surrounded by lava rock is in another corner, candles flicker in the rising steam. A TV screen any sports bar in the world would covet is against another wall, next to it is a small bar. Carol put the beer down on the table by a sofa. "Have a seat," she smiled and walked toward the bar. She mixed a drink and came back.

"Watching her walk, bounce, jiggle, sway, vibrate, beats the heck out of eating pork chops," my Guardian Angel said.

Carol sat. She smells like the ocean. I sipped my beer. She sipped her drink. I took another sip of beer. She took her top off. I sipped my beer and felt perspiration run down my back. She slipped out of the bikini bottoms. She is like a golden goddess. Do I care if she might have killed her husband? Do I care if she might have slept with every man in town? Do I care if she had ten known sexually transmitted diseases and might have two or three that aren’t known?

"Forget the small stuff," my Guardian Angel said.

I stood. "I can't. I'm sorry. I don't mix pleasure with business," I said, trying to sound calm. "And I have made a vow with myself I will only sleep with a woman I love."

My Guardian Angel started crying.

Carol looked shocked, put her bikini back on and then started to laugh.

"It's not funny," my Guardian Angel said.

"A regular knight in shining armor," Carol said.

"No, an idiot," I said.

"Some other time, big boy," Carol said and winked at me.

I went to my room and got my notebook and pencil and started writing down everything I knew about dead cats, stolen hearts, dead gamblers, Thai hot women, lonely women, hippie girls who had been to the nut house, unfriendly mayors and somebody who goes shooting at night but can't hit the side of a barn - me being the barn.

I do not own a laptop. There is something about batteries that bothers me. I also do not own a cell phone. Cell phone conversations are considered open airways by law which means they can be listened to by anybody, including your friendly police, without a warrant for a phone tap. So, I make all my phone calls from pay phones. I don’t want anybody listening in on my conversations even if they are boring. Also, with so many laws on the books right now who knows when they are breaking a law and might end up doing five years - trust me - I didn’t know I was breaking the law is not an excuse that will hold up in court.

I wrote and then reread my clues. It might not be a bestseller but at least it is a draft. One has to start from somewhere.

CHAPTER FIVE
HEY MISTER WOULD YOU PLAY WITH ME?

In the morning Carol was gone. I did the toothbrush, deodorant thing, and headed out of the house as quickly as possible - taking my pistol with me - this boy only has to be shot at once to get smart.

I put my pistol under the car seat. Matilda cranked right up and I headed for Albert Lee. I want to talk to Detectives Bill Buffalo, Pete Rosebet and Paul Binyon.

Saint Ansgar is twelve miles from the interstate and before I knew it I was putting north. A Volkswagen bug does not zoom.

It feels good to be driving. Driving is like a sedative to me - a period of time when I am stuck up in between and it doesn't matter if I am stuck up in between. I drove past farmhouses, around little towns, trucks, cars, busses - all in themselves different worlds. All of us separated, but a part of the same pattern even if we don't know what the pattern is.

The police headquarters in Albert Lee isn't too impressive - a one-story brick building surrounded by dirty snow. A lady receptionist, who looks like her hobby is milking cows, directed me to Bill Buffalo's office. I knocked on the door. "Enter," came gruffly from behind the door.

Detective Bill Buffalo scowled at me from behind his desk. His desk is a pile of papers so unorganized it looks like a mailman had dumped his pouch on it. "You porkin' Carol yet?" he asked me, which I thought was a strange way to say hello.

"What's do you think I am, a barbecue?" I said.

He started to laugh. It is a deep, hearty laugh, a laugh Santa Claus would be proud of. "You know, Roosevelt, I think I like you," he said. "What brings you to beautiful Albert Lee?"

"I want to ask you a few questions," I said.

"That's my job, not yours."

"If we work together we might be able to get to the bottom of Franklin Trouble's murder."

"I thought murders got solved not bottomed," he chuckled.

"This guy is funnier than you," my Guardian Angel said.

"What makes you think we need your help to solve the murder?" Bill Buffalo asked.

"Roosevelt has a big head," my Guardian Angel said. "He thinks the world needs him."

"I figured you boys would be so busy busting small time dope dealers you wouldn't have time to go back and forth to Saint Ansgar for a measly small town murder."

"I wish these new dopers were like you old hippies." Bill Buffalo said, completely changing the subject. "It was easy then. You peace and love freaks didn't carry guns. Busting you guys for pot and acid was a snap. Now it's crank, heroin, crack, ecstasy, and everybody owns a machine gun and isn't afraid to use it."

"It's not my fault the government created an industry that's so big organized crime got involved," I said, adding. "A government cannot control morals."

"Pays my check," he smiled, but there was no joy in his smile, he knew I was right. "Sit down Roosevelt. Ask me as many questions as you'd like?"

"Is your girlfriend pretty?" I asked.

"I don't have a girlfriend, I have a wife and she is uglier than a tax form. But I love her"

"Did you find anything in the bedroom?" I asked Detective Bill Buffalo.

"Nothing, no fingerprints except yours and Carol's, no hair, no blood on the floor, we even used a laser on the floor for any blood spots that couldn't be seen by the naked eye."

"Why do you have Carol's prints on file," I asked.

"She got picked up on a D.W.I. once."

"Do you think Carol did it?"

"Her alibi checks out. According to United Airlines she got back from Florida at 10:00 p.m. the night before you found the body. It's about a three-hour drive from Minneapolis to Saint Ansgar, which would have put her in around 1:00 a.m. According to the coroner Franklin had been dead at least 24 hours."

"He was stiffer than a piece of Japanese plywood made off the coast of Washington when I found him," I said.

"Did you find anything?" he asked me.

I shook my head. For some reason I decided not to tell him about the heart.

"The autopsy didn't discover anything either," he went on. "There were no drugs in his system, no poison, a low level of alcohol, no knocks on the head, no cuts, no bruises on the body, and no skin under the fingernails. All we know was somebody cut his throat with an extremely sharp knife, maybe a straight razor the wound was so clean."

"I understand Franklin was a gambler. Do you think he owed any money? Enough to get killed over?"

"The boy was a big gambler but from what information we have on him he never lost a lot. He knew when to quit. A pro doesn't take long shots or ride a losing string. He knows it comes and goes."

"Was he a crook?"

"If he was he was the best crook I've ever heard about. No arrests, no rumors, no connections with known crooks. I don't think so. He was a big card player. There's a slight chance whoever killed him owed him. But I don't think so. I don't think Franklin had any muscle around him to collect on bets and maybe scare someone into killing him. Like I said, he was a pro. A pro can't be bothered by people who can't pay and probably wouldn't sit down at a game unless there was cash on the table. I.O.U's don't cut it in the gambling business."

"Do you think somebody killed him who knew he had a lot of cash on him?"

"It's possible."

"Anything crooked going on around Saint Ansgar that you know of? Meth Labs, stash houses, anything?"

"That town is cleaner than a hotel room at the Hilton. The only thing going on in Saint Ansgar is the town is so small people get divorced and marry their neighbor's husband or wife."

"We know one thing," I said. "We know whoever killed him killed him someplace else and carried him into the closet."

"Why?"

"No blood in the house. The body was stiff. And there was no blood on the floor around his head. If he had been killed in the house there would have been blood everywhere. Blood shoots everywhere when a throat gets cut."

"I guess we have to find out who killed him, where he was killed, and why would they want to take him to Carol's?" Bill Buffalo mused.

"It would be a bingo," I answered.

"How long are you going to hang around, Roosevelt?"

"Until he tries some Thai food, I hope," my Guardian Angel answered.

"I'll snoop around until I figure I can't find anything out."

"People tell me Carol is one hot package."

I wonder what it is but people always want to know who you are sleeping with and when you slept with them. We are a sick society.

"Do you know a Sheila Harberts?" I asked.

"She's a nice kid. Got strung out on ecstasy last year. People found her running around in a cornfield naked. I've always liked her mother but her father is strange. When Sheila went over the deep end her father put her in the nut house. Her mother was opposed to it. I've heard they've been fighting every since."

"Sheila's out now. I saw her the other evening."

"You might be able to help her. Like I said, she's a nice kid, you being an old hippie might be able to get her on the straight and narrow path. Somebody has to tell her there's nothing to this peace and love garbage. She has to face the real world."

"The real world sucks," I said.

"I know," he agreed. "But what can we do about it?"

"Have millions of people believe like the hippies did but without the dope."

"Roosevelt, in this modern world we all have our own form of dope."

I changed the subject. It was getting depressing. "Are Detectives Pete Rosebet and Paul Binyon around?"

"No, they're over at Fairmont. A farmer over there was letting car thieves strip cars in his barn. One of the thieves got busted and snitched him."

I couldn't think of anything else I wanted to ask Detective Bill Buffalo and stood and held out my hand to shake. "If I stumble onto anything I'll let you know," I told him.

"You let me know when you stumble onto Carol," he laughed.

I was halfway down the hall when I turned around, knocked on Bill Buffalo's door and walked in without waiting for him to say, enter. He was about to make a phone call. "One more thing, do you know anything about Fanny Ruth?"

He put the phone down on the receiver. "She is a lonely lady who has had some problems but nothing to be afraid of."

I think there is more to the story but I could tell by his expression he wasn't going to tell me.

"When you guys came down after Sheriff Jack Benning called why didn't you search the entire house?" I asked.

"If you killed your wife would you stuff her in the closet and make dinner? If I killed my wife at night I'd throw her in a field somewhere before the sun came up. We didn't search the rest of the house because there was no need. Now get out of here."

I know when I have overplayed my welcome.

"You should have told him you got shot at," my Guardian Angel told me as I started Matilda.

"I felt like it but something held me back," I replied.

Back on the interstate I wondered what problems Fanny Ruth has? And I don't know if I believe Bill Buffalo's reasons for not searching the entire house.

I stopped at a McDonald's. After a day of roast beef and pork chops, with all the essential food groups, I need to get my feet back on the ground. Limp French fries, an overcooked hamburger with a soggy bun and a flat coke, served by a kid who thinks polite consists of the words, yea and nope, will do it every time.

It was 4:00 p.m. when I pulled into Saint Ansgar and time for a beer. I parked in front of the bar. My first time into town I couldn't read the sign. Now, up close, I could make out the faded word: MOM'S. I guess Mom and Pop has gone out of style.

Since it is the middle of the winter and no farmers were planting crops, there are no whore houses in town, no bingo parlors, gambling joints, or topless bars, the bar is packed - the general mode of dress for the men is bib overalls. About fifteen men are standing elbow to elbow at the bar while couples are at the tables either talking or playing cards. Cigarette smoke hangs in the air in dark stagnant clouds but the air is still fresher than a good day in Dallas. A waitress with sandy red hair and a cigarette hanging out of the corner of her mouth is waiting on the tables. She is a big, strong woman that looks like she could make the Russian women's weight lifting team.

A lady, who could have been 40 or 50, depending on the light, is behind the bar. "I bet that's mom," my Guardian Angel said.

I went to the end of the bar. The guy at the end of the line scooted over making room for me, causing everybody else along the bar to scoot over. It looked like a mini wave at a football game. The lady behind the bar came over to me. "You must be that dick, Roosevelt," she said to me in a deep scratchy voice caused by too many years in a smoke filled bar. "I'm Mom."

"It's detective, not dick," I smiled at her.

"He's more of a dick than a detective," my Guardian Angel said.

Mom raised her arms up and instantly the entire bar became quiet. "Ladies and gentlemen, bums and misfits, I want to introduce you all to Bob Roosevelt, he's the detective that was on TV and found Franklin."

There were comments ranging from, "I'll be damned. What the hell is he doing here? To, we don't need no more cops in town."

"First beer is on the house," Mom told me, "what will it be?"

"Have any dark beer?"

"This is Minnesota we have every beer in the world. What else is there to do up here in the winter except drink?"

"Ice fish," the man next to me said seriously.

"Guinness," I ordered.

I noticed every man at the bar was looking intently at me. I wondered if I had an outbreak of acne. I also wondered if two of them had been the ones to take a pot shot at me.

"Why do you think it was two men who shot at you?" my Guardian Angel asked.

"A driver and a shooter. The car went by me on the shotgun side."

I can be very, very, very smart. But I can also be very, very, very, very, dumb.

"Are you going to stay in town and try and find Franklin's killer?" the ice fisherman asked.

"I don't know. I was hoping to spend a few weeks and relax?" I replied, loud enough for every man at the bar to hear me.

The answer seemed to satisfy everybody at the bar and they went back to their conversations that ranged from women, to clutches on John Deere tractors, to warm boots.

Mom brought me the beer and set it down with her left hand. She has a rock on her finger big enough to make Elizabeth Taylor come back to life. "I don't know how you ended up in this 'berg?" she said to me. "Most people are trying to get out of here."

"Life is a funny thing," I replied.

"About as funny as hemorrhoids," she said in a voice that let me know she had a good grasp of life.

I sipped the beer. "I stopped by to talk to you," I said.

"My husband sent you over?"

The reply took me by surprise. "I don't know him."

"I moved out on the jerk three days ago. I thought he might be getting horny?"

"Mom is down to earth," my Guardian Angel said.

"No, I wanted to talk to you about Sheila."

The hard features of her face softened. "She's a good kid, mixed up, but a good kid."

"Is there someplace we can talk alone?" I asked.

"Sure, follow me. I'm tired of looking at these bums anyway."

She hollered to the waitress, "Cover the bar for me, Ginger."

I followed Mom through the bar and into a small cramped office. She sat in a wood swivel chair that Wyatt Earp might have used while supplying the bars with whores and robbing all the ranchers in Arizona while he was pretending to be a cop in Tombstone.

"Kids can drive you nuts," she said to me.

"I don't know," I said. "I've never been married."

"That's too bad."

"It is too bad but a story too long to tell."

"We all have bodies in the closet," she smiled.

"There are real bodies in closets around here?" my Guardian Angel said.

"It's a phrase, you idiot," I told him.

"Testy, testy," he quipped.

"Should I call you Mom?" I asked Mom.

"My name is Brenda Harberts, married to Earl Harberts, currently living alone while my husband and daughter are living at the house."

"Where are you staying?"

"Here at the bar."

"I met your daughter the other evening at the HOME OF HEARTS. Fanny told me she was a nice kid and had some problems. I'm an old hippie and thought I might be able to help her."

"What, teach her how to smoke dope? Group sex? Not take a bath? Where cheap perfume? Say intelligent words like wow, groovy, far out man?"

"I quit dope before your daughter was born. Everything she is going through I've been through. She seemed sad to me and I thought it would be worth a shot."

"You don't look like the helping kind of guy to me?" Brenda said.

"I'm no Joan of Arc," I replied curtly.

"If you were a cross dresser," my Guardian Angel said.

Brenda took a deep breath. "I'll talk to her. If she wants to talk to you, you can see her. Anything might help. It's all worth a shot. Where are you staying?"

"I rented a room at Carol Trouble's." I have a feeling she already knew where I was staying.

"Strange, you finding Franklin's body. I always had a feeling he'd get killed. The way he messed around with women and being a gambler he was asking for it."

"Were a lot of his women from around here?" I asked.

She hesitated for a brief moment before answering, "More than one and less than twenty."

"Did he play cards with any locals?"

"Nothing big. He'd play dollar pitch or two bit poker here at the bar every so often but never any big money. You can't live in a little town and fleece the local boys."

Franklin had been a smart guy.

"Not that smart, he got his throat cut," my Guardian Angel said.

Some reasoning is beyond reproach.

"I understand when your husband committed Sheila you were against it," I said.

Brenda's eyes grew fierce. "There was no need to put my baby in the nut house. We could have worked everything out at home," she snapped at me.

Brenda stood. I take it our tut to tut is over. I didn't want to push my luck and followed her back to the bar and stood where I had been before. The guy who had joked about ice fishing was gone. Two men, each one big enough to pick up a truck, looked at me like they wanted to use me to mop the floor. "Trouble in River City," my Guardian Angel warned.

"So you are a detective," the man closest to me said like being a detective is lower than a cow patty. His face is pudgy, red lines crisscrossed his cheek from too much alcohol, his eyebrows are more scar tissue than eyebrows. His buddy laughed like his friend is funnier than Hitler.

I noticed the other men in the bar watching us intently and the women in the bar had worried looks on their faces.

"I am a detective," I told the man looking directly in his blood shot eyes.

"I don't like cops," he snarled straitening up and pushing out his chest. He had to weigh close to 300 pounds and not all of it is fat. His hands are the size of small pumpkins.

"He is a funny looking little guy," his buddy agreed, also straightening up. He is a little guy compared to his friend, no more than 280 pounds.

"I think you can whip these guys," my Guardian Angel said.

"Not a problem," I said.

The bar got quiet. The good people of Saint Ansgar are waiting for me to get stomped flatter than an extra thin pizza crust.

"Bill and Joe leave him alone," Mom's voice echoed around the bar.

They both glared at her and while they were busy glaring I heard a voice from the back of the bar say, "those Schneider brothers are going to knock the livin' dog spit out of that poor boy."

I've never been full of dog spit and I've never eaten dog spit therefore it can't get knocked out of me.

"You boys look more like Mutt and Jeff," I said to the Schneider brothers with a grin on my face.

"You be asking for it, Roosevelt," my Guardian Angel said.

"You some kind of wise guy," Mutt asked, sticking out his chin like his chin alone would frighten me.

"What did I tell you, Bill?" Mom hollered.

He ignored her, growled, he must think he is a dog, and lunged at me. Before he had moved six inches I grabbed his windpipe with my right hand and squeezed hard. His eyes bugged out in surprise and he clawed at my hand and said something like, "goog, googie, aggg."

I squeezed harder. I didn't like the tone in his voice. Joe moved away from the bar and started cautiously towards me. I stepped back, pulling Bill with me, who was still trying to communicate in a foreign language and kneed him in the groin. As he fell forward I pushed him into the advancing Joe. Joe tried to get around Bill, but as he did I round house kicked him on the side of his big ugly head. He staggered backwards but didn't fall down. Bill was holding his family jewels and squirming on the floor, I gave him a solid kick to the ribs as I went for Joe. Joe is more surprised than dazed. I hit him with a left to the head, a right to the gut, another left to the head, two shots to the ribs, and then head butted him in the nose. Blood shot everywhere. He fell backwards to the floor, hitting the floor harder than a big pine tree. I kicked him in the groin. He knew the same language as Bill - "argg, goggle, googie."

Bill is groaning, I gave him two more kicks to the ribs, reached over and grabbed him by the collar and pulled his face to within an inch of mine. "You listen to me, you and your brother ever mess with me again you won't get out of the hospital for months. You understand?"

He mumbled something but didn't even see me. His eyes are shut. It's rude to mumble to people with your eyes shut unless you are a reincarnated Truman Capote.

I head butted him in the nose. The sound of crushed cartilage was sickening. "Understand?" I asked.

He muttered what I took to be a yes. I shoved him back down to the floor and kicked him in the ribs again.

"And don't you forget it," my Guardian Angel said.

I went back to the bar. "I'll take another Guinness," I told Mom, barely out of breath, "and somebody take the garbage out."

The bar is as silent as a church.

It took four men to drag Bill and Joe out of the bar. When they came back in the bar was still silent. "Those boys have needed a good whipping for years, round on the house," Mom hollered.

The men in the bar waved at me. Ladies smiled. I feel good. Sometimes this old hippie has to ruin his image. I do know one thing for sure, nobody in town will pick on me now. But, I also know, I have made two enemies. What I didn't know was if they had already been my enemies and were lousy shots?

Mom walked around the bar with a draw beer for herself and another Guinness for me. "For a skinny little runt you handle yourself pretty good," she said, "those boys are tough guys."

"I learned how to fight while making peace signs in Nam," I told her.

She laughed. She thought I was joking. She then put her face about three inches from mine. "I'm about two or three years younger than you I'd guess, close enough it doesn't make a difference, but you ever want to get it on hippie, cowboy, Viet Nam vet, whatever you are, you come see old Mom here and I'll put down whatever I'm doing and put one on you, you will never forget. Comprendo?"

"Si, Si," my Guardian Angel said.

I smiled and nodded my head. She walked away to talk to some other men.

I finished my beer, a few men nodded at me as I left, a few women smiled. Mom, alias Brenda, waved and blew me a kiss.

I decided to walk to the HOME OF HEARTS. A fifty-yard

walk would do me some good.

I once again marveled at the rooms filled with hearts as I went through them. "You're getting sentimental," my Guardian Angel said.

"You don't know me at all," I said.

"I suppose people who are close really don't know each other," he said.

Fanny is not in the Tea Room. Clyde is on top of a table eating a piece of sliced apple. "Crap," he squawked when he saw me and went back to eating.

I called for Fanny but there was no answer. I saw a note taped to the cash register. BACK IN A FEW. IF YOU WANT SOMETHING LEAVE CHECK OR MONEY ON COUNTER.

"No wonder her heart got stolen," my Guardian Angel said.

"Some people desperately hang onto trust," I said.

"Have you?"

I didn't answer him. I don't want to accept the truth.

I went into the QUEEN OF HEARTS ROOM and examined the floor. In front of the table the wooden floor had an area that would not be seen unless someone was intentionally looking for it. The wood is slightly lighter in color. Looking closer I saw an area where a 3' by 5' area rug used to be on the floor.

I went outside through the door in the Tea Room and went to the cellar. The two black cats did not have nine lives and were still lying where I had left them. I knelt down and examined their slit throats. Their throats were cut straight across and directly underneath their jaws. Looking down at them the left side of the wound is deeper. "This is strange," I said out loud.

"Why?" my Guardian Angel asked.

"You figure it out," I told him.

I like keeping my Guardian Angel in the dark.

I stroked the dead cats until I had rubbed up a small amount of their hair, which I put in my shirt pocket.

"I'm not even going to ask why you are taking cat hair," my Guardian Angel said.

Heading back into Fanny's house there is a boy about ten years old standing in the backyard of the yellow house. He has on a big tan floppy hat with ear flaps that aren't tied, a blue parka several sizes too large for him, a black pair of mittens that were attached to his coat with red yarn, baggy Levi's with a hole in the knee and is wearing tennis shoes. His little face is beet red. He waved at me the way a little puppy wags his tale when playing with children. Smiling, I waved back. He waved again. I waved. "Hey mister, would you play with me?" he called, with a beseeching tone to his voice.

"I can't right now I'm busy, some other time," I called back, waved goodbye and went into the house.

"You should have played with the boy," my Guardian Angel said. "There's nothing in your life so important you can't take a few minutes for a child."

I feel bad. He is right. Going back outside the boy isn't in his backyard. "Hey kid!" I hollered. "Hey kid! Where are you?"

No boy.

"Hey kid!"

No boy.

I feel terrible. "Hey kid!" I called.

No boy.

Turning, I walked back toward the house feeling lower than a skunk's belly.

I was halfway up the steps. "Mister! Mister!" the boy's voice sang out to me. "I'm here! I'm here!"

I ran down the steps and the little boy ran up to me. Green snot is running out of his nose. His dark eyes are shinning. A tuft of sandy red hair hung down almost to his eyes. He is smiling like I am Santa Claus. I reached out and put my hand on the top of his head. "You wanta' make a snowman?" he asked me excitedly.

"Son, that would be the best thing I've done in years," I told him as I handed him my handkerchief.

CHAPTER SIX
LEAVE THE LIGHTS ON

"What's your name?" I asked the boy. We are in his backyard and he is about to roll a ball of snow to start the snowman.

"Jimmy Page," he answered, grinning at me so happily it made my cold heart warm. "I'm almost eleven years old."

"I'm Bob Roosevelt. You can call me Bob." I didn't feel the need to tell him I am 62 years old.

Jimmy pushed the snow, stopped, and looked back at me with a heartwarming grin on his face and started to push again. He pushed until the ball of snow was so big he couldn't move it anymore. "Help me Bob, help me."

Helping push we added another foot to the circle. He started another snowball. He would push, stop and look back at me, push, stop and look at me, it was though he was afraid I would leave. When he was done I lifted it on top of the other one. It didn't take him long to finish the face and I perched it on top of the other two. "He's a good-looking snowman," I said, "at least six feet tall."

"He needs arms," Jimmy said and ran to the side of Fanny's house. He scurried back with two long sticks in his arms. He stuck them in the sides of the snowman and darted to the front of his house and came back with an arm full of pinecones. The pinecones became eyes and buttons for the snowman's coat. He ran into his house and came back with a carrot and it became a nose. A nice nose it is.

"He needs a mouth, a happy mouth," Jimmy told me. "I want my snowman to be happy."

"Happy is a nice thing," I said.

"Happy is the most important thing," my Guardian Angel said.

Jimmy and I pondered the mouth problem. There is too much snow to find rocks. "What are you two boys doing?" Fanny called from her yard.

"It's a snowman problem. We can't decide what to make the mouth out of," I called back.

"Come on over I have just the thing."

Jimmy and I started toward the house. I walked in front of him and he scampered behind me trying to place each of his steps into my footprints.

Fanny is sitting at a table going through a gold fish bowl full of buttons. Clyde is looking intently at each button she pulls out of the bowl and sets on the table. "Pretty, pretty," he squawked and pecked at one.

"No you don't," Fanny scolded him and shoed him away.

I could have sworn he gave her a dirty look. "Not you, not you, not you," he squawked.

"How about raven tail feathers for a mouth?" my Guardian Angel suggested.

"Ask Clyde," I said.

"Crap," Clyde squawked.

I wonder if Clyde can read minds or if he can hear my Guardian Angel?

"Oh boy, Fanny, those would be a great mouth," Jimmy said looking at a dozen quarter sized bright red buttons.

Jimmy had taken his cap off and I noticed how greasy his hair is. It is not dirty greasy but hair lotion greasy.

"You can use these buttons, but when the snowman melts I want them back," Fanny said.

Jimmy scooped the buttons up and clutched them in his hand tighter than if they were gold coins. "Come on Bob, come on, we have to give the snowman a happy mouth," he said excitedly.

He pulled on my coat sleeve. Fanny smiled at me the way a mother smiles at her children when they aren't looking.

Jimmy put the buttons on the snowman. "That is about the best smile I have ever seen on a snowman," I said.

"It's the loveliest snowman in the world," he said with pride.

Looking up at me and I could swear there were tears in his eyes, but he is smiling. I took his hand in mine and we stood looking at the snowman. He let go of my hand and put his arm around my waist. He snuggled his head into my side. I put my arm around his shoulder. He gave me more warmth than I gave him. "How about we go have Fanny make us a cup of tea?" I asked Jimmy.

"Please," Jimmy said.

Fanny brewed Jimmy and her a cup of tea. Thankfully, she made me a cup of coffee. "How's your mother doing?" she asked Jimmy.

"She cries all the time, Fanny. She cries and I don't know what to do. It hurts me in here." He held his hand over his heart.

"Poor little kid," my Guardian Angel said.

"Remember, you can come over here anytime you want," Fanny told Jimmy.

"I know, but mom says I shouldn't come over a lot. I would get in the way and bother you."

"You tell your mommy you don't bother me. I can always find something for you to do to help me."

"How about you, Bob, are there things I can do to help you?"

"I'm sure there is Jimmy," I said. What, I don't know? But I couldn't tell the kid no.

"Will you play with me again, Bob? We can throw snowballs at cars or play cards. I have a train set."

I haven't tossed a snowball at a car in years. It sounds like fun. Splat a few cars and go hide in the bushes. "I'll play anytime you want. But I have to do things sometimes. You have to understand," I answered him.

"I understand. My mom is always busy, too. You big people are always busy."

"Busy with things that have no importance. Busy with wanting things, buying things, paying off things. Needing things," my Guardian Angel said in a way he knew it would never change.

Jimmy finished his tea. "I have to go Fanny. Mom will be home soon and I have to set the table."

He stood, holding out his hand for me to shake. We shook hands. "It was a lot of fun, Bob," he said and turned and ran out of the room. The door banged behind him. I rubbed off the hair grease from his hand on my pants.

"He's such a nice little boy," Fanny said sadly. "His father was killed four years ago. A tractor rolled over on him. His mother hasn't been the same since. She scratches out a living working at the bar."

"Her name is Ginger," I took a guess.

"I take it you've been to the bar?" she said in a tone that bar is a four-letter word.

"Does Jimmy have any friends?" I asked, changing the subject - bars aren't good man, woman, conversations.

"No, he doesn't seem to make friends. He is a quiet, lonely little boy," Fanny said sadly.

I feel useless. There is nothing I can do to help the boy.

"What were you doing the day your heart was stolen?" I asked Fanny.

Business has a way of getting people back to earth.

"I was here until around 2:00 in the afternoon and then I went to run some errands. I got back about 4:30. I didn't discover my heart was gone until I turned the downstairs lights off around 9:00 in the evening."

"When you leave do you always leave a note by the cash register like you did today?"

"Yes."

"Was there any money for a sale when you came back the day your heart was stolen?"

Fanny shook her head.

"Where did you find the cats?"

"They were outside by the steps?"

"Where they were when I saw them?"

"No, they were about ten yards from the steps. I put them beside each other."

"Wasn't there a lot of blood?"

"There was, but I shoveled it up and put it in the trash."

"When you saw the heart was gone was anything out of the ordinary in the room?"

"The only thing that was different was the dome was not on its base. It was standing straight up but off to the side."

"Where was Clyde?"

"I normally put Clyde on the table when I leave and feed him an apple. He loves apples."

"Good, good," Clyde squawked.

"How did Clyde and the cats get along?"

"Clyde didn't like them but they never bothered him."

"Raven must be tough meat," my Guardian Angel said.

"I'd like to take the glass dome with me, if you don't mind," I told Fanny. "Do you have a box it will fit in?"

Fanny didn't question why I wanted the dome. She went upstairs, to, I presume, her storage room, and came back with a box.

We went to the QUEEN OF HEARTS room and I picked up the dome, holding it as far down toward the bottom as I could as I set it in the box.

"What are you going to do with the dome?" Fanny asked me when we sat back down in the Tea Room - her curiosity had gotten the best of her.

"I don't know," I lied to her.

I looked at my Kmart watch. It is almost six. The sun has gone down and the sky is a pale gray. I stood. "Will you come back tonight? A cup of tea, a beer?" Fanny asked me. Her voice sounds like a little girl whose friends have all gone home and she didn't want to be alone.

"Only if Thai food has indigestion," my Guardian Angel said.

I want to come back and I don't want to come back. Fanny's sad eyes searched my face. "Around eight, how's that?" I said. "I'll have a beer."

She looked relieved.

I went to Matilda carrying the box with the dome in it. "That was a nice thing you did with Jimmy," my Guardian Angel said. "Poor little guy. It's tough when your father is gone."

"He seems like a nice kid. A sad little boy but he seems like he has a great big heart."

"People with big hearts often times get hurt the most."

"I know," I said.

Thankfully Mutt and Jeff, better known as Bill and Joe Schneider, in retaliation had not stuck a knife in Matilda's tires or ball-batted the windows. I started Matilda and while driving to Carol's took the pistol out from under the seat and stuck it underneath my jacket.

The door is locked. I didn't have to read the sign to know to push the doorbell.

Carol answered the door wearing a light blue summer dress and is barefoot. I don't know what she is cooking for dinner but it smells great. "Clean up, dinner will be ready within an hour."

I can be such an obedient guy when I want to.

I went to my room, put the box in the closet, which was better than a body, put my pistol in the suitcase and got my pad and pencil. I started writing faster than Louis L'Amour knocked out westerns while drinking espresso.

"You have a lot of clues there for not much going on," my Guardian Angel said as I wrote.

"Everything is a clue."

"Not all of those."

"How am I supposed to write if you keep running your head?" I grumbled. He wouldn't know a clue from a fact.

"You're not an artist. Don't be so touchy."

Finished writing I put the notebook in my suitcase and took a shower. Building snowmen is hard work.

Carol is singing in the kitchen, something about if she was carpenter and having babies.

Fried chicken, rolls, Jell-O salad, and green beans were on the table. "This is the kind of woman to have. All you have to do is come home, eat, have sex and leave," my Guardian Angel said.

Carol and I sat. "I heard you got into a fight at the bar," she said.

"It wasn't much. A couple of boneheads who got up on the wrong side of the bed."

I didn't want to talk. I want to eat.

"Those boneheads as you call them could be big trouble, Roosevelt. They have been in and out of trouble for years, mostly for fighting. They might try and get back at you. I'd stay out of the bar."

I didn't reply and stuffed my mouth with green beans.

We finished our meal in silence. If I keep eating regular meals

I will gain about fifty pounds.

"How about a little dessert?” Carol asked.

I could visualize cherry pie, ice cream, a cup of coffee. "Love some," I said.

Carol stood up and quicker than a June Bug crawls out of its shell her dress slipped to the floor. "She sure beats cherry pie and ice cream," my Guardian Angel gulped.

Shaking my head I went to my room. I have a half-hour before I am going to Fanny's and I hope she doesn't want to have dessert. I looked at my clues. "I told you before, Roosevelt, your clues are nothing," my Guardian Angel said.

"What do you mean? I have 68 clues here."

"I didn't know you could count that high."

It’s hard to be a non-licensed private detective trying to solve three crimes at once when a Guardian Angel is a non-believing sarcastic jerk.

I continued reading my clues. I don't want to admit to my Guardian Angel that he is right and there is little information in my clues. But, at least it beats having writer’s block.

I stopped reading at a quarter to eight, put my pad under the chair cushion and headed for the door.

"Hey famous one with short-term memory you're forgetting your pistol," my Guardian Angel told me.

"I don't think I should carry it with me all the time. I bet it's against the law to carry a pistol in your car in Minnesota."

"You'll be sorry."

I didn't like the tone in his voice and I stuck the pistol in my belt, hidden by my jacket.

I started to get into Matilda but decided to walk to the HOME OF HEARTS. I am starting to get a truck driver gut.

"Not to mention your rear," my Guardian Angel said.

"Is there a Guardian Angel hot line I can call when a Guardian Angel is getting on your nerves?"

"Death," he replied bluntly.

Not a good hot line and I hope I never find the number.

I walked to the red light. It is about 10 degrees or so, not too bad. Looking up and down each street there are no cars. Turning right I can see a lot of cars at Mom's. Like most small towns the main entertainment is called drunk. I noticed for the first time Main Street has street lamps.

I hadn't gone ten yards from the light when I heard what I thought was a firecracker, until the sound of a bullet whizzing over my head and hitting a tree close to me told me I should duck.

Pulling out my pistol I jumped behind a tree as another slug hit the tree. I peeked around each side of the tree. Nobody had come out of their houses. "You didn't warn me," I chastised my Guardian Angel.

There was no reply.

Another pop and a slug hit the tree.

"God will take you back and assign you to a nun if you don't stay on top of your job."

There was no reply.

Peaking around the tree I saw movement in a bush to the front left of the corner house across the street. The bush is no more than thirty yards away. I aimed at the bush. A figure ran out of the bush toward the road. I lost sight of the figure as it went around the corner of the house. I ran after the fleeting person but when I went around the corner of the house nobody was there.

"What would you have told your boss if I got shot?" I asked my Guardian Angel angrily.

There was no reply.

At least my Guardian Angel isn't like most people when they make a mistake. He wasn't telling me excuses or making up alibis or trying to blame somebody else.

I ran away from the house, across the street, cut between two houses, cut left and ran until I reached Fanny's and went into the house through the side door. Fanny and Clyde were at a table when I barged in. I was out of breath and hadn't put the pistol back behind my coat. Fanny eyes got as big around as California strawberries. I feel bad. "Damn farmer, damn farmer," Clyde squawked.

"Don't worry, Fanny, it's not what it looks like," I said, which didn't make any sense but sounded good.

I put the pistol back behind my jacket.

Fanny took a deep breath. "I never thought you would carry a gun?" she said like I am Jack the Ripper with a 9 m.m.

I suppose she thinks detectives hang around with nice people and if a crook is about to shoot me all I have to do was hold my hands up and tell him I am only kidding.

I decided to tell her the truth. "I was shot at the other night and I thought it might be a good idea." I didn't tell her I had just been shot at again.

She covered her mouth like she was watching some low budget horror flick. "No," mumbled through her fingers.

"Yes," I said.

"Not in this town. People don't shoot people in this town."

"They only try to," I said as I sat down. "Most of the time they miss"

I guess she forgot people cut other people's throats in this town.

"I could really use that beer," I told Fanny.

She got up so fast she reminds me of a waitress who had three Colombian drug lords come to her table and she knew she would get a hundred dollar bill for a tip.

Waiting for Fanny I know one thing. The first time I got shot at the report was loud - a 243 or a 30/30. This time it was no louder than a 22. Two different guns. Does this mean two different shooters? At this rate I'd have all 564 residents of Saint Ansgar wanting to kill me. Little towns can be pretty cliquey.

"You now have 69 clues," my Guardian Angel said. "70 if you count little towns being cliquey."

"Don't push your luck," I warned him.

"Just trying to be oh so nice and oh so good," he said.

"Well then be oh so quiet," I said.

Fanny brought me a beer. She has a bottle of organic grape juice with a label that makes it look like a bottle of wine. She poured herself a glass of fake wine.

"Don't you think you should call the police about being shot at?" Fanny asked me nervously.

"I don't know if I trust your Sheriff Jack Benning and besides, if I felt like calling him right now, you don't have a phone."

"I've never had a phone. Never wanted one. I don't have a TV either. I like to read. I had a TV for a long time and it seemed to steal my mind. I'd sit and watch things I had no interest in, but still I'd watch. One day I gave it away."

She and I agree about TV's. They are like a big suction tube that sucks your brains out until all you can talk about are TV programs and remote controls.

"If there ever was an emergency you'd need a phone," I said.

"It's a small town. I have neighbors," she replied with a tinge of sadness in her voice.

The fact Fanny doesn't have a phone bothers me - why it bothers me I don't know?

"You never know anything, come to grips with it, Roosevelt," my snide Guardian Angel said.

"Somebody in town must not want you looking into Franklin's murder," Fanny said.

"I don't think I got shot at because somebody doesn't want me to find your heart or who killed your cats, unless you told someone?" I said, meaning it as a joke.

"I haven't told a soul," Fanny said defensively. "Nobody in this town knows about my missing heart or the dead cats."

I had a sudden insight. A flash bulb went off in my head.

"What, you figured out you're stupid?" my Guardian Angel said.

"You don't own a car? Do you Fanny?"

"I guess I should tell you before somebody else does. I was an alcoholic for years. I lost my license so many times I can't remember. Five years ago, while driving without a license, I swerved across the centerline and rolled my car. I was lucky I didn't get hurt but when they were checking me over in the hospital I overheard an intern tell his friend, 'good thing nobody was coming the other direction.' I could have killed an innocent person. It scared me. I quit drinking and never got another car. I can walk anyplace in this town I have to go to."

Maybe this was the trouble Fanny had been in Officer Bill Buffalo had told me about? Maybe it isn't?

I didn't want to pursue the matter but I think there is more to the story.

"How long has Dale Boraxe been mayor?" I asked Fanny, watching her face carefully.

She tried not to show it, but hearing his name made her wince. She sipped her fake wine and I could sense her mind playing back some scene she did not want to remember. "He's been mayor for two terms. This term is about half over," she said with a strain to her voice.

"You don't like him, do you?"

Her eyes had a momentary glare to them. "No I don't. He is a selfish egomaniac who only thinks about himself," she snapped, started to say more but stopped.

"I don't see why you are asking me questions that have nothing to do with getting my heart back or finding out who killed my cats?" she said to me in an accusing manner.

"I'm also trying to solve a murder, Fanny."

"I don't care about any murder. I only care about my heart and my cats," she blurted and then started to cry.

"You've done it now, Roosevelt," my Guardian Angel said.

Fanny is a good crier. She could make a good living as a professional crier at funerals for people who have died that nobody really liked.

"I bet Carol has already got you in bed?" she cried. "I bet she had you naked within twenty minutes after the police left," she cried. "And she asked you to find whoever had killed Franklin while you were both naked."

"Roosevelt is too dumb," my Guardian Angel said.

"I don't mix pleasure with business, Fanny," I said.

"She's slept with half the men in the county," Fanny said not paying any attention to my comment. "Why haven't you made a pass at me? Am I ugly? Too plain?" Fanny sobbed.

"I'm on your side, honey," my Guardian Angel said.

Women in Saint Ansgar don't want me to solve crimes. They only want me for my slightly over the hill body, which is better than being in California where most women are only into young boys.

"I don't think going to bed with you is the right thing to do," I told Fanny.

"Is it a wrong thing to do?"

"Only to Roosevelt," my Guardian Angel said.

"I like you a lot, Fanny. But I am trying to find who stole your heart and killed your cats."

"Are you telling me you will only sleep with somebody you

know you are in love with?" she said, looking confused and not crying anymore.

I nodded my head.

"That is so noble," she said.

"I want to barf," my Guardian Angel said.

We talked for about an hour and I left. Late in the evening Saint Ansgar does not have a pedestrian or traffic problem. I went to the bush I saw the figure run from. I examined the ground as closely as I could in the dim street lamp light. I didn't find any spent brass but I saw where a person had knelt down behind the bush and a set of footprints coming from the street and returning in almost the same route. The prints are of a winter boot with rubber soles. They are a popular winter boot and at least half of the people in Saint Ansgar probably have a pair. The prints in the snow are clear and clean, no sign of a nick or wear on the bottom of the boots. The prints are not huge but are not small. I followed the prints to the road. Not far from where they stopped at the road is a driveway to a house. The house has a wraparound porch with steps to it that are not far from the driveway. There is a door facing the street that is not the main entrance. I headed for Carol's.

"You be in trouble," my Guardian Angel said. "You don't have a key to get into Carol's and it's late."

It is cold. I am cold. I looked at the Ring Bell sign. I started to ring the bell and stopped - people don't like to be wakened by stupid people who forget their key. I started to ring the bell again and stopped.

"Try the door, idiot child," my Guardian Angel said.

I tried the door. It is unlocked. Before I went into the house I took off my boots. The house is dark. I tippee-toed oh so carefully to my room. Opened the door oh so carefully, shut it oh so carefully, turned on the light oh so carefully and jumped back in fright.

A naked Carol is on my bed. "Bring that hippie cowboy body of yours over here," she ordered.

Women are bossy in Saint Ansgar.

"I like Carol," my Guardian Angel said. "I don't trust her but I like her."

The, I don't trust, stuck in my mind.

I shook my head at Carol and pointed at the door. She grinned seductively, got out of bed and pranced by me like she was the lead dancer in a review in Reno.

"I hope you can't sleep," my Guardian Angel said.

CHAPTER SEVEN
FLY OR DIE

The sunlight is glaring through the window. "Good morning, oh don't mix pleasure with business," my Guardian Angel said.

"Is Carol gone?" I asked.

"Carol left the house about an hour ago."

I cleaned up as fast as I could and then went downstairs to Carol's room. When I was in the basement the first time I hadn't seen a closet. I opened the door to what I presumed was the bathroom. The room, from the outside looks small, but inside it is large - at least 15' by 15'. One entire wall is a walk in closet. I slid open the door. On both ends of the closet are full-length mirrors. There are enough dresses to supply the Salvation Army in Toledo and on a shoe rack, running the length of the floor, are enough shoes Shoe World would have been envious. Looking at the shoes, they are normal shoes as ladies shoes go, nothing made to be comfortable, until I got to the end of the rack and there is a pair of rubber soled, winter boots with leather tops and felt liners. I picked up one of the boots, the bottom is damp. I examined the soles. They look like the imprints I saw by the bush.

"Oh, oh," my Guardian Angel said.

"I don't like this," I said.

"Beat feet for Pittsburgh, shuffle on down to Buffalo, slide into Crested Butte," my Guardian Angel said.

I picked up the other boot. The bottom was also wet. The boots were new and there are no nicks on the bottoms. I put the boots back as if they were bombs.

There was nothing else of interest in the closet unless I was a cross dresser. Back in the main room I went to the bar. I need a belt of something stronger than orange juice. I should have gone downtown. The bar has two shelves. The top shelf has the normal bar stuff - on the bottom shelf are two rifles.

"Oh, oh," my Guardian Angel said.

"I'm getting tired of you saying oh, oh, all the time," I said.

I picked up one of the rifles. It is a bolt action 22 without a scope. It had recently been cleaned, oil still shone on the barrel. It is loaded and has a shell in the chamber. I set it back down like it was a poisonous snake.

I picked up the other rifle. It is a semi-automatic 30/30 with no scope and had recently been cleaned and is loaded.

It is time for me to exit stage left. I went up the stairs, had the box with the dome in it, my few cat hairs in my shirt pocket, my pistol stuck in my belt, my coat on and was out the door quicker than a robber can say, "Give me the money before I blow you away."

I didn't let Matilda warm up but putted up the street as quickly as her cold little engine would go. I am headed for Albert Lee.

"I'll tell you one thing, Roosevelt, you have some good clues now," my Guardian Angel said.

Clues I didn't want.

Detective Bill Buffalo was out of his office. The receptionist said he had to testify in court and would be gone all afternoon.

Detectives Pete Rosebet and Paul Binyon share an office. It is so small the front parts of their desks are only about a foot apart. To get to the window they have to walk sideways between the desks. "Cons get better rooms in the joint," I told them as I sat down in a green folding chair the state had probably stolen from the National Guard.

"They get free food, too," Pete Rosebet said glumly.

Rosebet had a coffee maker on his desk and offered me a cup. It tastes about three days old and melted the enamel on my teeth. "You boys been doing more than busting car thieves?" I asked whichever one wanted to answer.

"It's been slow," Rosebet said. "A few petty robberies. Some domestic violence stuff. Kind of boring."

"Mostly we've been trying to sell tickets for our police dinner. It's a pain. People don't like cops. They blame us for everything that goes wrong and bitch when we beat the pulp out of some street punk who has been robbing old ladies. But when they need us boy do they cry. We need to sell a few lousy tickets and we can't give them away," Paul Binyon said sounding depressed.

"Get a new cook," I said.

They didn't like my funny and gave me a stern look.

"Nothing personal," I told them.

"How about you?" Paul Binyon asked. "Doing anything besides letting Carol crawl all over your body?"

They both laughed. They like their own funnies.

"She should either be locked up or sent to Vegas," I said. There was no need to tell them I wasn't sleeping with her. They wouldn't believe me.

They nodded their heads in deep thought.

"When you guys checked the bedroom for blood did you go all the way to the front door?" I asked.

"Buffalo told us to only worry about the bedroom, but we did the hall and living room and all the other bedrooms. There was nothing," Binyon said.

"Did you do the bathroom?" I asked.

"I don't do bathrooms," Paul Binyon laughed and then looked at me seriously. "No trace of blood in the bathroom."

"It's a tough one. Carol's alibi checks out. We don't know where to turn," Pete Rosebet said.

I suddenly felt dumber than a flounder. I had completely spaced out Franklin's house.

"Did you guys search Franklin's house?" I asked.

They both looked at me with blank expressions on their faces.

"I take it the answer is no," my Guardian Angel said.

"What?" Pete Rosebet asked.

"Franklin's house. Did you search it?"

"We didn't know he had a house."

"I understand he bought a house a few months ago," I said.

"I'll be dipped in chocolate?" Pete Rosebet said.

"Roosevelt, it seems to me you have been running around in

circles and doing everything backwards. You should have already gone through the house," my Guardian Angel informed me.

"We'll have to tell Buffalo about the house when he gets back and go check it out," Paul Binyon said.

I wondered why they wanted to wait until Buffalo got back.

None-the-less I wanted to get my business done and beat them to the house. "I need a favor from you guys," I said, putting on my need a favor face.

Police normally don't do favors but they do take bribes.

"What kind of favor?" Pete Rosebet asked cautiously.

I put the box with the dome in it on his desk. "I need this dusted for prints."

He didn't open the box to see what was in it. "Maybe," he said.

I fished around in my shirt pocket and took out the small amount of cat hair. "Do you have an envelope?"

"You should change shirts more often," my Guardian Angel said. "You've been wearing that shirt for two days."

Pete Rosebet handed me an envelope and I put the cat hair into it. "I need this hair run through the lab to find out if there is a trace of poison?"

"I can do these things for you only if you promise to talk at our fundraiser," Paul Binyon said taking the envelope from me.

"About what?"

"Anything, it doesn't matter. We put the word out a detective who has been on TV will talk and we'll sell out. People who live here are starved for entertainment."

"That makes me feel real good," I said.

"You are an entertaining guy even if you need a haircut and a new pair of boots," Paul Binyon said.

They waited for an answer. I have never been good at public speaking. When I had to give a speech in high school for English class I almost wet my pants. But, what could I do?

"It's a deal," I agreed.

"Give us a few days," Pete Rosebet said like he had gotten the better part of the deal. He doesn't know I am going to talk about police brutality.

"The dinner is in ten days," Paul Binyon said.

I drove back to Saint Ansgar as fast as Matilda would go, 70 downhill. The problem is southern Minnesota doesn't have many hills. It's flatter than a female 18-year-old Olympic swimmer.

Fanny is dusting the hearts in the front room when I walked in.

"Where did Franklin live?" I asked, skipping all the small talk.

"Out in the country," Fanny said.

"Tell me how to get there."

"You would never find it. Do you want me to show you how to get there?"

I wanted to say, no, I don't want you to, but I said, "Yes I do."

"Pretty please with sugar on it."

"Fanny, I'm trying to find a murderer, please, get your coat and let's go."

"Pretty please with sugar on it."

I can never win with women. "Pretty please with sugar on it," I said.

"Roosevelt, you are a disgrace to all men in the world," my Guardian Angel said.

"Not to the Italians, Greeks, or any Arab race," I said. "They'll do or say anything to go out with a white woman."

Fanny put on her coat and hat and gloves and we were about to leave when I had an idea.

"Be careful, Roosevelt, ideas have never been good for you," my Guardian Angel said.

"Do you have any dishwashing gloves?" I asked Fanny.

She went upstairs and brought back a pair of yellow rubber gloves - she didn't ask me why I wanted them.

"She's known you long enough she knows there is neither rhyme nor reason to anything you do," my Guardian Angel said.

"This is a funny car," Fanny said as we headed out of town.

I drove about a mile past the Saint Ansgar Church. Turned left on a gravel road and went a quarter of a mile, turned left again and went another quarter of a mile, turned right and went about a half a mile, past two oak trees and turned right into a small driveway that on either side of it has a half buried tractor tire.

The house is not what I expected. I figured Franklin, the big gambler, would have a large brick home with a 25,000 station satellite dish out front. This house is a small, square, painted white, has no porch, and has a brick chimney. There is no garage. A white, one-year-old Cadillac is in the driveway. Wind had blown snow over the tire tracks since it had been driven in. Wind had also blown snow over any footprints that would have led to or from the front door.

I put on the rubber gloves. The wind is blowing and it is cold as hell.

"How can it be cold as hell?" my Guardian Angel asked.

I had to think. I thought more. I thought some more. There was no answer. "Everybody knows what it means," I said in defense. "It means really cold."

"You people can mess up a good language," he said.

I examined the Cadillac. The windows are iced over so I could not see inside. I tried the driver's door. It is unlocked and the keys are in the ignition. "Everybody leaves their keys in their car around here," Fanny explained.

"I bet they leave the back doors to their houses unlocked, too," I said.

"Yes we do," she replied in a tone that I was a low life big city guy who shouldn't be allowed in a trustworthy small community.

"I hope all the crooks in Detroit and New York don't find out about Saint Ansgar. It will start the biggest turf war in recorded history," my Guardian Angel said.

I looked through the Cadillac. There is nothing under the seats, behind the seats, or under the foot mats. In the glove box was the registration, two decks of cards, which I put in my pocket, and a bottle of Maalox, which I also put in my pocket. The registration was for Franklin R. Trouble. I put it back in the glove box.

I opened the trunk. Cadillac's have a great trunk. A family of three could live comfortably in them. Fanny looked in the trunk the same time I did. The next thing I knew she fell backwards, stone cold out. I guess a trunk covered with dried and frozen blood is not her cup of tea. I have no doubt who the blood belonged to. Also, no doubt he wished he had it back.

"Fanny should get together with Carol and Sheriff Jack Benning. They could start a getting the vapors' club," my Guardian Angel said.

I shut the trunk. Fanny got over her attack of the vapors and I helped her up and steadied her as we walked.

The back door is not locked. I should have known better than to doubt a woman. The back door went into a small kitchen. The kitchen is sparse, I know because everything that had been in the cupboards or in the drawers was on the floor. The refrigerator door is open. There is a head of lettuce that had seen better days and a twelve pack of beer. The ice cube trays had been emptied.

The living room is plain. A throw rug that should have been in front of the fireplace was tossed in a corner. The ashes in the fireplace are scattered around the room. The sofa and a single chair had been slashed open so many times Good Will would not want them. There are no pictures on the walls.

There is a short hall with two bedrooms and a bathroom off of it. The first bedroom is bare. The second bedroom has an unmade king sized bed that looks like Alli Babba and his thieves had used the mattress for sword practice. The two sheets on the bed are mere ribbons. The dresser drawers are on the floor along with normal dresser drawer things. On top of the dresser is a magnifying glass. The tattered remains of four suits that I figured had been in the closet are on the floor. In the corner are two books by some guy out of Vegas on how to play stud poker and the secrets to Omaha - the card game not the city.

"I have to go potty," Fanny told me, which in women's talk means, I have to go to the bathroom.

The word potty has always amazed me but I suppose in polite society it is better than saying, "I have to go take a dump."

The bathroom must be unique because no sooner had Fanny shut the door then she screamed and I heard a thump. Pulling out my pistol I rushed the door, slamming into it with all my might. The door crashed open. Fanny is passed out on the floor. I don't know what it is but people from Saint Ansgar seem to get attacked by the vapors more than people from the rest of the country. I looked at her. I looked at the tiny window nobody could have escaped through. I looked at the sink. It is a normal sink. I looked at the commode. It is a normal commode. I looked at the bathtub with attached shower. What makes the bathroom unique is the blood splattered all over the mirror, all over the walls, the shower curtain and even the ceiling. It was definitely not caused by shaving with a safety razor. Adding to the charm were the pill bottles and other medicine cabinet stuff that had been opened and tossed around the bathroom. Whoever had ransacked the house was not a neat person.

Fanny moaned. I grasped her under the armpits and dragged her out of the bathroom. If she had to go to the bathroom she could play pioneer woman and go outside.

I left Fanny lying in the hall and went back into the bathroom. The mirror is almost completely covered with blood. A large circle of dried blood is on the floor. It is strange. There is blood in the trunk of the car. But there is no blood on the floor leading from the bathroom to the back or front door.

Fanny was sitting in the living room holding her head when I went through the living room. I noticed she still has her gloves on. I found a mop in a closet in the kitchen - it is stained red. Somebody killed Franklin in the bathroom, took him to the trunk of his own car, mopped the blood off the floor but didn't clean the bathroom. They were either scared off or were lazy.

I decided to make a closer inspection of the kitchen. It was not worth the time. The only thing I found of any interest was a set of steak knives, which weren't sharp enough to cut margarine.

I poked around in the ashes in the fireplace thinking the demolition crew might have missed something. There is nothing but ashes. I helped Fanny to Matilda.

She did not say a word on the way back to town until we were sitting in the Tea Room. I still have on the rubber gloves. "You might as well do the dishes," Fanny said.

"I don't do dishes," I said.

"How about windows?"

"I don't do windows," I said.

"You have to call the police," she told me.

I don't know what police, windows, and dishes have in common, but whatever works, works.

"They'll be down soon enough. I told them about Franklin's house. They didn't know about it. And besides, I don't think they'd appreciate me snooping around a crime scene before they did."

"It's terrible, all that blood," Fanny said, adding, "would you like some tea?"

"How about some of that green tea. I haven't been too regular lately."

I took off the gloves.

"You have so many clues now, Roosevelt, you're going to get writer's cramp," my Guardian Angel said.

Clyde walked into the room from the direction of the QUEEN OF HEARTS room, flapped up onto a chair, and swung himself up onto the table. He looked at me, looked over at Fanny but didn't utter a word. I guess he is having a bad feather day.

Fanny brought us tea.

Fanny didn't drink any of her tea. She sat, gazing at the cup and started to cry. She looks like a lost little girl. I touched her on the shoulder. "It's all so terrible," she sobbed. "A man is murdered, my cats are murdered, my heart is stolen. I don't know what to do, Roosevelt. I feel so useless."

Her loneliness radiated out of her and filled the room with emptiness. I looked at her tear stained face. "It will all work out, Fanny," I said to her trying to sound comforting.

She sniffed. "It probably will, but I will still be lonely, and nobody will love me. Why doesn't anybody love me, Roosevelt?"

"I like you a lot," I said.

"But you don't love me."

Standing up I held her hand and gently pulled. She stood up and I hugged her. She sobbed quietly on my shoulder. In a few minutes she stopped, took several deep breaths and stepped back. "I have to go potty."

She must have a cast iron bladder. It had been over thirty minutes since we were at Franklin's house.

Fanny trudged upstairs. After a few minutes I had the urge for a snack and went upstairs to the kitchen. The first thing I saw was a set of knives in a knife block by the sink. There are nine knives - three big knives and six steak knives. I pulled out one of the big knives and tested the blade. Most women who live alone have dull knives. I could have shaved with the knife. All nine knives are as sharp as a razor.

"Don't you dare say oh, oh," I told my Guardian Angel.

Looking in the refrigerator I took out a block of Colby cheese, tore a corner off and went back downstairs.

Fanny came down in a few minutes. "Do you think the same person who killed my cats could have also killed Franklin?" Fanny asked me.

"Why do you say that?" I mumbled, my mouth is full of cheese.

"Franklin had his throat cut and my cats had their throats cut."

"If it is, then he is a serial murderer, that is if cats getting their throats cut is called murder," my Guardian Angel said.

"I doubt it. I think it's all a coincidence," I told Fanny.

There was a loud knock on the back door. Fanny opened the door. Jimmy ran in all sparkling eyes and grinning. "Bob, Bob, can you play?"

It's hard to tell a kid that after a day of finding guns, knives, bloody trunks and bloody bathrooms, it's hard to get into the mood to play.

"Sure he will," Fanny said.

We must have gotten married but I don't remember the ceremony.

I followed Jimmy outside. "It's too cold to play outside. Why don't we take a look at your train set?" I said.

"Anything you want, Bob," he grinned.

Jimmy could corner the market on grins.

When I walked into Jimmy's house I knew Ginger was on hard times. The living room has a wood stove, wood is piled by it, a cheap throw rug is on the floor and a sofa covered with a tattered blanket is along a wall. There are no vases filled with flowers, nothing feminine in the room. It looks more like a line shack cowboys would live in except it is clean.

We went to Jimmy's room. He has a bed that is the bottom bed of a bunk bed set, an old wooden chest painted red for a toy box, and a dresser that should have been in a flophouse in Baltimore. His closet is open and there are only a few pairs of pants and shirts. There are no models, no pictures of football or basketball players on the walls, no trophies from little league ball, none of the signs of a normal kid. It is sad - the room is dreamless.

Jimmy tossed his coat on the bed and opened his toy box. He pulled out a cardboard box.

The train track is only about three feet around. It has a wind up engine and one car. I feel like a little kid looking in a store window at a giant train set with hills, and trees, and people, little houses, water towers, bridges, and three trains running all at the same time and knowing I would never, never, have a train set half that size.

Jimmy wound up the engine and the two-car train went slowly around and around the track. "My dad gave me the train. Isn't it great?" Jimmy said.

His sad eyes followed the little train round and round.

"It's a nice train."

It doesn't take too long for a kid or a man to tire of train sets, unless you are into things going in small circles forever and ever. I remembered the two decks of cards I took out of Franklin's car. "Let's go sit at the kitchen table and I'll show you a card game," I told Jimmy.

"Oh boy," he said. "But first I have to put up my train."

Jimmy's mom is teaching him good traits.

The kitchen is also neat. There is small metal table with four chairs. I took a deck of cards out of my pocket. "Mr. Trouble always had cards," Jimmy said. "I want to be a gambler just like he was when I grow up."

"Did he come over and play cards with you."

"He and mom used to play cards and they would let me watch. It's too bad somebody killed him. He always gave me a quarter when he came over."

"Did he come over a lot?"

"He used to and then he and mom got into a great big fight and he stopped coming over."

"Did you like Fanny's cats?" I asked Jimmy.

"No," he said sadly. "They always scratched me."

I felt bad about grilling a kid and stopped the questions.

The deck of cards had been opened. I shuffled the deck and started to count them. It is a marked deck. I could feel the tiny nicks in the corners. No wonder Franklin was such a good gambler. But it wasn't a deck he could pass off on a pro. The only thing a marked deck used on another pro gambler would get him is busted fingers or how he ended up, a slashed throat.

I showed Jimmy how to play clock solitaire and the next game I let him play by himself.

"Fanny's green tea hit home and I had to go to the bathroom. Jimmy kept playing cards.

I sat on the throne thinking over everything I had discovered during the day. Without the tea it was enough to give me the runs. After I washed my hands I opened the medicine cabinet. I'm a snoopy type of guy. There is the normal medicine cabinet stuff. The front drawer of the sink cabinet also wasn't too exciting unless you're into combs and brushes. The other drawer is in a world of its own. Next to a box of Q-tips were two stainless steel straight razors. I took my handkerchief out of my pocket and picked one up and opened the blade. It isn't called a straight razor for no reason. If anything, the other razor was sharper.

"You be one clue finding guy," my Guardian Angel said.

"I wonder what Ginger does with straight razors?"

"Your guess is as good as mine but I know she doesn't pick her teeth with them."

"I like this game," Jimmy told me when I got back to the kitchen.

"I have to go," I told him. He frowned. "But you can keep the cards."

He has a great grin.

I walked slowly back toward Fanny's house feeling lost.

"Drive down to Mexico and buy a few buttons. Eat them, throw up, stick a few feathers in your hair and the answer to this case might come to you in a cat killing, heart stealing, gambler killing, vision, " my Guardian Angel said.

Fanny had two customers. I waved goodbye.

I decided to go to Mom's. Mom's is always a good place to go when you are feeling lost. I also decided to walk. If I kept walking a block every day for a year I might lose three pounds.

Mom's isn't jumping. Two men are playing pool. They stopped playing when I walked in and waved at me. They had probably heard about my run in with Bill and Joe - the Schneider boys. Ginger is sitting on a stool behind the bar reading a magazine. She smiled at me.

I sat down across from her. I hadn't really noticed her the first time we met. She is in her late twenties or early thirties, big-boned, sandy red hair, a good-looking girl but she would never make

Playboy. What stands out about her are her blue eyes. They are like the eyes of an Alaskan Husky. Eyes nobody could read. She is also strong. Saint Ansgar has its share of strong women. She got me a Guinness. "On the house, call it a payment for playing with Jimmy. He told me all about it. He really likes you Roosevelt," Ginger said, her Alaskan Husky eyes are not happy or sad.

"You from here, Ginger?" I asked.

"Why? Do you want to marry me and take me to some far off island where we can romp and play in the ocean all day and drink weird named drinks all night?"

"Only if you are rich," I said.

"Good one," my Guardian Angel said.

Ginger smiled. "Of course I'm from here. How else would somebody end up in Saint Ansgar?"

"I heard your husband was killed in a tractor accident?" I said.

Her blue Husky eyes didn't show any emotion. "He wasn't a good man or a bad man. He worked odd jobs around farms. But he was good with Jimmy. He loved that boy."

I could sense there had been no great love between them.

"Jimmy has never gotten over it. He won't make friends. His friends are all make believe. He will watch other kids play but he won't join in. I think he's afraid if he makes friends they will die and he will be hurt again."

"He and I played with his train today and I showed him a card game."

Ginger smiled a genuine warm smile. "Maybe you will cause him to come out of his shell," she said.

"He told me you and Franklin used to play cards together. He said Franklin used to come over a lot and then you two had an argument and he stopped coming over."

Ginger's smile vanished quicker than fleas jump off a dog with a flea collar on. "You think I killed him?" she said, looking at me so hard with her Husky eyes that if I said yes she would growl and bite my nose off.

"No, just asking questions, nothing personal."

The growl did not go out of her eyes but she relaxed. "He came over a lot for a few months. He and Carol split up and more out of boredom than anything else he came by the house in the evenings.

We'd play cards, eat dinner, little stuff. It was nothing serious."

I felt she had wanted it to be serious but I didn't feel she was the kind of woman to latch onto a man out of desperation.

"He used to practice card cheating on you, didn't he?"

"You're smart," she smiled, which I liked a lot better than her Husky growl. "He used to have me watch him deal and see when he was taking cards off the bottom of the deck. He was so slick I never caught him."

I was going to ask her if she slept with Franklin but I knew the answer. "What time does Jimmy get out of school?" I asked instead.

"At 2:30. Why?"

"I might pick him up someday and we'll go for a hamburger or something."

Three men came into the bar and Ginger went to their table. I left a dollar on the bar and waved at Ginger as I left.

Walking back to Matilda it is almost 5:00.

I wasn't paying much attention to anything as I started to open Matilda's door. The door was halfway open when I saw the message printed with a purple magic marker on the back window - FLY OR DIE.

It is short, it is direct, there is no way I can misunderstand the meaning - it is good writing except for the fact cars can't fly. The message should have said DRIVE OR DIE.

CHAPTER EIGHT
IN SOME DEEP FROZEN CACA

Carol was in the kitchen when I walked into the house. I went to my room and put the deck of cards and my pistol in my suitcase and set the bottle of Maalox on top of the dresser. The way things are going I am going to need the Maalox.

When I went to the kitchen Carol seems happier than a robin with two worms and no babies. Maybe finding an almost divorced dead husband in her closet and having a man around who she couldn't seduce is something to be happy about. Who am I to be a judge on what rings a person's bell?

Carol set a plate of goulash down in front of me. Whenever I eat goulash I feel like it's a hundred years ago and I'm serving fifteen years in Siberia for selling pictures to French tourists of the Czar doing nasties with his sister.

"Brenda Harberts called. She told me to tell you Sheila would like to talk to you this evening. You can go over to the house after dinner. Earl will be gone. There's a city council meeting and afterwards the men always play cards so he won't be back home till late," Carol said.

"Earl is president of the bank and also on the city council," I said.

"He is in the Rotary, the Masons, he's a Boy Scout troop leader, works for the F.F.A., you name it, he is involved."

"He's into funny little hats, secret handshakes, merit badges and sheep," I commented.

"What do you want to see Sheila for?" Carol asked.

"Her mother asked me to talk to her," I lied. "She thinks I might be able to help her."

"When you come back I want to get naked, put on a blindfold and have you rub my body with feathers," Carol said giving me a coy little wink.

"You should introduce her to Clyde," my Guardian Angel said.

I finished my goulash, glad to get out of Russia, the winters are worse than Minnesota, thanked Carol and went to my room. I have to write in my clue book before I forget everything I have discovered today.

I wrote and wrote and wrote and wrote...paused...and wrote some more.

"Some of those clues are pretty good," my Guardian Angel said. "In over eighty clues you should have one or two that mean something."

"At least ten," I informed him.

I finished writing, read over the clues until I couldn't take it anymore. I hate a book without a plot and stuck the pad back in the crease of the chair. Without my Guardian Angel telling me I stuck my pistol in my belt and headed for the door. I was about to open the door when I had a sudden insight and went to the kitchen. Carol was doing the dishes. "Carol, where does Sheila live?" I asked.

It is always a good idea to know where you are going. Something I have never been good at in life but still a good idea.

"You are a funny one," my Guardian Angel said.

"Go to the red light. It's the house on the other side of the street with the large bushes to the left of it."

I feel weak.

"I wonder if those bushes still have footprints by them made by rubber soled boots?" my Guardian Angel pondered.

I was opening the door to leave just as Sheriff Jack Benning was about to ring the doorbell. I wanted to tell him he should buy another pistol. It really wasn't necessary to wear an artillery piece on his hip. "How are you Mr. Roosevelt," he asked pleasantly like he was a male Avon lady and wanted to sell me nineteen bottles of wrinkle cream.

I liked the Mr. part. It made me sound mature, refined, a true member of society. "Fine," I replied.

"I heard about your little fist to cuffs at Mom's. I wish I could have seen it."

"It was nothing."

"If you have some extra time I'd like you to show me some of your moves," he said.

"I might. If I get time it would be my pleasure."

"That would be great."

"Are you here to see me or Carol or me?" I asked, for some strange reason feeling like Carol's father meeting some young punk at the door who only wanted to see my daughter naked.

"I came by to see Carol."

I stepped aside and let him in the house. I wondered if Carol liked guys to jump her bones who were wearing boots and pistols.

"I like that question," my Guardian Angel said.

"You like watching birds mate," I told him.

Before I walked to Sheila's I took some snow and washed off the FLY OR DIE from Matilda's window.

As I rang the doorbell to the Harbert's home I could hear an old Beatles's song, Ku Ku la Chew, or something like that, it sounded like a bad impression of a chicken trying to crow.

Sheila answered the door looking like a vision fresh out of the sixties. Her hair has a braid on either side of her face with red beads on the ends of the braids. She smiled shyly at me over the top of her wire-rimmed glasses. "I'm so glad you came by. Come on in," she said sweetly.

I followed her through the expensively furnished house to an entertainment room complete with stereo and a large screen TV. The lights are out but lit vanilla scented candles are scattered around the room, sending warm and comforting shadows dancing on the walls and ceiling. Sheila turned down the stereo. "I love the Beatles," she said to me and sat on the sofa.

"I've never been a big fan of bugs," I said and smiled.

I started to sit in a chair. "No, sit by me, please," she said and patted the sofa cushion next to her.

"Mom told me you are an old hippie?" Sheila said. "I bet it was wonderful."

Sheila has a faraway dreamy look in her eyes and seems so young and innocent.

"So naive," my Guardian Angel said.

"I guess I still try to be a hippie," I told her. "But it's hard."

"I know. You tell people about peace and love, how wonderful the earth is, and they look at you like you're crazy. They don't seem to understand we all have to toss away our differences and get along. If we all understood we were all human beings we could conquer sickness, war, famine. We could transcend the stars, be one with the universe."

What can I say? I can't tell her she is wrong. I have a feeling I should have kept my mouth shut to her mother and minded my own business. Maybe I should tell Sheila to move to San Francisco and teach a meditation class? I definitely am not going to tell her to buy a set of bongos.

"Dad makes me wear a bra but when he leaves I take it off. We should all be free, unrestrained, able to live our lives the way we want and need to be ourselves. If we were all ourselves we would all be happy. Don't you think I have nice breasts, Roosevelt?" She pushed her shoulders back and her perk young breasts pushed against the fabric.

"Peace, love, far out man, groovy, trip out, I can dig it," my Guardian Angel said.

It is a catch 22 question. I figured the truth was the best approach. "They are nice," I said at the same time wondering if freedom for women is not wearing a bra maybe men should go around not wearing pants.

She relaxed and smiled. "I knew you would understand."

"He is such a big hearted, understanding guy," my Guardian Angel said.

I have to get away from the topic of breasts. "Are you out of school?" I asked.

"I finished high school in the nut house. I'm 19 and trying to get into Berkeley or Michigan. Both of them seem to have more free thinkers. If I don't get accepted I am going to join the Peace Corp."

"You can't do drugs," I told her.

"Did you do drugs?"

It was the wrong question. "I quit years ago, short-term memory is what they call me," I smiled.

"I don't do drugs anymore. I never did until my parents really started fighting. Then it got too much for me and I got some pills from a guy out of Minneapolis and tried to fry my brain."

"What were your parents fighting about?"

"Dad was having an affair," she said matter-of-factly like dads always have affairs.

In this country it isn't true but maybe in France it is.

"Do you know with who?" I asked. It wasn't a nice question but it had to be asked.

"Fanny Ruth."

A ping-pong ball bounced around inside my skull. I couldn't say what I wanted to - duh, blah, whaaat?

"Mom asked for it though. She is always at the bar late teasing and flirting with all the men. I don't know what she expected? Men are men, even my Dad isn't perfect."

"You know that now. Did you know that before they committed you?" I asked, my mind still reeling.

"No, I hated him. It wasn't right. He should have told my mother to come home. They should have talked. A person has to trust their wife or husband. When I get married I will tell my husband everything. We will be one heart, one soul, one mind. We will share our experiences and grow with each day."

"This one for sure isn't into women's lib," my Guardian Angel said.

"No card games with the boys for her husband," I told him.

"She'd better find a blind, deaf mute, who can't walk," he said.

"People do things for strange reasons but a lot of time they don't want to hurt others, things happen," I told Sheila.

"Dad committed me not so much to straighten me out but to get me out of the way so he and mom could be alone. I think when it all comes down to it they are tired of me, Roosevelt. Dad doesn't like anything I do. He hates hippies. He thinks all 18-year-old kids should have to go into the military for two years right after high school."

"Good idea," my Guardian Angel said.

"It's tough being a parent," I said. "It will change after you have gone off to school and are away a few years. You will understand more."

"I don't want to wait. I want to understand now," she said bitterly but with a spoiled child undertone. "And besides, my Mom has moved out of the house."

"She told me they have been fighting since he sent you away. She didn't want to send you away. She wanted you to stay home."

"She hates me, Roosevelt," Sheila said angrily. The hippie was turning into a hawk. "She didn't want kids. I was an accident. She never loved me. I was always a burden to her."

"Most of us are accidents," I said. "And we are burdens to our parents."

Sheila glared at me. Her dark eyes were mere slits. The shadows from the candles were now ominous, deep and dark. I looked directly into her eyes. I didn't flinch. I've stared into the eyes of murderers, rapists, extortionists, heroin dealers and other scum of the earth. Being afraid of a young hippie would be like being afraid of a daffodil. She lowered her eyes and started to cry. At first a few sobs, then a big sob, and then a big, big sob. "I'm so confused," she big, big, sobbed. "I don't know what to do."

I let her cry. It is a feeble cry anyway. I don't want to hold her. There is nothing I can do. Time would either make it all work out or Sheila's life would turn into a nightmare. Maybe, in all truth, it's only luck some of us have good lives?

She stopped crying, sniffed a few times, and looked at me. "Are you an only child?" I asked her.

She nodded her head.

"Have you noticed that most women you talk to in this town end up crying?" my Guardian Angel said.

He was right. I wonder if it has something to do with my cologne.

I feel totally out of my element. I don't know what I had planned with Sheila? How I thought I could help her? I have to leave. "I should be going I have to see another person. We can talk another time," I told Sheila as I stood.

She didn't protest and opened the front door for me. "I have another question if you don't mind?" I asked her.

"Ask anything you want?"

"Does your father own any guns?"

"He has two gun cases full. I don't know exactly how many but at least ten."

"A regular militia type guy," my Guardian Angel said.

"I have a question for you, Roosevelt," Sheila said.

"Shoot, I'm a big boy."

"When you were a hippie were you ever into group sex?"

"No group sex. Sorry."

"I'm glad. I didn't think you were that kind."

"Will you come see me again?" Sheila asked me with a strange smile on her face.

"If you need somebody to talk to tell your mom," I said, not knowing why I committed myself and left.

"I don't know about that one, Roosevelt. You might want to be careful around her," my Guardian Angel warned me.

"I don't know about her either," I had to confess.

There is something about Sheila that scares me. I decided to do the man thing and go to the bar.

Mom's was hopping, if a full pool table and a jukebox up so loud you can't talk without yelling is called hopping? It doesn't take much to entertain the masses. Mom saw me walk in and flashed a smile at me that would have made The Thinker smile. I went to the end of the bar. Ginger walked by with a tray of beers. She looks tired and gave me a weak smile. Mom came up to me. "How was Sheila?" she asked, but not sounding greatly concerned.

"She's a young girl and I think she'll be fine."

"Was she wearing a bra?"

"No."

"Did she try to seduce you?"

"I'm the detective around here. I'm supposed to be asking all the questions."

"You sleep with my daughter I'll make you wish you never saw this town," she warned.

"That's a strange way to ask a man what he wants to drink."

Mom appraised me for a moment, then smiled and said. "If you want to ever get it on you call me."

"This is a weird town," my Guardian Angel said.

"I'll take a shot of Jack and a beer," I said.

Mom brought me the drinks. I gulped the shot and took a swig of beer.

"Sorry I was rude," Mom said. "I worry about my daughter."

"Sheila told me she thought your husband sent her away so you two could get back together. She thinks you don't love her."

Mom shook her head. "I don't understand. That kid has everything. Nice clothes, car, you name it, she has never wanted. But she's always been weird. We had a pet dog once and I came home and she had tied it up and was sticking straight pins in his hide. There's a dark side of her that nobody can touch."

"What did the doctors say about her?"

"They said she was basically a normal kid who at times had an identity problem."

"That's all of us," I said, but the sticking pins in a dog thing was discerning.

Mom laughed sadly. "What can we do, Roosevelt?"

"I have no idea," I said.

She shrugged her shoulders and went to the other end of the bar.

I looked around the bar and wondered what quirk in nature made us the way we are?

I waved at Mom and she brought me another round. The Jack is good. I had another round. It was still good. I had another round. It was enough. I had sufficiently dulled my senses to not think about cats, hearts, murder, straight razors, guns, hippie girls, and women who only want me for my body. I want to find a bed, read a few chapters of some cheap mystery, and fall asleep.

I put some money on the bar, waved at Mom, waved at Ginger and left. Walking toward Carol's I remembered an old song, "The old bars ain't changed much, just a new place in town when you're out of touch."

I didn't want to walk by Fanny's, she might see me, so I cut down a block. When I got to Carol's street I turned right. Sheriff Jack Benning's car was still parked out front. "I don't think you should go in the house unannounced," my Guardian Angel said.

I went to the side of the house. The curtains are drawn but there is a slight crack between them. Sheriff Jack Benning and Carol are on the sofa. They are not playing Monopoly. They are naked. Almost naked I should say. Sheriff Jack Benning has his boots on. The boots thing doesn't really bother me. What bothers me is my clue notebook is on the table in front of the sofa.

"They are trying to steal your ideas," my Guardian Angel said. "But I like the show."

I have two choices. It is too cold to stand by the window and watch a grade C porn flick so I could either go back to the bar or go to Fanny's. I decided to go to the bar and started back the way I had come. I was halfway down the street when a new blue pickup truck drove slowly by me and stopped a few yards in front.

I put my hand on my pistol, walked slower and watched the driver's window come down. I moved out and away from the truck so I could see directly in the window. A man I do not know looked at me. His left hand is on top of the steering wheel. "You Bob Roosevelt?" he asked. His voice was not menacing.

"If you have money for me I am. If you're a bill collector I'm not," I said watching him closely.

He laughed and suddenly his right arm moved quickly and before I knew it a pistol appeared in the window. I dove to my right, yanking out my 9 m.m. at the same time, two shots rang out, missing me by only a few inches. I rolled back to my left hoping to throw the shooter off target, another bullet hit next to me. I am not a Holy Roller and I stopped rolling and fired four quick rounds in the general direction of the truck door. The man's pistol clanked down the side of the truck and hit the ground. The man's head slumped forward and came to rest on the horn. The horn blared. I stood, pointing my pistol at the man's head. I nudged his head with the barrel. His head rolled to the side and the horn stopped blaring. Blood is pouring out of his nose and ears. This buy will never play the horn again. I put my pistol back in my belt. There are no bullet holes in his door. I figured all of the shots hit him in the chest. One probably went through his heart. Lights are coming on in houses on both sides of the street. A man wearing pajamas came out on his porch. People in little towns go to bed early. The excitement of being bored all day can be trying. "Call the police," I called to him.

"He's at Carol's house. They're probably messing around."

Little towns don't need newspapers.

"Call Carol's then," I called back.

He waved at me and went back in the house.

"Roosevelt, I don't know what's going on, this is the second time I didn't have any premonition at all there was any danger," my Guardian Angel said to me in an apologetic voice.

"Leave me alone," I ordered him. Jack and beer can make me surly.

The man came back out onto his porch. "I called the cops," he called to me. "Want to come in Roosevelt, and have a cup of coffee till they get here?"

You can't hide in a small town either. "Got any whiskey?" I asked.

"You bet."

I had better not leave the scene even if it was for a social engagement. "How about you bring me a shot of whiskey and a cup of coffee," I called to the man.

He came out with two cups of coffee and two shots. He had put a coat on over his pajamas and was wearing boots. He handed me the shot and a cup of coffee and looked at the dead man. "To his soul," he toasted and we drank the shots.

"You know who he is?" I asked.

"Never seen him in my life and I've lived in these parts for over fifty years."

By now other neighbors were standing on their porches. If they all offered me shots and coffee I could crawl back to Carol's.

The siren came on around the corner and Sheriff Jack Benning drove as fast as he could for about fifty yards. He got out of the car and walked toward us with his hand close to his pistol. He looked at me and my coffee drinking friend, looked in the car at the dead man, looked at me, looked back at the dead man. He opened the door and the body fell out of the truck. His side was completely covered with blood. Sheriff Jack Benning crumpled to the ground like a daisy getting hit with the first frost. The Saint Ansgar vapors had attacked again.

"I never did think he would be a good cop," the man said looking down at Jack Benning.

Sheriff Jack Benning stayed on the ground a few minutes and then slowly sat up, shook his head, made sure he still had his pistol and stood. "My God, Roosevelt, you killed him," he said.

"He shot at me. I don't even know who he is," I said.

"You see anything, Fred," Jack Benning asked my whiskey friend.

"I heard three shots and then four quick ones that were a different sound. I didn't see anything. But I know the three shots were first."

Jack Benning took a pen out of his shirt pocket with his left hand, stuck the pen in the trigger guard of the dead man's revolver and picked it up. He looked at the front of the cylinder and there were three spent cartridges. He put the pistol back down on the ground.

"Do you want to see my pistol?" I asked him.

"No, but I think I'd better call in."

I don't think Bill Buffalo, Pete Rosebet or Paul Binyon will be happy with me. They are going to lose out on their beauty sleep.

Jack Benning made everybody go back inside their houses and we sat in his car with the heater on. It would take at least an hour for the posse to arrive. I didn't want to sit in silence for an hour so I started the conversation.

"How long have you been popping popcorn with Carol?" I asked casually.

He squirmed around in the seat like a little kid who had been caught lying. He scratched his head. He rubbed his eyes. "I'm not," he said, looking at me and knowing I know he is telling a Pinocchio and recanted. "Only tonight," he admitted.

"Come on Sheriff," I said.

"No, really, scouts honor. She called me this afternoon and told me she had some information for me and I should come over. As you know I was about to ring the doorbell when you were leaving. After you left we sat in the living room and talked for a little while and suddenly she stood up and took all her clothes off. She told me to take my clothes off and leave my boots on."

"What did you talk about?"

"She wanted to know if we had come up with anything concerning Franklin's death. I told her the entire investigation was being handled out of Albert Lee and I had been told to stay out of the way. She also wanted to know if I had talked to you and if you had discovered anything?"

I wonder why she didn't ask me.

"What were you doing going through my clue book?" I asked him sternly.

"What?"

"My clue book."

"I don't know what you are talking about," he said in a tone I knew he was telling the truth.

"What do you know about Earl Harberts? Is he as good a guy as people say?"

"As far as I know he's never done anything wrong in town. It's rumored he's messed around with a few women, but I don't know for sure."

"I heard he had an affair with Fanny Ruth?"

"I heard it too, but I figure that's their business."

"How about Sheila? Has she ever been in any trouble besides going to the nut house."

Jack Benning looked bothered by my question but answered me anyway. "She drove around town once and shot people's cats and dogs. Because her father is the bank president people didn't press charges and Earl bought them another pet."

"That's a hippie with teeth," my Guardian Angel said sheepishly.

"Sheila has been caught a few times parking out in the country with different guys and they were doing more than kissing," Jack Benning went on.

"She ever steal anything?"

"Not that was ever reported."

I was fresh out of questions and starting to get a headache from too much whiskey. I need a shower and a good night's sleep.

We both heard the sirens on the edge of town.

Bill Buffalo, Pete Rosebet and Paul Binyon got out of the unmarked squad car. An ambulance pulled in front of the truck. I saw squad cars block off both ends of the street. I guess they figured the dead man would try and make a break for it. Benning and I got out of his car. "Roosevelt, give me your pistol, butt first," Bill Buffalo told me in a calm voice.

"It's loaded," I told him as I handed him the pistol.

He put the pistol in his pocket without looking at it. "I bet you a few years in jail you don't have a concealed weapons permit?" Bill Buffalo said to me in a tone that I knew I was in some deep caca - being in Minnesota it was some deep frozen caca.

CHAPTER NINE
A FEW DIAMONDS AND RUBIES

Detectives Pete Rosebet and Paul Binyon inspected the dead man. There was no identification on him and the pickup truck he was driving had been stolen out of St. Louis.

"Those were four good shots," Paul Binyon said to me. "You could cover them with a pie plate."

"Not my best," I said, after all, it had only been from a few feet.

"His heart must look like Swiss cheese," Pete Rosebet said.

Detective Bill Buffalo picked up the last of my spent brass. He was doing a good job. He even had his white rubber surgical gloves on. "9 m.m., good pistol," he said to me as he dropped the brass in a paper sack.

"I don't own it to shoot rabbits," I replied.

"Not unless that guy lying there thought he was the Easter Bunny," Bill Buffalo joked dryly.

"These cops have sick humor," my Guardian Angel said.

Sheriff Jack Benning and I stood together and watched as the detectives did their detective thing. Bill Buffalo kneeled down and took a close look at the shooter's face.

Besides looking there really wasn't much to do. Fred, my whiskey-bringing friend, gave his statement. The ambulance paramedics loaded the body and left. A tow truck pulled in a few minutes later and towed the stolen truck away. The police cars blocking off the street left and Saint Ansgar was back to normal.

"Take him to your office," Bill Buffalo told Jack Benning. "We have to talk."

I figure I am the him. When people are talking to another person about somebody who isn't cool or they feel superior to, they never use the person's name, but always use a pronoun like him, it, or them.

"I don't think we're going to talk about the police fundraiser," I told Jack Benning as I got in his car.

One nice thing about little towns is the driving distance. It took us forty-five seconds to get to the Sheriff's Office. Bill Buffalo and his crew were waiting.

It is a nice office as Sheriff Offices go - at least there were enough folding chairs to go around. All four of the men looked at me. If I had four sets of eyes I could have returned their stares.

"I could lock you up, you know that?" Bill Buffalo said in a matter of fact tone.

I nodded my head. I know better than to run my mouth to a cop if there is a chance I might go to jail.

He took my pistol out of his pocket, released the clip and pulled the slide back to eject the chambered round.

"You ever register this puppy?" Bill Buffalo asked.

I figured he was talking about the pistol and not a Labrador retriever I used to own. "In Florida it's a legal gun."

He tossed me the pistol - pushed the shell he had ejected from the pistol into the clip and tossed me the clip.

I put the clip in the pistol, did not work the slide to put a shell in the chamber, and stuck the pistol in my belt.

"Anybody here know who that dead guy was?" Bill Buffalo asked.

I for sure don't know. The others looked at each other like it was the million-dollar question but they didn't have a clue.

"That guy was Peter Thompson. He's been a contract killer out of Kansas City for years," Bill Buffalo said.

Saint Ansgar, Minnesota suddenly took a turn for the worst.

I wondered how Detective Bill Buffalo knew the shooter.

"There's more here than meets the eye," Pete Rosebet said.

"He is a master at the understatement," my Guardian Angel said.

"Why don't you tell us what happened?" Bill Buffalo said in a manner that let me know if I didn't he might be inclined to take my pistol back and see how I liked the jail in Albert Lee.

I told them everything, excluding the part about watching Jack Benning pinning the tail on the donkey with Carol.

"I wonder why he drove by you and asked if you were Bob Roosevelt." Pete Rosebet asked.

"He must have been getting lazy. Years of killing people he'd lost the edge," Paul Binyon said.

"He had to know what you looked like if he watched TV," Pete Rosebet said.

"Whoever hired him would have told him what Roosevelt looked like," Paul Binyon said.

"It doesn't matter," Bill Buffalo said. "He's dead, Roosevelt is alive. The boy screwed up."

The boy screwed up statement could be taken two different ways. One of which I didn't like.

"Why would a contract killer be in Saint Ansgar?" Sheriff Jack Benning asked.

"It wasn't to catch a cat killer or heart stealer," my Guardian Angel answered.

"Anybody from your past who would like to see you in hell know you are here?" Bill Buffalo asked me.

"Only my Guardian Angel. He has dreams of being the guardian angel for some sweet young thing," I replied.

"It's not time to be a wise guy," Bill Buffalo said.

"It's a good thing I don't have an identity problem," my Guardian Angel said.

"Pete Rosebet and Paul Binyon told me you told them Franklin owned a house. We haven't been out there yet but I bet you have," Bill Buffalo said.

Bill Buffalo is letting me off a concealed weapons wrap and I didn't think it would be wise to lie to him.

"I went out. His car is there. There's enough blood in the trunk to fill a small town blood bank. The house was ransacked and there's blood all over the bathroom. I figure somebody cut his throat in the bathroom, stuck him in the trunk and drove him to Carol's and put him in her closet."

"Why would anybody want to do that? Why not kill him and leave him in the bathroom?" Pete Rosebet asked.

"I have no idea," I told him the truth.

"You take anything out of the house?" Bill Buffalo asked.

I didn't have to lie. I shook my head. I only took things out of the car but I wasn't going to tell Bill Buffalo about the two decks of cards or the Maalox.

"We'll go out there tomorrow, Roosevelt, you stay away, understand?" Bill Buffalo told me in a tone I understood completely.

Detective Bill Buffalo looked at Pete Rosebet and Paul Binyon and then at Jack Benning. "I don't want anybody besides who is in this room to know who was killed tonight." His eyes bore into each of their eyes. He looked at me. "Understand?"

We all nodded our heads. In life, one has to know when to bow to the power.

The room was silent for a few moments. Silent like the few moments before an infantry squad attacks. "I would like to know if you find any prints at the house," I said.

"You scratch my back I'll scratch yours," Bill Buffalo replied.

"I didn't know you both had fleas," my Guardian Angel said.

Detective Bill Buffalo stood like he was carrying the weight of the world on his shoulders. We all stood. Bill Buffalo, Paul Binyon, and Pete Rosebet headed toward the door. Jack Benning opened the door for them. "Detective Buffalo," I called.

He stopped.

"Thanks."

"Don't thank me. Whoever hired Thompson is now too far committed to stop. You're going to need that pistol, Roosevelt. Next time you might not be so lucky. But I don't want your blood on my hands. You can thank the N.R.A., I'm a charter member."

When they were gone Jack Benning and I sat down. He let out a deep sigh.

"Saint Ansgar has turned into New York," my Guardian Angel said.

"What are you going to do now?" Jack Benning asked me.

"I'm going to Carol's."

Want a ride?" he asked.

"No, I'm going to walk."

I walked slowly toward Carol's. During my brief stay in Saint Ansgar I have been shot at three times and for some reason I think it was three different shooters. The question that bothers me is - was it for three different reasons?

"What happened? What happened? What happened?" Carol asked after I shut the door. She is doing her repeating nervous bunny hop routine.

She didn't give me time to answer but hopped up and down and sputtered so fast I could barely keep up with her. "I heard the shots and the neighbors called and then Benning got called and then the sirens and when I tried to go down the block the police said no and I came back here and I've been so afraid."

She does a really good run on sentence but not as good as her repeats and her hopping.

"Tell this rabbit to shut up. Would you, Roosevelt?" my Guardian Angel pleaded.

"It was nothing much. I had to kill a guy who took a few shots at me," I told Carol.

She stopped hopping. Her face went blank. She starred at me like I am transparent and all she could see was the door behind me. She suddenly threw her arms around my neck. "You poor, poor man," she soothed. "It must have been terrible. Let mommy help you."

I pushed her away from me. "Right now I am going to take a bath and I want to be left alone."

She put a little girl pout on her face. "But mommy wants to help."

I went to my room. "The next time you don't do your duty I'm going to start praying for God to come get you and I will tell him to assign you to a Buddhist Monk who lives so far back in the boonies all he does is sit around and watch trees grow," I said to my Guardian Angel.

"God wouldn't do that."

"God listens to all prayers."

He was silent for a moment. "Please?" he asked in such a beseeching voice it almost made me sick.

My clue book was back in the crease of the chair - my writing probably bored Carol. I took it out and started writing. When I was done I read over the clues one time, stuck the clue book back in the chair, took off my clothes, and with my pistol in hand I headed for the bathroom to take a bath. I have learned in Saint Ansgar one can't be too careful.

"It's a sad state of affairs when you can't trust anybody," my Guardian Angel said.

When the tub was half full or half empty, however you look at life, of steaming hot water, I tossed in some lavender bubble bath that was under the sink. When I slid into the tub the bubbles were over two-foot tall. The hot water feels wonderful. I don't know what it is about a hot bath but the water seems to pull all the worries and problems out of my head. I rested suspended between here and now, or there and then, or this and that, and shut my eyes. My mind slowly drifting away. Away to a land where hippie girls stuck flowers in soldiers rifle barrels. Away to a land where you could drink the water and eat as many fresh fish as you wanted without fearing your children would be born green. Away to a land where more money was spent on helping the poor, combating sickness and educating the young than on presidential election races. It was soothing. I fell into a deep dreamless sleep.

I woke up not knowing where I am. Nothing new, but I had an eerie feeling. I opened my eyes slowly. My magic wonderland bubbles were gone. The steaming hot water is tepid. A naked Carol was standing a few feet from the tub. A gorgeous sight she is but she has my pistol in her hand and it is pointed in my general direction. "I tried to warn you, but you were sleeping," my Guardian Angel said.

I sat up in the tub slowly. Carol gave me a crooked little grin. There was no way I could make a move for her before she shot. It is not a bad way to exit stage left - shot in a tub by a naked woman. I can think of a lot of worse ways to die. "Why are you taking a bath with a pistol by the tub?" Carol asked me.

"It's a man thing," I told her.

She set the pistol on the sink. "Well get out of the tub and let's go do a man, woman, thing," she said.

"Please, Roosevelt," my Guardian Angel begged.

"I'll say one thing for you, you are persistent," I said to Carol.

She smiled.

I shook my head.

She left but was not smiling.

My Guardian Angel started crying.

I woke up in the morning and Carol was gone. I wonder where she goes every day. I have never seen her blue Mercedes around town.

I ate some peanut butter on toast and looked in the phone book for the Boraxe number. Merriam and Dale Boraxe have four phone numbers. I figured they must own a house in town and have three phones on the farm, or the other way around, or two at each place. I dialed the first number.

A lady answered with a refined and confident tone to her voice. "Hello."

"Mrs. Boraxe, this is Bob Roosevelt."

"The detective that was on TV?"

"Yes, can we meet. I have a few questions."

"Come by the house here in town in about an hour."

"Thank you. I'll see you then." I hung up.

If everyone could be as simple and straight to the point as Merriam Boraxe life would be much easier.

I got out my clue book and started to read. Read for a few minutes and had a thought. "Now we are skating on thin ice," my Guardian Angel said.

I stuck my pistol in my belt and left the house. Matilda cranked right up - she is confident with her place in life and knows who she is so it isn't necessary to stroke her ego all the time.

I expected the house in town to be the biggest and grandest of all the houses in town. I was wrong. The house is a one level brick. Nice but not ostentatious. I rang the doorbell. Mrs. Boraxe answered the door. I had seen her at Fanny's but had not paid much attention. She is a striking woman in her early to mid-fifties and stands about 5'5". She has shoulder length auburn hair that I figured was dyed, but not so dark it looks cheap. Her wedding ring has enough large diamonds to fund a small college in Pennsylvania.

"Mr. Roosevelt, it is a pleasure to meet you, won't you please come in," she said to me with a smile that was so natural I felt instantly at ease. "Would you like coffee?"

"Yes please," I said.

"Black," I presume.

Merriam went to the kitchen and came back with a silver coffee serving set. She poured my coffee, served me and poured her own. She did not put cream or sugar in her coffee. She sat. "I like my coffee straight, just like I like my men," she told me with a glint in her eyes.

"Straight helps," I agreed.

"Now tell me why a famous detective like yourself is in Saint Ansgar?"

I don't think Merriam would understand following the sun so I didn't know what to say.

"I bet you were driving around in your cute little Volkswagen and your destiny told you, you should stop," she said.

I nodded - at times people are amazing.

"It must be wonderful to have the freedom to do what you want and when you want," she said in a wistful tone. "I've always been stuck here. Stuck like super glue," she said not sounding bitter but not happy either, more resolved to her fate.

"I bet you and your husband have traveled all over the world," I said.

"We have and we do. But we always come back here," she said here like here is a dirty word.

"But, enough about me, why, exactly, do you wish to talk to me?" she asked.

"I'm trying to find out who killed Franklin Trouble and thought you might be able to tell me some things I didn't know."

"I thought you might ask me who I thought stole Fanny's heart and killed her cats."

Her comment shook me for a brief instant. Fanny told me she did not tell anybody about the heart or the cats.

I shook my head.

"I knew Franklin for years. He was a nice man in his own way but he was a private man. He didn't need people around him all the time. He didn't have to go to the bar and be part of the crowd. But Franklin was also a lazy man. He didn't want to work but he liked nice things. He was a born gambler, a good gambler, but like most gamblers, I imagine he also had a few shady friends, the type of friends that if he made a mistake they would kill him. Like in the movies, nothing personal, it's only business."

Merriam sounded like she had more of an education than what having money and being comfortable had taught her.

"Do you know any of the people he played cards with?" I asked.

"He always took his action out of town. The police should be able to tell you though."

"I understand he chased a lot of women."

"Comes with the trade, easy money, easy women."

I like Merriam. Her feet are firmly planted on the good old mother earth.

"I understand he had an affair with Fanny?"

"Fanny is a strange girl. She has never tried to make close friends. She spends most of her time alone. She scared a lot of the local people off several years when she got into the occult. She wore all black, started reading books about witches and warlocks and the devil. A few people saw her walking around in the country singing chants."

"Better start wearing a cross or get some garlic," my Guardian Angel said, "and remember my warning when we first got to this iceberg."

"Garlic is for vampires, you idiot," I said, but the news about Fanny being into the occult is disturbing.

"But Fanny stopped all that occult nonsense," Merriam went on. "But even when she was being weird Franklin always liked her. He gave her the money to start her business. I suppose he could have had an affair with her. I know he had one with Mrs. Harberts but at the time Brenda was getting back at Earl for, rumor goes, sleeping with Fanny. Rumors about who is sleeping with who are the main topics of conversation in little towns. I take them with a grain of salt. I've always felt men and women should run around sleeping with anybody they wished then we wouldn't all be hung up on the jealousy thing so much."

Maybe Merriam was an old hippie but she has forgotten about AIDS.

"Do you have any idea who would have stolen Fanny's heart

and killed her cats?" I asked.

"Some sicko killed the cats, I know that. But, since she never locks her store when she leaves who knows who stole her heart. The strange thing about it, Roosevelt, is, there's thousands of hearts in the store and only one not for sale. Whoever stole it also wanted to hurt her. They had to know it belonged to her grandmother."

I didn't know a nice way to ask the next question and I figured Merriam would probably kick me out of the house, but I had to ask it.

"Do you think your husband has ever slept with Fanny?" I asked in a tone that I hoped let her know I am only doing my job.

Merriam pursed her lips. Her eyebrows arched. She took a sip of coffee and set her cup down. She looked at me like I had to be dumber than a Tootsie Roll Pop. "My husband is one of the wealthiest men in southern Minnesota. He owns over 5,000 deeded acres. We have three large houses on the farm. He flies his own airplane. He gives me more than I need and doesn't ask me any questions. We have been married almost thirty years. I know who butters my toast. When it comes to him and other women I have only told him one thing. If he ever gives me a disease I take half of everything he owns. If you want to know who he has slept with or is sleeping with ask him, I'm not his mother."

"I should have known, it was a dumb question," I told her trying to sound apologetic.

"If you want to see my husband he is out at the north farm," she told me and walked to the door and opened it. "It was nice meeting you."

I wanted to ask her where the north farm was. North is a vague direction but as I walked by her she pinched my rear and shut the door.

"Reverse discrimination," my Guardian Angel said.

I stopped at the convenience store and asked the clerk to draw me a map on how to get to the north Boraxe farm. He drew me a map on a paper towel.

The house is right out of Gone with the Wind before the Civil War started. A twin Beechcraft was in front of an airplane hangar. At the end of a landing strip is a snowplow to keep the snow off of the airstrip. Three metal barns are behind the house, so big B-25's could be parked in them. There is an eight-car garage next to the house. A new black Lincoln is in the driveway. I have a feeling the Lincoln is the run around car.

I parked next to the Lincoln and hoped Matilda didn't get an inferiority complex.

Before I knocked the massive oak door swung open. Mr. Dale Boraxe had a cigar the size of Rhode Island stuck in the corner of his mouth. Even being short, dumpy and bald, he reeks of power. He looked at me, puffed on the cigar, looked like he was going to say something but didn't. I waited patiently and noticed he had a Rolex watch on and a pinky ring any black jack dealer in Vegas would love. Something in his mind clicked. "You're that detective Roosevelt, that shot that old boy last night," he said casually, like shooting old boys in Minnesota is an everyday occurrence.

There really was no answer to his statement so I nodded.

"Come on in, unless you're passing out Watch Towers," he told me and chuckled.

The living room is the size of a high school gymnasium. Following him toward the back of the house we went to a glass enclosed patio. We sat. I don't know where she came from but a young lady with short blond hair, about 5'8", wearing a form fitting brown knee length skirt and a white blouse with cleavage so low she really didn't have to wear it, walked into the room. Her legs are so nice she could make a fortune modeling nylons. She made Carol look like yesterday's toast. My Guardian Angel howled. "Bring me a screwdriver, Lisa," Mr. Boraxe told the lady.

"And you, sir?"

"How about a beer?"

"You look like a beer type guy," she told me with a slight smile on her full ruby red lips.

I don't know if I liked her comment or not. I guess it depended on what a beer type guy was to her. My beer type guy might be entirely different from hers.

"Look all you want but don't touch that one. She's mine," Mr. Boraxe told me in a way I understood he was a powerful man with powerful friends who would do bad things to my skinny, poor, unpowerful, self.

"If Lisa is his property I don't know why he would have an

affair with Fanny?" my Guardian Angel said.

Lisa came back with the drinks. She poured my beer in a glass. I noticed she had enough gold on her fingers to give Norway a loan. She smiled at Daddy Sawbucks and ignored me. I guess her definition of a beer type man didn't match mine.

"Next time order a screwdriver," my Guardian Angel said

"So what brings you out to see me, Roosevelt?" Mr. Boraxe asked puffing on his cigar.

"I was wondering if you had any idea who Franklin Trouble played cards with."

Mr. Boraxe looked at me carefully. "Why would I know that?"

"A man of your position and wealth has to know the shakers and normally only the shakers have the money to play big poker," I said, trying to grease his ego a little.

"Franklin was a no good low life gambler who never held down a real job in his life," Mr. Boraxe said with an edge of hate in his voice. "This country didn't get strong because of men like him. It's because of men like him that we are getting weak. I never associated with the man or kept up with his business."

"You wouldn't happen to know anybody who might be able to tell me who Franklin played poker with?" I asked.

"Roosevelt, I'm the mayor of Saint Ansgar and I have hopes of being governor of this fine state. I keep my nose clean and I mind my own business. A man lives longer and goes farther if he lives that way."

"I can't argue with your wisdom," I said casually, bowing to his power. But I didn't buy the keep the nose clean bit. There is a raw side to Mr. Boraxe, a side that somebody somewhere knew about, and if he really wanted to be governor he should start hiding his other women, unless Minnesota is the only state in the union that the moral Christian voting block doesn't see anything wrong with the governor having a mistress.

"This is a nice house," I told him. It was time to change the subject.

"I got the place when my father died. I have built it up to what it is today. It's the envy of every farmer for miles."

"What do you grow here?" I asked. "I'm a city boy and don't know much about farming."

"You look like you are part hippie and part cowboy to me," he laughed, then sipped on his drink and took a puff on his cigar.

The cigar might have cost fifty bucks but it smelled like moldy alfalfa. I've always figured if they would make a cigar that tasted and smelled like pot they would sell a million of them. If nothing else it would drive the cops and dope dogs nuts.

"I grow 3,000 acres of corn and wheat and run cattle on the other 2,000 acres," Mr. Boraxe informed me. "The land is in constant rotation."

"I bet you have a lot of men working for you."

"Why? You looking for a job?"

"No. I'm more the Franklin Trouble type now," I said to him with enough starch in my voice so he knew he couldn't push me around.

His eyes twitched and I knew he didn't like my comment but he kept himself under control. "If you don't have anything else to ask me I have some important business to do today. I'm taking Lisa to Minneapolis and buy her a few trinkets. Girls like her need trinkets. If you know what I mean?" he said to me and winked.

"I only have one more and then I'll leave you alone. Why don't you like Fanny Ruth?"

"It's none of your business," he snapped, glaring at me like I would get up and run away.

My assumption about Mr. Boraxe and Fanny is right. Now I have to find out what the bad blood is between them.

I finished my beer and let Mr. Boraxe calm down. He is puffing on his cigar so quickly it looks like rain clouds are filling the patio.

"Would you care if I walked around outside and looked at your place? I've never seen a farm like this. It's really impressive?" I asked calmly.

He hesitated before he answered. I could tell he really didn't want me snooping around but there wasn't a good reason to tell me no. "Sure, take your time. One day you'll be able to say you toured the governor of Minnesota's farm headquarters."

I stood. "No need for you to get up. I can find the door."

We didn't shake hands. I guess he felt he wouldn't need my vote.

I was about to the door when Lisa walked up to me. "What's a girl like you doing in a dump like this?" I said to her.

"Diamonds, rubies, gold, cash, fur coats, expensive clothes, are a few reasons."

Lisa opened the door for me and as I walked by her she whispered. "I might be able to help you. Come out here tomorrow night at midnight. I'll be here alone."

She shut the door.

"You have any extra diamonds or rubies or a few fur coats lying around?" My Guardian Angel asked me.

I was halfway to the large metal barn when Lisa and Mr. Boraxe drove away in the Lincoln.

CHAPTER TEN
TWO DUMB DEAD BULLS

I really didn't know why I wanted to walk around Boraxe's farm unless it was an unconscious reason to stay away from all the women in Saint Ansgar.

Heading toward the twin Beachcraft I noticed an older Ford truck parked by one of the barns. The plane is a beauty.

I was going around the plane when two men walked out of the closest barn. I was as surprised to see them as they were me. Bill and Joe Schneider, alias, Mutt and Jeff, stopped in their tracks and glared at me. It is a double glare day.

"I haven't seen you boys in a while?" I said, smiling at them the way a cat smiles at a mouse.

Dashing back into the barn Bill came ran back with two tire irons. He handed one to Joe. He likes to share his toys. "I don't think they plan on changing a tire," my Guardian Angel said.

Bill and Joe started toward me, spreading apart from each other as they advanced. About five yards from me they stopped. Bill is on my left and Joe is to my right.

"We've been thinking a lot about you lately," Bill snarled in a bad impression of a guard dog.

"You could have written. I would have written back," I replied as calmly as if I was lying on a beach in Costa Rica.

"I'm glad that boy that shot at you last night missed. Now we can have some fun," Joe grinned.

"You shouldn't grin so wide, Joe, your teeth would frighten a scarecrow," I said. "You should see a dentist and look into some cheap caps."

He didn't laugh at my joke but he shut his ugly mouth.

"I don't know if this is a good time to be telling jokes," my Guardian Angel said.

I feel like a quarterback who had angered his lineman and they were going to miss their blocks on purpose to let him know he had better learn how to cultivate and keep friends.

Bill and Joe looked at each other and nodded. It was the old silent signal and nod routine. They suddenly rushed at me like two bulls after the same cow - two stupid bulls after the same cow. I took two quick steps back, yanked my pistol out of my belt, shot Joe in the right foot, turned left quickly, and as Bill's tire iron was about to change the shape of my head, I shot him in the left knee and ducked under the tire iron. Both men were flopping around on the snow, holding their wounds and howling like two coyotes that had been caught in leg traps. Only I don't think Bill or Joe will chew their legs off to escape.

"That wasn't fair. They didn't know you had a gun," my Guardian Angel said.

"Before people blunder into things they should ask questions," I replied.

I have a deep desire to walk up to each man and put a slug through his head. I know it isn't a good peace, love, thing to do and I could get a bad hippie demerit, but at the moment it didn't matter. I know Bill and Joe had hurt people badly. If I put them out of their misery they would never hurt anybody again. It would also save the earth a little precious oxygen and feed a few more people - Roosevelt's mini population control - I might even get on the Green Peace mailing list.

Joe is holding his foot and grimacing. It was a good grimace. At least he is good at something. I pointed the pistol between his eyes and about an inch from his face. "No, please," he whimpered.

"Who killed Franklin Trouble?" I demanded.

"I don't know, really, I don't know," he squealed.

I moved the gun barrel several inches to the right of his head and pulled the trigger. The concussion knocked his head sideways. It was an old interrogation trick the North Vietnamese used on captured soldiers - what did they care about the Geneva

Convention?

I stuck the pistol on his forehead. I could tell by Joe's eyes I'd taught him fear.

"Who killed Franklin Trouble?" I demanded again.

"Really, really, I don't know, don't shoot me, please, don't shoot," he begged.

"Don't do it Roosevelt. It isn't worth it," my Guardian Angel said.

I want to pull the trigger. I want to send Joe straight to fertilizer. My finger tightened on the trigger and then I slowly lowered the pistol. I stepped back and kicked Joe in the mouth, knocking him stone cold out. Now he can get his teeth fixed.

Bill had seen and heard everything. Turning toward him he is trying to crawl away. His bleeding knee is leaving a blood trail a businessman from Chicago, who had never been hunting in his life, could follow. I kicked Bill in the ribs so hard he rolled onto his back. I stuck the pistol into his belly.

"Who hired you guys to try and beat me up at the bar?" I asked him, putting a lot of emphasis on the word, try.

"I won't tell you anything, you skinny cop," he spat.

I swung the pistol up into his chin with such force it crushed bone and sent blood squirting like a small Old Faithful.

"One more time, who hired you?" I asked calmly, sticking the gun against Bill's forehead.

"I think you might have other problems," my Guardian Angel warned me.

I ignored him.

I could tell by Bill's eyes I had also taught him fear. He gurgled and spit out a mouth full of blood and was about to speak when a rifle shot report came from the direction of the house - a split second later Bill's head exploded like a water balloon hitting pavement. I dove to the ground and hid behind his body. Another shot slammed into his body.

"I told you, you might have another problem," my Guardian Angel said.

At least he is back on the job.

Joe was coming to and making an effort to sit up. A bullet hit him in the ribs. A surprised look covered his face, but wasn't there for long as a second bullet hit him in the temple. His head blew up like a pumpkin hit by a shotgun blast. I peered over Bill but could not see anybody. I heard an engine start in front of the eight-car garage. The engine had a deep powerful sound like a V-8. I ran toward the back of the garage in a zig zag pattern. When I got to the back of the garage I turned left and followed the wall until I got to the front left corner of the garage. I peered cautiously around the corner. All I saw was good old Matilda and I knew she wasn't shooting at me.

I saw footprints in the snow. Somebody had run alongside the garage, stopped, hurried back, and run back along the garage again. The footprints matched the footprints behind the bush at Sheila's. I followed them to the corner of the garage. From the corner I could see Bill and Joe's bodies. There is no imprint in the snow where the shooter had lain down. The shots had been fired from a standing position - it was over a hundred yards to the bodies - the shooter is an excellent shot.

There is no brass in the snow but I could see where it had hit after being ejected and a depression made by fingers where the shooter had picked it up.

I followed the footprints back to the driveway. It would be impossible to get a single tire print off of the driveway with all the compaction of the snow and ice.

I went to Bill and Joe to search their bodies. There is nothing out of the ordinary in Joe's billfold, a driver's license, a few credit cards and twenty bucks. There is nothing in his pockets. Bill's billfold could have been Joe's billfold twin - a driver's license, a few credit cards and twenty bucks. But in his shirt pocket there is a black, well-used, personal phone book. I put it in my pocket. In his pants pocket is a set of car keys that I figure fits the Ford pickup in the second barn.

I went to the house, hoping the door was open, which is was, and gave Sheriff Jack Benning a wakeup call and told him to call Bill Buffalo. Heading back to the plane I had a question for myself. "Self. Why had the shooter shot Bill and Joe and not me?"

"Maybe they owed him money," my Guardian Angel said.

"Maybe the he is a she," I said.

"Interesting, very interesting," my Guardian Angel said.

Standing in front of the garage my Guardian Angel said, "Roosevelt, you had me worried the way you acted with Bill and Joe. It's not like you. You're going to have to chill. You can't change the world or let bad people get the best of you and become like them."

Everything is peaceful now, the slight sound of the wind hitting the buildings, the smoothness of the snow, the tranquil overcast sky. "How do you take a violent world and change it through peace?" I asked my Guardian Angel.

"I don't know."

"Not even God knows," I said.

"Sad," he said.

"It's more than sad," I said.

I heard the approaching sirens. The real world can be a lousy place.

Sheriff Jack Benning is in the lead car. I was surprised to see Detectives Bill Buffalo, Pete Rosebet and Paul Binyon following him. Two Highway Patrol cars were behind them and then an ambulance. The ambulance didn't have to be in a hurry.

Sheriff Jack Benning was excited but at least he wasn't talking in triplicate. "Man, what a couple of days you've had," he said.

"I didn't think you boys could make it that quick. What did you do fly?" I asked Detective Bill Buffalo.

"We were just finishing going over the Franklin house when Sheriff Benning called us," Pete Rosebet replied.

"Is Dale Boraxe home?" Bill Buffalo asked me.

"He left before any of the action. Nobody is in the house," I replied.

"Why don't you show us where the party was," Bill Buffalo ordered more than asked. He told the Highway Patrolmen and the ambulance guys to stay put.

"Follow me gentlemen, the tour starts right here," I said and then looked at Bill Buffalo. "Thanks again," I told him.

"For what?"

"Letting me keep my pistol."

"I hate crooks. I don't care who kills them, as long as they end up dead," he said.

I know he isn't lying.

I showed them the footprints, where the shooter had picked up the brass, explaining on the way what had transpired from the time I ran into Bill and Joe.

Bill Buffalo looked at the two dead men. "I'll tell you one thing, Roosevelt. Whenever we get a call over a shooting involving you we know for sure there aren't going to be any wounded."

Sheriff Jack Benning looked at Bill's head, or what had been Bill's head, looked at me, looked at Bill once more, got attacked by the vapors and fell straight backwards. He is sprawled out on the snow like he is going to make snow angels.

"That ruins his chances of ever getting into a homicide department," Paul Binyon said casually.

None of the men made a move to help him.

The detectives did all their investigating things while I watched. They put Bill and Joe's personal things in two paper sacks. I told them I thought the keys went to the Ford truck by the barn. Pete Rosebet snapped photographs of the bodies and took one of Jack Benning just for kicks. They paced off the angle of the shots that killed Bill and Joe, made notes in their pocket sized notebooks, talked into tape recorders and all in all did a good detective job. I figured I would give them a B plus if I was teaching a crime scene class.

Sheriff Jack Benning stood, looked at Bill again and decided it was time to take a twenty-yard jog and puke.

"He must be on one of those new diets," Pete Rosebet said.

"You have a sick sense of humor," my Guardian Angel said to Pete.

"You'd have to be a little twisted to do his job," I told my Guardian Angel.

Detective Pete Rosebet found the three shell casings from my 9 m.m. and put them in a sack. The detectives had enough sacks they could sell them to pot dealers. They didn't have sacks big enough to hold the two tire irons.

When the detectives were done Bill Buffalo waved at a watching paramedic.

"Morticians must love you," a paramedic who had bagged Peter Thompson the night before told me as he zipped the body bag around Joe.

Bill Buffalo, Jack Benning and I walked back to the garage while Pete Rosebet and Paul Binyon went to check out the Ford truck. Buffalo told the Highway Patrol guys they could go back to giving little old ladies speeding tickets and eating at Hardy's.

"Get in my car, Roosevelt, I want to talk to you alone," Bill Buffalo said.

Jack Benning gave him a 'little boy left out look' and got in his own car.

Bill Buffalo's car had been left running and it is warm inside. I didn't know how cold I was until I got in the car. Cold or not cold I figured I was going to hand over my gun to Bill Buffalo, go to jail, pay a big fine and be told by the judge, who didn't like long hairs, to boot scoot it out of Minnesota and never come back.

"What did you take off of the bodies?" Bill Buffalo asked me calmly.

"Nothing," I replied.

"Roosevelt, I've been a cop for years. I've seen it all. If you haven't noticed too much gets me excited. When I leave my office at night I leave my job behind. I go home. I eat. I drink a few beers. My wife and I watch the tube. We go to bed. Sometimes we mess around, sometimes we don't. When I get up in the morning I go to my job and do my job. I'm a good cop. I'm a fair cop. Now don't make me kick the tree sap out of you for lying to me. I saw your footprints all around Bill and Joe."

"Do you think you can kick the tree sap out of me?" I asked.

"I have no doubt."

"Since you put it that way I took a personal phone book out of Bill's pocket," I said with respect.

He held out his hand. I gave it to him. He looked through the book and handed it back to me. "I don't have a big staff. You might be able to get more done than we can," he said.

I was thrown totally off guard.

"I like you Roosevelt. I ran a check on you. You might want to write for your F.B.I. file. It's a good read. But, back to what I was saying. I like you. You remind me of my son. He's an old freak, lost, dreaming, thinking the world will change. It won't change. It will run its own course and we have to hang on for the ride. Life is harder on people who look for the sunny side. You look for it but I think you know you'll never find it and you have to live with that knowledge. Now tell me what you think about Franklin Trouble's murder?"

I feel honored by Bill Buffalo's words. I feel a kinship with Bill Buffalo. If he wasn't a cop and I still smoked pot he'd be fun to smoke a few joints with. "I don't know a thing. I have a notebook I write clues in. When I add today's clues I'll have close to ninety clues. None of them mean a thing. Nothing makes sense," I told him, hiding the fact I was lying.

He laughed, letting me know he understood. "It will, you just keep bumbling around and you'll stumble onto something."

"The bumbling and stumbling he's good at," my Guardian Angel said. "It's the solving that's the problem."

"I only hope you don't get killed before you find something out," Bill Buffalo said.

"Me too. It would ruin my plan of living forever."

"I have the results for you on the dome and the cat hair. The dome had Fanny Ruth's prints on it, which only stands to reason, and a few sticky smudges, which we didn't have analyzed."

"How did you have Fanny Ruth's prints on file?" It was a confirming question.

"She used to be a drunk and got picked up a few times so she got printed."

"Was Fanny ever in any other kind of trouble?" I asked.

"A few years ago a rumor was going around Fanny thought she was a witch. A few cats and dogs disappeared and people blamed her. Nothing serious. I don't think she kills babies and drinks human blood," Bill Buffalo said.

"Clyde might," my Guardian Angel said.

"How about the cat hair?" I asked.

"Why did you want cat hair analyzed?" Bill Buffalo asked me.

"Poison."

"The cat hair had arsenic poison in it."

"Oh, oh," my Guardian Angel said.

"Oh, oh," I said.

"You think a cat killed Trouble?" Buffalo asked and then chuckled.

"What were you doing out here today?" he asked me after

enjoying his own funny.

I told him about hoping Boraxe could lead me to men who played poker with Franklin. But it hadn't panned out. I didn't tell him it might pan out with a certain young, good looking blond, with pouting red lips.

"Your pan out and my pan out are sadly two different things," my Guardian Angel said.

"Both Merriam and Dale Boraxe are under investigation by the Feds, for what I don't know, it's a hush hush deal. I don't want you messing with either one of them. Understand?" Bill Buffalo told me in a tone I knew he was serious.

I nodded my head but his statement confused me.

"I'll call Mr. Boraxe tonight and talk to him and send somebody down tomorrow to take his statement. I'll also find out where he was during the shooting," Bill Buffalo said.

"Did Bill and Joe work for Boraxe?" I asked.

"Not that I know of. But he might have hired them recently to do odd jobs. Neither one of them was any good. They did some time for car theft and were always in and out of jail for assault."

"Did they live in the area?" I asked.

"They have an old trailer on the edge of town. I don't care if you check it out before we do. It might take us a couple of days. Take the road behind the bank. You'll go right by it. It's blue, you can't miss it."

"What do you think about Carol Trouble?" I asked.

"She didn't kill her husband," Bill Buffalo said.

"What do you think about Franklin's house," I asked.

"Strange. It doesn't make any sense. Why would somebody kill him, haul him off, drop him at Carol's and bring the car back. And what were they looking for?"

A thought shot through my mind like I had stuck a spoon in a light socket.

Bill Buffalo noticed my reaction. "What is it?" he asked.

"Nothing, just thinking."

"Don't hurt yourself."

"If Roosevelt does have a thought it won't last for long," my Guardian Angel said.

"When you get the finger print reports back I'd like to know who was in Franklin's house," I told Bill Buffalo.

"Not a problem."

Paul Binyon and Pete Rosebet walked around the corner of the garage. Bill Buffalo rolled down the window. "The truck belonged to Bill Schneider," Paul Binyon told Bill Buffalo.

"That's a lot of Bill's," my Guardian Angel said.

Bill Buffalo looked at me in a way I knew our little tut to tut was over. He said, “Good luck,” as I got out of the car.

"Don't forget about talking at our fundraiser," Paul Binyon said as he got in the car.

"You only have to stay alive a few more days," Pete Rosebet smiled.

Sheriff Jack Benning didn't look at me as he drove away. Maybe he was embarrassed about having a snow angel attack.

Looking at my watch it is 4:30 and I am hungry. I thought about going to Fanny's but I am really not in the mood to see her. I decided to go to the cafe.

There was nobody in the cafe. The decor is late 50's. I sat at the counter. There is a serving counter between the kitchen and the cafe but it is so high I can't see into the kitchen.

After five minutes I am getting bored. The menu isn't exciting reading - there is no sex or violence. I started to get up, resigned to my fate of going to Fanny's, when Ginger walked out from the kitchen and flashed me a big happy smile. "If I was you I wouldn't eat here. The food sucks," she told me.

She isn't the employee of the month type.

"You make breakfast all the time?" I asked.

"It's hard to mess up eggs."

I ordered bacon, two eggs over easy, hash browns, and to have something healthy, wheat toast. Ginger poured me a cup of coffee that had been sitting in the pot since dawn.

She hollered to the back. "Pig, chick’s light, spuds and brown T."

Companies have to teach their employees their own jargon so the poor saps working their lives away for minimum wage feel they are part of a team.

"Jimmy told me you and he are going to throw snowballs at cars," Ginger said, looking at me like she really didn't care if we threw rocks at cars.

"He's a great kid. Nice little boy."

Her face got serious. "It's too much about that guy trying to kill you the other night. Everybody in town is talking about it. What's going on Roosevelt?"

"I can't say," I told her, which is better than saying, "I have no idea."

"Wait until they hear about Bill and Joe," my Guardian Angel said.

"You should go by and see Fanny. She is really worried about you," Ginger said.

"Oh, oh," my Guardian Angel said.

"Do you have a car?" I asked Ginger, dropping a question out of nowhere.

"If you want to call it a car. It only runs half of the time. But yes, I have a car, a 1976 red Pontiac."

"It's got a big eight in it," I said.

"When she's running she will flat eat up some highway."

"Slop up," somebody yelled from the back.

Ginger brought me the slop. It was good slop, even if the bacon was half-raw, the eggs were hard, the hash browns soggy and the toast burnt.

I paid the bill and tipped Ginger two bucks. "Tell Jimmy I'll drop by and see him," I said to Ginger as I headed out the door.

"Are you going to see Fanny?" she asked.

I nodded.

Fanny wasn't home. The sign was back on the cash register. Some people will never learn. Clyde was on a table eating an apple. He didn't look at me or say a word. Birds can get that way when the spark has died out.

I went up the steps two at a time and into Fanny's bedroom. I went through her dresser. There is only girly stuff in the top drawer and since I don't collect under panties it didn't interest me. The second drawer was still girly stuff. But in the bottom drawer, underneath the girly stuff, is a box of 308 rifle shells - 150 grain copper jacketed with lead tips - four cartridges were missing out of the box.

I opened the closet dormer and sorted through the clothes. I don't like her choice in clothes but I don't have to wear them and my opinion really doesn't count. There are several sets of shoes, the ugly comfortable type. And there is a pair of rubber soled, felt lined boots. Picking them up, they are new boots, the bottoms are wet, and the souls matched the prints from the bushes by Sheila's and the garage.

"You are mired in a quagmire of contradictions," my Guardian Angel said.

I didn't know his vocabulary was so good.

I moved a coat that is hanging in the corner of the dormer.

"I'm glad I'm not you, Roosevelt," my Guardian Angel said.

Propped in the corner is a rifle with a sling and a scope.

I picked it up. The rifle is a Sako 308. The sling is the quick adjust type and the scope is a variable 4 through 12 power. A good shot could shoot the heads off of matches at 100 yards with this set up. The gun had been recently cleaned. I opened the bolt. It is not loaded. I put it back in the corner.

"I'll say one thing about the people in Saint Ansgar. They take care of their weapons," my Guardian Angel said.

I went into the bathroom. There is nothing out of the ordinary in the medicine cabinet or underneath the sink unless blue towels with red hearts on them are clues to a murder.

I poked around the bedroom for a few more minutes but didn't find anything of interest and was about to leave the room when I saw a book on an end table by a chair. The title jumped out at me - "Spells and Incantations."

"I wonder where she keeps her broom?" my Guardian Angel said.

Hearing the front door open I dashed downstairs. I was sitting at the table watching Clyde eat when Fanny walked into the Tea Room. "You had me scared to death," she hollered at me.

Her hollering sparked Clyde. "Damn farmer, bad cat, bad cat, coffee sucks," he squawked and looked at me like it was my fault his peaceful dinner had been interrupted.

"In my line of work I never know what's going to happen," I said to Fanny.

She stomped over to the tea counter and made herself a cup of tea. Stomped to the table and sat down. I knew I was in deep doggie poop as she hadn't offered me a cup of coffee.

"Don't count on it," my Guardian Angel said.

Fanny sipped her tea. Glared at me. Sipped her tea. Glared at me. Sipped her tea and then smiled at me.

"I'm happy you are ok," she said, all the anger had been tea'd out of her.

"Thanks," I said. "It's been a rough day."

"Tell me about it, it might help," she said to me while looking in my eyes like if I told her my problems they would all go away. I decided I wouldn't tell her about Bill and Joe. She could find out from somebody in town and then accuse me of keeping secrets from her.

"I don't feel like talking," I said.

"Then let's get naked," she said.

"Pretty please," my Guardian Angel said.

"Fanny, please," I said.

"I know, I know, business," she said, but with a tiny smile.

"You're the one who should be a monk," my Guardian Angel said.

"Do you ever hunt?" I asked Fanny.

"No. People should leave the animals alone," she said.

"Do you ever target shoot?" I asked her.

"No."

"Do you own a weapon of any kind?"

"No."

"Liar, liar, pants on fire," my Guardian Angel said.

"Do you ever go hiking?" I asked her.

"No."

I didn't ask her if she owned any rubber soled, felt lined boots. I know what the answer would be.

"Bye bye love, bye bye sweet caress, hello loneliness," my Guardian Angel sang. What little he knows.

"Cowboy, cowboy," Clyde squawked so loudly he could wake up the neighbors.

"I wonder if he would make good pie?" my Guardian Angel said.

I stood. "I think I might be getting close to who stole your heart and killed the cats," I said.

She gave me a puzzled look as I left.

The sun is beginning to go down. When I turned the corner to Carol's, Jack Benning's car was pulling away from in front of her house.

"That sheriff is starting to become a nuisance," my Guardian Angel said.

I didn't turn into Carol's but followed Jack Benning. He drove past the sheriff's office for a block and turned left, I slowed down. When I turned the corner I didn't see his car, but passing a small blue house I saw the rear of his sheriff car and another car that was dark blue seconds before an electric garage door came down.

I don't want to go to Carol's. I don't want to go to the bar. I thought about going to see Sheila but decided it was not a good idea. I am not in a playful enough mood to go see Jimmy. "There isn't much entertainment around here," my Guardian Angel said.

I have an idea.

"No, not you," my Guardian Angel said in astonishment.

"Yes, me," I said.

"I can't believe it," he said.

I decided to drive to the Saint Ansgar Church.

"When I told you, you had to chill out I didn't mean you had to take a cold bath," my Guardian Angel said.

CHAPTER ELEVEN
THE MONEY GOD

A light is on in the house behind the church. The four door Chevy was there but the van I had seen when I first arrived in town was gone. Standing by the door to the house I feel like a twelve year old kid standing in the confession line and I am going to have to tell the priest, who is also my gym coach, I am having carnal thoughts about Julie Frost over the knee high white socks she wears and how her blue pleated skirt hikes up to the middle of her thighs when she sits.

I knocked on the door. Bless me father for I have sinned.

A priest opened the door with a glass in his hand filled with a light brown liquid. I knew it wasn't Pepsi. Unless priests have the power to drink Pepsi and make their breath smell like whiskey. "Roosevelt, come on in," he said pleasantly.

"These little towns are something," my Guardian Angel said.

Soft orchestra music greeted me as I entered. A fire is blazing in the fireplace and there are two dark brown leather chairs facing the fire. "Sit down," the priest said. "I was having my nightly whiskey and water and listening to some music. Would you like a drink?"

"Please." It's hard to say no to a priest.

I sat. There are easy reading books on the end table - Public Theology in the 21st Century, The Contradictions of Saint Luke, The Promise of Postmodern Apologetics, The Realization of Atheism, The Changing Catholicism, and Satanism in Modern

America. I doubt if any of them are on the bestseller list.

The priest handed me the drink and sat down. "To the defeat of sin," he toasted with a wry grin on his face.

We both drank. It is a good whiskey. Maybe it is the company I am with.

The priest gazed into the fire. I knew it wasn't his place to start the conversation. Most people go to a priest to talk about their own problems. Priests are like good bartenders they keep their mouth shut and listen to everything a person says.

I studied the priest. He has to be in his sixties. He isn't tall, maybe 5'7", his hair is white with a light sheen to it from hair oil and combed neatly. He is slightly overweight and has a double chin that hangs over his priest collar. He looked at me and in the glow of the fire his eyes radiated understanding of the human condition. "My name is Father Fisher. If you're not a Catholic you can call me Sam," he said in a deep slow voice that was both soothing and comforting.

"I don't know what I am anymore, and if I don't know, I don't really know what to call you," I said truthfully.

"Welcome to earth," he smiled in a way that I knew his smile covered up a deep sadness. True men of God have to be sad. It has to be a futile battle.

"You have caused quit the stir since you have been in town," Father Fisher said to me in slow even words.

"I can't say that isn't true," I agreed.

"I would imagine people in your line of work draw trouble like a magnet."

"I'm not a detective anymore. I've been trying to get away from it all but it doesn't seem to work."

"You don't have to help people," he said soothingly.

The statement surprised me.

"I've been trying to find myself, but it seems the more I travel and the more things I see, I get farther and farther away from finding me."

"Everything is inside yourself, Roosevelt. You don't have to travel far," he said with no trace of sympathy in his voice.

"I know. Maybe I can't face who I am, and I tell myself I'm looking for myself, while in reality I'm trying to run away from who I am and I really don't want to know the true me."

My Guardian Angel was being quiet. In the presence of a true man of God he knew he should keep his big mouth shut.

"You didn't come here to talk philosophy. What is on your mind?" Father Fisher asked me.

"I really don't know. I didn't want to go to where I'm staying. I didn't want to get drunk. It's too cold to go sit under a tree somewhere and contemplate some question that has no answer. So I thought I'd come out to the church. I haven't been to a church in years."

"Interesting," he mused and looked at his empty glass. "Want another one?"

I gave him my glass. Like I said, it's hard to say no to a priest even if he might get me pie eyed.

Father Fisher brought back the drinks, handed me mine and sat with a contented look on his face. "To finding oneself and liking what you find," he toasted.

We drank.

"Now, Roosevelt, ask me some questions. I would feel jilted if a famous detective didn't ask me any questions," Father Fisher said. His eyes had a twinkle of mirth in them and I have a darting feeling he was toying with me.

"Is Fanny Ruth a Catholic?" I asked.

"Why yes she is. She comes to church a few times a month."

"Did she ever talk to you about Satanism or witchcraft?"

"I can't answer that, Roosevelt, what people talk to me about is between God, them and me. But I can tell you that Satan is alive and well."

"It must be nice to have God on your side," I said.

"It beats having the Cleveland Browns," he grinned.

"Or Notre Dame, the way they've been playing lately."

He gave me a look that let me know I'd better stay off the subject of Notre Dame.

"Do you know anything about Franklin Trouble?" I asked.

"Franklin Trouble, whatever he was or did, gave this church a large donation once a year. Normally around Christmas time," he said in a tone that made me think even bad people have a trace of good in them. But even if that is true I don't think one can buy grace.

"How about Jimmy Page?"

Father Fisher's eyes lit up. "He is a lonely little boy. A boy, who, if he can stay mentally strong will grow up to be a great thinker, maybe a good writer or a painter. In the summer Ginger brings him out and he mows the churchyard."

"Do they come to church?"

"The competition got them, they are Baptist," Father Fisher replied sadly.

"Do you have any idea what's going on in this town?"

"Adultery, fornication, stealing, larceny, greed, murder. The same things that are going on everyplace else, only this is a smaller fish bowl," Father Fisher replied with no tone of defeat in his voice - only understanding.

"How long have you been here?" I asked.

"Fifteen years. I like this church. I like the people," he replied simply but with a solemn tone.

"What do you think about Carol Trouble?"

"She is every priest's nightmare," he said and grinned like even he had a few carnal thoughts.

I glanced at the fire. It is peaceful. I've always wondered why people, no matter what their religion, choose to represent God.

"Why did you become a priest?" I asked Father Fisher.

"I became a priest to try and help mankind," Father Fisher said.

"I don't know if I help or hinder mankind," I said.

"You help more than you hinder," my Guardian Angel said.

I finished my drink and stood. I feel like I am wasting the good priest's time. Father Fisher walked with me to the door. "I'm sorry I can't be of any help but I did enjoy our conversation," he said, holding out his hand to shake.

He has a firm handshake. To do battle with Satan a person cannot be a wimp.

"You did help me, Father Fisher," I said, as I released his hand.

He gave me a searching look. "I can tell you one thing, Roosevelt. I wouldn't trust Fanny and there is something about Sheriff Jack Benning that gives me the willies. Now go in peace."

He shut the door.

It is a clear dark night with no wind. The stars are little glows of hope radiating down onto earth. I went inside the church and lit a candle for every person who is caught up in a trap but will never escape. I didn't pray, praying is for other people, but I stuffed a fifty-dollar bill in the donation slot and went back outside to the real world.

Driving back to town I could see Father Fisher sitting in his chair with a book in his lap and gazing into the fire. He might have mixed another drink. What the hay? He deserves it.

"He's a nice man," my Guardian Angel said simply.

Looking at my watch it is almost 9:00 p.m. I have run out of excuses. It was time to go to Carol's. Thinking about Carol's I felt like an idiot. I still don't have a key to the front door.

"Glad you are back to normal," my Guardian Angel said. "There for a few minutes I thought you might sell everything you own and fly to Tibet and spend the rest of your life selling prayer flags to American tourists."

"Not to fear my lecherous friend."

I hit the red light and had to wait for it to turn. Merriam Boraxe drove through the intersection. She was driving a white Ford van with a dent on the right side. The van I had seen by the church when I first drove through town.

"Oh, oh," My Guardian Angel said.

He was back to being a birdbrain.

When Carol answered the door I knew by her face Miss Cosmopolitan was having a bad make-up day. After I stepped in she slammed the door. "Where have you been? Where have you been? Where have you been?" she screamed and hopped, hopped, hopped.

"I've been so worried. Officer Benning told me about Bill and Joe. Where have you been? Where have you been? Where have you been?"

I started hopping up and down. "Thinking, thinking, thinking," I said.

There is only so much hopping I can take.

My reaction shocked her and she stopped hopping and slapped me. "Quit acting ridiculous, Roosevelt. It doesn't suit you," she chastised me. "And you haven't been thinking you've been drinking."

Her reaction surprised me plus the slap hurt.

Carol gave me a haughty look. "I don't want to see you until in the morning," she informed me, spun around, and headed for her basement playhouse.

"You're relieved she didn't want to do kissy, kissy," my Guardian Angel said.

"Now that she has rejected me that isn't true," I said.

I took a leisurely bath and then lay on the bed. The heart I found in the chair, the deck of cards from Franklin's car, the phone book I removed from Bill's body and my clue book are scattered around me. Somewhere in the gibberish are the clues I need to solve the trio of crimes - the stolen heart, the dead cats and Trouble's murder. I know I have one good clue. It came to me in a flash of insight while talking to Detective Bill Buffalo, but one clue isn't enough, but, it is a beginning.

"Being a beginning is better than no beginning at all," my Guardian Angel said.

I started writing in my clue book. It wrote for about thirty minutes. When I was done I know my clues needed a good editing job but I wasn't in the mood.

I examined the deck of cards. They were marked like the deck I gave Jimmy.

I looked at the little black book I took off of Bill Schneider. I wonder why most pocket phone books are black? Do we all think we are spies? Are phone numbers deep dark secrets that should be shrouded in black? Are girlfriends supposed to be secrets? It's weird.

There are six phone numbers in the black book. The book is not being utilized to its highest potential. I picked up the quarter sized-blue glass heart and looked at the faceted sides. The thought of a stolen heart is strange. The thought of a broken heart is sad. The thought of having no heart is morbid.

I slowly read through my clues. I did my same old routine - I read them from beginning to end and then from end to beginning. If I could read them from side to side I would, but it's impossible, I don't write in Chinese.

I decided I would make a list of what I thought were good clues by going through my clues in the order I had written them down. I wouldn't discard my list of not so good clues as I have always had a problem in life discerning good from bad, and I know good clues could only be in the mind of the beholder.

"Roosevelt, just write the clues," my Guardian Angel said.

I wrote.

"Roosevelt, those clues are terrible," my Guardian Angel said when I finished.

"Then write your own," I snapped. I hate people or angels who criticize my writing.

"Now, now, oh non-literate one, I'm only trying to help."

"Then you should learn how to spur people on by using subtle suggestions and not caustic sarcastic remarks."

"I'll work on it," my Guardian Angel said.

I read my new list of clues. I have to admit my Guardian Angel is right.

"Wise one, who makes the words of Ernest Hemingway seem like dribble, I think you should make a list of questions you will have to answer before you might, one chance in a million, solve this triple case you got yourself into," my Guardian Angel said.

"That's a good idea about the questions," I replied. I couldn't argue with him about the odds of solving the case.

When I finished writing the questions I put the clue book, heart, cards and phone book in my suitcase. I gave my pistol a good cleaning and made sure the clip was full.

"Every man should have a good clean pistol with a full clip," my Guardian Angel said.

I turned off the light and went to bed. I am tired and I have a lot of things to do tomorrow.

I was halfway into deep sleep when the door banged open and the light snapped on. "Get your rear out of bed and come down to my room. I want to play," a naked Carol ordered.

"Cribbage?" I said sleepily.

"Roosevelt you're one big romantic love muffin," my Guardian Angel said.

"You, you, you man," Carol stormed and slammed the door.

Cold wet noodles have more energy than I did when I woke up. I swigged down a cup of cold coffee, stuck my pistol in my belt, got the little black phone book out of my suitcase and headed out the door. My first stop was the bank.

"Are you going to rob it?" my Guardian Angel asked.

I wonder why all banks try to emulate churches. Workers talk in whispers and wear nice clothes. The windows are always big, the carpet a good industrial grade that will last until the next ice age, and what isn't carpeted is marble or tile so when you walk your steps echo through the whole building. A bank is a temple to the money god where most people don't have a problem throwing their money at his feet and praying, "Forgive me Money God, I would give more, but I didn't find enough people to over charge this week."

Mr. Earl Harberts sat behind his large spit-shined desk. He is wearing a gray suit, a white shirt with a collar so starched it wanted to join the army, and a tie that cost more than my boots. He smiled at me like a bass smiles at a goldfish and pointed at a chair in front of his desk. "Sit down, Roosevelt, I figured you would come see me sooner or later."

"I want to borrow ten million dollars, buy a Lear Jet, and fly five tons of whatever they cut cocaine with to Colombia. I'll pay you double your money within two months," I told him.

"You have to go to the Cayman Islands for those types of loans," he told me seriously and then gave me a banker smile, which is very close to the way a mortician smiles as he takes the check for $10,000 to put old Fred in the ground.

There was no need to beat around the bush. "I understand you slept with Fanny," I said.

He glared at me. "I thought you were trying to solve a murder, not check into people's sex lives?" he said, trying to act more perturbed than he was.

"I also understand your wife slept with Franklin Trouble," I said, "who, in case you've forgotten, was murdered."

His facial features softened. "She only slept with him to get back at me. It was all my fault. Sheila was getting into trouble. I felt alone and lost. I didn't know what to do. I went to Fanny's one day to buy a heart for Sheila and one thing led to another and Fanny and I had a short fling."

"How short?"

"A month, maybe a month and a half," Earl said.

"What color of heart did you buy?" I asked.

"It was dark blue, about the size of a quarter, faceted and had a gold clasp. Why do you want to know?"

"I'm thinking about buying one and wanted some advice."

He looked at me like I am the main attraction at a freak show.

"How long did your wife see Franklin?"

"Only once that I know of."

"Are you and Brenda living together again?" I asked.

"She came back last night. We've been together a long time Roosevelt. Marriage is not always a smooth road."

"Sheila told me she thinks you admitted her to the nut house to get rid of her."

"She has been a difficult child. A strange child. I love her, she is my daughter. But it has been difficult. Difficult for me and difficult for Brenda."

"I understand she went through a spell of shooting dogs and cats."

Earl nodded his head.

"She also went through a year when she thought she was a witch. She thought she could talk to demons and goblins."

"She's done everything Roosevelt. She's a bright kid but she's done everything. Kids here age when she was in school were afraid of her."

"How many rifles do you own?"

Earl gave me a worried look. I guess it is a worry question. "I have a dozen rifles ranging from 22's to 30/06's. I have five pistols and six shotguns. They are all collector items. I used to collect guns but I don't anymore. The ones I have left are the cream of the crop."

"Did you ever teach Sheila how to shoot?"

"Brenda, Sheila and I used to go shooting all the time. Sheila isn't very good but Brenda without a rest can shot the eye out of a mosquito at a hundred yards. She loves to shoot."

"How about you?"

"Not too bad but not as good as Brenda."

"There are some good bug shootin' and some bad bug shootin' people around here," my Guardian Angel said.

"Did Franklin Trouble ever borrow money from your bank?" I asked with a pleasant tone to my voice. It was time to lay off

Earl's family and I have a gut feeling he is on the up and up.

"Gamblers don't need banks. All they want out of a bank is a safety deposit box."

"Did he have one here?"

"No, but I bet he's got a wade of cash buried somewhere around Saint Ansgar. Trouble always dealt in cash. Maybe somebody killed him for cash he was carrying?"

"I wish it was that easy," I said.

"What do you think I should do with Sheila?" Harberts asked me.

I wanted to tell him to make her wear a bra but I couldn't. "I don't know. I'd hate to be a kid this day and age. I'd be as messed up as most of them are."

"Your more messed up than they are, Roosevelt, don't kid yourself," my Guardian Angel said.

"I hope I haven't upset you too much, Mr. Harberts. I'm only trying to find out who killed Franklin. It's a bad deal."

He looked relieved and gave me an, I understand, look. The same look he would give a guy as he repossessed his car.

"On a lighter note I was wondering what the corn, wheat and cattle prices have been for the past few years? I've been thinking about doing a little gambling on the commodities market.
This detective stuff doesn't pay all the time."

"I'd think about putting my money someplace else. Corn, wheat and cattle for the last three years are selling for the same thing they sold for in the 1940's. With the cost of equipment, fertilizer, herbicide and everything else, most farmers are losing everything. It's been rough. If something doesn't break soon most farms will be huge corporate operations. It's already happened in the hog and chicken market."

"How about Dale Boraxe?"

I noticed a slight twitch in Earl's jaw and it took him a split second too long to answer me. "Dale still has money but his farm is carrying a huge debt load and he has never been good at investing."

"Does Fanny owe the bank any money?"

"I shouldn't be telling you all these things," he said.

"Better than a visit from the cops," I replied, but only bluffing.

Why would the cops want to see Earl?

"Fanny owes a lot, all she ever pays on her loan is the interest."

I stood. Earl stood. We shook hands. He shakes hands like a mouse. "You need anything let me know," he told me as I left.

"People who shake hands like mice can't be trusted," my Guardian Angel told me.

"Bankers can't be trusted," I said.

I need a hamburger fix but don’t feel like going to the cafe. I stopped at the convenience store and bought a pint of chocolate milk and a sandwich - white bread, chopped and pressed animal guts made to look like slices of beef - I smothered the sandwich with mustard. It wasn't half-bad.

I followed Bill Buffalo's instructions and drove to Bill and Joe's trailer. The trailer was out of town a few miles and set back in a grove of trees. It looks like it was hit by a tornado and beaten back in shape with a hammer. It had been hand painted blue. The screen to the door is half off. It is a place a junkyard dog wouldn't want to live.

The door wasn't locked, which would have been a waste of time anyway, the walls are so thin a person could break in with a can opener. I went in. The heater is on. The place smells somewhere between a men's locker room and the inside of a garbage can. I pawed through the mess, checking drawers, closets, under the sofa, under the sink. I didn't find anything until I found two purple magic markers on the table. I put them in my pocket. I was about to leave when I saw a calendar on the back of the door. It is a calendar of biker chicks wearing a few strips of black leather and gazing out with drooping eyes like they wanted to suck Harley Davidson exhaust pipes.

I took the calendar down and flipped through it. There was nothing written on the calendar until the last week and then there were four circled dates with phone numbers by them. I folded the calendar and stuck it in my pocket.

"With Fanny, Carol, Merriam and Lisa, you don't have to look at pictures if you don't want to," my Guardian Angel said.

I went outside. There are only two animals that will live in the filth that they create - human beings and rats.

I needed to use a phone but I didn't want to use Carol’s. The only pay phone I had seen in town was inside the convenience store but there would be no privacy. I drove toward the interstate and the nearest truck stop. Truck stops are good for bone sticking greasy food, phone booths, and steaming hot showers.

When I got to a truck stop I changed a twenty-dollar bill into quarters and sat down in a private phone booth.

I took out Bill's little black book.

"I bet two of the numbers are massage parlors in Minneapolis, two of them are hookers, one is to a garage, and the last one is Bill and Joe's mother," my Guardian Angel said.

I dialed the first number. "Secret of Sin Escorts," a little old lady knitting a sweater for her granddaughter answered.

I hung up.

I dialed the second number. "Maxine's Massages, in or out call line, please...."

I hung up.

I dialed the third number. The girl who answered had to be a hooker. When she answered, "honey I want to lick you all over," I knew she wasn't a teacher.

I dialed the forth number. "Brenda the total dominator," she answered.

I hung up.

I dialed the fifth number. "Please hold."

I didn't know what they wanted me to hold but I didn't hang up. "Frank's garage."

I hung up.

I dialed the sixth number. A lady answered in a raspy feeble voice. "Yes."

I could picture an old lady happy somebody had called her.

"Is Bill or Joe there?" I asked pleasantly.

There was no reply but I could hear the lady breathing. Then in quiet voice she said. "I am sorry but the stupid jerks got their ass blown away so don't call me again sonny."

So much for the theory a bad home environment doesn't affect the development of children.

"Remember what I said those phone numbers were too," My Guardian Angel said.

"You were six out of six," I said begrudgingly.

He was so happy at being six out of six he started singing a song if he had a hammer, he'd hammer in the morning and he'd sing.

I wished he'd stick his head in a commode and flush it.

I took out the calendar of the exhaust pipe suckers and dialed the first phone number. "Carol Trouble's."

I hung up.

"Lord have mercy," my Guardian Angel said.

I dialed the second phone number. "Hello, Mr. and Mrs. Borax's house. May I help you?" Lisa answered the phone.

I didn't want to hang up but I did.

"Boy," my Guardian Angel said.

I dialed the third number, which, if I had been paying any attention I would have known. "This is Sheriff Jack Benning."

I hung up.

"I don't know Roosevelt," my Guardian Angel said.

I dialed the forth number. "Detective Bill Buffalo."

I hung up.

I feel like a six-ply tire that had run over a nail.

"Why would Bill and Joe be calling Carol, Boraxe, Benning and Buffalo?" my Guardian Angel asked.

"I have no idea and I don't know if I want to know," I replied truthfully.

"I know one thing. You are good at hanging up a phone," my Guardian Angel said.

It was a good thing there were no more phone numbers because I was dialed out, although I hadn't been dialing I'd been pushing buttons.

"You have hours to kill before you go see Lisa. What are you going to do?" my Guardian Angel asked.

"I'm going to go have a conversation with Bill Buffalo."

"I don't know if that's a good idea," he warned me.

CHAPTER TWELVE
CAPTAIN KID'S LAIR

Driving to Albert Lee all I could think about were the phone numbers on the biker chicks sucking exhaust pipes calendar. I don't think Carol, the Boraxe's, Sheriff Jack Benning, and Detective Bill Buffalo get together once a week to play bridge with Bill and Joe Schneider. If they did they had to find two new players.

"Tony's Pizza," I said loudly as I knocked on Bill Buffalo's door.

"Come on in, Roosevelt," Bill Buffalo said.

Bill Buffalo is behind his desk and Pete Rosebet and Paul Binyon are sitting in metal folding chairs. It reminds me of a bookie convention. "How did you know it was me and not Tony?" I asked.

"I saw you drive into the parking lot," Bill Buffalo said and pointed at the window.

I'd never noticed his window had a magnificent view of the parking lot. We miss so many little things in life.

"Did you bring a draft of your speech?" Paul Binyon asked.

"I hired a speechwriter that used to work for the president and told him to send you guys the bill," I said and sat.

For a moment they took me seriously and then I smiled and they relaxed.

"Get shot at or kill anybody today?" Pete Rosebet asked like he was trying to be funny.

I shook my head.

"Boring day then," Paul Binyon said.

I had driven all the way here to ask Bill Buffalo why Bill and Joe had his phone number, but now I had the feeling I had better not ask him. I feel like an idiot.

"Binyon and Rosebet were going to go to Bill and Joe's trailer today but we've had a rash of house burglaries where the burglar breaks in, ties up whoever is home and steals nothing but guns, so we're busy for a few days," Bill Buffalo said.

"If the homeowners had guns why didn't they shoot the thieves?" my Guardian Angel asked.

"I went through Bill and Joe's trailer. I couldn't find anything but a lot of garbage," I said Bill Buffalo.

"I sent a man down to see Dale Boraxe. He said he'd hired Bill and Joe to clean out the barns. Dale couldn't have been the shooter, he has enough alibis to write an alibi book," Bill Buffalo said.

"If he was involved with any of this mess I don't think he'd shoot somebody. He has too much to lose," I said.

"I got the prints back from Franklin's house. We found Fanny's, Franklin's and Carol's," Bill Buffalo informed me.

"Strange," my Guardian Angel said.

"How come your prints weren't on anything?" Pete Rosebet asked.

"I have sensitive hands and before I search anything I put on rubber gloves," I said, then felt dumb, "but you will find them at Bill and Joe's, sometimes my memory isn't long enough to remember to put on gloves."

"I have to tell you the truth, Roosevelt, right now there are no solid leads on Franklin's murder. We don't have any ideas on what else to do?" Bill Buffalo said.

"Did you run a check on the blood at the house and in the trunk of the car?" I asked.

"The blood matches Franklin's and we found a few hairs in the trunk that were his," Bill Buffalo said.

"How about the bullets that turned Bill and Joe's heads into silly putty?"

"The bullets were fired from a 308 and the slugs are 150-grain copper-jacketed lead heads manufactured by Savage Arms."

"Could they be matched by rifling marks?"

"There are enough riflings left on the slugs to match the rifle if we find the rifle."

"Tell them about Fanny's rifle," my Guardian Angel said.

I didn't want to. It's a bad deal in life when you can't trust anybody, not even the cops, but I knew what I had to do when I got back to Saint Ansgar.

"Go see Lisa," my Guardian Angel said.

"I might have a lousy memory but I won't forget her," I told him.

"Good," he said.

I looked at all the men. "I'm like you guys I have no idea what to do next. You would think finding a body in a closet in a small town would be an open and shut case."

"All we really know is Trouble didn't cut his own throat his house, drive to Carol's and put his own dead body in the closet, and then drive his car back," Paul Binyon said.

"There is only one main question that has to be answered. Why does somebody want to kill me? There has to be more going on than killing Franklin," I said.

I stood. They hadn't offered me coffee and I was too chicken to confront Bill Buffalo over finding his phone number. "I'll be in touch," I said and left. I've wasted enough time.

"Most of life is wasted," my Guardian Angel said. "Believe me, I know, I'm dead."

I am about ten miles from the Saint Ansgar cutoff. My mind is running like a rusty sawmill. An idea will pop into my head and be discarded as fast as it had entered. I have discovered enough on both cases that I should know more than I do. Like I had told the detectives it's a small town, this case should be cut and dried, over, a piece of cake to solve. What am I missing? It has to be something so obvious I keep overlooking it. It bothers me. I have a gut feeling if I don't get a handle on what is going on other people are going to die and I, for sure, don't want to be one of those other people. Life is nothing but a mind game.

"It takes a mind to play the game," my Guardian Angel said.

I saw a new yellow Volkswagen by the side of the road with the trunk up and I pulled over. Sheila got out of the car. "Roosevelt, I don't know if I want you to help me. You're dangerous to be around," Sheila said, looking worried and nervous.

"Maybe I can fix your car," I said, wishing I hadn't stopped.

She popped the hood. Everything is diodes and computers. The engine isn't like Matilda's engine which can be fixed with a can opener. This engine would take a masters in electricity. None-the-less I shook a few wires, jiggled a few computer boxes and motioned for her to try and start the car.

Sheila turned the key and the engine fired to life. It sounds like a 1965 V-8 Mustang, a Volkswagen with teeth. She gunned the engine several times before the engine sputtered, backfired and died. It would not start again. I went to the back of the Volkswagen. It has two oversized tail pipes. Putting loud mufflers on a Volkswagen is like believing the turtle really did beat the rabbit. Sheila got out of the car.

"I'm not that dangerous, come on, I'll give you a ride to town and you can call a wrecker."

"My dad can get it hauled in," she said.

Sheila reluctantly got into the car. She is wearing patchouli oil. I have always hated the stuff. If a girl in the 60's didn't own sixteen gallons of the perfume she definitely was not in the hippie in-crowd and was forced to turn in her beads.

I smiled at Sheila, trying to quell her fear of me, which did nothing for my fear of her. She is a cute little thing with her wire-rimmed glasses - and her rubber soled, felt lined boots, I have a strong feeling would match the foot prints behind the bush by her house.

"I heard about the guy who tried to kill you and you killed him," Sheila said. Her eyes moved in quick jerky movements as she talked.

"There was nothing I could do. I didn't tell him to try and shoot me so I would have the excuse to shoot him."

"Then somebody shot and killed Bill and Joe after you had already shot them.” Her eyes darted again.

"It wasn't my idea to run into them and for them to try and beat my head in with tire irons."

She thought about my statement for a while, relaxed, and then smiled at me. "I suppose none of it is your fault but your karma must be terrible. You need a deep soul and spirit cleansing, Roosevelt," she said. "I could give you a deep muscle massage and it would release some of the bad spirits that have slipped into your muscles."

"Only if you give massages topless," my Guardian Angel said.

"Be kind, she's a young girl," I told him.

"She can vote," he retorted.

"I don't think your father or mother would approve of you giving older men massages," I said trying to find a polite way to tell her no.

"Let them watch," my Guardian Angel said.

How can I not have bad spirits in my body when my Guardian Angel is a bad spirit?

"My parents trust me," Sheila said. "And besides they are going to a steak house in Austin tonight."

"Texas?" I said truly astonished.

"No, silly, it's about thirty miles north of here."

"So your folks are back together," I said. I didn't want to tell her I had spoken to her father and already knew.

"They're so happy it's almost sickening. They're like a couple of newlyweds."

"Good?" I smiled.

"They have been nice to me too. They think it's a good idea if I go to Berkeley or Michigan."

"Have you been shooting lately?" I asked Sheila.

She tensed for a moment but as quickly relaxed. "Who told you I used to shoot?"

"It's a small town. I'm a detective. Remember?"

"I used to shoot a lot but I don't anymore. Guns are evil things. They have no purpose except death. People who target shoot will tell you it is a sport but deep down in their hearts they would really like to be killing something."

"Guns are used for defense too. What are we supposed to do when only the bad guys have guns but we don't have guns to defend ourselves?"

"All guns should be against the law. They should be all confiscated and melted down and turned into plows or birdbaths."

"Such a young mind she has," my Guardian Angel said.

I stopped in front of her house. She got out but didn't shut the door and said to me. "Are you sure you don't want that massage?"

"I'll take a rain check."

"I am no virgin, Roosevelt, and I would love for you to make love to me," she said and ran the tip of her tongue over her lips.

"Do you need ChapStick?" I asked.

She lowered her voice and said. "I bet you really know how to please a woman. I would do anything you ask to be your love goddess. You could teach me what really turns you on?"

"I'm sorry Sheila, but not tonight," I told her in voice that hopefully sounded like her father.

"Then stick it up your nose," she shouted and slammed the door.

"Some college boy is going to fall in love with that one and after three months of great sex he is going to find out that sex isn't everything," my Guardian Angel said.

It is close to 4:00 p.m.. I have eight hours before I am supposed to meet Lisa. Passing time in a small town is a harder job than one thinks. I decided to go to Fanny's. Walking into Fanny's I knew I should have gone to the bar. Fanny is hanging hearts in the window. When she saw me she set the hearts down on the window ledge, gave me her Mussolini impression with her hands on her hips, stuck out her jaw and said in a tone that would only be friendly to a boa constrictor. "When you were here the other night why didn't you tell me about Bill and Joe? You don't trust me enough to tell me what you are up to."

If her eyes were scud missiles she would have blasted me back out the front door.

"Is it that time of the month?" I asked her.

"Yes it is," she hollered. "What do you want to do about it frog face?"

"There has to be a tea on your shelf that will help. I'll even make it for you," I said trying to help.

I have never had that time of month but I have suffered through at least 65,000 of them.

Fanny started crying. It is a good cry. She let he arms fall to her side and big tears almost dented the floor when they hit. I took her hand and led her to the Tea Room. Clyde is sitting on the counter.

"Cowboy, crap," he squawked.

"Nice to see you too, Clyde," I said.

I pulled out a chair for Fanny and she sat. She had her crying under control but her nose was running. She wiped her nose on the sleeve of her dress, took two deep breaths and seemed to be fine. "You are a nice man, Roosevelt, but you worry me to death. I would hate to see anything happen to you."

I brought Fanny a cup of tea. According to the box it was supposed to help menstrual cramps, promote sleep, cure cancer, shrink hemorrhoids and reduce smile wrinkles.

"Would you go up to my bathroom and bring me down two Midol?" Fanny asked with a small pleading smile on her face. The tea works quickly.

I went upstairs and when I got to her bedroom door I tip-toed to the dresser, opened the bottom drawer, and rummaged around but the box of 308 bullets was gone. I tip-toed to the closet dormer and the rifle was gone.

"You know. Any of the women in this town could be the killer," my Guardian Angel said.

"One of them is," I said.

"Which one?" he asked me excitedly.

"I'm not telling," I said.

"You're nothing but a tease," he said.

I got Fanny two Midol out of a bottle that held 10,000. When I gave them to Miss Anne Oakley with no more bullets or rifle she smiled at me like I am the best thing that happened to pants since the zipper.

I feel like I am a pair of pants without a zipper.

"I suppose you are working on solving Franklin's murder more than on finding my heart," Fanny said.

"It's a complicated mess. Right at the moment I don't know what I'm doing."

Fanny gave me a sad look. "I've never met a man that makes me feel like you do. Men have never made me angry like you do. I worry about you. I miss you when you are gone. But I don't want to hinder you in anyway. But please, tell me what is happening so I don't worry so much. Would you do that?"

Looking at her sad face I know she owns a 308 Sako with a quick adjustable sling and a sniper scope. I know she has shells for the rifle. I have strange suspicions about her cats. I know she says she has no friends but she sleeps around. But, even with what I know, I still like Fanny. "I'll keep you posted," I told her and patted her hand.

"Peace, peace, pretty, pretty, me love you, me love you," Clyde squawked.

"I think you're making a big mistake with Fanny," my Guardian Angel said.

Fanny and I sat and didn't talk. She sipped her tea. Clyde walked around like a vaudeville actor who had forgotten his lines. We had almost reached the thirty-second silence limit when insecure people have to say anything when there was a knock on the door. "Come on in Jimmy," Fanny called. "I know the way he knocks," she explained to me.

"Fanny and Bill Buffalo should get together," my Guardian Angel said.

Jimmy came in, saw me, and is all smiles. He ran over to the table, took his hat off and his gloves, ran his hands through his greasy hair, wiped his nose on his sleeve and started talking excitedly. "Boy, Bob, my Mom told me about that guy who tried to kill you and you shot him. It's just like in the movies. And then Bill and Joe tried to bean you with tire irons and you shot them and then somebody killed them. I want to be just like you when I grow up, Bob. I want to travel all over the whole wide world and catch the bad guys. Can you teach me how to catch the bad guys?"

"He can't teach what he doesn't know," my Guardian Angel said.

I bet when my Guardian Angel was alive he didn't even try to be good with children.

"First off you have to finish high school and get good grades. After high school you go to college and study criminology and try as hard as you can. Then you can get a job as a real detective with some police force around the country. Maybe even get into the F.B.I. or the C.I.A. and really catch the bad guys," I told Jimmy.

His little eyes looked like they would pop out of his head as his fantasized about being a real detective. I didn't want to tell him most detectives drink more coffee and smoke more cigarettes than they catch the bad guys. Life will break his fantasy bubble, there is no need for me to help it a long.

"You want to play, Bob?" Jimmy asked.

How do you say no to a greasy-headed snot-nosed kid?

We went outside and I noticed Jimmy had forgotten his hat and gloves. I didn't want to tell him to go get them and sound like an adult. The snowman was still doing his snowman thing in Jimmy's backyard. "Do you want to see my secret place," Jimmy whispered.

"Sure," I whispered back. All secrets have to be whispered.

"You can't tell anybody. Promise?"

"I promise."

"Cross your heart and hope to die?"

I crossed my heart.

I followed Jimmy around the house and to the cellar. He pulled open the doors and I followed him downstairs. He turned on the light switch and opened the door to the cellar. We walked in and he shut the door behind us. The cats were gone. "This is a nice secret place," I whispered.

He put his finger to his lips and then walked behind the furnace. I didn't move. Getting behind a furnace has never been my thing. He came back out from behind the furnace and motioned for me to follow.

"While you are at it check the pilot light and filter," my Guardian Angel whispered.

I stooped down to walk under a heater duct that was behind the furnace. Between the back of the furnace and the wall is about two feet. There is a door about three feet tall behind the furnace. Jimmy opened it and went into the darkness. I heard the sound of a match striking and then light from a candle flickered out to me.

"Come on in, Bob, but be quiet, Fanny could hear us and I don't want her to know about my secret place."

I ducked and went into the room. The room is about ten feet by ten feet. It has a concrete floor and walls and the roof is the house flooring. Shelves line two of the walls from the floor to the ceiling and are lined with plastic models of cars, airplanes and ships, coffee cans filled with crayons and marbles, toy soldiers, broken dolls, rusty Red Ryder wagon wheels, rocks, pine cones and everything imaginable a kid would find interesting. Jimmy had a wooden fruit crate in the middle of the room with a candle on it. A throw rug was by it. I figure it was the rug that had been in front of the QUEEN OF HEARTS.

"It's the best place in the world," Jimmy said to me. "I can come here and nobody knows where I am. Nobody bothers me, nobody picks on me. It's my own secret place."

It is its own world, a world of dreams, a world of cowboys with tall boots and spurs that jingle when you walk. But it is a clubhouse with only one member. "It's a great place, Jimmy. I feel honored you would show me," I said.

"It's my secret place with all my treasures," he said.

I reached over and jostled Jimmy's greasy hair and smiled. He smiled but it was not hard to see the sadness and loneliness that lived behind his eyes.

"We should be going. I have to go do my detective thing," I said.

He blew out the candle and we left Captain Kidd's lair.

Outside Jimmy ran toward his house. He stopped, made a quick snowball and threw it at me. I side stepped it. I made one and smacked him in the belly. He laughed and ran home.

"Jimmy forgot his hat and gloves," Fanny told me when I sat at the table.

"He'll be back."

"What did you two do?" she asked.

"Nothing," I said.

"Boys will be boys," she said and smiled at me.

"Did you use to have a throw rug in front of the table where the QUEEN OF HEARTS was?" I asked Fanny.

She looked puzzled. "I did, and one day I came home and it was gone."

"Was it missing the same day you lost your heart?"

"No, it was during the summer. Why?"

"I was just wondering. Nothing important, but it seems like you should have more throw rugs around the place."

"I used to but it's easier to mop than wash rugs," she said. "I gave them all away except the one by the QUEEN OF HEARTS."

"Did you get rid of your cats?" I asked Fanny.

She gave me a strange eerie look.

"I put them in the cellar and they're gone."

"I didn't touch them," she said, like more than the cats being gone bothered her.

It is time for me to go. I feel restless. There are answers churning in my brain I can't quite reach. So close yet so far away. It is frustrating.

I stood. "Will you be back tonight?" Fanny asked me.

"If you say yes I'm going on strike," my Guardian Angel said.

"Not tonight. I think I'm on to something and I won't be back in town until in the morning," I said.

"It's good to have a positive game plan," my Guardian Angel said.

"It's nice to have a profession you can lie and get away with it," I said.

Fanny looked at me like she knew I was lying as I kissed her on the forehead. She gave me an, I am alone sad smile and I left. It is close to 6:00 p.m.

I drove past Merriam's house and saw Dale's black Lincoln in the driveway. I then drove to the bar.

There are only a few people in the bar. To my surprise Brenda was washing glasses behind the bar. I take it the dinner at the steak house was off. I sat at the bar. She looked at me and I got the feeling she didn't know if she wanted to smile at me or slap me across the face. "You must be one hard man to kill," she said.

"When you're on a lucky streak you have to ride it out," I said.

She gave me a Guinness. "This one is on the house for not letting Sheila give you a massage," she said.

Moms always know what their daughters are up to.

"And thanks for giving Sheila a ride to town when her car broke down."

"Brenda is a poet and doesn't know it," my Guardian Angel said.

The beer tastes good. Maybe I should sit at the bar and drink about twelve of them and forget Lisa.

"I understand you and Earl are back together?"

"I was getting horny and since you wouldn't come over what could I do?" she said and winked at me.

"Good sex can solve a lot of problems," I said, ignoring the feeble attempt to lay a guilt trip on me.

"It doesn't have to be good it just has to be sex," my Guardian Angel said.

"It's better for Sheila you two are together. It should help her solve some of her problems," I said.

"Going away to school will help a lot. She has to get out of this town and see what the real world is like," Brenda said, sounding concerned but knowing she couldn't do anything about it.

"Did Earl ever give you a deep blue heart pendant?" I asked.

"As a matter of fact he did. I was looking for it a few weeks ago and I can't find it. I broke the gold chain it was on and I was going to Albert Lee. Albert Lee has a jewelry store that carries a lot of inexpensive gold chain. I don't know where I could have lost it," she said. "I hate the feeling when something is missing and I can't find it."

The bar got busy and Brenda walked around being the psychologist to people trying to get drunk.

I was on my third Guinness when the ice fisherman I had met the evening I fought Bill and Joe sat beside me. "The way your life is going you should settle down and take up ice fishing. The walleye are biting like crazy and they don't shoot at you," he said like I should have more friends that were fish.

I was about to order another beer and engage in some trivial conversation when I looked at my watch. It is 10:00 and time for me to leave. Time flies when one sits in a bar and accomplishes nothing. "Lisa told you midnight," my Guardian Angel said.

"I'll surprise her," I told him.

"She might not like surprises."

I should have known he would be right.

CHAPTER THIRTEEN
GOLD AND SILVER OLYMPIC SIZED BUMPS

My plan isn't to surprise Lisa but I want to see if anybody will leave the house before I was supposed to arrive.

I figured it would be better to drive by the house and park the car, most people leaving the house would head back to the main highway, which is in the opposite direction.

I parked Matilda about five hundred yards from the house and walked a wide arch behind the house. I didn't see any people moving around in the house and snuck up to the side of the garage farthest away from the house.

All the garage doors have Plexiglas windows in them. I take it the cars like to look out. There is a door immediately around the corner from where I am and I tried the doorknob. It is unlocked. I went into the garage. There is enough light coming through the windows I can see fine. The first parking space is empty. The next six spaces are filled with cars I can't even afford their tires. The seventh space is a big surprise - Carol's baby blue Mercedes.

"Oh, oh," my Guardian Angel said.

The words had no sooner come out of his mouth when the garage door directly behind the blue Mercedes started up and the lights came on in the garage. I darted behind the car next to it.

"What do you think about Roosevelt?" Lisa asked.

"I don't think he could solve a crime if it came with a guidebook. And, he is a strange monkey, he won't sleep with me," Carol said.

Carol and Lisa laughed.

"No sex is not funny," my Guardian Angel said.

"How much longer do you think it will take with Dale?" Carol asked.

"I don't know. Sometimes I think I'm getting close and then he shuts up. He is no fool," Lisa said.

"I wish it was over. I want to get out of this stinking town," Carol said bitterly.

Carol got into her car and started it. I heard the car window go down. "I'll be back out soon," she said.

"Do you want a report on Roosevelt after I get him in the sack?" Lisa joked.

Carol backed out of the driveway. I heard the garage door close, Lisa walking, and the door open and close.

"It's a good thing you're an old hippie and got over the ego thing," my Guardian Angel said.

"I've never got over the ego thing, as you put it, since I never thought having an ego was a problem. Besides, hippies had as much ego as everybody else."

"How can you say that oh long haired one?"

"Easy. Long hair was ego. Beads were ego. Hand carved stash pipes were ego. Who had the best dope was ego. Who had the best tickets to a rock concert was ego. Whose Volkswagen van had the most peace signs painted on it was ego. Who had knee high moccasins in downtown L.A. so they could track busses without being heard was ego. Need I go on?"

My Guardian Angel didn't say anything. He doesn't like to be proven wrong.

I inched over to the door Lisa had gone out, opened it slowly until it was partially open, and stuck my head out to look around. It was not a smart thing to do. Whatever the heavy object was that crashed down on the back of my head had enough weight distribution and velocity to knock me to my knees. The second blow sent me to da da land.

Everything is warm. Little sparkling flashes of silver are cascading behind my eyeballs. My name drifts peacefully between the flashes. "Roo...se....velt, Roo...se....velt, Roo....se....velt."

Whoever is calling me has to be an angel, a beautiful angel with a voice like soft falling snow. The sparkling flashes of silver slowly blinked off to be replaced by the worst headache I've ever had. The back of my head feels like it has its own heart and its main function is to pulsate pain. My eyes feel like one-inch midgets are using them for a trampoline. "Beautiful Angel," I mumbled.

"Beautiful angel, bull, you idiot," my soft falling snow angel said.

I opened my eyes. "Lisa," I said groggily.

"Sit up," Lisa ordered.

I am lying on the kitchen floor. I sat up and felt the back of my head. I have an Olympic gold medal winning bump next to a silver medal bump.

"What were you doing in the garage and don't tell me changing oil?" Lisa asked.

"I was going to surprise you," I said while standing up. "How did you know I was there?"

"This house has sensing devices everywhere. I saw one of the monitors after I came back inside. An ant can't sneak into this house?"

Lisa helped me to the kitchen table. "What did you hit me with?"

"There's a ball bat by the door."

"Good thing they don't keep a gun by the door," my Guardian Angel said.

Propping my elbows on the table I rested my head in my hands.

"If I had known it was you I wouldn't have beaned you," Lisa said with no remorse in her voice. "But most people who get invited to a house ring the doorbell."

"Roosevelt wouldn't think of anything that easy," my Guardian Angel said.

Lisa wet a wash towel with hot water and handed it to me with her left hand. "Hold it on your head," she told me.

I take it she doesn't have to prove she is a woman by displaying any motherly instincts.

"Would you like something to drink hard head?" she asked.

"Fifteen gin and tonics with a lime wedge half-squeezed and only two ice cubes per drink," I told her.

Lisa left the kitchen.

"I bet Lisa knows you were in the garage when she and Carol came out," my Guardian Angel said.

"Bummer," I replied. "What should I tell her?"

"You're good at lying to women, you should be able to figure that out by yourself," he said.

Lisa came back with a serving tray that had fifteen drinks on it. Each has two ice cubes and a lime wedge. She set it down on the table, smiled at me, and picked up a drink.

I picked up a drink. "To a 300 batting average," I toasted.

"To coming in the front door," she toasted.

I drank five drinks before I couldn't feel the pain. I also couldn't feel my lips, my tongue, my feet, or my hands.

"Thiiis isss goooood giiiin," I slurred, faking being more smashed than I am while picking up another drink.

Lisa looked bored. Beautiful women have had more drunks drooling over them than there are stolen American cars in Mexico.

"Do you have a sister?" I asked Lisa, who had had three drinks.

"You're one in a million. How did you ever solve a kidnapping case and get on TV?" she asked, not answering my question.

"It was all luck," I told her the truth, but wondered why she didn't answer my question.

Lisa finished her drink and picked up another one. I watched her as she sipped the drink. There is something about her that is familiar. I don't know if it is the way she moves, the tone in her voice, or the way she looks at me, but there is something about her I can't put my finger on.

"You told me the other day you might be able to help me?" I said.

"I know a few people who Franklin played cards with," she said.

Lisa must have been little Miss Eavesdropper when Dale and I were talking.

"How would you know? I've asked everybody in town and all I've heard is he played out of town."

"Look at me Roosevelt. Do you think I have a problem finding out information?" she asked me in a low seductive voice and a knowing smile on her lips.

"I'll tell you anything you want to know about me," my Guardian Angel said.

What could I say to Lisa?

"Do you like foreplay?" Lisa asked me.

How we got from who played cards with Franklin to foreplay I don't know.

"About two minutes of foreplay is enough," I said.

"I was only wondering, Roosevelt. You'll never get to find out," Lisa said, giving me a look like I am a dust ball in the realm of her superior vacuum cleaner self.

I laughed. It is a good hearty laugh. A from-the-gut laugh. Lisa gave me a strange look. I laughed harder. My sides started to hurt and still I laughed. I laughed more and then I suddenly stopped, looked at Lisa, grinned like a wise old sage - which is hard to do - not the grinning, but the wise old sage bit, and said. "Lisa, you are one of the prettiest women I have every ever seen in my life. You are living with a man who is married and one day you will dump Dale and another man who has enough money to buy Japan will pick up your poor little heartbroken self and spend another fortune on you. But you know what? I like you. A woman has to do what she has to do. It beats working in a factory."

"I do what I have to do, Roosevelt. It's nobody's business but my own. But I am glad you like me. Why I'm glad I don't know?" she said and smiled a genuine smile at me.

"Who are the local people Franklin plays cards with?" I asked, getting back to the fat of the matter.

"Earl Harberts, Father Fisher and Dale Boraxe," she said.

"Can you believe that," my Guardian Angel said.

In my surprise I sprayed gin and tonic all over the table.

"Good touch," my Guardian Angel said.

"I can see Earl and Dale playing, but not Father Fisher. He's a priest," I stammered, but I wondered why Merriam had told me Franklin only played out of town? And why Dale had lied to me?

"They used to play out here once a week, Roosevelt. There is no need for me to lie to you. I want to see whoever killed Franklin caught and it isn't going to happen if you don't catch him. The police in this part of the country don't care what happens in the little towns."

"A priest couldn't afford to play big stakes poker," I said.

"Franklin staked him. They were good friends. If the priest won he gave half his winnings to the church. He is a conservative player and never won or lost much," Lisa explained to me.

"How much did they play for?"

“Ten dollar anti, two hundred-dollar max bet with no check and raise, and only three raises allowed.”

"That's enough money to make a bald man grow hair," my Guardian Angel commented.

"What did they play?" I asked.

"Seven-card stud and five-card draw with no wild cards. Sometimes they'd play high hand and low hand and split the pot but it was normally high hand takes it all."

"You seem to know a lot about cards," I said.

"I dealt for their games, Roosevelt."

I was flabbergasted over the information. So flabbergasted I was no longer half drunk. But being flabbergasted didn't help my headache, it only added to it.

"Who was the best player?" I asked.

"Franklin. He could read every one of them like a book. It was almost like he knew the cards."

"Who supplied the cards?"

"Franklin normally brought the cards but there was no way he could have marked them. The decks were always sealed. I took off the wrappers myself."

I've known more than one guy who made a good living steaming wrappers off card decks and putting them back together but I didn't tell Lisa. She might not approve of my choice of friends.

"Did any of the men bother you?" I asked.

"They came over to play cards, not worry about Dale's mistress," Lisa said matter-of- factly.

"What does Merriam think of the arrangement between you and Dale?"

"Merriam knows about me. She doesn't come out here and I don't go into town. I don't know if she likes it but she doesn't do anything about it. Dale treats her well, buys her what she wants. Dale never spends the nights here. It's life, nobody's hiding what's going on."

I pondered my next question.

"You're not pondering life and death, the creation of the universe, is there an end to time, what causes love, will Star Trek come back? Ask the question," My Guardian Angel said.

"I heard you and Carol in the garage. She told you she didn't think I could solve a crime if I had a guidebook."

"Poor little boy, did him get his feelings hurt?" Lisa chided.

"Then she asked you how long you thought it would take with Dale and you said every time you thought you were getting close he shuts up."

"I was wondering if you were going to be brave enough to tell me you heard us talking." Lisa said.

I thought my question about her and Carol would surprise Lisa or make her mad.

"Not so, oh non-seducing one," my Guardian Angel said.

"Do you remember a question you asked me earlier?" Lisa asked.

It was the old double question routine.

"How earlier?"

"Earlier, earlier."

I tried to remember. The trying was good. The remembering was not so good. I shrugged my shoulders.

"You asked me if I have a sister?"

"Do you have a sister?"

"Carol Trouble is my older sister."

I grabbed a drink and gulped it down. I grabbed another one and gulped it down. Lisa picked up a drink and sipped it. She has better social graces. I picked up another drink and sipped it. It helps to hang out with refined people.

I looked at Lisa closely. Lisa and Carol have the same features.

"Carol comes out here a lot, doesn't she?" I asked.

"Whenever Dale isn't around. It gets lonely out here."

Now I knew where Carol went all the time.

"Why didn't Carol tell me she had a sister?" I asked.

"You probably never asked. Everybody in town knows who Dale Boraxe's mistress is, but it is something people don't talk about."

"Every person in town I've met sleeps with other people's spouses and they tell me," I said.

"You're a detective, you ask questions. If you didn't ask they wouldn't tell you," Lisa said.

"What did you mean about getting close and then Dale shuts up?" I asked.

"Carol and I have dreamed for years about getting a house in Florida. Carol met Franklin and although she didn't love him she married him. Franklin didn't love her either but they offered each other what the other one wanted. Franklin wanted a pretty woman - Carol is that - and Carol wanted someone with money that would enable her to reach her dream without having to work."

"Why did they separate if everything was peachy keen?"

"Carol has saved most of the money Franklin gave her. She told Franklin she was going to move to Florida and anytime he wanted he could come visit her. Franklin told her they might as well get a divorce and he would give her the house and money to live on. She has the house up for sale and she is also getting a nice life insurance policy."

"Why does Carol rent rooms when she is set?" I asked.

"She meets men from out of town and she likes to cook," Lisa said.

"There are a few answers in life that are too simple," my Guardian Angel said.

"Back to my question. What is it you're looking for that Dale has?" I asked.

"I was married for ten years and single for four. I had a lousy marriage and didn't like working at the bar for minimum wage. One day Dale showed some interest in me and I played it along. He has taken me on trips, bought me nice clothes, jewelry, a car, but he only gives me a couple hundred dollars a week. I'm tired of it Roosevelt. Smiling for the little king, bringing him drinks, sleeping with him - he is faster than a rabbit and the only thing foreplay is to him is taking his pants off."

"Sounds like Roosevelt when he is in the mood," my Guardian Angel said.

"I figured if I stayed with Dale for three or four years I'd have enough money saved up I'd be able to get out of here but it hasn't happened. I know Dale does something that is against the law. What it is I don't know? But a few months ago he started keeping a lot of cash here at the house. I've seen him counting money, big money. It isn't in the safe. I've checked. I've looked everywhere and never been able to find it. When I do I'm taking it and Lisa and I are getting out of Saint Ansgar. We're going where nobody knows us and start a new life. Dale won't be able to report it since it's illegal money. That's what Carol and I were referring to."

"Why don't you ask him where it is?"

"I do. I tell him he should tell me so in case anything happens to him. He has been about to tell me several times but he always stops. I don't think he trusts me."

"Most crooks don't trust anybody," my Guardian Angel said.

"If he is a big crook he can find you Lisa and he might kill you. Did you ever think of that?" I said.

"He wouldn't do that. I know him too well," she said confidently.

"Somebody killed Franklin," I said.

My statement shocked her. Maybe it had never entered her mind Dale Boraxe might be a killer.

"You told me one of the women killed Franklin," my Guardian Angel said.

"They did."

"Dale isn't a woman," my Guardian Angel said.

"So," I said.

"So, you need to take an anatomy class," he said.

"If I were you I wouldn't steal his money. I'd sell the car, all your jewelry and leave," I told Lisa.

She gulped the rest of her drink and reached for another one.

I finished my drink and picked up another one. There is one drink left. It's amazing how much gin a guy and woman can drink when they are talking about foreplay, sisters, murder, illegal activities and trying to steal large sums of money.

"Do you have any idea at all, even a guess, what Dale does that is illegal?" I asked Lisa.

I noticed Lisa's face is getting flushed. Her speech is slower and in my gin haze she is turning from prettier, to prettiest, to - hot dang son that babe is prettier than Hefner's second wife.

"I really don't have any idea what it is, Roosevelt, but people fly here that he never invites over to the house. They stay out at the shed by the airport sometimes for hours and then they fly off."

"He's smuggling illegal wheat and corn seed," my Guardian Angel said.

I thought about Bill Buffalo telling me Dale and Merriam were under investigation by the Feds but there was no way I could go knock on the F.B.I. office door in Minneapolis and ask what they were looking for. The F.B.I. doesn't like people meddling in their affairs. I'd tried it once in Iowa and almost got killed.

"Do you ever notice what type of planes they are?" I asked Lisa.

"All I know is most of them have two engines."

Lisa reached for the last drink. Her eyes are glazed. Her facial features have softened. Her shoulders are sagging. Gin has a way of turning a person into putty. She sipped on the drink and looked at me over the edge of the glass. Maybe with only a partial view I look better. Her eyebrows arched and she set the glass down and smiled. "I've changed my mind," she said.

"That's nothing new for a woman," my Guardian Angel said.

"About what?" I asked Lisa, thinking she might tell me something she had not intended to tell me.

"I want to get naked and sleep with you."

Am I nothing but a piece of meat?

"It would be an honor, Lisa, but I don't mix pleasure with business," I said.

Lisa must not have heard me. "I want you to carry me to the sofa, set me down and take all my clothes off. Then you undress slowly for me."

"Please Roosevelt, you can pretend you are the warm up act for the Chippendales," my Guardian Angel said.

"Then I want you to start kissing me on the forehead and slowly kiss me all the way down to my toes and back up. What do you think Roosevelt? Do you think you can handle me?"

"Maybe not, but it's worth a try," my Guardian Angel said.

"You must not have heard me. I'm sorry, but I don't mix pleasure with business," I said again.

Lisa giggled, gave me a crooked little smile and then her head plopped on the table. She was stone cold out.

"Gin vapors," my Guardian Angel moaned.

I picked Lisa up and carried her to a sofa in the living room. There is an afghan on the back of the sofa. I put the afghan over her and left.

It is cold outside. The night is cloudy and a stiff wind is blowing out of the north. I hurried to Matilda. Good old Matilda cranked right over. I let her warm up while watching my breath form clouds in front of my face.

"If you ever get out of here I want to go someplace where it's warm. I want you to go where the women carry a matchbox around to put their wet swim suits in. I want to see the ocean, seagulls, seals, and sailing ships. I want you to go where you will not stumble onto a murder and you can have a sex life. What do you think?" my Guardian Angel said.

“I don’t know of any place place where there isn’t murder, although the Vatican City might be close, but Vatican City is out for a place for wet bathing suits in match boxes,” I said.

“Bummer,” he replied.

“What could Dale be doing that is illegal?” I asked.

"A man as ugly as he is having Lisa should be illegal," he said.

"Since Father Fisher liked to play poker with the big boys do you think he could be involved in anything else?"

"No, he is too nice of a man."

I turned Matilda around and drove slowly past the house. There are times in life when we miss opportunities and we know we will never have the opportunity again. These moments are the reason for love songs and country western feel sorry for me songs.

When I got back to Carol's it was 3:00 a.m.. I feel like I've been awake for five days. The blue Mercedes is in the driveway. As I walked to the door snowflakes the size of silver dollars started falling out of the sky. Carol had left the door unlocked.

I went to my room, didn't turn on the lights, and lie on the bed fully dressed.

"You know Roosevelt, I don't think you're going to solve this triple case. I think it would be a good time to pack your few belongings and get out of here," my Guardian Angel said.

"Life is a game of futility," I said gazing into the darkness.

"If you keep 'futiliting' around I think you're going to get hurt real bad," he said.

Maybe it is the two bumps on my head, maybe it is because I have been shot at three times, maybe it is because a message had been written on Matilda, maybe I am dumber than dumb but I am not going to leave. "I can't leave yet," I told my Guardian Angel.

"Will you write a letter of recommendation for me?" he asked.

"Sure."

"Goodnight Roosevelt. When it's all over I will miss you."

"Goodnight Guardian Angel."

I tossed and turned all night.

CHAPTER FOURTEEN
A LONG BLACK ROBE WITH A BLOOD RED LINER

Waking up it is not a blue-collar morning. It is more of a ring around the body day and I don't know of any manmade chemical I can spray all over my body to make the ring go away, unless the chemical is so strong it would kill all the fish in Lake Michigan.

I cleaned up and went to the kitchen. Carol is sitting at the table drinking coffee and thumbing through a travel magazine. "Did you sleep with Lisa?" she asked casually.

"I didn't do anything."

"How's your head?" she asked. She and Lisa must have talked on the phone.

"It hurts," I said as I sat.

Carol poured me a cup of coffee.

"You should learn what a doorbell is for," she said and then smiled at me.

I don't know what it is but there are a lot of people in life who find humor in other people's pain.

"Did you find out anything of interest from Lisa?" Carol asked.

I wasn't getting any sympathy so I figured I might as well answer the question. "She said Franklin played cards with Dale, Father Fisher and Earl Harberts and that she was the dealer."

"I could have told you that," she said. "Why didn't you ask me?"

"Yes, why didn't you ask her?" my Guardian Angel said.

"People in town told me Franklin didn't play with local people," I said.

"People in town don't know everything. They only think they do," Carol said.

"Lisa said she is trying to steal a pile of cash from Dale and then she and you will get out of here."

"He deserves it," Carol snapped. "He's only using her."

"Being used is the main job of being a mistress," I said.

Carol gave me a dirty look.

The way I feel I really don't care.

"Why didn't you tell me you had a sister?" I asked.

"You haven't asked and it never entered my mind."

"Lisa said your marriage with Franklin was a marriage of convenience. He gave you the house when you separated and you are getting a large insurance settlement. You have it made. Why ask me to solve his murder? Let the cops handle it."

"Franklin was good to me. We might not have been in love but we were good friends. I don't trust the cops around here. I only asked you for Franklin's sake."

"You must trust Sheriff Jack Benning?" I said.

Carol gave me a knowing smile. "Roosevelt, he's only a little boy. I like to give him a thrill. Are you jealous?"

She caught me off guard. "I have to think about it?"

"If you have to think about it then you are jealous."

"Strange world isn't it?" I said.

"Stranger than fiction."

"Why don't you trust the cops around here?" I asked, still amazed I was jealous.

"Lisa and I think Dale is doing something against the law. Dale is mayor of this town and one of the big boys in the area. It only stands to reason he has to have the cops in his pocket. And if he has cops in his pocket they aren't going to do much snooping around and shake things up."

"Are you talking about Bill Buffalo and his men?" I asked.

"Who else is there?"

"They seem straight arrow to me. Bill Buffalo has done everything a cop is supposed to do on the case."

"Are you sure?" she asked.

She caught me off guard again. "No, I'm not really sure. But when he came over here right after we found Franklin he was nice to you. It seemed to me you two were old friends," I said.

"I don't know Buffalo from beefsteak," she said.

"I decided to shock her, "I know who one of the killers is," I said.

Surprisingly she didn't show any shock but she looked puzzled. "You mean there is more than one?"

"There has to be?"

"Why?"

"I'm not telling. I'm taking no chances until I know for sure who the other person in is."

"You have to have an idea who the other one is?"

"I don't have a clue. I only know there was more than one person. And even the person I know was in on Franklin's murder I can't prove yet."

Lisa started to say something but didn't.

"Franklin didn't have anything in his pockets when we found him. How much money did he normally carry around with him?" I asked.

"He always had at least a thousand, but when he was going to a card game sometimes up to ten thousand."

"Do you know where he hid his cash?"

"I have no idea Roosevelt. He never told me. I never asked. I do know he never kept a bank account or a savings deposit box."

"Do you think Dale Boraxe ever had a thing going with Fanny?" I asked.

Carol looked at me like I was dumber than a goose that flew north during the winter. "Look at my sister and look at Fanny, and answer that question."

"That's a good point," my Guardian Angel said.

I was about to tell Carol that Franklin had loaned Fanny money but I decided not to.

"Let's say Dale is doing something illegal. We really don't know if he is. But if he is who would he trust in this area?"

"If I was going to do something illegal I wouldn't let anybody in the area know," Carol said. "I'd think he would be smart enough to keep his mouth shut."

"One would think so," my Guardian Angel pondered.

It's nice to have someone ponder for me every so often. Pondering too much can become a real pondering drag.

"Lisa told me she was married for ten years and was single for four before she took up with Dale. What did she do for those four years?"

"Her husband was a jerk. After the divorce the best thing that happened for her was when he got killed in a car wreck in Chicago. The only good thing was they didn't have any kids. But to answer your question she worked at the bar for a while. She worked at the cafe for a while. She went to Vegas and went to dealer's school and came back and dealt cards at a Casino by Albert Lee. She thought she would like the job but it was nothing but long hours and lousy tips and having truck drivers and farmers hit on her all the time. Men think that every woman that works in a casino is a hooker."

"There's a good clue for you Roosevelt," my Guardian Angel said.

"What did she deal?"

"Black Jack and poker. I never went so she could have dealt other games. I don't gamble. Money is too hard to come by to toss it in some machine on a payoff schedule or bet it on a deck of cards."

"I know you've been sneaking into my room and reading my clue book," I said like I was scolding a kid for stealing from the cookie jar.

Carol, to my surprise, wasn't alarmed by my accusation. "I was vacuuming one day and I found the notebook in the chair, which I didn't know what it was until I read a few scribbles and then I read all of it. I like your writing but you seem to wander a lot," she said.

"I saw it on the coffee table when you and Jack Benning were together. You must have shown it to Benning," I said.

"I saw you looking in the window you little window peeper you. Did you like the show?" she grinned at me.

"He's not into watching. I am. And yes, I did like the show? I like the way you moan and hold your ankles above your head," my Guardian Angel said.

"I didn't like the show," I said.

"Don't worry, Roosevelt. I didn't let Benning read the book."

I didn't have any more questions.

"I'm going out and see Lisa, Roosevelt," Carol said. "If you want to make yourself breakfast go ahead, but clean up when you're done."

I wondered if Lisa would tell Carol I'm so exciting I put her to sleep.

I don't feel like cooking. I don't feel like eating. I poured myself another cup of coffee. Looking into the coffee cup I wondered why fortunetellers always use tea to read the future. Coffee would be much better - it's always deep and dark.

"You seem stuck, Roosevelt," my Guardian Angel said.

"I hate to admit it but I am stuck," I agreed.

"I have a cat killer and now no cat bodies, a heart stealer, more than one murderer, all going on at the same time, but I have a gut feeling they are all connected. Why, I don't know, but I am sure they are."

"You also have a fat cat that might be a crook?"

"I don't care if Dale Boraxe is a crook. All I want to do is figure out this mess I got myself involved with and then I'm going to go to a warm place like you suggested."

"You've got ten minutes to solve this case and then let's get out of here," my Guardian Angel said excitedly.

"Get real," I told him.

"I can't. I've been dead too long."

I finished my coffee and decided to go see some people I haven't talked to yet.

I stuck my pistol in my belt and headed out into the real world. About six inches of snow had fallen during the night. It is pretty if you like scraping car windows.

I drove to the house next to Jimmy's. Fanny had told me a retired couple lived there. I could hear a TV blaring from inside the house as soon as I got out of Matilda. I knocked on the door. Waited. There was no answer. I knocked on the door harder. Waited. There was no answer. I beat on the door. The TV volume was turned down and a shriveled up old man who had to be in his late 80's answered the door. "I don't want no Watch Tower. I don't want no siding on my house. I don't want no encyclopedias. I don't want no house numbers painted on the curb. I don't need my porch fixed. I don't need new shingles. If you want to mow the yard come back in the spring," he hollered in a shrill scratchy voice and started to shut the door.

"I'm a detective and I'd like to ask you some questions," I said quickly.

"What?" he hollered.

"I want to ask you some questions?" I hollered louder.

"My gutters don't need cleaning out," he hollered back.

An old woman, shorter than he, came to the door. "It's that detective who killed that guy down the street, George," she hollered directly in his ear.

"Kill about twenty of the worthless scum around here," he hollered to me. "Start with the slob down on the corner that won't clean his yard."

"Mr. Roosevelt, don't mind my husband, but what do you want?" the lady said sweetly. Her face is wrinkled like a prune. She has white hair pulled back into a bun. She looks like her hobby is making fudge.

"I'd like to ask you two some questions," I said.

"Come on in. But when it comes to questions you have to ask me. My husband is crazier than a bed bug."

"I don't want my fence painted either," the old man hollered at me as I entered the house.

"Excuse me for a minute," the lady said and helped her husband back to a recliner which was directly in front of a TV. She turned the volume back up on the TV, patted him on the head lovingly and walked in slow jerky steps back to me. "We can sit in the kitchen," she said. "Each day at this time my husband watches the Playboy Channel and drools a lot."

She poured a cup of coffee for each of us, smiled at me, wrinkled her nose, which had to be hard to do with all the wrinkles on her face, and said. "I heard you shot that guy four times in the heart. I bet that surprised the pee donk out of the scumbag."

"It surprised him dead," I said.

"There are so many bad people in the world today they should line them all up and shoot them in the head and be done with it, she said."

"Oh granny what language you have," my Guardian Angel said.

I don't know what to say to granny.

"I suppose, young man, that you came by to ask us who we think killed Franklin?" the lady asked.

"I would like to know your names first," I replied.

"Grace and George Brethren," she said. "We have lived in Saint Ansgar our complete lives," she added proudly. "I wouldn't want to live anywhere else. Everywhere else is full of commies."

"Yes, I would like to know who you think killed Franklin Trouble," I said.

She sipped her coffee and set the cup down carefully. "Mr. Roosevelt, whoever killed him did him a favor. He was a gambler. He wanted to die," she explained.

"I don't understand," I said.

"He lived on the edge. He did everything to the extreme. He carried cash money on him all the time. People were always wondering where he kept his money. It was only a matter of time before somebody would bump him off. Franklin had to know that."

"But who do you think killed him?"

Grace looked around the kitchen like somebody might be listening and then whispered to me. "Ginger and Franklin used to argue all the time. I could hear them. When Franklin was seeing Ginger I bet he told her he would marry her just so she would sleep with him and when Ginger found out he had only used her she killed him."

"But they found Franklin in Carol's closet," I whispered back.

"If I killed some no good lying man I wouldn't put him in my own closet," she said almost righteously.

"Can't argue with that," my Guardian Angel said.

"Why would somebody put the body in Carol's closet?" I asked.

"Because they didn't like Carol and wanted to pin the murder on her or at least have the police suspect her."

"Makes sense to me," my Guardian Angel said.

"Do you ever notice who comes in and out of Fanny's?" I asked.

She wrinkled her nose again like she was debating whether to answer my question or not. "Not too many people come visit George and I. When you get old younger people are afraid of you. They think old is a disease they can catch and they avoid you. So I stand by the back window or the front window and watch the world go by. I watch the birds and the squirrels. I watch the people. I watch them go to work, come back from work. I know their routines but it's like there's a big tall wall between us. It's very lonely Mr. Roosevelt."

"I've been that way all my life," I said.

Grace patted me with her tiny gnarled hand. "Don't worry son, it will all work out," she said.

I smiled.

"I guess you can call me a snoop. Jimmy goes to Fanny's a lot. He is such a nice boy. It's a wonder with the mother he is saddled with. Merriam Boraxe goes a lot. Dale Boraxe used to go but I haven't seen him in a long time. I saw Carol there a few weeks ago. The hippie Sheila Harberts goes by. When Earl was sleeping with Fanny he went over. Then when Franklin was sleeping with her he went over. For the locals that's been about it. And, of course, I've seen you come and go a lot, you sly devil you," she winked at me.

I feel like I am the caboose of a train.

"Do you like Fanny?" I asked.

"Yes I do. We have one thing in common," she said.

"What's that?"

"We both like black cats."

"Oh, oh," my Guardian Angel said.

"Does Father Fisher ever visit you?" I asked.

"God never did anything for George and me. We don't want any stinking priest coming to the house."

The last answer shocked any other questions out of me.

"I should be going," I said.

"I suppose trying to find a killer is hard work," she said.

I followed Grace to the front door.

George hollered at me as Grace opened the door. "We don't need no Medicare supplement policy either."

"You be careful now. The next person that tries to pop you might not miss," Grace warned me and shut the door.

I drove to the convenience store to use the pay phone. There were three men inside drinking coffee and betting if spring would come in June or July.

"Detective Bill Buffalo speaking."

"Where's your next Wild West show?" I asked.

"Roosevelt, I figured you would be dead by now."

He is not a funny guy.

"I want you to do something for me," I said. "You should search Franklin's car for a place he might have hidden money."

"Roosevelt. You must think I'm stupid. We tore that car apart. The only thing hidden in the car was grease."

"Did you print it?"

"The car doesn't have hands," he chuckled.

"He's funnier than Paul Binyon and Pete Rosebet," my Guardian Angel said.

"Franklin's were the only prints on the car we got a match on," Bill Buffalo told me. "Is there anything else? I have to work."

"You'd better be nice to me or I won't talk at your fundraiser."

"Yes you will."

"You can't make me."

"I'll drum up some charge and put you in jail for a few months."

"Do you want a five or ten minute speech?"

"Roosevelt, be careful," Bill Buffalo said and hung up.

"You know, oh Chicken Little, one of these days you are going to have to ask him why Bill and Joe had his phone number?" my Guardian Angel said.

"I know."

I've had enough coffee to make my toes vibrate and need some food. The cafe is empty. Ginger is sitting at the counter filling salt and pepper shakers. I waved at her and sat at a table. She continued to fill the salt and pepper shakers. When she was done she ambled over in slow motion. Up close she looks like she had been drunk for three days. Her eyes are puffy, her lips are chapped and her hands are shaking. "I'll take a bowl of oatmeal, a double order of wheat toast and a large orange juice, no coffee," I told her.

She grunted something and left. "Gruel, double B and O.J.," she hollered to the back.

"What do you think?" I asked my Guardian Angel.

"You want my opinion, oh famous private detective without a license, who is running around in circles asking more questions than he can keep up with and is about to run out of both questions and people to ask questions to. I am humbled by the honor. I am graced by your appreciation."

"Answer the question Pea Brain."

"That's more like you. I was getting worried. I think it was either Jimmy, Sheila, Merriam or Earl Harberts that stole the heart. I think it was either Jimmy, Sheila, Dale Boraxe or Grace killed the cats. I think it was either Carol, Lisa, Sheila, Earl, Fanny, Ginger or Dale, killed Franklin. I think it was either Sheila, Brenda or Fanny shot at you the first two times. I know Peter Thompson shot at you because you dusted him."

"The next time I ask for your advice tell me to shut up," I said.

"I think it was either Dale, Earl, Carol, Lisa, Sheila, Ginger, or Fanny who hired Thompson to try and dust you. I think it was either Dale, Lisa, Carol, Fanny, Sheila, Earl or Merriam who killed Bill and Joe. I think the next time you go and see Lisa you shouldn't let her drink as much gin."

Ginger brought me my good for your colon breakfast and without being invited sat down.

"There were two men in here this morning asking questions about you?" Ginger said.

I took a bite of gruel.

"They looked like cowboys and wore sunglasses and were driving a black four door Chevy."

I sipped my orange juice.

"They were in their late thirties and had short hair. They had to be cops."

"What did they ask?"

"They wanted to know if you hung out with Dale Boraxe. They wanted to know if you were in town before Franklin was killed. They wanted to know if you flashed a big roll of cash. They wanted to know where you were staying. And they wanted to know who you hung with and who you were seeing?"

"What did you tell them?"

"I told them if they were so interested in you to go ask you.

I'm no snitch."

The mob would like to have more people like Ginger around them - there men seem to talk a lot now.

"It's big tip time," my Guardian Angel said.

"Did they show you a badge?"

"No."

"You have been drinking too much," I told Ginger.

"Things haven't been good. It's the old money game. More bills than money."

"Were you with Franklin only for the money?" I asked.

"What else is there?" she replied.

A customer came in. Ginger got up without saying goodbye.

I finished my gruel, double B and O.J. and left the money on the table along with a big tip.

"Why are the cops looking for you?" my Guardian Angel asked.

"I don't know if they're cops," I replied.

As I was driving toward Fanny's, Sheila and Fanny, in Sheila's yellow Volkswagen, drove by me going the other way. I turned around at the next block and followed them. I didn't have to go far. Going by the Saint Ansgar Church I saw Sheila's Volkswagen and Carol's Mercedes parked in front of Father Fisher's house. The Ford van and the four door Chevy were also there.

"I doubt if it's a sewing class," my Guardian Angel said.

I kept driving for a few miles and turned around. The cars were still there when I went back by. I went to Fanny's.

Clyde is sitting on a table peeling an orange. "Damn farmer," he squawked when he saw me.

"Crap, cowboy," I said.

"Bad cat, bad cat," he squawked.

"Not you, not you, not you," I said.

He tilted his head as if he was taking a better look at me. "Peace," he squawked and went back to his orange.

I darted up the steps and went directly to the room where Fanny stores her inventory. I opened boxes and closed them as close as possible to the way they had been. After ten boxes I was growing tired of looking at hearts. I had no idea the heart market is as big as it is. There are no hearts in the next box. There is a long black robe with an attached hood. The robe is lined with blood red silk. There is a book bound in black leather with a gold embossed symbol of an inverted star with a goats face in the middle of the star and the words - SATAN MASTER OF ALL - underneath the symbol. I did not open the book. There is also a large silver bowl and two extremely sharp silver knives in the box.

A dark eerie feeling engulfed me. I shut the box and put it back on the bottom of the stack and went back to the Tea Room.

"Witches belong to covens. There are thirteen people or less to a coven and they have four major celebrations a year, one for each season," my Guardian Angel said.

I sat at a table with Clyde. He has the orange peeled and is happily eating away.

"October 31st in ancient times was their biggest celebration," my Guardian Angel went on. "It's now celebrated as Halloween."

"How do you know so much about witches?" I asked.

"We burnt a lot of them," he said.

"Do they kill people or animals during their ceremonies?" I asked.

"I don't know. I never wanted to get close enough to find out," he told me. "But rumor goes they do. When they want to cast spells on people or invoke Lucifer they must shed blood."

"I thought all this witchcraft and warlock stuff had died out," I said.

"Remember my warning when your worthless destiny told you to stop here. Witchcraft has been on the rise in Europe and America for years. There are covens all over the world."

"I bet they try and recruit converts like organized religions do," I said.

"They seek out the lost and lonely, people who only feel hate and only want to spread hate, people with no compassion or feelings, people who blame all their misfortune on other people," he said.

"Sounds like half of the world," I said.

"Maybe that's why the world is in deep crapola," he said.

"Coffee sucks," Clyde squawked.

"Do witches have a thing with ravens?" I asked.

"Not that I know of. They are into goats and black cats. In my day sorcerers were into ravens."

Looking at Clyde he is kind of cute as birds go but his feet are too big.

I decided to go back to my room and go over my clue book - there are some additions and subtractions to make.

I parked in the driveway and saw Sheriff Jack Benning's car a few houses away. For all I know he is sleeping with every woman in town. I cursed myself for still not getting a key to the house from Carol.

"I don't know if you want to go over your clues right now," my Guardian Angel said.

"Why?"

"I really don't know. My powers seem to come and go any more."

"I have things to do," I said. "You have to be more definitive."

I was in luck once again. The front door is unlocked, Carol knows how stupid I am. As I shut the door I heard noise coming from the hallway. Taking two light steps I could see my door was open. I never leave the door open. Pulling my pistol out of my belt I inched along the wall toward my room. By the door jamb I stopped, took a few deep breaths, and then stepped into the doorway with my pistol fanning the room. A man with short hair, who looks like a cowboy, even though he doesn't have a cowboy hat on has my suitcase on the bed and is in the process of going through it.

"Don't shoot. Please don't shoot," he pleaded when he saw me and stuck his hands in the air. He is wearing white surgical gloves.

"You'd better have a warrant," I told him and pointed the pistol at his belly.

"I'm only doing what I was told to do," he said nervously.

"Bill Buffalo told you to search my place?"

The way he looked at me I knew he didn't know who Buffalo Bill was let alone Bill Buffalo.

"Who sent you?" I demanded. I should have stayed away from questions and thought more about the situation I was in. Two men had talked to Ginger. Where was the second man?

"Lookout!" my Guardian Angel yelled.

My Guardian Angel was too late, as was my question, as

somebody behind me slammed a granite hard fist into the side of my head. I hit the floor stone cold out for the ten count.

CHAPTER FIFTEEN
SHAKE THAT BOOTY

I heard a faint voice like somebody was shouting at me from across a wide canyon. "Wake up, Roosevelt, wake up."

Groaning and opening my eyes I started to sit up but slumped back down. The room is a pulsating blur. I feel like I am drunk and riding a spinning mattress.

"It will be ok, just take it easy," the wide canyon voice said.

My head feels like I had been hit by a truck. I tentatively touched the right side of my face. My cheek is bleeding profusely but it is not a large cut.

"Here, hold this on your face," the wide canyon voice said and put a cool wash cloth in my hand.

Holding the wash cloth on my cheek my vision began to clear. I blinked several times. A blurry face is looking down at me. It slowly came into focus. "Sheriff Jack Benning, you are uglier than sin but boy I'm I glad to see you," I said feeling relieved.

Sheriff Jack Benning helped me up and I sat on the edge of the bed.

"What are you doing here?" I asked Sheriff Jack Benning.

"A couple a few houses down were having an argument, or domestic dispute if you want to be politically correct, and the neighbor lady called. I was leaving after the couple got settled down and saw two men who look like cowboys, although they didn't have cowboy hats on, leaving Carol's. They walked around the corner and drove off in a black Chevy. After seeing the men I figured you had to be home and I came down to talk, but instead I found you on the floor playing a Rocky victim. That's a nasty cut on your face, Roosevelt."

The wash cloth was turning red. It's strange how little cuts on a person's face bleed so much.

"You're not going to get an attack of the vapors are you?" I asked Sheriff Jack Benning.

"What's that?" he asked me, looking highly confused.

"Forget it. It's nothing," I replied.

I went to the bathroom and looked at the cut. It had almost stopped bleeding and I put a small piece of toilet paper on it and went back to my room.

"Do you think the guys that hit you were hit men?" Sheriff Jack Benning asked me.

"No."

"Why not?"

"I'm not dead."

"Good deduction skills," my Guardian Angel said.

"That's smart thinking, Roosevelt. But who were they then?" Sheriff Jack Benning asked.

"Who does he think you are? A mind reader?" my Guardian Angel asked.

"I think they were Federal agents," I answered Sheriff Jack Benning.

"No," Sheriff Jack Benning said although he really meant, "I'll be danged."

My pistol is on the floor and I picked it up and stuck it in my belt. Everything that had been in the suitcase was on the bed. Sheriff Jack Benning picked up the biker chicks in leather exhaust pipe sucking calendar and started flipping through it. I noticed the drawers to the dresser were open and the bottle of Maalox had not been moved. I take it my sneak thief friends have good stomachs. I didn't have anything of importance in the dresser unless the men needed some off white T-shirts.

The cushion to the chair is on the floor. I ran my hand through the creases of the chair. My clue book is gone.

"Lord, Roosevelt, what a waste, you must have worked on your clues for at least thirty minutes," my Guardian Angel said.

"You look in shock. What's missing?" Sheriff Jack Benning asked me as he tossed the calendar back on the bed. I take it women who are into exhaust pipes don't ring his bell.

"They took my note book I write all the clues in and all the questions I have to answer before I can solve this case," I replied feeling devastated. I might have only worked on my clues for thirty minutes like my Guardian Angel said, but it was a serious deep in thought thirty minutes and they were my words, my unique words, now gone forever, flushed down the commode of life, lost. I could never write the words the same way. I might not ever pick up a pencil and notebook again.

"Don't worry, Roosevelt. When the guy sits down to read your clue book he won't be able to figure out what you were trying to say anyway. The only thing he will know for sure is that you are a terrible writer and if you really want to get serious you should take a few English and writing classes," my Guardian Angel said, sounding like a college professor who teaches creative writing and the only thing of his that had ever been published is a book on how ants reproduce.

"As smart as you are you shouldn't need your notebook," Sheriff Jack Benning said.

"Keep your mouth shut and don't ruin your image," my Guardian Angel coached me.

He is right. I'm taking this notebook thing a little too far. I have to get back to earth - a Pulitzer Prize is way beyond my grasp.

I decided to break my detective code of honor.

"The other day out at Boraxe's, after somebody used the Schneider boy's heads for target practice, when I sat in the car with Bill Buffalo he told me something he didn't want me to tell anybody else."

"You can tell me, Roosevelt. I promise I won't tell anybody else," Sheriff Jack Benning almost begged me.

"Bill Buffalo told me Dale and Merriam Boraxe were being investigated by the F.B.I. and it was so hush hush the Feds told him to stay away."

Sheriff Jack Benning looked shocked.

"Do you have any idea what Dale and Merriam could be up to?" I asked.

Sheriff Jack Benning started pacing back and forth across the room with a serious look on his face. If he smoked a pipe and shot cocaine he could have been a skinny reincarnated Sherlock Holmes.

Sheriff Jack Benning stopped pacing. "I have no idea what Dale and Merriam could be up to," he said.

"That was a lot of pacing for no idea," my Guardian Angel said.

"Do you want to do some investigating for me?" I asked Sheriff Jack Benning. "But don't tell anybody if you do."

Don't tell anybody are the words, that in a small town really mean, everybody, including Aunt May who is blind and deaf, will know what was said or done within fifteen minutes.

"I'm like you, Roosevelt. I would never tell a secret."

I was afraid of that.

"I'd like you to keep an eye on the Boraxe home where Lisa lives and see if anything strange is going on. I especially want you to let me know how many airplanes fly in and out of there and what type of planes they are."

"I can't keep driving by in my Sheriff's car. I'll have to figure something out," Sheriff Jack Benning told me already mentally engrossed in his mission.

"I'm sure you can figure it out," I told him reassuringly.

He put on his Sherlock Holmes face. "I'll report to you in a timely manner," he told me like he had been transformed from a lowly sheriff to a spy for the C.I.A. and left.

"Telling him about the Boraxe's and asking him to investigate for you was a big mistake," my Guardian Angel told me.

"Maybe, maybe not," I said.

"Do you really think the guy that searched your room and the guy that sent you to 'stars are dancing in my head heaven' were Federal Agents?" my Guardian Angel asked me.

"No I don't. The Feds wouldn't have had to go to the coffee shop and ask where I was and if they wanted to search my room they would get a warrant. Contrary to popular belief the Feds normally follow the law."

"What were the, not the Feds, looking for?"

"I don't know but Franklin Trouble was into something

besides playing high stakes poker."

"I think somebody killed Franklin who had nothing to do with what Franklin was involved in. But, when Franklin was killed, he had something in his possession the people he was involved with now want and don't know where it is," my Guardian Angel said.

"That's a good idea," I said, truly impressed by my Guardian Angel's cognitive thinking.

"I have a lot of good ideas if you would listen to me more often and not ignore me. If you would listen I wouldn't have to be such a wise guy all the time to get your attention," he said.

"Being a wise guy suits you," I said.

I straightened up my room and put the deck of cards, the heart, the calendar and the purple markers back in my suitcase and then went to the bathroom to check the cut on my face. It is nothing major.

I was looking in the mirror when I thought. "Self. Where was the guy who bushwhacked me when I was standing in the doorway to my room pointing my pistol at the guy looking through my suitcase?"

"Maybe he had to go to the bathroom," my Guardian Angel said.

"Nothing has been disturbed in the bathroom," I told him I went to the bedroom. The dresser drawers are open and the mattress and bedding are on the floor. I pulled out the drawers to see if something was taped to the back of them. There isn't. I checked the bed frame and there was nothing. I put the mattress back and made the bed.

The other room had also been searched in the same manner and I checked the dresser drawers. There was nothing. I made the bed.

"When you grow out of this detective phase of your life you can work for a hotel as their number one bed maker," my Guardian Angel said.

I went downstairs. Carol's room had been ransacked. I went into the bathroom. All the clothes in the closet had been gone through and tossed on the floor. The shoes were tossed everywhere. The drawers by the sink were dumped on the floor. I didn't find anything of interest. I walked around the bedroom looking at all the stuff. It's funny how much unnecessary stuff people own. I know there is a money god. I wonder if there is a stuff god. If there is he lives in a room he can barely move around in debating what he should keep and what he should toss out. There is also a good possibility the stuff god could be female, which would be a big stride forward for women's equal rights.

I was standing in the middle of the room thinking about how angry Carol was going to be when she saw the mess when I saw a small green leather hand bag on the floor. I really don't need one, but I picked it up and opened it. Inside there are several credit cards and a driver’s license. The credit cards are for a Carol Maidenform. Carol's photograph is on the driver’s license. She looks like we all do in our driver’s license photographs - needing sleep and hung over. Her name is clearly typed underneath her photograph - Carol Maidenform.

"Go ahead and say it," I told my Guardian Angel.

"Oh, oh," he said.

I put the credit cards and driver’s license back in the purse and tossed it on the floor. I'm not going to clean up the mess and I'm not making another bed.

"What are you going to do now?" my Guardian Angel asked.

"It's time to go for a drive."

"Let's drive out of here?"

"Soon, I hope. This small town living is getting me down."

I am going to Lisa's but I took a detour. I went by the Saint Ansgar Church. Sheila's yellow Volkswagen and Carol's Mercedes were still there. Checking the time, they have been at the church for over two hours. When I went to catechism it only lasted an hour and that included a coffee break for the priest.

"It's funny, Franklin had an affair with Fanny, which Carol knows, and yet they go to church together," my Guardian Angel said.

"People around here don't seem too hung up on who sleeps with who," I said.

The Lincoln is not in front of the Boraxe house.

Lisa answered the door before I rang the bell. The security system had to scan the front. Lisa hasn't changed, she is still beautiful. "Come on in, Roosevelt. It's about time for my nap," she said.

"Where's Daddy Big Bucks?" I asked Lisa.

"He doesn't leave me notes and tell me where he goes funny guy," she replied tersely.

"Did I drop in at the wrong time?" I asked her.

"I made a mistake asking you out the other night. I should have never told you the things I did. It would be better if you never come out again and let me get back to my life."

I appreciated her truthfulness. Each of us should have in our life the right to do what we want to do, but, there was one big problem - it's called murder.

"I don't care if you steal every illegal dime Dale has ever made, I only came out for one reason. I'm going to ask you a few questions and I want the truth. Not part of the truth but the whole truth. Do you understand?"

Lisa looked me in the eyes as if her beauty would melt me. I don't melt. There have been too many times around the block for this kid. I returned her gaze. For a few moments our eyes crossed swords and then she looked away.

"You're a jerk," she told me sheepishly.

"True," I replied.

"Maybe that's why I like you."

"Don't trust her," my Guardian Angel told me.

"Not to worry old friend."

I may argue with my Guardian Angel but he is a friend. He knows me. He isn't afraid to tell me the truth. Remember boys and girls only your true friends tell you the truth - everybody else butters you up and wants to see you fail.

"Ask away. I'll tell you the truth," Lisa said.

"Ask her if she is better in bed than her sister?" my Guardian Angel said.

"Come on, Roosevelt, let's go to the kitchen. By the size of that knot on your cheek you look like you need a beer," Lisa said.

"I ran into a door," I told her.

Lisa brought me a beer and herself a glass of water. The beer tastes good. I'm surprised the government hasn't tried to make beer illegal again because it tastes so good.

"Did Carol change her maiden name when she got married?"

I asked Lisa.

"No. But everybody knows her as Trouble. Franklin and Carol flew to Vegas to get married so nobody from around here knew she didn't change her name."

"Did you change your name when you got married?"

"I did, but after the divorce I took my maiden name back. I didn't want to be branded my whole life by some jerk I'd married."

"Can I see your driver's license?"

"It's a terrible photograph. It looks like I needed sleep and was hung over," she said. "You don't want to see it."

"I like hung over pictures," I said.

She left and came back with an alligator purse that is so big I could have put Matilda in it. She rummaged around in her purse for about thirty seconds - she has enough stuff in her purse she could open a thrift store - and then handed me her driver's license.

I looked at the driver's license. Lisa Maidenform.

"You look exactly like your sister," I commented and handed the license back to her.

"When we were children people had a hard time telling us a part," she said.

"You knew they were sisters. It would stand to reason they had the same last name. So what's the big deal?" my Guardian Angel said.

"It could be a really big, big deal," I said.

"A really, really big, big, big deal," he said.

"Has Dale had any visitors lately?" I asked Lisa.

"A couple of guys flew in the other day but they didn't come to the house."

"Is their plane still here?"

"No, they were dropped off and Dale took them someplace."

"Did you get a chance to see them?"

"I watched them walk to the garage. They looked like cowboys but they didn't have cowboy hats on," Lisa said.

"How can they be cowboys without cowboy hats?" my Guardian Angel said. "A cowboy doesn't go anywhere without his hat."

"How can you be a birdbrain but you can't fly?" I said.

"I can fly oh mortal one."

He has me there.

"Does Dale have any more cars than the ones in the garage?" I asked.

"Not that I know of."

"How about at his other houses on the farm?"

"The other houses are farmhouses that his full time employees live in. There are three of them."

"Do you know where the houses are?"

"Of course, Roosevelt, I sleep with Dale. I know everything about him except what he does and where his cash is."

"Bummer," I said.

"It's more than a bummer it's a drag," Lisa said.

"Want to go for a drive and show me the houses?"

"I'd like to get out of the house. Dale won't be here this late in the afternoon."

"This little car is cute," Lisa said as we drove. "It kind of makes me want to hug it."

"Matilda's not into women," I said. At least I don't think she is. If she is she's kept the closet door tightly sealed.

Driving, Lisa pointed out fields that belonged to Dale. After a while one snow covered field looks like all the rest. We drove by the first house slowly. The house is a typical one story Midwest farmhouse with no garage or outbuildings.

"A Mexican man and his wife live there. In the summer his four grown boys come up from Mexico and work," Lisa told me.

The second house was like the first house - a nice small farmhouse with no outbuildings and no garage.

"A Norwegian man and his wife live here. They have three kids. He's worked on the farm since he was a young man. I have only met him a few times," Lisa told me.

I feel like I should be in a bus and Lisa is a travel guide.

The third house is run down and needs a paint job. There were fresh tire tracks in the snow-covered driveway going to and from the house. There is a new metal storage building. I noticed the metal shed's doors were chained and padlocked shut.

"Dale keeps this house empty. Workers stay here during the summer and deer and bird hunters stay here during hunting season," Lisa told me. "And a lot of town kids like to come out here and park behind the barn."

"Does Dale have any brothers or sisters?" I asked.

"He had a brother but the brother was killed in Vietnam."

I felt sad for a moment but being a Vietnam Vet I have suppressed most of the memories.

"Did Dale go into the service?" I asked.

"No, he was married and had a college exemption. I also think you didn't have to go if you ran a farm," Lisa told me.

"I suppose wars are only for poor uneducated people and city boys," my Guardian Angel said.

I headed back for the Gone with the Wind house.

Lisa is relaxed. "It's nice to get out and go for a drive," she said.

She reminds me of a pretty song bird locked in a cage. The only difference is Lisa had made her own cage.

"Have you ever heard anything about an occult group in the area?" I asked.

Lisa licked her top lip before answering me. "I heard Fanny was into the occult for a while. I also heard Sheila Harberts thought she was a witch but with all the dope she was doing back then it's a wonder she thought she was anything."

"Were there ever any rumors about other people being involved with them?"

Lisa licked her top lip again. "Not that I've heard," she said and added. "Do you believe people that get into the occult really think they can conjure up the devil?"

She sounded apprehensive but also slightly nervous.

"I don't know. I've never been to a black mass nor do I want to go."

"Anybody who would get involved with devil worship is weird," Lisa said, adding, "Weird and sick."

The sun is setting when we got back to the house. I opened the door for Lisa.

"You're nothing but a little boy at heart, Roosevelt, will you ever grow up?"

"I hope not."

"Would you like to come in for a bite to eat?" She smiled a smile at me that would make a Born Again Christian become a

Muslim.

"What's for dinner," I asked, afraid she was going to say carrot sticks, bean sprouts, tofu and seaweed, chased down with a multivitamin drink that tastes like weak Tang.

"Me."

"Don't give her any gin, Roosevelt," my Guardian Angel ordered. "In fact you might want to hint at a few cups of coffee."

“I’ve already eaten,” I told Lisa.

“At this rate you are going to starve to death,” my Guardian Angel said.

I drove slowly by the first house Lisa had shown me. There is a red Dodge pickup parked in front of the house.

I headed for the second house. The lights are on but there is no vehicle out front.

"I think you'd better turn around and head back to town," my Guardian Angel said.

"I am a detective. I have to take risks," I said.

"I wish you would make up your mind. First you're not a detective and now you are a detective. Now which one is it going to be? You can't go through life being confused all the time."

I slowed up as I got to the third house. All the lights were on in the house. I don't have a problem with people keeping all their lights on when it isn't necessary. Everybody alive knows we have an energy shortage but if they want to be wasteful it's their business. But I do have a problem with the four door black Chevy that is parked in front of the house.

"Oh, oh," my Guardian Angel said.

"Oh, oh" I said.

"Oh, oh, oh, oh," my Guardian Angel said.

I know what I have to do. I also know it is a bad idea.

"It is a bad idea," my Guardian Angel said.

It is time to make an unannounced visit, which I know is rude, but people who bushwhack me from behind have a way of getting my dandruff up.

"You'd better think more about your scalp than your dandruff," my Guardian Angel said.

CHAPTER SIXTEEN
SURREALISTIC PAINTING

Parking Matilda about 500 yards from the farmhouse I walked away from the road, into a field for several hundred yards, and then made my way cautiously to the side of the metal barn. I inched my way to the front of the barn. The doors are locked with a chain and padlock. At times people push in a lock and think it's locked but it isn't. It was not the case this time. I went to the side of the metal barn and examined the house. All the lights are on but the curtains are drawn so I can't see inside.

"If you had a squad of Navy Seals this assault would be a piece of cake," my Guardian Angel said.

"If I had a tank it would also be easy, if I had a 105 recoilless, if I had a grenade launcher, if I had wings, if I had a million bucks I'd hire a mercenary force from Louisiana. If, if, if, shut up with the if thing."

"What are you going to do now that you're hiding beside a barn and freezing to death?" he asked nonchalantly.

"I don't know."

"Good, that's good," he said. "That's real good."

There is a front porch that runs the entire width of the house. The front door is in the middle of the porch and a window is to either side of the door. There is a screen door and I figured the screen door swings out and the main door swings in.

"Have you ever seen a screen door that didn't swing out?" my Guardian Angel asked.

"Yes, when the screen door is on the inside," I said.

I started moving cautiously around the house, keeping out of the light that radiated from the house. There is one window on the side of the house with the curtains open about two inches. There is a small back porch with four steps.

A phone rang inside. It rang five times and then stopped. I figured it had been answered. The phone rang five more times and then stopped. I knew then the phone had not been answered - it is a code. A few minutes later the phone rang three times and then stopped.

Pulling my pistol out of my belt I ran to the side of the house and then inched along the wall until I was underneath the window with the curtains slightly open. I flattened myself into the wall. "Do you feel like paint?" my Guardian Angel asked.

The window is low to the ground and if I stood up the windowsill would be even with my waist. I heard a TV and a man talking on a telephone. The window had to be in the living room.

"I don't know why you don't want us to kill him. Yes, I understand. Of course we'll be careful." The man hung up.

"I think you are the, kill him," my Guardian Angel said.

I've been a lot of things in my life but I can't remember ever being a, kill him.

Now that I am pressed up against the wall of the house I am really in a bind as to what to do next. I can't stand up and look through the crack in the curtains. If I did common sense tells me I would get a bullet in the eye, which is far worse than a stick in the eye. I can't stand up and yell at whoever was inside, "come on out you clue book stealing cowards."

"Why don't you take the direct approach and knock on the door," my Guardian Angel said.

His advice is good - the simple things in life are normally the most practical.

Keeping low to the ground I inched around the corner of the house. I tip-toed across the front porch, knocked loudly on the door, ran off the front porch, around the house and went up the back porch steps in one stride. Waiting for a few moments I then beat on the back door and ran around to the side of the house.

I heard both doors open and after a few moments close.

"What is going on?" I heard a man say angrily from inside the house.

"Must be some farm kids," another man answered him.

"If I catch them they'll think farm kids," the first man said.

Waiting for about five minutes I crept once again to the front door. I knocked on the door, stepped back, and turned my back to the door, holding my pistol against my chest. The front porch light came on, the door was yanked open and the screen door pushed out so hard it banged against the wall. "What are you doing?" the man yelled as he came out of the house.

I recognized the man's voice - it was my old clue notebook stealing cowboy buddy. I spun around quickly and hit him on the side of the head with my pistol. As he thudded to the porch I rushed into the house. A man was sitting in a recliner watching TV. He started to reach for a pistol that was on an end table by the chair.

His hand circled the butt of the pistol. "Not a good idea," I said pointing my pistol at his head.

He released the pistol and put his hands where I could see them.

"You must be the guy who knocked me out," I said.

He didn't answer me.

"Get up and move slow, real slow, and put your hands above your head," I ordered.

He got out of the chair so slowly he was trying to make slow motion look fast.

When he was standing I took two quick steps toward him and kicked him in the stomach. When his head came down I kicked him in the face. When his head snapped back I slammed the pistol into the side of his head. He hit the ground like he was a practice dummy for the Green Bay Packers.

"That was dirty but that boy is definitely out," my Guardian Angel said.

I ran through the house, jumping in front of every door in a firing position. There were two bedrooms, a kitchen and a bathroom. There is nobody else in the house. I went quickly back to the front porch. The man was starting to sit up and was moaning. Blood is pouring from the side of his head. Grabbing him by the back of his shirt collar I drug him next to his friend and again smacked him in the head with my pistol. He joined his buddy as a practice dummy. There is a pole lamp in the room and I ripped the cord out of the socket and broke it off of the lamp. I placed the men back to back and wrapped the cord around their chests, pinning their arms to their sides, and pulled the cord as tight as I could before tying it. There is another lamp next to the TV and I used the cord to tie their feet together.

"Put a lampshade on each of their heads and stick a light bulb in their mouths and you're done," my Guardian Angel said.

I searched the men, neither one had a pistol or knife. I took their billfolds and set them on the table by the recliner. The pistol on the table is a snub nosed Colt 357. I stuck it in my belt.

I knew there had to be at least two weapons in the house and before the men came to I wanted to find the other one. The first bedroom has two beds and on a table between the two beds was a Walther P.38. I also stuck it in my belt.

"With all that fire power in your belt you can try out as an extra in an action movie," my Guardian Angel said. "Of course you'd have to play a bad guy."

Going back to the living room I shut the front door and locked it, made sure the back door was locked, and then I went back to the living room, turned off the TV, sat in the recliner and waited for my two cowboys without cowboy hats to wake up.

The two men look like undercover cops. It suddenly dawned on me that my deductive skills might be faulty and if they were undercover cops I was in deep grease.

"Deeper than deep grease," my Guardian Angel said. "Deep, deep, deep, deeper, deeper, deepest, deepest deep grease there is or ever will be deepest deep grease."

"You'll be there with me," I said.

"I hope they're not cops," he said.

When the two cowboys that I hoped were not cops regained consciousness they struggled into a sitting possession. It is like watching two Slinky's that are stuck together trying to go up a stairway. "Good evening, gentlemen," I said.

They turned their heads sideways to see me. I pointed the pistol at them to make sure they understood I am not on the rural Saint Ansgar welcoming committee.

Neither of the men spoke but I could tell by their eyes they would like nothing better than to draw and quarter me. People who have been hit in the head with a pistol a few times and then tied up usually aren't ready to forgive and forget.

"Where's my clue book?" I asked in a fashion I wanted them to know I am not going to waste any time on them.

Once again, neither of the men spoke.

I pulled the hammer back on my 9 m.m.

"It's in the first bedroom in the drawer of the table between the two beds," the man closest to me said quickly.

They are not cops.

I went to the bedroom and I got my clue book. I feel like a new man. What had been lost is now found. My words, my beautiful words are back in my possession.

"Don't get back on the Pulitzer Prize kick," my Guardian Angel said.

I took the men's billfolds from the table next to me. Looking at the driver's licenses I compared the photographs to each man.

"Mr. Sam Sheeps and Mr. Row Harper. I, as you know, am Bob Roosevelt. I presume it is a mutual feeling that we are not glad to meet each other."

Neither man spoke.

If they are pro crooks I didn't expect them to say a word, unless they are Mafia under bosses then they would snitch out their mother. But I have the advantage over normal police. I don't have to be Mister Nice Guy or worry about losing my job if I decide to turn Mr. Sam Sheeps and Mr. Row Harper's faces into shredded chicken.

"Roosevelt, don't go there. Remember, peace, love, take yourself to a calm place," my Guardian Angel said.

It's bad enough fighting my conscious, but also trying to justify things with a Guardian Angel makes it extremely difficult to be violent and not feel guilty afterwards.

"You boys are lucky. My Guardian Angel tells me I should cut you some slack," I said to Sam Sheeps and Row Harper.

"Stick your Guardian Angel where the sun doesn't shine," Sam Sheeps said and glared at me.

"Beat the peacock out of that low life. Rip his ears off. Cut out his tongue. Pull his fingernails out. Pinch his toes with pliers," my Guardian Angel shouted angrily.

There are not many people alive, or angels who are not alive, that have beliefs they can stick with when they are insulted.

"Are either one of you guys into cutting black cats throats?" I asked.

They looked at me like I am dumber than a P.E. teacher.

"How about stealing small diamond hearts from lonely witches?"

"What are you talking about?" Row Harper demanded.

"It was worth a try," my Guardian Angel said to me. He is relaxed again. He must have found his quiet place.

"Which one of you read my clue book?" I asked.

"I did," Row Harper said. "It's terrible. Your sentences aren't complete. You never finish a thought. Your punctuation is terrible. There is no continuity. Your plot wavers and the beginning is too slow."

For a guy who is tied up he has a lot of gall - of course it's easy to be a critic.

"What were you guys looking for at Carol's?" I asked.

I got the silent treatment.

"Who are you working for?"

I got the silent treatment.

"Who called you on the phone tonight?"

"We're not telling you anything," Sam Sheeps said.

"Nothing," Row Harper said.

"Are you sure?" I asked.

"Sure as sure," Sam Sheeps said.

"Surer than sure," Row Harper said.

I kicked Sam Sheeps in the chest, not hard but hard enough for a wakeup call. It knocked the wind out of him and he gasped for breath.

"You lousy," is all Row Harper got out of his mouth as my boot hit him in the chest. I don't want him to feel left out and not be able to gasp for breath like Sam Sheeps.

I sat back down. Watching two crooks gasping for breath is more entertaining than TV.

"Let's try this again, Mr. Sam Sheeps and Mr." is all I got out of my mouth when my Guardian screamed. "Dive! Now!"

I dove out of the chair at the same instant the window with the crack in the curtain exploded into thousands of tiny spinning knives. The curtains stood straight out like they were in a tornado. Pieces of glass hit my face and hands. The back of the chair disintegrated as shotgun pellets ripped into it. I hit the floor and rolled past Sam Sheeps and Row Harper who were jerking around trying to loosen the lamp cords that bound them together. I kept rolling and heard two more explosions. I rolled until I hit the front wall, stopped rolling, and fired three shots through the window. The report from the shots is deafening in the small room. I jumped up and ran outside through the front door. A figure is running at the end of the driveway. I fired three quick shots. A car drove up with its lights out and the passenger side door opened, but I could not make out who was driving from the faint dome light. The figure jumped in. I emptied my pistol at the fleeing car. I heard a ping as several shots hit the vehicle. With the speed in which everything had happened I couldn't make out the type of car. All I know is that it was a dark sedan.

Sticking my empty pistol in my belt I pulled out the snub nosed Colt 357 and went back inside the house. It is not a pretty sight. Sam Sheeps and Row Harper each had been shot in the head. Blood, bone and tissue are splattered all over the floor and wall. I can't recognize either of the men. The shotgun had won.

"I might get the vapors," my Guardian Angel said. "I'm going outside."

"Thanks for the warning," I said as he left.

I called Sheriff Jack Benning.

"Sheriff Jack Benning, speaking, how may I help you?" he answered, sounding out of breath.

"Sheriff, this is Roosevelt, guess what?"

"Who is it?" I heard Carol's voice in the background. She was giving young men thrills again.

"You killed somebody else," Sheriff Jack Benning kidded.

"No, two more," I said.

"Roosevelt, are you ok?" he sounded truly concerned.

"Call Bill Buffalo. I'm at the Boraxe farm at their hunting house."

"I'll be there as soon as I can. Don't go anywhere."

I guess he thought I am going to go to a pot luck dinner or

maybe take in a movie.

I went outside and looked at the stars. I don't feel sick. I don't feel much at all. I do know for sure that this time the shooter wanted to kill me.

I headed for Matilda. She has been sitting by the road lost in an old Volkswagen bug dream. I wonder if Matilda ever wishes she was a four-door sedan or if she is intelligent and accepts her lot in life. Matilda cranked right over and I drove back to the house.

I walked through the living room without looking sideways and went to the kitchen.

"Aren't you going to search the house?" my Guardian Angel asked me.

"No. I've had enough for one day. I'm going to let Bill Buffalo and his posse have first crack."

There is a small mirror over the sink and I looked at my face. There are a few cuts from the flying glass but they are no more than shaving nicks. The backs of my hands are also cut slightly. I washed my hands and face.

Sitting at the table I suddenly feel tired and wondered why things happen the way they happen? What is it in life that had put me in a farmhouse in Minnesota with two dead men in the living room? What cosmic happening set a course for my life that I will never have any rhyme or reason. What made it that I can't believe in governments or corporations but can understand their worth and their disadvantages? What makes me a pessimist never believing all will work out for the good, but still have the strength to go on?

"Life is a weird trip," my Guardian Angel said. "It's worse than bad acid."

I sat at the table thinking about skinheads, hate groups, folk music, trout fishing, Lisa's legs, Carol's laugh, Fanny's heart, my grandmother's cherry pie. It was taking too long for Sheriff Jack Benning to get here. I wondered if I should invest in a 401 K? I was running out of things to think about when I heard a siren. There was only one. I knew I should go to the living room and try and catch Sheriff Jack Benning before he stormed into the house and was attacked by a severe case of the vapors. One of these times he will break his neck.

Sheriff Jack Benning left his flashers on but turned off the siren. I waited for him on the front porch.

"I think we should go around back and wait for Bill Buffalo in the kitchen," I told him.

"No. I am the first police officer on the scene and I am supposed to secure the area," he informed me. He must have been spending time reading police procedure manuals in case he ever got transferred somewhere where they had police procedure.

"Fine with me," I said.

I followed Sheriff Jack Benning into the house. Three steps in he stopped and stared at the two headless horsemen. He looked at the pieces of brain and bone and tissue splattered on the wall, which looked like a surrealistic painting that the painter would tell you were salmon swimming through the river of life, and represented people searching for their true meaning while living on pot, speed and Hostess Twinkies.

Sheriff Jack Benning turned and looked at me. I was positioned to break his fall. "Those boys won't be answering any questions," he said calmly. "Do you think there's any coffee in this house? It will be a while before Bill Buffalo gets here."

I pointed in the direction of the kitchen. Sheriff Jack Benning is now a veteran or he finally understands that the vapors are out of fashion.

Sheriff Jack Benning made instant coffee and we sat at the table. I gave him a brief rundown on what had happened. I don't want him to feel left out when Bill Buffalo arrived.

"I wonder why Carol likes me to wear my boots while we do it?" he asked, which is a better topic than surrealistic murders.

"I think Carol likes him to wear his boots because he has ugly feet," my Guardian Angel said.

"I used to have a hippie girlfriend who wore an Indian Headdress to bed," I said.

"Why?"

"I never asked her. I felt if she didn't like my lovemaking she might scalp me."

"Do you know where she is now?"

"The last I heard she owned a jewelry shop in Santa Fe and was married to a real estate salesmen who had succeeded in jacking the prices of houses and real estate up so high the locals have had to leave town."

"I've been by Boraxe's place several times but haven't seen anything out of the ordinary," Sheriff Jack Benning told me.

"This detective thing is a slow process," I said and sipped my coffee.

"I won't give up." He sounded like Napoleon after drinking too much poison thinking about taking on Russia again.

"Why do Carol, Fanny and Sheila go out to see Father Fisher?" I asked him.

Sheriff Jack Benning's rubbed his chin. "I don't know. I've never seen them at the church."

"Have there ever been reports of mutilated cattle or anything like that in this area?"

"I've heard there were a lot when I was a little kid - that would have been twenty years ago or so and then they slowly trailed off. But then a few years ago there were a rash of mutilated horses and cattle and a lot of missing dogs and cats. The big TV station out of Minneapolis even came over and did a broadcast. There were reports it was aliens doing it. Some people thought it was a satanic group that had moved into Minnesota. Other people blamed it on kids. Nobody has been ever caught."

"Have there ever been anymore?"

"One every three or four months."

"Remember what I told you?" my Guardian Angel said.

"Witches have masses for every season," I said.

"You get a gold star by your name on the bulletin board," my Guardian Angel said. "But think about how long the mutilations have been going on?"

I did and the correlation I made was surprising.

Sheriff Jack Benning and I were on our third cup of bad coffee when we heard the cavalry arriving. We went to the front porch. Two Highway Patrol cars slid in with their sirens blaring and red lights flashing, followed by Bill Buffalo and his troops, followed by two more highway Patrol cars in their full glory, followed by an Ambulance.

The Highway Patrolmen spread out and secured the area from being attacked by skunks or deer. Bill Buffalo, flanked by Pete Rosebet and Paul Binyon walked toward us. He reminds me of a college football coach walking onto the football field being guarded by two state policemen.

I still had my pistol and Sam Sheeps and Row Harpers pistols stuck in my belt. "Roosevelt, you look like a mini Rambo," Paul Binyon commented.

"Rambo can't speak good English and gets paid more than I do," I said.

The three men put on surgical gloves and handed Sheriff Jack Benning and I a pair to put on.

When we went into the living room Pete Binyon looked at the mess and ran to the bathroom - I don't think it was a sudden attack of the runs.

"You always do a good job of it, Roosevelt," Bill Buffalo said.

"It looks like a surrealistic painting," Pete Rosebet said.

"Too much red for my taste," Sheriff Jack Benning commented.

Paul Binyon came back from the bathroom several shades lighter than most white men.

"You two get to work and explain to Benning what is going on. Roosevelt why don't you and I go to the kitchen," Bill Buffalo said.

Sitting at the table Bill Buffalo took a small tape recorder out of his pocket and turned it on. He didn't have to tell me to explain everything that had gone on. I knew he didn't have the tape recorder to record our breathing.

I told Bill Buffalo my story. When I was done he clicked off the tape recorder.

"Why would they want your clue book?" he asked himself as much as he did me.

"Franklin had something, whoever these two guys worked for wants, and he must think I know something about it. Whatever they were looking for they didn't find."

"It has to be more than money," Bill Buffalo said.

"Either that or it's a lot of money," I said.

"I told you to stay away from Boraxe. Why would you go see Lisa?" Bill Buffalo is not happy with me.

"She said she wanted to put little love nibbles all over my body," I said.

"That's a good reason," he said. Men understand the important aspects of love nibbles.

"Did she cover your ugly body with little love bites?" Bill Buffalo asked.

"No, I wouldn't let her."

"You sound like my wife," he said.

I still have the two pistols in my belt and I slid them across the table to Bill Buffalo. He didn't seem too impressed by the pistols. Real crooks carry machine guns.

"You are going to have to go see Boraxe since these guys were staying at his house," I told Bill Buffalo.

"When we went through town I went by his house. His car is in the driveway and we have his house being watched in case he tries to go somewhere. I'm going to drop in on the way back to Albert Lee."

"Can I come with you?"

"I don't know if I want to hang out with you. Everyplace you go you get shot at," he joked. "But I don't see why not."

"There's one thing I forgot. When I was outside under the window they got a phone call. You should be able to find out where it originated," I told Bill Buffalo.

"They should know better than to use phones," he said.

"When you find out about the phone call I'd like to know," I said.

He nodded.

We went back to the living room. Paul Binyon and Pete Rosebet were busy doing their detective things. Sheriff Jack Benning followed them around like a little puppy. They had three fired twelve gauge shotgun shells they had found outside the window in plastic bags, shotgun pellets from the chair in plastic bags, the billfolds, spent brass from my pistol, car keys, all in plastic bags."

"They must be out of paper sacks," my Guardian Angel said. "Normal police procedure calls for evidence to be put in paper sacks."

"They care about trees," I said.

"I'd like to know if the I.D's are real and who the car belongs to," I told Bill Buffalo.

"You should have called us before you broke into the house," Bill Buffalo said. "You're skating on thin ice on this one. These guys could have been undercover cops."

"I knocked on the door," I said.

"Vigilantes aren't allowed in this country," Bill Buffalo informed me solemnly.

He's never been to the south or Idaho.

Pete Rosebet, Paul Binyon and Jack Benning stayed in the house and Bill Buffalo and I went outside. He got a flashlight out of his car. I showed him where I had shot at the car. I showed him my route from the road to the barn and to the house. My footprints were clear. Beneath the window there is a set of boot prints that match the prints by the bush at Sheila's. The tracks were coming to and from the driveway. We followed the tracks. The shooter was dropped off at the end of the driveway, walked to the side of the house, fired, and ran back to the driveway where he or she was picked up.

"It's obvious there were two people," Bill Buffalo said.

"I wonder why the shooter didn't come to the door." I asked.

"They might have seen your car down the road."

It made sense only if they had driven by and then turned around, which I had a feeling they did not do.

"Five men have now been killed trying to kill you," Bill Buffalo said.

"It's five men the world doesn't need," I commented dryly, meaning every word of it.

"You could take a job with police departments all over the country. If you worked an area for a year all the criminals who tried to kill you would end up dead and there would be no more crime."

"Somebody would get me in time," I said

"Somebody will get you, Roosevelt," Bill Buffalo told me and patted me on the shoulder like he was my father and he knew I was in for a rough time if I didn't change my ways.

Going back toward the house my Guardian Angel had been silent for so long I was worried.

"Not to worry," my Guardian Angel said. "I've been analyzing the murder part of this case."

My Guardian Angel at times likes to think he is a private detective.

"What have you been analyzing?"

"I think Sheriff Jack Benning is involved?"

"That's ludicrous. But tell me why you think that?"

"Not now. There are too many cops around."

"They can't hear you."

"The bugs N.S.A. have developed you can't be sure of that," he whispered.

"We're done," Pete Rosebet told Bill Buffalo when we got back to the house.

The paramedics had loaded up what was left of Sam Sheeps and Row Harper and were leaving with their flashers blinking and their siren blaring. I suppose it's the only taps many of us will be honored with.

"Let's go pay a visit to Mr. Dale Boraxe," Bill Buffalo said. "Pete, you drive Roosevelt's car. He can ride with me. Sheriff Benning thanks for your help."

Sheriff Jack Benning saluted and winked at me. I take it he has kept our little secret. He got in his car and drove off.

Paul Binyon didn't look too happy about driving Matilda. I know Matilda isn't happy about the situation at all. She was illegally strip searched over fifty times during the hippie days and still hasn't recovered enough to trust cops.

I suddenly remembered something. "Did any of you guys search the metal barn?" I asked.

Paul Binyon and Pete Rosebet looked at each other like they both were stupid.

"The metal barn is locked with a chain and padlock," I said.

Pete Rosebet got a set of bolt cutters out of the trunk. Every good cop car has a set of bolt cutters.

Pete Rosebet snapped the lock on the metal barn. There is a light switch on the wall. There are several stacks of wood pallets in the barn and a forklift but nothing else.

I shrugged my shoulders.

All the lights except the front porch lights were out as we drove by Gone with the Wind.

"Have there ever been reports of satanic markings anywhere

around here?" I asked Bill Buffalo.

"No."

"Are you a Catholic?" I asked.

"Lutheran."

"I'm a believer in football," Pete Rosebet said.

"Sheriff Benning is a Catholic," Bill Buffalo said.

"I'll be," my Guardian Angel said.

I thought it was strange. Not so much that Sheriff Jack Benning is a Catholic. But why didn't he know Fanny, Carol and Sheila went out to the church? Saint Ansgar is not the size of Rome. People don't get lost in the crowd here.

It was 3 a.m. when we got to the Boraxe home in town. It took Dale Boraxe ten minutes to answer the door. Dale looked at Bill Buffalo, Pete Rosebet and Paul Binyon and smiled. He looked at me and made a face like he had swallowed unsweetened grapefruit juice. "Come on in gentlemen," he said, not looking nervous at all.

"Sit down," he told us.

"Would you make us some coffee?" he told Merriam.

Merriam headed for the kitchen like a good little wife should.

"I'm not going to go into all the details but two men were killed tonight at the house you rent out to hunters. Whoever killed them also tried to kill Roosevelt," Bill Buffalo told Dale.

Dale didn't bat an eye. "Roosevelt, you should paint a target on your back," he said.

I thought it strange he didn't wonder why I was at his house.

"I saw two men get dropped off at your airstrip yesterday," I said to Dale Boraxe. I couldn't tell I didn't really see them but Lisa had told me. "And you drove them somewhere."

Bill Buffalo gave me a surprised look letting me know if I didn't start telling him everything I was doing or had found out I was headed for the jail house.

Dale gave me an amused smile, which I didn't expect.

Merriam brought in the coffee.

"Go wake up Mr. Mahan and Mr. Foreman," Dale told Merriam and continued. "I rented the house to two men who called last week. They said they were looking at property in the area and needed a place to stay for a few days. I met them in town at the bar three days ago and led them out to the house."

"Who was at the bar when you met them?" Bill Buffalo asked.

"Brenda."

"What were they driving?" Bill Buffalo asked.

"A black Chevy four door. Seemed like nice guys. If I remember, their names were Mr. Sam Sheeps and Mr. Row Harper."

Two men in their early forties came from the back of the house. Their bathrobes cost more than my car and even woken up from a deep sleep the men reeked money and power. "These are the two men I picked up at my airport, Roosevelt. This is Mr. Shawn Mahan and Mr. Don Foreman from the Law Firm of Mahan and Foreman out of Kansas City. They are my attorneys and for the last day and a half we have always been together."

"Have you ever felt about an inch tall?" my Guardian Angel asked me.

The next few minutes were spent listening to Bill Buffalo explaining what had happened at the house and apologizing for the inconvenience.

After we left the house Bill Buffalo put his stubby finger about an inch from my nose. "If you hold information from me I'm going to stuff your head in a pop bottle," he threatened.

"You should run a check on those two attorneys," I said.

"Idiot," he snarled, which I don't know if that meant he was or wasn't going to run a check on Shawn Mahan and Don Foreman.

CHAPTER SEVENTEEN
OH FANNY WHAT A BIG NOSE YOU HAVE

It was close to 4 a.m. when I got to Carol's. The living room light is on but the door is locked.

"Don't even say it," I warned my Guardian Angel.

I rang the doorbell.

To my surprise Carol answered the door immediately. She didn't even say good morning but turned around and headed for the kitchen. I know I am supposed to follow her. Sitting at the table she started to pour me a cup of coffee. "No coffee, I've had enough in the last two hours I won't be able to sleep for two years," I told her. "How about a beer?"

She got two beers out of the refrigerator and sat. I guzzled the beer. She gave me hers and she got two more. She took a swallow of her beer, studied me carefully for a few moments and said. "I'm glad you're not dead."

"You stayed up all night to tell me that?"

"I had company for a while," she smiled coyly.

She didn't know I knew she had been playing black boots with Sheriff Jack Benning.

"Did Sheriff Jack Benning stop by here about an hour ago or call you?" I asked Carol.

"No," she said.

I finished my beer and opened another one. Beer is always a better early breakfast than bacon and eggs - beer has more carbohydrates.

"What were those men looking for when they broke into my

house?" Carol asked. "It took me hours to clean up my room."

"Franklin must have been involved with some tough people. He had to have something they wanted. Something so important they are willing to kill for it. The problem is neither the police nor I have any idea what the people are looking for."

"I don't know who Franklin could have been involved with to cause this much trouble?" Carol said sounding perplexed.

"That is the big question?" I said.

I finished the beer. "I'll see you when I get up," I told her and headed for my room.

I put my clue book on top of the dresser. With all the beer and coffee I'd drank, with no food, my stomach feels like it is a sailboat. Aluminum Sulfate isn't really one of my favorite things but I picked up the bottle of Maalox I'd found in Franklin's car. I unscrewed the cap and started to lift it to my mouth but stopped - there is a slight odor that isn't right. I've never heard of Maalox spoiling. I smelled the Maalox again. I decided I would take the Maalox to Bill Buffalo and have it tested.

Waking up at 9 a.m. I feel surprisingly good. It is a new day. My whole life stretches out before me. There is no past, no future, only now, the moment.

"You sound like a college freshman, grow up, Roosevelt," my Guardian Angel said.

I started worrying about everything I had to do. But at least I feel normal, feeling free and carefree could screw everything up.

Carol was gone and I took an extra-long shower, took time to trim my beard - everything is vanity - and put on clean clothes. I even took time to fry some bacon and eggs.

Over the past two days I'd learned a lot concerning the murder. Concerning Fanny's stolen heart and her dead cats I think I know who did it but I'm not certain. I cleaned my pistol and refilled the clip - carrying an unloaded pistol is a false sense of security. I got my clue book and added everything I had not been able to add since a low life scumbag, who is now dead, had stolen it, and not appreciated what he had read. When I finished writing I read all the clues. When I was done I put the book in my suitcase, stuck my pistol in my belt, put the bottle of Maalox in my coat pocket and started to leave.

"Aren't you forgetting something?" my Guardian Angel asked.

"Carol is gone. It's too late to get a key," I said.

"Guess again oh one who thinks short-term memory is caused by genetics?"

"Do I get a clue?"

"Clue number one. Sheriff Jack Benning?"

"You told me last night you think Sheriff Jack Benning is involved with the murder and you would tell me today?"

"Yes.” There was a long pause.

"Well, why?"

"You have to apologize.”

"Apologize for what?"

"Last night you implied my thinking was ludicrous."

"I'm sorry," I said, but didn't really mean it. Sometimes in life it's easier to tell little white fibs. I suppose I could tell little black fibs if I wanted, but I don't know what the difference would be.

"Ok, listen to this reasoning," my Guardian Angel said. "After Sam Sheeps and Row Harper were killed you called Sheriff Jack Benning. You heard Carol's voice in the background. You assumed Carol and he were at Carol's house playing the old skin game. But, they didn't have to be. Sheriff Jack Benning has a cell phone. They could have been in his car or another car. Carol could have dropped him off, he could have tried to shoot you, missed only because of me, thank you, dusted Sam Sheeps and Row Harper because they might talk, and Carol could have picked him up.”

"That's not bad," I said. "But how would Sheriff Jack Benning known I was at the house."

"Either Lisa called Sheriff Jack Benning or they were coming out to see Sam Sheeps and Row Harper."

"Why?"

"I don't know everything. You're the detective I'm an analyzer."

"Sorry oh analytical one," I said.

"There's more. When Sheriff Jack Benning walked into the room and looked at Sam Sheeps and Row Harper he didn't get an attack of the vapors. The reason he didn't was because he was the one that turned their heads into cherry jelly. What do you think?"

"I am truly intrigued but I'll have to think about it and see how it fits in the scheme of things," I said. "But don't quit your day job."

"I can't quit," he replied sadly.

I drove to the bar. Two old men are playing cribbage and Ginger and Brenda, alias Mom, were cleaning. They both smiled at me but kept working. I sat at the bar and let them dust and empty ashtrays. I never like to get in the way of women's domestic instincts. When they were done they came over.

"I heard you thinned out two more of the criminal element," Brenda said not sounding greatly concerned. "And your room was ransacked."

"It had to be the two men that were asking about you at the cafe," Ginger said.

"Did Dale Boraxe meet two men here a few days ago?" I asked Brenda.

"Yes he did. He met two men who looked like cowboys only they didn't wear cowboy hats."

"They had short hair?" Ginger said to Brenda.

"Why yes," she said, sounding surprised.

"Did they get here before Dale did?" I asked.

"Yes they did?"

"Did they ask you any questions?"

"They wanted to know where you lived," Brenda said and then covered her mouth with her hand. "Oh no, it was the men, I told them where you lived, Roosevelt. I'm so sorry."

It's the little things in life that tend to topple the mountain.

"Who told you two about the two guys getting killed?" I asked.

"Sheriff Jack Benning ate at the cafe this morning. He told me about the men breaking into your room. How you got busted in the head and getting shot at out at the Boraxe house and the men getting killed," Ginger said.

Brenda set a Guinness in front of me and poured Ginger and her a shot of peach schnapps. It had to be noon somewhere in the world. "The beer is on the house and I promise I will never tell anybody anything about you again," she said and we toasted.

"I don't like people who make promises," my Guardian Angel said.

"Are you and Earl still together?" I asked Brenda.

"Yes we are, but my invitation to you is still open. Variety is the spice of life you know," she smiled and she and Ginger laughed.

It was my cue to exit stage left. I am demoralized. All the women in Saint Ansgar only want me for my body. Not one of them has even attempted to get to know me, to see my inner self, to once look at me from the shoulders up. What is a man to do who is trying to find meaning in life and is considered nothing more than a sex object?

I headed to Fanny's. If Fanny was gone I'd talk to Clyde.

Fanny was gone. She and Sheila and Carol might be out having a heart to heart with Father Fisher again. The note was on the cash register and Clyde was on the table eating grapes. I noticed Clyde's bird stand was by the window. Clyde swallowed a grape - I felt like telling him to be careful of the seeds - he looked at me, took a couple of hops, which were cute in a raven sort of way, and squawked, "Crap, cowboy."

I sat down at the table with Clyde.

"Clyde. Who killed the cats?" I asked.

"Bad cat, bad cat," Clyde squawked.

"Clyde. Who stole Fanny's heart?" I asked.

"Damn farmer," Clyde squawked.

"Clyde. Who killed Franklin?" I asked.

"Not you, not you, not you," Clyde squawked.

The conversation with Clyde isn't going anywhere so I went upstairs to Fanny's storage room. I had found the robe, silver plate, knives and satanic bible in the bottom box of the stack of boxes in the corner. I pulled out the bottom box again. It is empty.

"Oh, oh," my Guardian Angel said.

I searched all the boxes in the stack. There was nothing except hearts.

I quickly went through every box in the room and found nothing out of the ordinary.

I went to Fanny's room and looked in her clothes closet. The rifle was still gone. I checked her drawers, there were no bullets.

I scanned the room the way people do when they are going on a trip and know they are forgetting something but don't know what it is. My eyes stopped on the table by the chair. There is a book and next to it a phone pager. I picked up the pager like it was a hand grenade.

"Why little Miss Fanny Ruth, what a big nose you have," my Guardian Angel said.

I was about to put the pager down when it beeped and a number appeared on the screen. "Memorize this," I quickly told my Guardian Angel.

I went downstairs. There is a pad and paper by the cash register and my Guardian Angel told me the phone number.

Clyde is still munching grapes.

I went out the side door and looked over at Jimmy's house. The snowman is still a snowman and makes me smile. I walked to the convenience store and called the phone number I had written down. The phone rang three times. "Saint Ansgar Bank, President Earl Harberts speaking."

I hung up.

I called Detective Bill Buffalo. "How'd you like to have lunch?" I asked him.

"Get up here. I want to talk to you," he replied gruffly and hung up.

I take it missing out on sleep makes Bill Buffalo a not too happy camper or he wasn't hungry.

The drive was enjoyable and the sun was out. When I walked into Bill Buffalo's office I knew he couldn't care less about the sun.

"Sit down bongo head," he grumbled as I put the bottle of Maalox on his desk.

My rear had no sooner hit the chair then he started in on me. "That little deal last night when you told Boraxe you'd seen him with two other men peeved me off."

I started to say something but he held up his hand in the common gesture of don't talk you jerk.

I didn't talk so I guess I'm a jerk.

"I have given you a lot of slack. I've given you back your pistol when by all rights you shouldn't be allowed to carry a pistol. I've told you everything that we have uncovered. I know you haven't told me everything you've found out so start talking and talk fast. If you don't your pistol is going into the evidence room and I'm going to give you free room and board until you decide to talk."

"Run your head, spill your guts, talk," my Guardian Angel

implored me.

"Are you afraid of small dark cramped rooms?" I asked him.

"No, jailhouse sex," my Guardian Angel said.

I started to spill my guts. I told Bill Buffalo everything that had gone on since I have been in Saint Ansgar, finished, I told him, "I'm told out.”

"Tell him about my theory about Sheriff Jack Benning," my Guardian Angel said.

"No, I'm told out," I told my Guardian Angel.

"You're selfish. You want all the glory for yourself," he pouted.

"Are you sure you're told out?" Bill Buffalo asked.

"I'm positive I'm told out," I said..

"In other words, a lot has happened to you that you have not reported to me, but you don't know anything?" he said.

"I know for sure who one of the people is who killed Franklin. I am almost positive I know who another one is. But I don't know why he was killed," I said.

"Who are they?" he demanded.

"I'm not telling," I said. "Not until I wrap this thing up."

"I can lock you up for withholding evidence," he threatened.

"I'm not withholding evidence. There is no evidence," I said.

Glaring at me he asked, "Who stole Fanny's heart and killed the cats?”

"I have two ideas but nothing solid," I answered him truthfully, but not all that truthfully.

Bill Buffalo started laughing and picked up the bottle of Maalox. My tolding him everything must have cheered him up or he thinks Maalox is funny.

He looked at the bottle of Maalox. "Thanks for the gift but my stomach is fine," he said.

"I want that tested. I think it might have poison in it," I said.

He put the bottle of Maalox back down like it was a poisonous spider.

"Remember the cat hair I had tested and it had arsenic poison in it?" I said.

Bill Buffalo nodded.

"I think that Maalox will have the same poison in it."

"We have a lab here in town. I can get you the results by this evening."

"Did you find out who called Sam Sheeps and Row Harper?" I asked.

"The call came from the pay phone at the convenience store in Saint Ansgar, so no lead," Bill Buffalo said, "but their I.D.'s checked out. They were really Sam Sheeps and Row Harper. They came from Kansas City and the car was registered to Sam Sheeps."

"That's three guys from Kansas City who should have stayed home," I said.

"Both men were in and out of jail on charges ranging from assault to extortion?"

"Any mob ties?" I asked.

"Not that I know of," Bill Buffalo answered.

"Strange, first it's a professional hit man and then it's two amateurs," I said.

"Maybe the wise guys are running out of money. Their lawyer bills have been high the last few years," Bill Buffalo said.

"I have a question for you," I said.

"Shoot," he said.

He might shoot after I asked the question.

"When I was searching Bill and Joe's trailer I found a calendar of pin up girls who look like they enjoy sucking Harley Davidson exhaust pipes."

"Did you bring it," Bill Buffalo said sounding excited.

"No."

"Too bad," he said.

"On the calendar were four phone numbers that had been recently written down. There was Carol's, Boraxe's house in town, Sheriff Jack Benning and your office number. What gives?"

Bill Buffalo took a deep breath but he didn't look angry or guilty. Most of the cases I've worked on recently have involved dirty cops and I really don't want Bill Buffalo to be a dirty cop.

"Why Carol's number is on the calendar I don't know. I know Dale Boraxe did hire them to clean up his buildings around the house, which might be the reason they had his number. The reason they had my number and Sheriff Jack Benning's number is because they were snitches for me and I told them if they couldn't get hold of me to contact Benning."

"Low life snitches," my Guardian Angel said.

Nobody likes snitches. Not even angels.

"Remember the time I told you about the car ring we'd busted and the farmer who was letting the thieves strip the cars at his farm. Bill and Joe turned us on to the operation."

"That still doesn't mean they weren't doing things illegally themselves," I said.

"Birds of a feather flock together," Bill Buffalo said, which isn't original but is easy to understand.

"You told me the Feds were investigating Dale and Merriam Boraxe. Have you heard anything from them?" I asked.

"Nothing."

"Strange," I commented.

I was still hung up on the strange while Bill Buffalo picked up a box from behind his desk. "This dome has been here for days," he said and slid it over to me.

"Did you check into Shawn Mahan and Don Foreman?" I asked.

"I made a call but haven't gotten anything back yet."

Standing I picked up the box. I gathered Bill Buffalo wasn't going to take my pistol and lock me up. "You keep me posted," he told me sternly. "You're not off the hook yet and I'll call you this evening on this Maalox. I'll be here, I have tons of paper work to catch up on."

Driving back to Saint Ansgar the news about Bill and Joe being snitches didn't settle right.

"This is one complicated case," my Guardian Angel said.

Fanny was in the Tea Room stringing hearts on fishing line to hang in the rooms - the needle was in her left hand. She smiled at me like I had been gone for a week and she was Bonnie and I was Clyde and I'd robbed a bank in Missouri, killed four guards, three kids and two dogs and now I was going to take her to a big hotel in Kansas City for the weekend.

I sat down. "Here's the top of your dome," I said.

"It's no big deal," she said.

"You look happy," I said.

"It's hard to get depressed when somebody tried to kill you but you didn't get killed," Fanny said.

In its own weird way the statement made sense.

"Me love you," Clyde squawked.

I don't know if he was talking to Fanny or me but I really didn't care. Most love is bird brained anyway.

"You have become the talk of the town," Fanny said with a tint of pride in her voice.

"Why do you and Carol and Sheila go out and see Father Fisher?" I asked.

Fanny looked startled for an instant and as quickly regained her composure and said. "We have discussions about life. We are all trying to get over our fears and find a deeper meaning than everyday life gives us."

"You should go," my Guardian Angel said.

"How are you coming on Franklin's murder?" Fanny asked.

"I know who killed Franklin," I told her. My answer startled her and she dropped the heart she was stringing.

"Who killed Franklin?" she demanded more than asked.

"I can't say."

"You can tell me, Roosevelt, I won't tell a soul."

"She might not tell a soul but she'd tell a person," my Guardian Angel said.

Looking at my watch it is 3:00 p.m. "I have to do some money transfers. Maybe we can get together tonight."

"I'd love to," Fanny replied but her heart didn't seem to be in it.

I walked to the bank and got there fifteen minutes before closing time. I went directly to Earl Harberts office. Protocol is for sissies. When Earl saw me standing in the door he looked at me like I am the grim reaper.

I got right to the point. "Has Fanny paid off the loan you told me she's only been able to pay interest on?"

"I can't tell you that. I've told you too much already," he said.

"I wonder if your wife would like to know that you are calling Fanny." I said.

He looked startled, which meant he was dialing more than Fanny's phone number.

"How do you know about Fanny?"

"A man has to have his little secrets," I replied implying that I know more than I do.

"She hasn't paid off her note."

"Thank you, you sly devil you," I said, winked at him, and left.

"Blackmail does not become you," my Guardian Angel said sounding disappointed.

"I know. It's a lousy thing to do."

"But if you're ever going to try it again ask for some money and not just information," he said.

On the way to Ginger's house I had a small insight.

"It has to be small for you to have an insight," my Guardian Angel said.

The hit man had been from Kansas City and Sam Sheeps and Row Harper had been from Kansas City. It stood to reason whatever Franklin had been involved with was from Kansas City, and if Dale Boraxe was involved with something crooked, like Lisa suspected, it might stem from Kansas City.

"I thought Kansas City was only famous for its barbecue," my Guardian Angel said.

"They have top of line organized crime in Kansas City," I informed him.

Jimmy wasn't outside so I knocked on the door. After a few moments I heard his voice. "Who's there?"

His mother is a smart lady. She has taught him not to answer the door when he is alone.

"It's Bob."

The door swung open. Jimmy grinned at me like I am one step higher than the Tooth Fairy. "Bob, come on in. I've missed you."

It's nice to be missed by a little boy.

He grabbed my hand as soon as he shut the door and started pulling me toward the kitchen. "I want to show you, hurry, hurry."

Jimmy had the deck of cards spread out in the game of solitary I had shown him. "See, I play the game you taught me," he said excitedly.

Jimmy picked all the cards up and shuffled the deck. "I can shuffle now," he smiled.

"I'm real proud of you. Let me see the cards."

I tapped the cards even, split the deck and felt a small

indentation on one of the cards. "Let's go to the store and I'll buy you a new deck of cards if you let me have these back. What do you think?"

"You bet," he grinned and ran and got his coat.

I put the old deck in my pocket.

"How's your mom?" I asked Jimmy as we walked.

"She seems happier, Bob, she hasn't been crying as much. I like it when she doesn't cry. When she cries it makes me sad but there is nothing I can do. I think it's my fault."

"Moms have to cry sometimes. But it's not your fault."

I put my hand on his shoulder. His little shoulders are too small to have to carry a heavy load.

We went into the convenience store and Jimmy couldn't decide if he wanted a red deck or a blue deck. I bought him one of each. He was so excited as we walked back to his house it was like I'd bought him a new car.

We sat at the table and he opened the blue deck and practiced shuffling. Because it was a new deck, cards shot everywhere each time he shuffled. We laughed.

Jimmy shuffled and shuffled and then had to go to the bathroom. As soon as the bathroom door shut I went to Ginger's bedroom. There is a king-sized bed, unmade, a small dresser with a few photographs of Jimmy on the top. I looked under the bed, nothing. I quickly went through the drawers, nothing. I looked in the closet. Ginger doesn't own many clothes but there is Fanny's Sako 308 in the corner with a box of shells on the floor that had four missing. Also in the corner is a Mossberg semi-automatic twelve-gauge shotgun.

"Women in this town don't trade recipes. They trade guns," my Guardian Angel said.

Hearing the toilet flush I hurried back to the kitchen.

Jimmy sat down and started to pick up the cards. "I want to ask you a few serious questions and I want you to tell me the truth, Jimmy. Will you do that?" I said seriously.

Jimmy looked me in the eyes and then bent his head and looked at the tabletop.

"Will you tell me the truth?"

"I will," he replied quietly but he wouldn't look at me.

"Did you take Fanny's diamond heart from underneath the dome?" I asked him.

He looked me straight in the eyes. "No, I didn't," he said.

I rubbed his greasy head. "I didn't think you did," I said, relieved by his answer.

"Now, did you do anything with the dead cats that were in the cellar?"

Looking away from me he fidgeted in his chair. He picked up the deck of cards. "Come on Jimmy. I'm your friend," I said.

"I took them and put them in a ditch on the edge of town. I didn't like them, Bob. They were creepy," he said in a voice like he thought I would punish him.

"That's ok. I can understand," I said.

He grinned at me in relief.

"Do you happen to have a magnifying glass I can borrow?" I asked Jimmy. I had one when I was a kid but all I did with it was burn ants.

"Roosevelt, that was a terrible thing to do," my Guardian Angel said.

"It's always bothered me," I confessed.

"I have one," Jimmy said, running to his room. He ran back and handed me a magnifying glass. "My mom got it for me last year for my birthday."

"I won't lose it, I promise," I said, and for some reason asked. "When is your Mom's birthday?"

"It was last week?"

We practiced shuffling cards until I felt it was time for me to go. I have some card shuffling to do myself.

"I would never lie to you, Bob," he said as he opened the door for me.

"I hope not."

"Next time you come let's go to my secret place. Ok?"

"Ok."

I didn't tell him since I know about the room it no longer is a secret place.

CHAPTER EIGHTEEN
THE 13TH FLOOR ELEVATORS

It is close to 5 p.m. and Carol is not home. I have luck on my side - she left the front door unlocked.

"How can you keep forgetting to ask for a key?" my Guardian Angel chastised me.

"How can you talk so much and say nothing?" I told him.

"I won't talk then."

"Good."

"You'll miss not hearing my voice."

"I promise you I won't miss it for a while."

I went to my room and got the other deck of Franklin's cards, my clue book and pencil and sat on the floor.

I took the deck of cards I got from Jimmy and sorted it by suits in the way a new deck of cards comes in the pack - spades, diamonds, clubs, and hearts. I then put each suit in numerical order.

I did the same thing with the other deck.

"See how bored you get when I'm not talking to you," my Guardian Angel said.

"Shut up."

"Testy, testy."

"If you would give me some time to think I'm pretty sure I can solve this case and we can get out of here. When I do we will go where it's warm and women only wear bikinis when the nude beach is closed."

"My lips are sealed, zipped, clamped, fastened, glued, stapled, sewn."

I picked up the ace of spades and looked at the back of the card with Jimmy's magnifying glass. In the upper right corner is a tiny 9 that had been made by poking dots with a needle or pin, but had not gone completely through the card. Running my finger over the 9 I could feel the indentations, but without looking at the dots with a magnifying glass I would not have been able to tell they formed the number 9.

I remembered the magnifying glass that was on top of Franklin's dresser when Fanny and I searched his house. I should have known it meant something.

On the back of the two of spades there is a 1. On the back of the three of spades there is a 3. There were marks on the rest of spades but no numbers. I wrote the numbers in my clue book.

The ace through six of diamonds each has a number on the back: 4, 4, 6, 7, 4, 6, 3. I wrote the numbers in my clue book.

The rest of the deck has marks on the cards but no numbers.

I repeated the process with the other deck. The ace through three of spades has three numbers: 9, 1, 3. I didn't have to write them down - my memory isn't that bad.

The ace through six of diamonds has seven numbers - 4, 4, 6, 8, 1, 1, 7. I wrote them down.

The rest of the deck had markings but no numbers.

I have eighteen numbers. "What do you think? I asked my Guardian Angel.

There was no reply.

"Answer me. What do you think?" I demanded.

"You have to be a Pisces, Roosevelt. You are confusing to be with. First you want me to shut up and then you want me to speak."

"I want you to shut up until I ask you to speak and I'm not a fish I'm a Taurus. Now answer my question."

"You are a good Taurus, Roosevelt. You're bull headed, you used to be a hippie and liked to roll in the dirt and you're full of manure," my Guardian Angel said, and then answered my question. "It's obvious, the numbers are two phone numbers: 913-446-7463 and 913-446-8117," he said like he was an English butler who was talking to the cleaning lady.

It is slightly after six and time to call Bill Buffalo. Driving to the convenience store the sun started to set.

Bill Buffalo picked up the phone but before he could speak I said, "I have some information for you to check out. Got a pencil handy?"

Bill Buffalo grunted which I took for a yes. I gave him the two phone numbers. "How long will it take to find out who they belong too?"

"As fast as my little fingers can do the walking," he replied.

"How about the Maalox?"

"How about it?"

Everyone thinks they are a comedian anymore.

"The Maalox is full of arsenic. It is the same poison that was in the cat hair."

"Oh, oh," my Guardian Angel said.

"Have you found out anything on those two attorneys Shawn Mahan and Don Foreman?"

"Not yet."

"I'll call you back in thirty minutes," I said and hung up.

I have thirty minutes to kill. I decided to go for a drive. Driving clears my mind. I headed toward the Saint Ansgar Church. When I past the church I saw, in the pale light, the Chevy sedan but not the Ford van. I continued on for a quarter mile, pulled over, got out of Matilda and jogged back to the church. It is now dark. I snuck around the church until I was between the church and Father Fisher's house. The lights are on in the house and the curtains are closed. Making my way quickly to the Chevy I looked for bullet holes. There weren't any. I barely made it back to the rear of the church when headlights swung into the driveway. I pressed up against the wall of the church as the Ford van pulled in and parked, luckily for me on the far side of the Chevy so the headlights did not shine on me, but hit the front of the house. The headlights went out. I heard many people walking to the front door, a loud knock and the door open. When the door closed I went to a side window of the house and put my ear against the glass. Over the next few minutes I heard many voices: Sheila, Fanny, Brenda and Earl Harberts, Ginger, Grace and George Brethern, Lisa, Dale and Merriam Boraxe, Officer Jack Benning and Father Fisher. I couldn't make out what they were talking about.

"Oh, oh, oh, oh, oh, oh, oh, oh, oh, oh, oh, oh," my Guardian

Angel said.

I was about to leave when I heard a car pulling into the driveway and I ran toward the side of the church, but before I could make the corner, the headlights hit me in the back. "Who are you? Stop!! What are you doing?" Carol hollered as I sprinted around the corner.

I ran to Matilda as fast as my 62 year old legs will let me, jumped in and drove away. I didn't see anybody behind me but, if there is, Matilda, no matter how hard she tries, is not a good getaway car.

"I hope Carol didn't recognize you," my Guardian Angel said.

Hearing all the people together set off a series of bells in my head.

"You're a regular ding-dong," my Guardian Angel said.

I drove for a few minutes and turned around. When I went by the church I tried with all my cosmic powers to turn Matilda and myself invisible. I don't have to worry about my Guardian Angel, he is invisible. The Ford van and Chevy were still in front of Father Fisher's house and I didn't see anybody outside.

I called Bill Buffalo from the store. He must have caller I.D. because he started right off. "Where did you get those phone numbers?" he demanded, reminding me of a S.S. officer in an old World War II war movie who is grilling a French resistance fighter that has been caught with a satchel full of photographs of German women playing with donkeys.

"Would you believe in a box of Cracker Jacks?" I replied.

"Not funny."

I explained the deck of cards. When I finished there was a long silence and I could hear Bill Buffalo tapping a pencil or pen on his desk. "How did you get the idea to check the cards? he asked.

"Pure luck," I told him the truth. "It's the old bumble and fumble along thing you and I talked about once."

"Those phone numbers belong to Mr. Dale Owens. Dale Owens runs the biggest illegal gambling operation in Kansas City. The first number is to his home and the second one is to a place where bets are dropped off. Word is Owens has spread his operation over the past several years into St. Joseph, Omaha and Minneapolis."

"Owens doesn't sound like a wise guy name," I said.

"He's Irish and hates Italians. His favorite pass time is whacking mob guys when they get in his way. With all the heavy fire the mob guys are under from the Feds they try and avoid as much trouble as they can so they have learned to leave him alone. Word is Dale Owens also has a few key politicians in his pocket and more than one judge. People around him who get busted always seem to get probation or light prison time."

"I'll be dipped in snuff," I said. "What do you think it all means?"

"Maybe Franklin was taking big bets for Owens and decided to keep the money and Owens sent boys to kill him. Maybe somebody knew Franklin was handling big money and they killed him and stole the money?"

"Maybe," I said, but I don't think all of Bill Buffalo's assumptions are true.

"What do you think?" he asked me, letting me know by the tone in his voice it wasn't time for me to be keeping secrets.

"I have an idea but I don't know for sure," I said.

Bill Buffalo was satisfied with my answer. "You'll like this," he said, like he was going to give me a present. "Those two attorneys, Shawn Mahan and Don Foreman are Dale Owens's attorneys. He has them under exclusive retainer. Both Mahan and Foreman are under investigation for setting up off shore corporations for the sole purpose of laundering money."

"Life has many twisting roads," my Guardian Angel said.

I have wanted to ask Bull Buffalo a certain question for several days but have not. Now is the time. "How did you know right away that Peter Thompson, the first man who I killed, was a hit man from Kansas City?" I asked.

"Are you insinuating I'm a dirty cop?" Bill Buffalo asked, but not angrily.

"I hope not," I told him the truth.

"I have two brothers on the police force in Kansas City. One's been in an organized crime unit for fifteen years and the other one has been in homicide for twelve years. We have traded information for years. How do you think I checked those two phone numbers so quickly? And how do you think I found out about Mahan and

Foreman?"

"I had to ask," I said, trying to sound apologetic.

"You keep me posted," Bill Buffalo said, now angry, and slammed the phone down.

An honest man does not like his integrity questioned.

"Why would an honest man care?" my Guardian Angel asked.

I bought two pre-made sandwiches, a bag of chips and a carton of chocolate milk. Standing outside I ate the sandwiches and chips and drank the milk. I should have thrown the sandwiches and chips away and eaten the wrappers - the wrappers would have more vitamins in them.

I went to Carol's and got out my clue book and collection of things I've found, tossed them on the bed, took my boots off, propped the pillows against the head board, sat down on the bed, leaned back against the pillows, stretched, shut my eyes and started breathing slowly and deeply. In goes the good air out goes the bad air. With the condition the air is in now the statement should really be - in goes the heavily polluted air out goes the heavily polluted air. I repeated the process for ten minutes. The tension slowly drained from my body. My mind became clear.

“Your mind becoming clear, that’s a good one,” my Guardian Angel said, “All you are getting is pollution high.”

Opening my eyes I read slowly and deliberately my clues and questions.

When I was done my Guardian Angel said. "I think you should make out a will."

"Is it that bad?"

"Bad vibes man, really bad vibes."

"I wonder who I can leave Matilda too?"

"Who would want her?"

"Be careful. You know how women are when they are scorned?"

The idea of bad vibes doesn't really bother me. Bad vibes have always been a part of my life. If it wasn't for bad vibes I'd have no vibes at all.

I read all the clues one more time. I feel like I am standing on a diving board and the pool below me is the cat killing, heart stealing, murder case, water. All I have to do is jump off the board and the solution will come to me before I hit the water. The only problem is I swim like a rock and I am afraid of heights.

"You told me you know who killed Franklin," my Guardian Angel said.

"I do."

"I think you know who killed the cats and stole the heart," he said.

"I think so."

"So let's get out of here. You're alive, that's all that matters."

"If I did my mind would always be puzzled."

"Your mind's a riddle anyway. What does it matter?"

I ignore questions about myself that have too much truth to them.

I put my collection of things and my clue book in my suitcase, put my boots and coat on, stuck my pistol in my belt and headed for the door.

The night is clear and the moon is almost full. In the Southwest it's called a smugglers moon. The starlight sparkles off the frozen snow. The sparkles remind me of lost dreams trying to escape the confines of earth. I wonder why so many years of our lives are wasted trying to gain things that have no intrinsic meaning. Why the majority of our decisions revolve around what we want other people to think of us? It is like we are puppets but we can't pull our own strings. Who is the puppet master?

Walking toward Sheriff Jack Benning's house I was passing houses with husbands and wives in them, children, each house a little world of it's own, a world of individual wants and needs, desires and hopes, each lost and out of control, only trying to hold on until things get better, maybe until the complete earth is one united family.

"You're acting strange, Roosevelt," my Guardian Angel said.

"I've come to accept myself," I said.

"There is hope," he said.

"Where?"

"Somewhere far away and hiding, afraid to come out, but there is hope."

"Will I ever find it?"

"I doubt it. But don't quit trying. Ok?"

"I hope not."

There were no lights on in Sheriff Jack Benning's house. I walked by the house. The neighbors to either side of the house had their curtains closed. I turned around and when I was even with Sheriff Jack Benning's driveway I ran to the side of the garage. There is a small window but I couldn't see in. I went to the back of the garage but the garage door is locked. "Not to worry," I told my Guardian Angel.

Using my driver's license I had the door open quicker than Jimmy the Cricket can do a back flip.

I couldn't risk turning on the light in the garage so I felt my way around the sheriff's car to a dark Chevy sedan parked next to it. I walked around the car running my hands all over the car. There were no bullet holes.

"I'll be dust," my Guardian Angel said. He was surprised.

The back door to the house is also locked. It was too risky to break into the house so I backtracked to the street. I didn't want to go back to Carol's so I decided to walk to the bar. The cold air feels good.

"You have the case about all figured out, don't you?" my Guardian Angel asked. "You won't admit it, but you do. I can tell."

"I have the who done it figured out, but the why the who done it did it, I don't," I said.

"What you know doesn't make you feel good, does it?"

"Part of it does and part of it doesn't."

"The Yin and the Yang. You can't have one without the other."

"Why? Why can't there be all good? And don't give me the old original sin excuse either," I said.

My Guardian Angel thought for a few moments. "I don't know," he admitted.

"The Yin and the Yang only try to explain why the system works the way it does. But there could be a better system. The question is why did this system get the way it is?"

"Too deep for me," my Guardian Angel said.

A lady in her late 50's with bleached blond hair, slightly overweight and bright red fingernails about two inches long is working the bar.

I sat down at the bar. "You're that detective that drinks

Guinness," she said. "Brenda says all your beer is on the house."

She got me a Guinness. "I'm Lou. Enjoy your beer."

She walked to the other end of the bar where the conversation might not have been so lopsided.

"Ok, tell me who done it," my Guardian Angel said.

"I'm going to sit here and drink a few beers. Not enough to get pie-eyed but enough to get a good buzz. Then I'm going to my room, sleep, get up in the morning, pack all my things and drive to Albert Lee, tell Bill Buffalo everything I know and then you and I are getting out of this freezer. I'm going to drive until the ocean impedes my forward motion, buy three or four pairs of ugly baggy swimming trunks and lie on the beach and hopefully I will meet a woman that hasn't killed somebody or is in trouble and we will fall in love."

My Guardian Angel started singing a bawdy blues song 14th century monks would sing after drinking the senior Abbot's private wine stock and were sufficiently smashed enough to want to go into town and break their vow of chastity.

"Which ocean do you want to head for?" my Guardian Angel asked me.

"Why don't we go to California and get on a freighter. A freighter will take Matilda and us to Hawaii. I went to jungle training school there and have never been back"

"How were the beaches and the babes?" he asked.

"We were quarantined. The only beach I saw was when we were on the ship and headed for Nam."

"Bummer," he said.

"I'd like to see it."

"Promise me we'll go?"

"You keep me alive and I promise we'll go."

"I'll do my best."

I waved at Lou for another beer. "How many people in a witches' coven?" I asked her as she set the beer down.

"Thirteen, that's why thirteen is an unlucky number," she said. "Did you know there are no hotels or skyscrapers with a 13th floor?"

"No I didn't."

"Did you know on any Friday the 13th that one third of the

work force in the country stays home?"

I shook my head.

"Did you know that at gambling casinos slot machines are always set in rows of even numbers?"

I shook my head.

"Did you know that back in the 60's there was a rock group in Texas called the 13th Floor Elevators that were killed when they rolled their van on Friday the 13th exactly thirteen miles from El Paso, Texas, and thirteen days after their last gig, and the odometer on the car read ninety nine thousand and thirteen."

"No I didn't."

Lou started to say something else but thankfully a man at the other end of the bar called her for an order. If I had known she was an expert on the number thirteen I would have kept my mouth shut.

"Weird stuff about that band," my Guardian Angel said.

I drank my beer and the bar seemed to melt around me. I heard bits and pieces of conversations that even if I were part of the conversation would mean nothing to me. All I can think about is we are all running as fast as we can to die - to mean nothing to the world - to make no changes - to utter nothing that means anything - to live in our little fish bowls and convince ourselves that by looking out at the world we are safe.

"Don't drink any more beer," my Guardian Angel said. "You're too close to the truth and the truth will only depress you."

"Why do people kill each other?" I asked my Guardian Angel.

"I don't know. Nobody knows, Roosevelt. But, let's get out of here," my Guardian Angel said.

I am not drunk, but I reached a good buzz. Getting up I waved goodbye at Lou. I don't think she saw me but it wouldn't have mattered if she did or not - a wave is as important to the waver as the one receiving the wave.

Walking toward Carol's I didn't feel the cold. I didn't think about the moon or the stars. "You know," I said to my Guardian Angel. "I don't care who stole Fanny's heart. I don't care who killed the cats. I don't care who killed Franklin. I don't care who tried to kill me."

"Roosevelt?" my Guardian Angel said in a quiet distant voice.

"What," I said.

"You care."

"No I don't."

"Yes you do. I know you do. I wouldn't have been sent to protect you if you didn't care. If you don't care than my mission means nothing."

It is a great blessing in life to have a friend.

"I don't know what I would do without you," I told my Guardian Angel.

"Don't get slobbery on me now," he said.

"How can I? I can't even hug you?

"Thank God."

My Guardian put his hand on my shoulder, which I can't feel, even so I imagined the touch.

It is amazing in life what a touch can do.

I wasn't paying much attention when I went into Carol's house nor was my Guardian Angel. I wasn't paying much attention when I turned on the light to my room. Sheriff Jack Benning sitting on my bed did get our attention. "Oh, no," my Guardian Angel said. "I've missed again."

A man in another man's bed is not that big of a deal anymore, but when a man is pointing an overly large pistol directly at the center of my chest, it makes a bigger than big deal.

"What big eyes you have," Sheriff Jack Benning said to me with a big bad wolf grin on his face.

I didn't say anything. I'm not into fairy tales.

"Pack your suitcase, we're going for a ride," he told me as he stood and moved to the far wall, never letting the pistol stray away from my body.

I put everything I owned in my suitcase. I am a one-suitcase type of guy. I was about to shut the suitcase. "Put your pistol in it too," Sheriff Jack Benning ordered, "but move slow and easy."

I put my pistol in the suitcase and shut it.

"I can't believe you'd stoop this low," I said to Sheriff Jack Benning.

"I haven't stopped I've crawled," he said with no trace of remorse in his voice.

I thought about my predicament and my options. My back is to the open door to the room and I figured I could make it to the door in one leap. I might get lucky and Sheriff Jack Benning would shoot and miss. I am two steps from Sheriff Jack Benning. He seemed so confident I might surprise him if I feinted to my left and then took a quick step and tried to kick the pistol out of his hand. I weighed both scenarios and decided attacking would be the best gamble.

"I don't think it will work," my Guardian Angel said.

"Why not?"

I didn't hear his reply because a heavy blunt object crashed against the back of my skull and sent me postage free to the land of oblivion.

CHAPTER NINETEEN
CUT YOUR HEART OUT AND EAT IT

It's a strange feeling to wake up in the trunk of a moving car. My feet are tied together and my hands are bound behind my back by what feels like hemp rope - at least my captives are into organic materials. A handkerchief is stuck in my mouth and my mouth is taped shut with duct tape. It is so dark all I can see is a small amount of light that radiates from the back of the rear taillights. The only conciliation I have is the trunk is big enough I don't have to curl up into a ball like an armadillo.

"I'm sorry, Roosevelt," my Guardian Angel said.

"Not as sorry as I am," I said and winced.

"How's your head?" my Guardian Angel asked sympathetically.

"I like big knots the size of baseballs on the back of my head that radiate excruciating pain from the top of my head all the way to my toes," I said more angry than sarcastic.

"Looks like we won't make Hawaii," he said sadly.

"Don't talk. Don't think. Don't do anything. And you can kiss my letter of recommendation goodbye, adios, sayonara, au revoir, arrivederci, don't come back you American pig tourist unless you bring cash - understand me?" There was no sarcasm in my outburst, only anger.

My Guardian Angel did not reply. He understands completely.

"You listen up my not even at 50% at protection Guardian Angel, even though I am tied up in the trunk of a speeding car, being taken who knows where, I am not giving up. You understand? I am not giving up. So you stay on your toes. Do you understand?"

I shut my eyes and tried to rest. I know I will need every ounce of mental and physical energy I possess to get myself out of this jam.

"The Jaws of Life would help," my Guardian Angel said.

I bounced and jiggled and rolled for what had to be more than an hour. But, it seemed to me, whoever was driving, I presume it is Sheriff Jack Benning, is turning around a lot and making more left turns than right - we were going around in circles and not driving far from town. Sheriff Jack Benning is trying to disorientate me. I take it he doesn't want me to know where I am when he kills me.

"I am glad to see you still have a sense of humor," my Guardian Angel said, adding, "and it is Sheriff Jack Benning driving the car."

"Another reason Sheriff Jack Benning might be driving around in circles is that he isn't going to kill me, and there might be a slim chance I can escape, and if I did escape he doesn't want me to know which way to run," I said.

"That is really reaching for straws," my Guardian Angel said.

"I'm not reaching for straws. I'm angry, mad, peeved, enraged, furious, irate, wrathful, annoyed, exasperated, irritated, piqued, antagonistic, bitter and hateful."

"Good, there are a lot of those feelings in the world, draw inner strength and fortitude from them," my Guardian Angel said.

Shutting my eyes I thought about everything I hated or had hated during my life. I let the fury inside of me start to glow, then glimmer, than burst into flame. I directed the flame at the ropes around my wrists and feet. I am Super Man, I am Super Demon. I twisted and turned my hands. I exerted all the pressure I could on the ropes. Sweat popped out on my brow, dripped from my armpits. I am either going to break the ropes or poop my pants. I did neither. I am going to have to learn how to hate better or I need more fiber in my diet.

I was about to try another hate induced try at the ropes when the car stopped. After the constant noise and vibration in the trunk the silence reminded me of the intense unnerving quiet after a gun battle.

Sheriff Jack Benning got out of the car - if my Guardian Angel is telling the truth. Another car pulled up beside us and stopped and somebody got out. Both engines were left running. Two people talked for several minutes in muffled voices. I couldn't understand what they were saying nor identify the other voice but I figured they were talking about me. Talking behind somebody's back is bad manners but talking about somebody who is locked up in the trunk of a car is worse than bad manners.

I heard the other the door to the other vehicle close and the car drive away.

My captor got back in the car and drove for several minutes and then did a U turn. He drove for another fifteen minutes and then stopped. I have a sinking feeling it isn't another conversation break.

"It's been a good run, Roosevelt," my Guardian Angel said.

"The way I've lived my life I suppose one has to accept the inevitable," I replied.

The key was inserted into the trunk lock. It had never once entered my mind that the fickle finger of fate would sound like a key turning in a lock. The trunk popped open. A strong flashlight beam immediately hit me in the eyes and blinded me and I had to shut my eyes. Someone yanked me into a sitting position and a hood was shoved over my head. I yelled at my captors, but with a handkerchief stuck in my mouth covered by duct tape, what I yelled had little effect. "Yooob moveeer feders! Yooob bamerds!"

Four strong hands grabbed me and yanked me out of the trunk and shoved me face first onto the snow. A hand hooked under each of my arms and I was dragged. If I was into drag it might have been ok, but drag has never been one of my things. "Yooob shem heds! Yooob ock ukers!" I duct tape hollered.

I was about to continue my outburst of obscenities when a hard object thudded into my skull and I went on another trip to the land of oblivion. If I keep getting hit on the head I will be going to the land of concussion.

I don't know if I am awake or dreaming but I know I am cold, so cold my bones ache. I also have a headache a bottle of aspirin wouldn't dent. My eyelids feel as though they are being held closed by tiny weights. I forced by eyes open. On the ceiling above me are hideous creatures and bodiless grotesque faces in bold bright colors that are outlined in black. The faces are filled with grief, hate, disgust - faces chewed on other faces - blood dripped from ears and eyes and noses, knives slashed flesh, eyes filled with pain and torment are clawed by hands with talons for fingernails. Bodies of beautiful men and women, only with heads of beasts and feet of goats and pigs, made love wildly - long tongues flying back and forth - teeth sinking into flesh and sending rivers of gushing blood - scaled forked tails whipped through the air madly, breasts were being ripped by hands with talons for fingers, young men with flowing hair and horns copulated with pigs and dogs. A goat with a man's head ravaged a woman who was tied to a stake while fire flamed around them. Snakes and scorpions and spiders crawled and slithered through the mosaic of pain and suffering. Everything was entwined by flames.

Turning my head sideways candlelight flickered off of a brown granite block wall, each block is at least three feet square. I tried to sit up but I can't. I feel dried blood on my forehead and on the back of my head. I lifted my head as far as I possibly could. I am naked and lying on my back on a solid granite table at least 8 feet long and 6 feet across. My arms extend straight out from my sides and my wrists are shackled by iron manacles to the granite table. The manacles are attached to several lengths of heavy rusty chain and the chain is imbedded into the granite table. My legs are spread apart in a V and my ankles are also shackled to the table. Between my legs, engraved on the table, is an inverted star with a goat's head in the middle of the star. There are two circles around the star about two inches apart. The complete symbol is about the size of a large pie plate. At each point of the star, but within the two circles, are symbols that have no meaning to me. They look Egyptian but could be early Albuquerque or lower East Manhattan. About three feet from the end of the granite table is a large black cast iron bowl that looks like the bottom of a barbecue. It is filled with firewood and there are steel rods sticking out of the wood that remind me of branding irons. Rolling my head back as far as I can there is another cast iron bowl that is also filled with firewood and steel rods sticking out of the wood.

By moving my head from side to side and rolling my eyes I am able to see the room. To my left is a small wood table with a black cloth draped over the top that almost reaches the granite floor. Two highly polished silver knives, a silver bowl and a black book are on top of the table. I am in the center of a round room that at the most is thirty yards in circumference. There are no windows. Spaced evenly around the outside of the room are thirteen black wrought iron candleholders that are taller than a normal man, each with thirteen lit candles. The candle flames dance to an evil unheard song, sending muted shadows drifting through the room that seem to spur the painted figures above me into a wilder frenzy of hate and depravation.

I can not make out a door in the granite walls but there has to be one. I know there is no need to cry out for help. If anybody had the remotest chance of hearing me my captors would not have removed the gag.

I strained against the shackles but they did not budge. Sampson I am not. Then I had a profound realization. What I am lying on is not a table - it is an altar - and I am the sacrifice.

Shutting my eyes I tried to ignore how cold I am. Hearing a scraping sound I opened my eyes. Three granite blocks slowly swung open. When the blocks stopped two figures wearing long black robes with hoods stood in the open doorway. The black robes touched the floor. The arms of the robes extended past their hands. The black hoods obscured their faces. The two figures glided toward me like they are riding on air. They stopped several feet away and I can see who they are.

"The Pope won't like this," my Guardian Angel said.

"Father Fisher," I said casually. "Would you like to hear my confession?"

He gave me a wry sardonic smile.

"Sheriff Jack Benning, black isn't your color," I said.

"It is the color of the great one. It is the color that will redeem us and drive from the heavens the false prophet," he replied in deep conviction.

"You have been chosen to be our sacrifice during tomorrow's black mass to honor Satan, the true one. You should feel privileged," Father Fisher said.

"Was the decision based on the fact Carol saw me by your house?" I asked.

"Satan sends us his desires," Father Fisher said piously.

"Screw Satan, screw his desires, I feel cold and hungry," I replied.

"Your nakedness is to show Satan we are all naked before his power. But the daughters of the true light will feed you."

"Since it is my last meal I want a sixteen inch rainbow trout pan-fried in bacon grease, not a pond raised trout either, but a trout caught out of a clear mountain stream, three wedges of lemon, a spinach salad with raspberry vinaigrette dressing, a twice baked potato with cheddar cheese on the top, and for dessert two scoops of Ben and Jerry's vanilla ice cream," I said.

Father Fisher and Sheriff Jack Benning laughed.

"Good food isn't funny," I said.

"You are a strange man," Father Fisher said. "But I admire you."

"You can stick your admiration up your nose," I told him.

Father Fisher only smiled.

"I knew you were behind something like this," I told Father Fisher.

"How?" he asked.

I thought Father Fisher wanting to know how was strange. Why would he want to know unless he is a mystery buff? But I told him.

"It came together slowly. The first hint was when I discovered Sheila and Fanny were at one time into the occult. Then I saw a book in Fanny's bedroom about curses and incantations. One afternoon I searched Fanny's house and discovered her black robe, two silver knives and a silver bowl, I bet they are on the table over there, and a satanic bible. When I searched Fanny's again the hood and everything was gone. I'd learned that at one time Sheila killed dogs and cats but because of her father nothing was ever done about it. I also learned that starting about twenty years ago there were cattle and livestock mutilations in the area but they tapered off to only four a year. Devil worshipers have a mass for every season. When I visited you, you told me you have been at the Saint Ansgar Church for twenty years which is the exact time the mutilations have been going on."

"You are astute," Father Fisher said. "But you had to learn more."

"When I was standing by your window I heard you, Fanny, Dale and Merriam Boraxe, Sheila, Brenda and Earl Harberts, Ginger, Lisa, and Grace and George Brethern talking. But then Carol drove up and saw me. As I was running it suddenly dawned on me. There were thirteen of you. Thirteen is the most powerful witches' coven."

"I gave you hints before that," my Guardian Angel said.

"You're supposed to protect me, not hint," I told him. "I ignore most of your hints."

"See what your ignoring has gotten you into," my Guardian Angel said.

"Satan will appreciate a man of your intelligence as our sacrifice," Father Fisher smiled.

"But why you a priest and a man people look up to and respect?" I almost pleaded.

"What better way to destroy your enemy than to live in his belly and learn his heart and lies?" he said confidently.

"A spy for the dark side," I said.

"I am not a spy but one chosen by the most powerful to fulfill his prophecies. To pave the way for Satan's return to his rightful seat of power over mankind," he said with a mad tinge to his voice.

"How did you recruit all these people?"

"People are drawn to the truth. God is the spreader of lies and deceits. God is not the redeemer. He is cloaked in the wool of lambs but he is not innocent. He seeks out mankind with lies? He does not protect. He fills men with false hopes and then bashes their hopes. Satan is truth."

"Satan is truth," Officer Jack Benning repeated.

Father Fisher reached into a pocket in his robe and took out a small clear bottle filled with a red liquid. He opened the bottle and walked around the alter seven times sprinkling whatever was in the bottle on the floor and repeating seven times, "Prepare our gift for the mighty one. Let the most high feast on the soul of a non-believer. We pay homage to the one of truth."

When Father Fisher was done he looked straight down into my

eyes. "Each member of my coven will visit you before the black mass tomorrow night. They come to show respect for the chosen one. You may talk to them. It is forbidden for them to lie to you. If they do the power from your death will be diminished. When the moon is full your life will be given so that others may see."

He then poured several drops from the bottle on my forehead. "We bless your sacrifice with blood chosen one," he chanted.

Father Fisher and Sheriff Jack Benning glided away. The granite door groaned shut.

"If Satan is the opposite of God, and a lie is the opposite of the truth, doesn't it seem reasonable that a witch who is telling the truth is in all truth lying, and when they are lying they are in reality telling the truth?" my Guardian Angel asked.

"Your question is a good one but I will stick with the literal meaning for truth and ask everybody who visits questions. At least before I die I will know if I was right about Franklin's killer," I said.

I feel angry. I want to rip Sheriff Jack Benning's and Father Fisher's hearts out. I yanked on the manacles that held me until my wrists and ankles hurt and I could feel blood dripping from my ankles. "There is hope. There is hope. There is hope," I repeated.

I don't know how much time past when I heard the door grinding open. Two figures in hooded black robes approached me. One holds a wooden bowl.

Sheriff Jack Benning and Carol Trouble looked down at me.

"Do you really have to tell me the truth?" I asked Carol.

"Yes."

"Is the truth really the truth to you or is a lie the truth?" I asked.

"Don't be stupid," Carol said.

"I know you didn't kill Franklin," I said to Carol.

"Why would I ask you to find his killer if I killed him?" she asked me.

"If I did find the killer you and Lisa thought I might find the money," I said.

"True," Carol said.

"I know who killed him," I said. "And I know I won't get the $3,000 you said you would pay me."

"Who killed him?" she demanded.

"Not telling," I said.

She started to hit me but Sheriff Jack Benning grabbed her arm. Which I thought was nice of him.

"Did you have a change of heart about asking me to find Franklin's killer and tell two people to follow me and try and kill me?" I asked Carol.

"No," she replied looking puzzled.

"I was shot at once from the bushes in front of Sheila's house. Did you shoot at me then?"

"Why would I want to kill you if you were my main hope of finding out where the money is?" she asked.

"I don't know?" I replied. "Merely asking?"

"You ask a lot of ridiculous questions," my Guardian Angel said.

"Sometimes I get way ahead of myself and lose track of what I've asked or not asked," I told him.

"When you read my clue book did you find anything that helped you?" I asked Carol.

"The only thing I found out was that you are a lousy writer," she said.

"That's an understatement," Sheriff Jack Benning said.

"The truth can really hurt," my Guardian Angel said.

"Did you kill Bill and Joe?" I asked.

"No I didn't and that's enough questions. I am here to feed you not play twenty questions," Carol said sternly.

Carol set the bowl on the altar and took a spoon out of a pocket in her robe. "What's in the bowl?" I asked.

"Chicken and rice."

"There seems to be some mistake. I ordered trout," I said.

"I don't think you are in the possession to order anything," Carol said.

I have more questions I want to ask Carol but even if I am going to die there is no need to die hungry. Carol put her hand behind my head and spoon fed me. The chicken and rice is not half bad - it tastes like Rice-a-Roni. I ate it all hoping I will have bad gas all during their ceremony.

"Did you kill Bill and Joe?" I asked Carol again, trying to catch her in a lie.

"Sorry, Roosevelt."

"You have a 22 rifle and a 30/30 in your basement," I said.

"So?"

"Did you kill Sam Sheeps and Row Harper?" I asked, not knowing how to answer her question.

"I told you I didn't kill anybody," Carol replied.

"You went out and ransacked Franklin's house after I found him in your closet didn't you?" I asked Carol.

"I did go out to his house. I was hoping to find the money or a clue to where he hid his money," she said. "But the house was already ransacked."

Sheriff Jack Benning gave me a strange look before they walked toward the door. When they got to the door I hollered at them. "Tell Father Fisher his fat lamb is thirsty and wants a Guinness."

The door ground shut.

"It will be hard to have gas," my Guardian Angel said. "When I was living rice always bound me up."

"It binds me up, too," I said sadly.

"Too bad," he said.

I tried to think of a way I could escape. I thought and thought and thought and thought and thought and thought. The thinking was good but the escaping was impossible.

It wasn't long before the door ground open again. Already people opening and shutting the door is getting annoying. Two black robbed and hooded figures stopped by me.

"What are you? A body guard for witches?" I asked Sheriff Jack Benning.

"I am the guardian of the temple. No person enters this room without me," he said proudly.

I wonder if there are guardian devils.

"Do you have a bra on?" I asked Sheila Harberts.

She didn't answer my question. "I practically crawled on my hands and knees for you to make love to me. But you think you are too good, too superior, for a person like me," she said in a voice filled with venom.

"You should have gotten out of town and gone to school," I said to Sheila.

"And then what? Be like everybody else in this screwed up world of ours. Spend my life working nine to five so I can pay my taxes and never get ahead? Marry some empty headed man who only thought about sports or his car? Or maybe have kids and then sit around the house all day wondering what life is really about. It's not for me Roosevelt. I know the truth. Most people only think about themselves. They are only out to use others for their own gain. I have found my home. Satan will lead his believers. Satan will smite our enemies. Satan will give his followers the power we deserve."

"Did you try and shoot me from the bushes in front of your house?" I asked Sheila.

"Why would I do that?" she asked.

"A witches' thing," I said.

She laughed.

"Why, at one time, did you go around town killing dogs and cats?" I asked.

"Satan told me I must. I had to prove myself to be accepted into the chosen ones," she said with no hint in her voice that what she had done was wrong.

"You're not lying to me, are you?"

"You are chosen for the supreme sacrifice. You are blessed. I can't lie to you even if I want to."

"There goes my witches' truth and lie debate," my Guardian Angel said.

"Did you kill Bill and Joe?" I asked Sheila.

"I didn't kill anybody, believe me."

"Did you steal Fanny's diamond heart?" I asked.

"I loved that heart. Before I went to the nut house Fanny used to let me wear it. I would never steal from a fellow witch. Never."

"Did you kill Sam Sheeps and Row Harper?" I asked.

"No," Sheila replied simply.

She and Sheriff Benning glided away.

"Warlock Benning," I called.

He stopped and turned around. "You forgot my beer. Don't do it again or you won't get a tip."

The door ground shut. "And oil the door," I yelled.

I gazed at the burning candles. As long as I don't look at the ceiling the swaying shadows are enjoyable. In the old hippie days when I lived in the mountains with no electricity I read by candlelight. I spent a lot of hours, when I wasn't reading, studying the different shades of colors candlelight brought out of objects. Candles are soothing, more soothing than an open fire. Open fires are primitive, candles have grace. Maybe that is why candle shops are in every city in the world.

The door scrapped open. Three black robed and hooded figures entered. One is holding a Guinness. I can't see Satan having anything against booze. Booze has probably sent Satan more followers than any other vice in the world.

The trio stopped by the side of the altar. It was Grace and George Brethern and Sheriff Jack Benning. Grace Brethern held up my head and put the beer bottle to my lips. I drank until the beer was all gone. "Aren't you the guy who wanted to sell me siding," George Brethern asked.

I nodded.

"And you wanted to paint my house."

I nodded.

"And you wanted to sell me a Medicare supplement policy?"

I nodded.

"Are you going to mow my yard this summer?"

I shook my head.

"Too bad," he said. "Kids aren't reliable anymore.

"At your age you should know better than to follow Satan," I told Grace.

She slapped me. "You are a believer in the false prophet," she snapped.

I won't make that statement again. She slaps hard for a little old lady, but I suppose with Satan on her side her slaps have a little more zing to them.

"When I went to see you, you told me you thought Ginger killed Franklin?" I said to Grace. "Do you still believe that?"

"Not really," she replied. "I was just making conversation with you. You seem like such a nice young man."

"Were you telling me the truth when you told me Franklin and Fanny fought a lot?"

"Yes I was," she replied. "Toward the end of their relationship all they did was fight."

"How long have you been a witch?" I asked Grace.

"Since the day the honeymoon was over," George said.

"Father Fisher led me to the truth and then Satan appeared to me in a dream. He told me he would punish my enemies. He promised me power and riches in the afterlife. I do as he commands."

"Even watch me die?" I asked.

"You will forever walk with the lord of darkness. Those who die in his name will be kings in the other life. You should be proud you were chosen."

"Do you know who killed Fanny's cats," I asked Grace.

"Probably some Christian," she said and then patted my shoulder. "Your blood will bless the believers."

They started to leave. "Wait. Tell me. How am I going to be sacrificed?"

"See those silver knives and silver bowl," Sheriff Jack Benning said. "Father Fisher is going to cut your heart out with the knives, put your pulsating heart in the bowl, and set the bowl on the fire. When your heart is cooked we are going to cut your heart into thirteen bite-sized pieces and each of us is going to have a snack."

Grace and George Brethern laughed. Sheriff Jack Benning had no expression on his face.

"I wish I wouldn't have asked," I said.

"You don't have long to learn when to keep your mouth shut," my Guardian Angel said.

CHAPTER TWENTY
A SLIP OF THE TONGUE

Waking up I knew I had been sleeping but I did not remember falling asleep. I tugged on the manacles that bound me but a good fairy had not unlocked them during my snooze.

"The way the world is anymore I don't know if people should even trust the Tooth Fairy," my Guardian Angel said. "She is most likely leaving gingivitis under kids' pillows."

The granite door ground open and three black robed figures approached me. I know it isn't the three Wise Men bearing gifts. Brenda and Earl Herbert's and Sheriff Jack Benning glided over. Brenda looked at me from the top of my head to the tip of my toes. "Not bad," she commented approvingly. "Too bad you always turned down my invitation."

"I bet in your coven you don't care who sleeps with whom," I said to whichever of them wanted to answer.

"It is our duty to share all with our brothers and sisters," Earl Herberts said.

"You've even slept with Sheriff Jack Benning," I said to Brenda.

"And Dale Boraxe," she smiled.

"Even George Brethern?" I asked.

"He is too old but he likes to watch," Brenda replied and winked at me.

"He and my Guardian Angel would get along well," I said.

Brenda, Earl, and Sheriff Jack Benning gave me a funny look

but didn't say anything. I suppose if you are a witch Guardian Angels are something you don't want to think about.

"So you didn't really have an affair with Fanny, it was your duty as you call it?" I said to Earl Harberts.

"Tough duty," he smirked.

"Then why when I came to see you at the bank did you pretend that you were afraid I was going to tell Brenda that you were seeing Fanny again?" I asked him.

"Father Fisher told all of us to answer your questions."

"So you've also slept with Merriam, Ginger, Carol and Lisa?" I said. I left out Grace - even witches have to have respect for older people.

"Everyone," Earl Harberts replied.

"How about your daughter?"

"Sheila's virginity was a gift to Father Fisher," Earl Harberts said proudly, not at all offended by my statement.

"The Arch Diocese won't like that," my Guardian Angel said.

"I bet you both knew Sheila was trying to seduce me but I always felt guilty and said no," I said.

"She wanted you in our coven. She's knows you are unhappy and lost. She thought if she slept with you, you might fall for her and she could lead you to the lord of darkness," Brenda said.

"Weird," my Guardian Angel said.

"Did either one of you ever try to shoot me?" I asked.

"Why would we want to shoot you?" they replied in unison.

"Did you ever find the heart Earl gave you?" I asked Brenda.

"No, I never found the heart," Brenda replied. "It's strange."

Earl had no reaction over my question.

"I have the heart," I said, watching their faces intently. "I found it in the chair in the room where Franklin was found dead in the closet."

Both Earl and Brenda looked puzzled.

"I suppose neither one of you stole Fanny's diamond heart or killed her cats," I said.

They both shook their heads.

I glanced at Sheriff Jack Benning and he is looking at me with a strange expression on his face that I cannot read. It is like he is halfway between being surprised or being amazed.

"Who killed Franklin?" I asked Earl.

"I have no idea and couldn't really care," he said.

"We tried to bring him into our coven but he refused. He told us we were all crazy and mixed up. All he was interested in was gambling and money," Brenda said. "But I don't know who killed him or why?"

"So I take it you slept with him for the same reason Sheila was trying to seduce me and not to get back at Earl?"

"That and for fun," she said. "We witches are into casual sex like you old hippies were."

"I take it you both had Sheila committed to the nut house and their really was no dissension between you two over it?" I said.

"She really did flip out on dope and Father Fisher said she might be able to make converts in the asylum," Brenda said.

"Then why did you two separate for a while?" I asked.

"Witches are normal people, too. We were bored with each other is all," Earl said.

The being bored I can understand, but witches' considering themselves normal people does not make any sense.

"Did either of you kill Bill and Joe or Sam and Row?" I asked.

"Sorry, wrong again," Earl said, "but not a bad poem."

"Not me either," Brenda said.

"You die for the great one," Brenda said solemnly.

"You die for the truth," Earl said.

Sheriff Jack Benning nodded at me as they walked away.

The door shut.

"For having the name of a saint this is a strange little town," my Guardian Angel said.

"Have you ever seen a devil?" I asked my Guardian Angel.

"No. And I never want to," he replied emphatically.

"Is God on the side of any government?" I asked him.

"I don't think so," he said.

"Then we fight and die for no truth," I said.

"You fight and die for reasons man invents and calls truth," he said to me sadly.

I was lost somewhere between good and evil and what truth really is when I heard the door scrape open again.

"You are one popular guy," my Guardian Angel said.

"It must be something to do with the chains," I said.

Two black robbed figures approached me.

"You're still ugly," I told Sheriff Jack Benning.

He must know it because he smiled.

"You should be ashamed of yourself," I told Ginger. "You have a little boy with a heart of gold and you have sold yours."

"You can't be the one to judge," Sheriff Jack Benning said.

Ginger's eyes are deep pools of sadness. "You have no comprehension about my life," she said barely above a whisper. "You have no idea what I have been through or how I have suffered."

"I know Jimmy deserves better than this," I said. "I know he loves you."

"Jimmy will make his own decisions when the time comes. I don't force my beliefs onto him," Ginger said.

I could see Jimmy's face as he and I made the snowman. I could see his sad smile as we played cards and watched his little train go around and round. I could see the happiness on his face when he showed me his secret place.

"Please, Ginger, for your son's sake, you can't embrace darkness. Get out while you can," I pleaded with her.

"It's too late for me, Roosevelt," she said simply.

"It's never too late," I said.

"It's too late for you," she said.

"Argue that," my Guardian Angel said.

It's a bummer when you are proven wrong in the pursuit of a noble cause.

"Why did you kill Bill and Joe?" I asked Ginger.

Sheriff Jack Benning looked alarmed.

"I didn't kill them," Ginger replied also looking alarmed.

"Why did you kill Sam Sheeps and Row Harper?" I asked Ginger.

"I didn't kill them," she replied.

"You have a 308 Sako with 150 grain bullets in your closet and a twelve-gauge shotgun," I said. "Bill and Joe were killed with 150 grain bullets and Sam and Row were killed by a twelve-gauge shotgun."

"The guns were my husbands and I've been trying to sell them.

I don't shoot them. The only time for years they haven't been in my closet was last week when I took the rifle to Fanny. She had a man in the store that was interested in buying them but he didn't come up with the money. I've never shot a gun."

"Why do you have two straight razors in your bathroom?" I asked.

"You're a regular little snoop," she said.

"It's my job."

"The razors belonged to my grandfather. I have never used them."

Sheriff Jack Benning gave Ginger a strange look.

"So you didn't cut Franklin's throat because he broke up with you," I said.

"He led me on but I didn't kill him," she replied angrily.

"And you didn't cut the throats of Fanny's cats?"

"Sorry, Roosevelt. I might be a lot of things but I'm not a killer."

"What are you when you watch Father Fisher cut my heart out," I asked.

"You are the chosen one. You will bring power to our coven. You are a gift to our leader," she said in reverence, adding, "I do appreciate what you meant to Jimmy."

"Did you at any time take any pot shots at me?" I asked Ginger.

She shook her head.

The door ground shut behind them.

Looking at the demons on the ceiling I hope Jimmy will be able to escape the clutches of the coven and keep his heart simple and pure.

"Are any of the things you thought about this case true?" my Guardian Angel asked.

"You may be surprised but there are more true than false," I said.

"It's too bad you are finding truth as you are about to die," he said.

"Better late than never," I replied. "Besides, I'm not dead yet. I do believe in miracles."

The door scrapped open. Sheriff Jack Benning and Lisa

Maidenform were laughing as they approached me. I hate being the focal point of an inside joke.

"Did you ever find the money?" I asked Lisa.

Sheriff Jack Benning gave me his strange look again.

"I haven't found the money," Lisa said sounding dejected.

"I guess you and Carol will never move to Florida."

"We'll make it, Roosevelt. Father Fisher knows of several covens in Florida and he has given us permission to leave."

"Is there a chance you shot at me in town?"

Lisa frowned. "No."

"Is there a chance you killed Bill and Joe and Sam and Row?"

"Bad poetry, Roosevelt, but the answer is no."

"The night I was in the garage, before you smacked me in the head, there was one car stall empty. The car that was gone wouldn't happen to be a dark sedan would it?"

Sheriff Jack Benning seemed momentarily shocked by my question. "I guess you will never know," Lisa smiled.

"Why did you kill Franklin?"

Lisa didn't flinch. "I didn't kill him. Why would I want him dead? I knew he and Dale Boraxe were involved with something illegal that involved a lot of cash, and Franklin was a chance of finding out where the cash was."

Sheriff Jack Benning looked me straight in the eyes like he was trying to read my mind.

"Carol didn't kill him, either," Lisa said. "Franklin didn't care about her being a witch and we all knew he would never snitch us. Being a crook and a gambler he hated cops."

"Franklin did sleep with Fanny," I said.

"Franklin slept with anybody who would sleep with him."

"Did Fanny love him?"

"I think so. Women have a way of falling for rogue men."

"What would Dale Boraxe do if he knew you were trying to steal his money?" I asked.

"You told me he would try and kill me. I believe that is true. But not if I killed him first."

"There is no honor among the disciple's of darkness," my Guardian Angel said.

Sheriff Jack Benning looked at Lisa with a blank expression

on his face.

"Do you know what Bill and Joe did for Dale Boraxe?"

"I don't know. When he talked to them they always went outside where I couldn't hear what they were saying."

"Did you ransack Franklin's house after he was killed?" I asked Lisa.

"Not me," she said.

The door ground shut behind them.

"I wonder if God can undo locked manacles?" I asked my Guardian Angel

"God seems to have an aversion with the dealings of man," he said.

I shut my eyes and listened to my heart beating in my chest. I wonder if when Father Fisher cuts my heart out if it will continue to beat in his hands? I wonder if for a few moments my mind would still work and I will see my heart? I wonder if I will see my complete life flash before my eyes as the shiny silver knife plunges toward my chest? I wonder if life itself is a joke?

I drifted off into a dark dreamless sleep.

The door grinding open woke me up. Merriam and Dale Boraxe and Sheriff Jack Benning walked over to me clad in the black robbed witches' fashion of the day.

"You people ever into white?" I asked. "Black is so drab and unimaginative."

"Everything was fine until you showed up here," Dale Boraxe said to me, sounding disgusted.

"You undo the chains that bind me and I promise you I'll be out of the area quicker than you can say baboon," I said.

Merriam giggled, which I thought was strange, as one would think witches wouldn't be into giggling.

"Since Franklin was running money for you, you should have known where he hid it in case something happened to him," I told Dale.

"He wasn't supposed to hide the money. He was supposed to bring it straight to the house," Dale said, perturbed.

"A little thing called murder got in the way," I said.

"It's the little things in life that mess it up," Dale said.

"It was bound to mess up," I said.

"You think you have it all figured out, don't you?" Dale asked me in a sarcastic voice.

Sheriff Jack Benning looked overly interested.

"I more than think I do," I said. "I think Franklin got you and Dale Owens, the bookie from Kansas City, together, and Owens put you in charge of expanding his operations in Minnesota. I figure Franklin was taking big bets from gamblers he knew all over the state. I believe you when you told me you have aspirations to be governor so you can't afford to do things yourself. Shawn Mahan and Don Foreman, Dale Owens's attorneys, would fly up, land on your private strip and pick up the money. It was all going good until Franklin decided to get his throat cut and by accident little old me decided to stop in Saint Ansgar."

"I told him it wasn't worth the risk," Merriam said and gave Dale a dirty look. "But with crop prices down and Dale's ability to invest in anything that will lose money he decided to take a chance."

"I figured as much," I said.

"How did you figure it out?" Dale asked.

"I found two decks of cards that belonged to Franklin's and by accident I discovered phone numbers hidden on them. They were numbers to Dale Owen's betting houses. Franklin needed them to call in and get the lines. And the two attorneys at your house are attorneys for Dale Owens. It all added up to four."

"You're smarter than I thought," Dale said.

"You had Bill and Joe shoot at me that night on the edge of town," I told Dale.

"I told them not to kill you but to shake you up a little. I thought you'd run out of town faster than a dope dealer with the cash. I didn't want you in town and maybe discovering what I was doing."

"He should have run," my Guardian Angel said.

"I should have run," I said.

"You should have run," Merriam said.

"How did you know who I was to have Bill and Joe shoot at me?" I asked Dale. Carol asked me to try and find out who killed Franklin so she wouldn't have called you. At the time the only other people who knew I am a detective were the cops from Albert Lee and Sheriff Jack Benning."

As soon as Sheriff Jack Benning was out of my mouth I felt like an idiot.

"Well duh," my Guardian Angel said.

Sheriff Jack Benning gave me that strange look again.

"The Sheriff called me," Dale said, which was an anti-climactic answer.

"You are in on the gambling operation?" I asked Sheriff Jack Benning.

"No. I didn't know anything about it until now," he said, with an undertone of surprise in his voice.

"Did you tell Bill and Joe to write FLY OR DIE on my car?" I asked Dale.

"No, they were mad at you for beating them up. I'd told them to stay away from you after you didn't run out of town."

"If you told Bill and Joe to leave me alone why did you hire Peter Thompson out of Kansas City to kill me?"

"I didn't. Shawn Mahan and Don Foreman thought it would be a good idea to get rid of you. I told them I'd have nothing to do with it. They called in Thompson."

"That's why he didn't know what I looked like and had to stop his car and ask if I was Bob Roosevelt," I said more to myself than anybody in the room.

I looked at Sheriff Jack Benning and he seemed to be deep in thought.

"Did you kill Bill and Joe after I'd shot them at your farm?" I asked Dale.

"Those two boys were dumber than woodpeckers but they didn't know anything. There was no need to kill them. They ran into some bad luck when you showed up is all."

"No, they ran into 150 grain slugs," I said.

"How about Row Harper and Sam Sheeps?" I asked.

"I had nothing to do with that either. Dale Owens sent them in."

"When they ransacked my room they thought I would have a map to where the money was?" I said jokingly.

"That's funny," Merriam said.

"Why don't you ask Dale how much money he's talking

about," my Guardian Angel said.

"How much money is missing?" I asked. It seems like a good question.

"$375,000 in cash," Dale said.

Merriam looked surprised.

"That's a lot of cash," my Guardian Angel said.

"That's not chicken feed," I said.

Sheriff Jack Benning looked like he had tried to swallow four aspirin without taking a drink of water.

"Then who shot Bill and Joe Schneider and then knocked off Sam Sheeps and Row Harper?" I asked anybody who wanted to answer.

"I don't know," Dale Boraxe said.

"I don't know," Merriam Boraxe said.

Sheriff Jack Benning shrugged his shoulders.

"I don't know," my Guardian Angel said.

Ask and you shall receive doesn't always work.

"You know if Fanny hadn't asked you to stay and try and found out who killed her cats and stole her diamond heart, you wouldn't have found Franklin dead in the closet and you could be as happy and carefree as an old hippie can be," Merriam said to me.

"Life has a way of keeping me in the muck," I told her.

"Well at least your life won't be a waste. Being chosen by Father Fisher as the supreme sacrifice is an honor," she said.

"I'd rather be drafted," I said.

The door ground shut behind them.

"I wonder who took the money?" my Guardian Angel asked me.

"I know but I don't care," I said.

"In your position I suppose there is no need for you to care," he said.

I am beginning to get hungry again. Chicken Rice-a-Roni is like Chinese food - it doesn't last long.

When the door started to creak open I hoped it was a person delivering a large supreme pizza with a thin crust.

It wasn't. It was Fanny Ruth and Sheriff Jack Benning.

"You've lost more than your diamond heart pendant," I said to Fanny.

"I didn't plan it this way, Roosevelt, believe me," Fanny said sadly.

"I only told you I would help find your heart and who killed your cats because I felt you were lonely and needed a friend," I said.

"I was lonely and I really do like you Roosevelt, but I spoke in haste and now I am no longer lonely. I have returned to my master. I know what is right and I follow the most powerful one," Fanny said, but she didn't sound convincing.

"Why did you tell me to go to Carol's when you knew Franklin was in the closet?" I asked.

Fanny's eyes darted from side to side and Sheriff Jack Benning looked alarmed.

"What are you talking about?" Fanny stammered.

"The first day I met you, you offered me an upstairs room, but I told you it would be better if I stayed someplace else and you told me I could get a room in town," I said.

"I don't remember saying that," Fanny said defensively.

"I do. But it wasn't until a few days ago I put it all together and knew you killed Franklin. Why you killed him I didn't know?"

Sheriff Jack Benning's eyes burned into mine. He glared at Fanny.

"I don't know what you are talking about," Fanny said nervously.

"When you asked me to stay at your house I told you I had better not. You then told me you knew of a widow in town who rented rooms. It was a slip of the tongue on your part. There was only one person at the time who knew Carol was a widow and that person was whoever killed Franklin," I said. "You."

"I'll be a Christian," Sheriff Jack Benning said.

"I'll be," my Guardian Angel said.

Fanny didn't say anything but glared at me with eyes that could have roasted hot dogs in less than a minute.

"What I don't know is who helped you kill Franklin, but I plan on finding out before my heart becomes an appetizer," I said.

Fanny started laughing. Her laughter is dark and sinister which is fitting for the room we are in. She kept laughing until her laughter was getting on my nerves and I cut in. "I also know you ransacked Franklin's house," I said.

She stopped laughing. I guess murder is funny but ransacking isn't. "How do you know?" she demanded.

"The day you and I went out to Franklin's you had gloves on and you never took them off. But when Bill Buffalo finger printed the house your prints were all over it."

She smiled.

"I figure Franklin came back to town with a lot of cash, $375,000 to be exact, and you killed him and took the money. You were planning on killing him when you went to see him. You took one of the sharp knives out of your kitchen with you. He went to the bathroom to clean up and didn't lock the door and you went in and cut his throat. It confused me at first because whoever cut his throat, by the angle of the cut, had to be left handed. You never use your left hand but a few days ago you were stringing hearts with fishing line and holding the needle in your left hand. You put the body in the trunk of Franklin's car and whoever was with you followed you to Carol's house and helped you put the body in the closet hoping Carol would get blamed. I think you hate Carol for being pretty. You then went home, cleaned the knife, and went about your business."

"I never thought you would figure it out," Fanny said. "But you are right. I did kill him, and I am naturally left handed, and I did ransack the house. But I only ransacked the house to confuse the issue. I didn't know he had a lot of money when I killed him, but when we put him in the trunk there was a suitcase full of money," she said.

Sheriff Jack Benning could not hide his shock.

"Why did you tell me to stay at Carol's," I asked Fanny.

"It was a mistake. I was lonely and you made me feel good and the words were out of my mouth before I thought," she replied.

"Nobody should have to be lonely," I said.

Sheriff Jack Benning's eyes seemed to soften.

"Franklin was laid in the closet on a king sized-sheet but his bed is a queen. Where did the sheet come from?" I asked Fanny.

"It was in the closet at his house," she said.

At times the answers in life are too simple.

"I really do like you, Roosevelt," Fanny said. "When you came to town I did need a friend. You are the only person whoever did anything for me out of friendship."

"I know. It's strange isn't it?"

She nodded.

"Why did Fanny kill Franklin?” Sheriff Jack Benning asked.

I thought it was strange for Sheriff Jack Benning to want to know, but to prove my worth as a detective I decided to tell him. "Fanny borrowed money from Franklin to open her HOME OF HEARTS, I presume when they were seeing each other. Franklin probably led Fanny on like he did Ginger. I imagine he told Fanny he wanted to marry her after his divorce with Carol went through.”

"The jerk used me. He lied to me. He never intended to marry me," Fanny hissed.

"Then Franklin must have gotten into a money jam and he needed the money back he had loaned Fanny. He probably made a big bet and owed Owen's. Fanny didn't have any money. He threatened her but Fanny couldn't come up with the money so he poisoned her cats and then cut their throats to show her he meant business. I found a bottle of Maalox in Franklin's car that was laced with arsenic poison. The poison showed up in the cat’s hair. When I found the dead cats I knew something was strange because the cats throats had been cut evenly and they had to have been on their backs when their throats were cut. A person trying to cut a live cat’s throat and holding a cat down on its back wouldn't have any skin left on their hands or arms and the cuts would have been jagged."

"He told me he would hurt me if I didn't get his money but he shouldn't have killed my cats," Fanny said sadly. "They and Clyde were my only friends until you came to town."

"Franklin must have been a strange man," I said.

"How did you know I hadn't paid him back?” Fanny asked.

"You told me you had the store paid for but I went to the bank and you haven't paid anything on your note to the bank except the interest. I presumed you didn't make enough to pay back Franklin either," I said.

"I could have killed you, Roosevelt," Fanny said.

"I know. Thanks for not killing me," I replied. "It's better to get killed later than sooner."

She smiled at me the way a person smiles at an old friend who is dying from cancer and they both know they will never see each other again.

Sheriff Jack Benning looked confused.

"The day I ran into Bill and Joe out at Boraxe's you and Sheila were driving around. Sheila had taken one of her dad's rifles. By chance you drove by Boraxe's house and you saw my car and heard the two shots as I shot Bill and Joe. Sheila stopped and you ran around the side of the garage, saw me, saw Bill and Joe, ran back to the car, got a rifle, ran back and shot Bill and Joe. I learned it was Sheila's car because I heard the exhaust noise as she drove away and later, by accident, I heard her exhaust when I helped her by the highway when her car was broken down, the sound was the same. You really did have a buyer for Ginger's rifle and that is why it was in your closet. If you would have used Ginger's rifle you wouldn't be dumb enough to keep it in your house."

"I like you, Roosevelt, I told you that. They would have only tried to hurt you again. I shot them for you," Fanny said.

"You really did want me to find out who stole your heart, didn't you?" I asked Fanny.

"It is the only thing in my life besides Clyde and my cats that I love," Fanny said sadly. "Who stole my heart?" she asked.

"I don't know," I lied to her.

"Did you shoot at me from behind a bush in front of Sheila's house?" I asked Fanny.

"No," she answered simply.

"How about the rubber soled, felt lined boot prints?" my Guardian Angel asked.

"They don't mean anything," I told him. "Everybody in Minnesota has boots like them."

"You didn't kill Sam Sheeps and Row Harper either," I said to Fanny.

"No."

"Where's the money, Fanny?"

Fanny looked nervously at Sheriff Jack Benning. "I will cut you in if you don't tell anybody else," she said to him.

"One third," he replied casually, like $125,000 dropped into his lap every day.

"I'm not telling you where the money is," Fanny told me.

"I feel sorry for you Fanny," I said. "You have a good heart but somewhere you lost it."

"Nobody has a heart, Roosevelt, we have either sold them or given them away," she said quietly.

I thought I saw her eyes mist up before they turned and she and the now rich Sheriff Jack Benning left the room.

"You solved this case better than any you have ever been involved with," my Guardian Angel said.

"The best for last," I said, feeling no pride or sense of accomplishment.

"But who killed Sam Sheeps and Row Harper and stole Fanny's heart?" my Guardian Angel asked me. "And who shot at you from in front of Sheila's house?"

"I can only answer one of your questions but I will only answer it if I get out of this jam alive," I told my Guardian Angel.

"I'll miss you," he said.

"After a few weeks with somebody else you won't even think about me," I said.

"At times," he said with a smile.

"Thanks," I replied.

CHAPTER TWENTY-ONE
IT ALL COMES TOGETHER

I believe in miracles but I am resigned to the fact there is no miracle in store for me. God, the fates, destiny, Mighty Mouse, Superman, Batman, the army, the national guard, the Marines - none of them are coming to my rescue.

It's strange. I have both feared and not feared death, but with death knocking on the door I am almost thankful that the battle is over - a battle I always knew I could not win.

"Life is always the underdog but it puts up one good fight," my Guardian Angel said.

"It has a lousy left jab," I said with no remorse.

Looking at the ceiling the portrait of evil no longer bothers me. It is a joke that caring people of the world should laugh at. But I wondered what would twist people's minds so badly that they would embrace hate and violence and only dream of personal power?

"Hitler, Stalin, mob bosses, skinheads, the KKK, any of them could answer your question," my Guardian Angel said.

"Sad," I said.

"If you had your life to do all over again what would you want to be?" my Guardian Angel asked me.

I thought seriously for a few moments. "I'd like to be a frog in Florida. I'd eat bugs all day and then serenade the ladies all night."

"Sounds like a good life, unless the people in the neighborhood like frog legs," he said.

We both chuckled. Life is beyond absurd.

"I'm going to sleep," I told my Guardian Angel. "I want to be fresh for my going away party."

"Rest in peace," he said.

I slept like a baby or as well as a baby could sleep on a cold granite slab. Hours of sleep went by without dreams.

I was rudely awakened by chanting voices. Whatever they were chanting I could not understand. Twelve hooded black robbed figures are standing by the walls forming a circle around me. Father Fisher, dressed in a white hooded robe is standing by the table with the knives, bowl, and satanic bible on it. Father Fisher has his eyes shut and his arms folded over his chest. Sheriff Jack Benning is at my feet. Ginger is by my head. I stuck my tongue out at Sheriff Jack Benning.

The chanting continued - a monotone of evil. After a while the tempo quickened and the chanters raised their voices. But it is not a song I can dance to. The tempo grew faster again and the voices of the twelve reached a feverish pitch.

Opening his eyes Father Fisher unfolded his arms and took a small vile out of a pocket in his robe. Walking around me he held out the vile for everybody to see. Stopping, he looked down at me and the chanting ceased. A devilish smile creased his lips as he removed the cap from the bottle. He held the bottle a few inches from my lips.

"If you're going to dope me up I want some good Sunshine Acid," I said.

"For the chosen," he said, and before I could turn my face he poured a small amount of the liquid on my lips. Instantly my lips went numb and the walls of the room started pulsating. The witches started chanting again, only this time their voices seemed to be miles away. I started spinning in circles as a universe of stars burst in front of my eyes. The chanting grew closer until it sounded like the voices were originating inside my head. My mind feels like it will burst into millions of bright shiny fragments, each fragment a hologram filled with a portion of the chant locked inside of it. Father Fisher's face is a smiling goat, he has horns and his eyes are burning red dots that drops of blood ooze out of and fall all over my chest. I can smell the sweet sticky odor of blood. The chanting stops and the silence is like no silence I have ever experienced - a silence of the dead - a silence of a world where there are no creatures to hear sound.

Father Fisher raises his hand and as if on command the steel pit filled with wood at my feet and head ignited in large swirling flames. Sweat drips from every pore in my body.

Father Fisher looks at the ceiling, holding his arms above his head he beseeches the evil sights to come to him - to embrace him - to lead him to the depths of darkness where pain and suffering nurture them before releasing them on a defenseless world. Father Fisher's image melts into the flames and seems to give him power. He cries out - "Lord of darkness we cry out to you. Lord of darkness accept the gift of death we send to you."

The twelve witches repeat his words.

Father Fisher steps over to the table and picks up the two silver knives, one in each hand, and raises them above his head. "The fatted lamb is our salvation. The blood of the non-believer is our strength."

Walking around the room, he stops at each witch and they kiss the knives. When he has completed the circle he looks down at me. The room is no longer spinning. I am at ease, every muscle in my body is relaxed, my mind is free of cares. I feel my Guardian Angel beginning to slip away from me. It is not a goodbye as soon I will be in his world.

"Do you accept Satan as your redeemer?" Father Fisher beseeches me as he slowly raises the knives over my chest.

"Your sacrifice is diminished. People in your coven are liars."

The knives go higher. The flames from the fires glisten from the silver blades. Father Fisher's face is filled with power and greed. The muscles in his neck tighten until they bulge out like steel bridge cables. "Do you accept Satan as your redeemer?" he screams at me again.

"He is not the truth."

A grimace of a smile creases his lips. I see his fingers tighten on the knife handles.

Like a faint echo I hear my Guardian Angel. "Goodbye Roosevelt, and in all truth you are not boring, you are a good man."

The knives start toward my chest and I shut my eyes.

A loud explosion reverberates through the room and I hear the knives clank to the floor. My eyes snap open, Father Fisher's left arm is hanging limply by his side, blood is pouring out of a wound in his shoulder. Father Fisher, his face ashen, looks in utter bewilderment at the hole in the robe and the ocean of blood spurting from it. He looks in amazement at me and then in shock at Sheriff Jack Benning. Sheriff Jack Benning has his 8 inch long barreled 357 magnum in his hand and a small wisp of white smoke is curling out of the barrel. Father Fisher crumples to the granite floor. The other witches and warlocks are frozen in astonishment.

No sooner has Father Fisher hit the floor than the granite door scrapes open and Detectives Bill Buffalo, Paul Binyon and Pete Rosebet run in with their pistols drawn, followed by a small posse of Highway Patrolmen. "Everybody hit the floor and put your hands behind your backs," Bill Buffalo orders.

The witches, all accept Ginger and Sheriff Jack Benning, sprawl on the floor quicker than a buck private ordered to do twenty pushups. Ginger runs over to me and looks deeply concerned. "Are you ok, Roosevelt?"

"I've never felt better," I grin like a cat on his tenth life.

"I'm sorry, I would have shot sooner but the pistol got stuck in my robe," Sheriff Jack Benning said.

I started to tell him, forget it, but the drug Father Fisher had poured into my mouth kicked in again. I went in and out of consciousness. I remember bits and pieces of movement, fading sirens, cursing men, crying women, being picked up, faces looking down at me, but it was mostly a blur, like a dream with no pattern, forgotten as soon as one wakes up. I feel like I am on a journey that will never end. Black empty time stretches before me. Then I woke up. I am sitting in Father Fisher's room in one of the leather chairs facing the fire place. Somebody had found my clothes and dressed me. Looking at the fire my first thought is I wished I had a stick and a bag of marshmallows. Detective Bill Buffalo is sitting in the other chair and he smiles at me. Nine witches, now devoid of their black robes are sitting on the floor with their backs to the wall not enjoying the security of handcuffs. Sheriff Jack Benning is standing by the fire. Detectives Paul Binyon and Pete Rosebet are keeping a close eye on the witches. "Welcome back," Bill Buffalo said.

"I can't believe it," my Guardian Angel said.

"Where is Father Fisher?" I asked.

"In an ambulance on the way to the hospital," Sheriff Jack Benning said. "The 357 made his shoulder look like Swiss steak."

Looking at the nine witches I said. "I guess your brooms ran out of gas."

Bill Buffalo chuckled, and then said, "we're waiting for a police bus to get here to move all the prisoners."

"You used me," I accused Bill Buffalo angrily.

"I told you to stay out of the way," he said.

"You knew I wouldn't."

"It worked, didn't it?" he smiled like a wise old owl.

"You're smarter than I gave you credit for," I said - one can't argue with success.

"Thanks."

"Ginger and Sheriff Jack Benning are the undercover people you told me about," I said. "But they're not Feds."

"So I lied, the rest is history."

"When I was in the trunk and the car stopped Sheriff Jack Benning got out and talked to you, didn't he?" I asked.

Bill Buffalo nodded.

Paul Binyon, Pete Rosebet, Ginger and Sheriff Jack Benning all smiled at me.

Carol, Lisa, Fanny, Earl and Brenda, Merriam and Dale, Grace and George, and Sheila glared at me. Witches who have been cheated out of their sacrifice are not happy campers.

"I could have been killed," I said to anybody who wanted to listen, but I wasn't angry anymore.

"We thought about that," Bill Buffalo said, "but then we figured nobody would really care and we took a course of action that would wrap everything up if it all went right."

"I won eighty bucks on you, Roosevelt," Pete Rosebet said.

"What?" I demanded.

"We had a pool and I bet you wouldn't get killed, so I won."

"Gambling on a man's life, you should be ashamed," I said to Ginger.

"Hey, sometimes this undercover thing isn't boring," she said, with an impish grin on her face.

"You are nothing but a big sap," my Guardian Angel said.

"I'll sap you," I warned him.

"Would you tell me what brought this about?" I asked Bill Buffalo.

"For years there have been cattle mutations and things like that in the area. We knew about them but we had no idea who was involved. Right after Ginger's husband died Ginger was approached by Fanny and slowly brought into the coven. What Father Fisher and the rest didn't know was that right after she was approached by Fanny, Ginger came to see me. We took her on as a paid informant and she has reported to us every since. Sheriff Jack Benning was pulled into the coven by Ginger. She quelled any fears Father Fisher had over the fact he was a cop."

"You made great bait," Pete Rosebet said.

"I had received reports from Kansas City from my brother, the one in the organized crime unit, that Franklin Trouble had been seen in Kansas City talking to Dale Owens and that it would be a good idea to keep an eye on him. So we knew something was probably going on, but being a small community it is hard to find out anything. You showed up and either by luck, skill, or a combination of both everything fell into place," Bill Buffalo said.

Sheriff Jack Benning walked over and set a small tape recorder on the table. "Whenever I came into the chamber I had the recorder under my robe," he said.

All the witches around the room suddenly wished they were Jewish.

Sheriff Jack Benning pushed a button on the recorder. I heard my voice and Father Fisher's voice on the tape. "It's all there," Sheriff Jack Benning said proudly. "Every last word from every little Halloween freak in this room. You nailed them all."

"I haven't nailed all of them. Somebody helped Fanny when she killed Franklin. Somebody killed Row Harper and Sam Sheeps. And somebody shot at me from in front of Sheila's house," I said. "And we don't know where the money is that Fanny found when she killed Franklin."

"You thieving witch," Dale Boraxe spat at Fanny, which was a fitting statement under the circumstances.

"I can solve one of them for you," Sheriff Jack Benning said sheepishly. "I shot at you from the bush in front of Sheila's house but I didn't try and hit you. At the time we thought you might get in the way of everything and we thought you would run like a scared rabbit."

Bill Buffalo shrugged his shoulders at me.

"But after your incident with Bill and Joe we knew we were wrong," Pete Rosebet said.

"You own a pair of felt lined, rubber bottomed boots?" I asked Sheriff Jack Benning.

"Everybody in this state has a pair of them. You don't think I'd wear my work boots do you?" he said.

"I would have never figured," I told him.

He smiled proudly.

"But why didn't you guys just ask me to leave?" I asked.

"We thought about that, but then we figured if we asked you you'd think we were crooked cops and stay and try and bust us like you did to that detective in Iowa," Pete Rosebet said.

The statement made sense in a twisted sort of way.

"Who helped you kill Franklin?" Paul Binyon asked Fanny.

"I don't know," she spat.

"You tell us and we might be able to work out a deal," Pete Rosebet told her.

Fanny laughed a crazy demented laugh. But the joke is really on her.

"I know who helped her," I said.

"Satan will eat your heart," Fanny cursed at me.

"Only in your dreams," I replied.

"Enough of eating hearts and dreams. Who helped her?" Bill Buffalo demanded.

"After I found Franklin's body I searched the room he was in and I found a small blue heart pendant in the chair. I found out that the heart had belonged to Brenda but she had lost it."

"I didn't kill him," Brenda cut in.

I ignored her.

"Earl told me he had given the heart to Brenda. I thought at first either Earl or Brenda had helped Fanny. I told them I had found the heart when they came to see me in the dungeon and neither one of them seemed surprised. There is only one other person who would have had access to the heart.”

I looked at Sheila. "You drove Fanny out to see Franklin and helped her move the body to Carol's house. You took the heart out of your mother's jewelry box and were wearing it and it fell off into the chair."

"I didn't know she was going to kill him," Sheila whimpered.

"Shut up," Fanny screamed at her.

"I don't think you did know," I said to Sheila, "but when you both found the money that was in the trunk of Franklin's car greed took over."

"She said she would kill me if I told anybody," Sheila cried. "But I don't know where she put the money."

I don't know if I believe her or not.

"I have known for a while Fanny killed Franklin but it wasn't until later it dawned on me she had to have an accomplice. Fanny doesn't own a car or have a driver’s license. She needed a ride to get to his house."

"Where's the money?” Bill Buffalo asked Fanny.

"Where is it?” Dale Boraxe demanded.

"Where you're going you won't need money for a long time," Pete Rosebet said to Dale.

Dale turned pale.

"I'll never tell anybody where the money is," Fanny said.

"That's some good detective work," Sheriff Jack Benning commented to me.

"Luck," I said.

"People make their own luck," my Guardian Angel said.

"Who killed Sam Sheeps and Row Harper?” Bill Buffalo asked me. He knew, in time, Fanny would tell them where the money was.

"There are only two people who could have killed Sam Sheeps and Row Harper," I said.

Everybody in the room looked at me intently. "Carol and her sister Lisa," I said.

Carol and Lisa tried to stand up like they wanted to run over and scratch my eyes out, which they couldn't do with handcuffs on. Pete Rosebet and Paul Binyon pushed them back down.

"You don't know anything," Carol snarled at me.

Lisa didn't say anything, like a guilty person should do.

"The night I went out to where Row Harper and Sam Sheeps were staying I called Sheriff Jack Benning after I captured them. I heard Carol's voice in the background."

"I was at her house," Sheriff Jack Benning said.

"I bet you told her where you were going."

"I did."

"When you left her house did you go straight out to the farmhouse?"

"No. I was dressed in civilian clothes and in my private car and had to go get the sheriff car and change clothes."

"Carol left right after you did and picked up Lisa. They got into a car that wasn't in the garage the night when I snooped around the Boraxe's place. I bet Dale Boraxe has a shotgun in his house they used. I don't know which one shot at me and killed Sam and Row but I know one of them did."

"You're only guessing," Carol stammered.

Lisa glared at me and said nothing.

"I wish I was lying. But I know I'm not. After the shooting I got off a few quick shots at the car as it was driving away. I know I hit it. When the police showed up and everything was done I went to your house, Carol, and you knew what had happened. I asked you if Sheriff Jack Benning had been back by your house and you told me no. There was no way you could have known unless you were there."

"Carol shot them, not me," Lisa blurted out.

"Shut up," Carol hissed at her sister.

"Lisa knew Dale Boraxe was doing something illegal and kept large amounts of cash around the house. She kept trying to find it but couldn't. She and Carol were going to take the money, Carol was going to sell her house, and with the insurance money Franklin left her they were planning on moving to Florida. I knew this and they had to figure I would ruin it for them."

Pete Rosebet whistled softly.

"I bet you will find the car I shot at. It's a dark sedan and belongs to Dale Boraxe."

Dale Boraxe looked at Carol and Lisa. All the witches' juice had been drained out of him. He had aged ten years in only a few minutes.

A bus pulled up in front of the house. The witches were lined up and marched to the bus. Bill Buffalo, Pete Rosebet, Paul Binyon, Ginger, Sheriff Jack Benning and I watched as the evil cargo was whisked away.

The sun cleared the horizon - rays of hope cleansing a dark world.

"The Feds are arresting Owens and his boys in Kansas City today under the organized crime laws. I have no doubt Dale Boraxe will spill his guts to get a lighter sentence," Bill Buffalo said.

"How about the others?" I asked.

"For Fanny I'm going to try and get the D.A. to go for murder one. Carol maybe murder two and attempted murder. Sheila as an accessory to murder. Father Fisher for attempted murder and the rest of them on conspiracy to murder. Dale Boraxe will also get charged with illegal gambling. Nobody is going to go free on this one," Bill Buffalo said, sounding tired but satisfied.

"Crime is a mess," I said.

"It's endless," Bill Buffalo said.

"You'll have to keep us posted where you are for when the trail dates come up," Pete Rosebet said. "You will have to testify."

The three detectives and Ginger got in their car. "I'll give you a ride to Carol's," Sheriff Jack Benning told me.

"Not in the trunk," I said with a grin.

The detectives started to drive off, but stopped. Bill Buffalo rolled down his window. "Don't forget your talk at the fundraiser in a few days," he told me and then sped away.

Sheriff Jack Benning and I didn't talk as he drove me to Carol's. I didn't say thanks to him for saving my life when he let me off.

"That was rude," my Guardian Angel said.

"I'm basically a rude person," I said.

"No you're not," he said.

I took a long hot shower and put on clean clothes. I packed my things and loaded everything into Matilda and drove to THE HOME OF HEARTS.

Walking through the heart filled rooms I am once again amazed. Even if Fanny was a witch she had to have a heart to surround herself with hearts. Clyde is pacing back and forth on a table in the Tea Room. When he saw me he stopped. "Coffee sucks, crap, cowboy, bad cat, bad cat, not you, not you, damn farmer, too cold, too cold, peace, pretty, pretty, good tea, me love you," Clyde squawked.

"Clyde must be happy to see you," my Guardian Angel said.

Holding out my hand Clyde hopped onto it.

Clyde and I went out the back door and headed for Jimmy's. I knocked on the door. Ginger answered. She looks tired. "I came to say goodbye to Jimmy," I said.

"He's in his room," she said, starting to follow me.

"I'd like to see him by myself," I said.

She gave me an understanding smile.

Jimmy is sitting on his bed. He jumped up excitedly. His little boy eyes shine and a large happy smile is spread over his face like a fresh spring day. "Bob, I'm glad you came to see me."

I ruffled his greasy hair. "Fanny is going to be gone for a while and she told me to give you Clyde," I told him.

"I love Clyde," Jimmy said excitedly.

"Me love you," Clyde squawked and jumped on Jimmy's shoulder.

The smile on Jimmy's face with Clyde sitting on his shoulder makes me warm and happy.

"Jimmy I'm leaving. I've come by to say goodbye," I said after a few moments.

"I knew you would leave someday," he said in a low distant voice, but looking in my eyes.

"But I have to ask you something before I go. Will you tell me the truth?"

"I've never lied to you Bob," he said.

"I know you took Fanny's heart that was under the dome, Jimmy. You have lied to me," I said, but not in any way he would think I was hurt or angry.

Jimmy fidgeted and looked away from me. "You asked me if I took Fanny's heart from underneath the dome?" he said.

"That's true."

"It was my mom's birthday, Bob, and I didn't have anything to give her. I was at Fanny's and the dome was lying on its side. I picked up the dome to put it back and saw the heart and I took it, but I didn't take it from under the dome, so I really didn't lie to you," his eyes pleaded with me.

"I guess we could call it stretching the truth a little but not an outright lie," I said.

"I wrapped the heart up but then I felt bad and I never gave it to my mom," Jimmy said.

"Where is it?"

"It's in my secret place, Bob."

"Let's go get it."

Ginger is in the kitchen. Jimmy ran to her and put Clyde on the table. "Fanny told Bob I could have Clyde," he chirped like a happy bird.

She smiled warmly at me. I told Ginger we would be right back.

Standing in Jimmy's secret room I look at all the little boy things and realize how much I have forgotten about my own childhood. I wonder what Jimmy will grow up to be and when he is older if he will remember me.

Jimmy took a coffee can down from the shelf and pulled out a balled up piece of wrapping paper, unfolded the paper and handed me the diamond heart.

I put it in my pocket.

When we got back to Jimmy's, Ginger told Jimmy, "You take Clyde and go play in your room."

Jimmy went to his room without an argument.

Ginger poured us each a cup of coffee. I took the heart pendant out of my pocket. "You make sure Fanny gets this," I told her and set the pendant on the table.

"Where did you find it?" she asked me, with surprise in her voice.

"A big black bird told me where it was," I smiled at her.

She smiled back.

"What are you going to do now?" I asked Ginger.

"I'm going to move to Minneapolis and go back to college. I want to be a teacher."

Finished with my coffee I stood. Ginger called for Jimmy. By the front door Ginger has her arm around Jimmy while Clyde perches on his shoulder. "You take care of your mother," I told Jimmy and shook his hand. "She is a good mother."

"I'll always take care of my mother," Jimmy said.

"Hug Jimmy," my Guardian Angel told me. "It will not hurt you."

I bent down and hugged Jimmy. His little hands on my back are like warm rays of sunshine.

I shook hands with Ginger. "Good luck with your life," I said.

"With our love we'll do ok," she replied.

"You are the best friend I've ever had," Jimmy said to me as I opened the door.

"You have done my heart well," I said and rustled his greasy hair one last time.

As I shut the door Clyde squawked loudly, "Crap, cowboy."

Driving west out of Saint Ansgar the sun glistens off of the snow bringing millions of tiny ice fairies to life. They dance and play as I speed by them.

I headed Matilda west. "Where are we going?" my Guardian Angel asked.

"I'm driving until I hit the ocean and then you and I and Matilda are getting on a boat and going to the islands."

"You are supposed to give a speech for the police fundraiser."

"I'm all speeched out," I said.

"Pete Rosebet told you to stay in touch. They will need you to testify at the trials."

"They have enough evidence on everybody they could put them in jail ten times over. They don't need me."

"Do you think you will find the love of your life in Hawaii?"

"I will find seafood, tropical flowers, the ocean, and hundreds of beautiful women sunbathing on the beach and maybe, just maybe, I will meet a lady I love and she loves me," I said.

"Somewhere over the rainbow," my Guardian Angel sang out happily, "keep chasing that rainbow."

He couldn't care less about any rainbow. He is only interested in the bikini-clad women.

THE END

OTHER BOB ROOSEVELT MYSTERIES

BOOK ONE – A BUCKET FULL OF LIES

BOOK TWO – TROUT FISHING FOR BODIES

BOOK THREE – DOUBLE BOGEY MURDE

BOOK FOUR – FROGS DON'T CROAK IN THE WINTER

COMING SOON – BEACH BUM TANGO

For more of Robert K. Swisher Jr's many novels visit

http://www.swisherbooks.com/

www.ingramcontent.com/pod-product-compliance
Lightning Source LLC
Chambersburg PA
CBHW022015120726
47902CB00012B/271

9780997909685